D0447514

a mother's
promise

a mother's promise

K.D. ALDEN

FOREVER

New York Boston

Copyright © 2021 by Karen A. Moser

Reading group guide copyright © 2021 by Karen A. Moser and Hachette Book Group, Inc.

Cover design by Daniela Medina
Cover photograph of girl by © Kerstin Marinov/Trevillion Images; photograph of woman by © Ildiko Neer/Trevillion Images
Cover copyright © 2021 by Hachette Book Group, Inc.

Forever
Hachette Book Group
1290 Avenue of the Americas, New York, NY 10104
read-forever.com
twitter.com/readforeverpub

First Edition: January 2021

Forever is an imprint of Grand Central Publishing. The Forever name and logo are trademarks of Hachette Book Group, Inc.

The publisher is not responsible for websites (or their content) that are not owned by the publisher.

The Hachette Speakers Bureau provides a wide range of authors for speaking events. To find out more, go to www.hachettespeakersbureau.com or call (866) 376-6591.

Library of Congress Cataloging-in-Publication Data
Names: Alden, K.D., author.
Title: A mother's promise / K.D. Alden.
Description: First edition. | New York : Forever, 2021. | Includes bibliographical references.
Identifiers: LCCN 2020030162 | ISBN 9781538718179 (trade paperback) | ISBN 9781538718186 (ebook)
Subjects: GSAFD: Legal stories.
Classification: LCC PS3611.E53378 M68 2021 | DDC 813/.6—dc23
LC record available at https://lccn.loc.gov/2020030162

ISBN: 978-1-5387-1817-9 (trade paperback), 978-1-5387-1818-6 (ebook)

Printed in the United States of America

LSC-C

Printing 1, 2020

This novel is dedicated to the memory of
Carrie Buck.

And to everyone who has experienced the loss of a
child or the heartbreak of infertility—
for any reason.

The United States in the 1920s was caught up in a mania: the drive to use newly discovered scientific laws of heredity to perfect humanity.

—Adam Cohen, author of *Imbeciles: The Supreme Court, American Eugenics and the Sterilization of Carrie Buck*

One

Dr. Price wore a three-piece suit with lots of authority and a kind smile.

As superintendent of the Virginia State Colony for Epileptics and Feebleminded, he looked like God, or at least Ruth Ann Riley's idea of God. She imagined He would wear a fine-cut, hand-stitched three-piece suit like the good doctor's, with a white coat over it, and have pale, narrow blue eyes, thin, refined lips with neatly trimmed whiskers and a beard. He'd smell nice, too, of shaving cream and cigar smoke and heavy volumes of learning.

Doc checked his gold pocket watch and wrote down the time. Time seemed important to him, not so much to her. Ruth Ann told time by how many peas she got shelled, or by how many shirtwaists, nightdresses, petticoats and overskirts she'd hung on the line.

Doc seemed to want more time, but she wished she had less, because it stretched and stretched and it wasn't ever over with. Not 'til she went to sleep. Then it started up all over again when the cock crowed.

She didn't want to be here, the focus of attention. Attention was guaranteed to be a bad thing. Better to be invisible. She tried her best to evaporate, like water into air.

But Doc Price wanted to talk to her again for some reason. He picked up a pen. And a file folder. Then he walked around his monster of a desk to sit down.

She eyed it with awe. *That desk is bigger than my bed.*

Ruth Ann knew he must be very smart, because he had read all those books that climbed his shelves to the very ceiling. She loved books herself—fiction that she snuck out of the Colony library. Not these tomes. How he remembered all the facts in these defied logic. But she was a working girl—what did she know? She didn't even know why she'd been called to his office.

Outside, the wind had picked up, torpedoing poor Clarence's carefully raked piles of leaves and ruining the handyman's work. Ruth Ann thought uneasily of what a storm might do to the mountains of laundry she'd wrung out until her arms ached. It all hung on the lines. She peered out the window. In the distance, beyond the neatly landscaped terrace outside of Doc Price's office, she spied a pair of long johns kicking, skirts flying up indecently, sheets billowing.

"Sit down," Doc Price said, waving his hand toward a chair on Ruth Ann's side of the desk.

She limped to the seat, gritting her teeth and sweating with the pain. She'd dropped an iron on her big toe in the laundry. Gotten screeched at by Mother Jenkins for burning her shoe, and the son of a gun still stunk of fried hide.

Doc Price didn't seem to notice the smell; his nose was buried in some scribbles in the file.

Ruth Ann wondered if she could ask him to examine her toe. But he looked very busy. *And what can he do? Tell me to go barefoot? Can't do that when you work in the laundry and the kitchen.*

Doc asked her questions he'd asked her before. This time he wrote down her answers, though, while she went halfway to somewhere else in her head. She did that a lot.

What's your name?

Ruth Ann Riley.

How old are you?

Sixteen.

Who is your father?

Cullen Riley.

Where is he now?

Dead.

Who's your mother?

Sheila Riley.

Where does she live?

Here.

Do you know where you are?

Yes, sir. At the Virginia State Colony for Epileptics and Feeble-minded.

Do you know why your mother is here?

Yes, sir. She don't have no other place to live. Ruth Ann winced. She should've said "doesn't." But Doc didn't seem to notice.

Do you know why *you're* here?

Her face heated. She looked down at her lap, at her red, raw hands with their gnawed nails. She just nodded.

Why *are* you here?

You know that, sir.

Yes, Ruth Ann. But I need to ascertain whether *you* know it.

Ascertain. Doc did drop some fancy words. *Sounds like a cross between a donkey and* enter*tain—like why you go to the county fair.*

Ruth Ann? His voice was sharper. *Like the butcher knife in Mrs. Dade's kitchen. The one I couldn't get to in time.*

Do you understand why you're here?

Pressure built behind her nose, tingling. It pushed unwilling tears into her eyes. She blinked. "Wasn't my fault." She couldn't look at him. *Write* that *down, mister.*

"You've said so before." Doc tapped his pen. "It's all right. It's not important."

The hell it ain't. Her anger startled Ruth Ann. It was usually like a toothache, a dull pain—not fierce, like this. It blew away her mental fog. All of her was present now, in this chair in front of Doc.

"Ruth Ann. Why are you here?"

"Can I just see her?" she blurted. She forced her chin up, her eyes to his. "Please? Can I just see my baby?"

Ruth Ann had been an open wound when they took her infant, bundled up and howling. Wasn't allowed to touch her. Barely allowed to see her. But she could still remember how she smelled. Raw and new. Coppery, a freshly minted penny.

For someone else to spend.

Ruth Ann pushed her swollen big toe hard against the top of her shoe, and agony shrieked through her nervous system, ricocheted through her brain, streaked back down to the injury. She did it again and again. Something was wrong with her; normal people didn't do stuff like this. But the pain in her toe felt better than the pain in her heart.

Doc packed soothing into his voice on purpose, like gauze into a wound. "Little Annabel is with Mr. and Mrs. Dade. You know that."

That's supposed to make me feel better. It makes me feel worse. So close but so far away. Safe, but for how long? Cared for, but only until she's old enough to care for them.

"Can't I hold her…just one time?" *Meh, meh, meh.* She hated the way her voice sounded. Like a goat's. Bleating.

Doc looked down, shuffled his notes. He sighed. "I'm afraid that's not possible."

Why? She didn't say it aloud. She knew it was against the rules. He'd told her before.

But who made the dang rules? An' if he's good as God here at the Colony, cain't he break 'em if he wants? She felt heavy and dark and tight, like her ugly lace-up shoes. Smudged, mud-crusted, burned out and smelly.

"Ruth Ann. Let's get back to the matter at hand."

Right. My matter don't matter. His does.

"I'm here," she said slowly, "because I ain't married and I had a baby. And that's bad."

Doc nodded. "And why else are you here?"

She stared blankly at him. Then she remembered. "Because…they say I'm feebleminded." News to her.

"And what does that mean, Ruth Ann?"

She looked over at the diplomas. She could easily read the letters that said where he'd studied, even the Latin ones. Mrs. Hawkins had taught her some Latin in fifth grade. She'd finished sixth before she'd gone to work for the Dade family. "*Feebleminded* means that I ain't smart." She winced again. But who cared if she said "ain't"…if she was a moron, like they said.

He stroked his beard. "Well, these things are relative."

What did that mean? *My only relative—here, anyways—is my momma, and I stay away from her. She's crazy. And when she ain't crazy, she's drunk. And they don't know where she gets the hooch. I know where: it's from any man on staff who wants a piece. But they don't really want those answers.*

Doc Price got up from his desk. He walked around it and folded his arms, looking down at her. "Ruth Ann, we're going to do an operation on you."

He's not asking me. He's telling me. She fixed her gaze on the third button of his waistcoat: shiny and brass, etched with a proud eagle in flight. "An operation?" She didn't like the sound of that.

"Yes. It's...for the greater good."

She dropped her gaze from his button to her lap. But then she didn't feel comfortable looking there, because that was where the baby came from. So she looked back at Doc Price's diplomas, at the curly handwriting that said how smart he was. Harvard said so. And so did somebody named John Hopkins—though there seemed to be two of him.

She liked to do good. *I'm a good girl. Well, I was. Until Mrs. Dade's nephew Patrick held me down and climbed on me and put the baby in me even though I said no. He just laughed at me, and I couldn't get to the knife. Because of him, I'm no longer a good girl.*

Doc Price snapped his fingers in front of her face.

She looked up, startled; afraid she'd made him mad. But he looked almost pleased at her wandering attention. Pleased with himself, though, not her.

"What kind of operation?" she asked.

"It's complicated, Ruth Ann," he said, dropping a hand onto her shoulder. He squeezed it.

Ruth Ann flinched, couldn't help it. She wasn't used to anyone touching her. *And it ain't never a good thing when they do.*

"You'll just have to trust me," Doc said. "All right?"

"But—"

Doc took out his pocket watch again and checked it. "Our time is up, my dear. I have to see another patient now."

Another one? But you don't really see me.

He smiled like a very kind uncle and gestured toward the door. The sunlight bounced off that third button of his waistcoat again, glinting on the eagle. It looked so graceful and free.

Ruth Ann got up, still feeling heavy and dark and even tighter.

Dirtier. Her toe screamed under the scab of burned leather. She didn't kick off the shoe, or ask Doc to look at it, or even scream back.

"For the greater good," he said, nodding and stroking his beard again, as if he were trying to convince himself.

She used to be a good girl. And maybe Doc was offering her the chance to be that girl again. Slip backward in time, wash off the filth and the sin.

She searched his eyes for what Pastor Miller called absolution, for redemption. Fancy words that meant God forgave a soul for being bad. Doc was saying she could do something for others? Everybody should. So even though it felt wrong, she nodded.

"We'll do the surgery soon, Ruth Ann."

Her breath hitched as her pulse kicked up. "Wait." She wiped her suddenly sweaty palms on her gray work dress. "What...what is it that you—"

"My dear, you've nothing to fear," he said in tones that were overly reassuring. "It will be over before you know it."

"What kind of surgery?" She hated the word. It started with a hiss and meant scalpels and slicing and scariness...pain. Pain much worse than the steady throb in her stupid toe.

"I'll give you a drug that makes you sleep," Doc Price continued, as if he hadn't even heard her words.

"But what are you going to *do* to me?" Her voice had risen. She knew she was supposed to be more respectful because he was a doctor and all, but now she was scared.

He sighed and walked to the window, gazing at anything rather than her. "This is an operation of a rather...delicate...nature."

She shook her head. "What's that mean?"

"It involves your, ah, female organs." He stroked his beard again, as if it were a small animal.

Ruth Ann clenched her hands. "But…there's nothing wrong with them."

A sigh reached her from the window. "Just so." His expulsion of breath clouded her view of the darkening sky outside and the now madly writhing silhouettes of laundry pinned to the lines. They looked desperate to escape, like tortured souls.

"Doc, there's nothing wrong with my parts. I'm fine since I had the baby. I get my monthly courses again and all." Ruth Ann's face heated in shame at the topic. *But he brought it up first. He's the one who wants to fix something that ain't broke.*

"Correct," he said, as if she needed him to agree with her on what she already knew about her own body. "That's rather the issue, Ruth Ann."

"Huh?"

"My dear." He gestured toward the other buildings and grounds of the Colony. "Given the facts of your life here, given your broken family history and your mental, ah, capacity…"

Why doesn't the man just use plain English and say what the heck he means?

"It is best that we curtail your ability to breed."

"What?" She had no idea what *curtail* meant. "I *can* breed. I just had a ba—"

Doc checked his watch again. "But you shouldn't," he said gently. "That's the whole point, Ruth Ann. It's in no way your fault, my girl, but you're the daughter of a drunken, defective, debauched…derelict. You live in an institution, and given that circumstance, it's highly unlikely you will ever wed. And"—he cleared his throat—"you're certainly no intellectual. So we have decided that it's best for all concerned that we sterilize you."

"Sterilize," she repeated. "Like boiling jars before canning vegetables?"

He chuckled. "Well, not exactly. But somewhat. That sort of sterilization does also reduce the risk of…toxic growth."

She blinked, unsure what he was talking about.

"Ruth Ann, I intend to simply cut your fallopian tubes and then neatly tie them. Sew you back up. And you'll be good as new."

"My what?"

"Fallopian tubes…think of them as pipes through which a fertilized egg travels on its way to your uterus—your tummy. Where the egg grows into a baby."

Ruth Ann absorbed this. *Eggs.* From there it was a short hop to chickens. Another of her tasks sometimes was to fetch the eggs from the chicken coop. *An' what happens to hens when they stop layin'? They become soup.*

A cramp seized her from deep inside, snatching her breath and twisting some nameless part of her listed in Doc's books. Clamping down viciously, wringing it like a hot, wet sheet. Ruth Ann pressed down hard on her belly with her clasped hands to make it stop.

They'd taken her baby, but she would find a way to see her and get Annabel back. Raise her: that was a promise. And one day, she'd have another. She would.

Doc snapped his fingers again in front of her face. "All right, Ruth Ann?"

"No," she said, surprising them both. "I don't want this."

He peered at her over his steel spectacles. Down his nose. "My dear girl, I regret to inform you that the choice is not yours."

Her mouth dropped open as he seated himself again behind his desk.

He didn't sound like he regretted anything except the time he was spending in discussion with her. He pulled out his watch yet again. She wanted to shove it down his throat. Or somewhere darker. "But you can't just...you can't do that."

Dr. Price steepled his hands upon his blotter, his thin-lipped mouth downturned. His gaze was gentle but firm. "I'm afraid I can."

"It's *my* body." Her voice was louder than she meant it to be.

"Indeed? Forgive me, but *your body*, as you say, is fed, clothed and housed by the government of Virginia. Therefore, the state takes an interest in it."

So I'm just an alley cat, living on scraps and shame? "I work for that food, these clothes that I sweat through every day and the leaky roof over my head," she said, as the sky rumbled in agreement. She pointed at the army of laundry trying to flee the coming storm. "I *work*."

"No." Doc sighed, pinching the bridge of his nose between thumb and forefinger.

No? Whatever did the man mean by *no?* Was *he* feebleminded?

His pale blue eyes honed in on her. "You defray the costs of your upkeep, which the state should not have to bear in the first place. So perhaps, young lady," Doc suggested, "you may wish to cultivate some gratitude."

"*Gratitude?*" Her voice rose involuntarily. "Is that right." *Man's clearly never worked a day in a laundry.*

"You need to calm down, Miss Riley."

"I am calm!" But she realized, too late, that she'd shouted. And at a doctor, of all people. Who was she to snap at a doctor?

He eyed her severely. "You're nothing of the sort."

Ruth Ann blew out a breath. She dug her fingers into her eyeballs to relieve the rising pressure there. She inhaled, counted to three. "I'm sorry. I 'pologize. I'm calm now. I promise. It's just that—"

Doc Price got to his feet. "Good. I trust you will remain so. Our interview is now completed."

In less than five seconds, Ruth Ann and her disrespect were outside his door, dismissed.

The bruised sky began to spit on her as the laundry flung itself desperately toward freedom—with no luck. It was well pinned.

Two

No time to feel sorry for herself; she had to rescue the laundry before it got soaked. As Ruth Ann ran headlong into the torrents of wind, the sky deployed buckets of cold water and pitchforks of lightning. Thunder shook the earth under her horrid black shoes. She sprinted despite the fire consuming her toe. The toe that felt what she could not feel.

The rain was blinding, the grass slippery underfoot. Her hair came loose and smacked wet mop strings into her eyes. She lost her footing, went down. Lay there with her face in the mud for a long moment, drinking in the disparate scents: tangy, grapefruity vegetation; the duskier, muskier earth it was rooted in; the drowned sunshine.

It was too late for the laundry.

As she raised her head, a small, ghostly pale hand with blackened nails appeared in front of her face, as if it had reached out of an unmarked grave. She screamed and recoiled, fell onto her back, panting.

A girl, not a ghost, stood there. She was about Ruth Ann's age and just as drenched. The girl looked vaguely familiar and wore the same gray work dress as Ruth Ann. She dashed water out of her huge brown eyes, then she covered her mouth and sneezed like a buffalo.

"God bless you," Ruth Ann said automatically. Not that she

thought it'd do the least bit of good. If a body at the Colony sneezed her soul out and a devil wanted to pop into its place, it would do as it pleased, blessing or not. Clearly Satan possessed Mother Jenkins. Her soul—if the witch had ever had one—had been dropkicked into a gulley and pissed on by an angry mule.

The girl grimaced. "You look like you could use some blessing yourself."

"What makes you say that?" Ruth Ann's tone was wry. But she took the girl's helping hand and pulled herself to her feet.

"I'm Glory."

It was the very last name Ruth Ann had expected, since Glory looked about as glorious as a rat caught in a bucket of wet cement. Her hair clung to her skull, her dress was stuck like glue to every bone in her body and any color that might once have crept onto her cheeks had been thoroughly rinsed off by the rain.

"Pleased to meet you," Ruth Ann managed. "Ruth Ann. Riley."

Glory's eyes widened. "Oh."

She wouldn't want anything to do with her now that she knew Ruth Ann's last name was Riley. That was for sure.

"Yeah." Ruth Ann turned to resume her trek toward the doomed laundry. Its former struggles had ceased; every piece hung like a sodden corpse, stretching the lines to breaking point. Mother Jenkins would be fit to be tied. Too bad nobody'd actually tie her. "Thanks for the hand up."

"Wait…" Glory sneezed again.

"God bless you," Ruth Ann repeated.

"Did you just come from Doc Price's office?"

Ruth Ann stilled. Nodded. Jammed her toe against the top of her shoe again, relishing the pain. And again. Her toe popped through the abused, burned leather. She registered it in disbelief. Now there'd really be hell to pay. Shoes didn't come cheap.

"'Cause I'm headed there now. I'm late. Mother J told me I had to get the oven scrubbed clean first—she didn't care if I had an appointment with St. Peter himself."

There was a long pause.

Glory swallowed. "Do you…maybe know…why he wants to see me? I don't feel sick."

Ruth Ann wiggled her purple toe. "You're new, right? I remember now when you came. About three months ago? And you were…"

Glory's face flamed. "Knocked up. You can say it."

"Yeah. Well, so was I. Um. Doc Price prob'ly wants to talk to you about that."

"Why?"

Ruth Ann shrugged. "It's a medical thing."

"What kind of medical thing?"

There was nothing Ruth Ann could do to help the girl. Heck, she wasn't sure there was anything she could do to help herself. "I got to go. Mother Jenkins is gonna take the Belt to me as it is, what with the wet laundry and all." Ruth Ann turned on her fat plum of a toe, dragging it through the muddy grass.

"What happened to your shoe?" Glory asked.

"Nothing." She wasn't going to waste her breath on sob stories. This girl wouldn't end up her friend, anyway. She'd shun her, like everyone else, now that she knew her momma was creepy, crazy Sheila Riley. And who cared? She sure didn't.

"What happened to your toe?"

"Nothing," Ruth Ann said. "See you around." Midstride, she stopped, somehow sensing the hurt in the gap between them. She turned around. "What happened to your baby?"

But Glory's face had hardened. "Nothing."

* * *

"You lazy, useless, stupid girl!" ranted Mother Jenkins as Ruth Ann shivered and dripped in misery on the mudroom floor. The matron didn't even hand her a towel, much less tell her to go find some dry clothes.

Mother Jenkins resembled a toad on stilts: bulging eyes set wide in a well-fed face, a bare blip of a nose and a broad, thin-lipped, foul mouth. She had no breasts to speak of; her girth was all in the belly, but she had curiously small feet. They might even be described as dainty, in contrast to her disposition. She was crusty on a good day. On a bad day, such as this one, Ruth Ann would swear that bats flew out of her behind, shrieking for blood.

"Hours and hours of labor, wasted!"

I should know. My labor.

"Cakes of soap, hundreds of gallons of hot water, down the drain!"

Who d'you think boiled that water to heat it?

"A whole day lost…"

Please, ma'am, may I lose another? How 'bout a whole week? A month?

"You're disheveled, you're filthy, you smell like a farm animal."

Moo.

"And you have utterly destroyed a perfectly good pair of shoes, you slattern!"

Not a word about Ruth Ann's toe, which was almost three times its normal size and turning black. It looked like an eggplant sprouting from the ragged, open hole in the leather.

"What in God's name is wrong with you?"

Don't be takin' the Lord's name in vain, Mother J. Not that I'd care, particular, if He struck you down and left you smolderin'. I might even toss a match at your carcass.

"What's wrong with you?" the toad-hag screeched, spittle flying from her wide mouth.

Long list. Pretty much everything.

"What is your excuse for that...that *mess* outside on the lines? Tell me!"

Wordlessly, Ruth Ann pointed up at the sky.

"Oh, it's the fault of the *rain*, is it? Really?"

Not much I could do to stop it, now is there?

"Impudent, impertinent, imbecile of a girl! If you weren't so slow, you'd have finished the laundry yesterday, and it wouldn't be hanging out this afternoon! Ever think of that?"

No, Mother Jenkins. After all, I'm feebleminded. As well as being all that other stuff you say. Besides which, it rained yesterday, too. Ruth Ann wiggled her eggplant of a toe. The scream of its pain tuned out Mother J, not all the way, but at least a little.

"What do you have to say for yourself?"

Ruth Ann knew better than to say anything at all. Wordlessly, she shook her head.

"I don't care for the look on your face!"

What look?

But Mother Jenkins didn't bother to get into specifics. There was a whoosh of air and then her beefy palm struck Ruth Ann's cheek, hard, with an audible crack.

Ruth Ann reeled backward, her flesh stinging. She put her own cold hand up and covered the heat with it.

Mother Jenkins tossed three big sacks at her. "Now get outside, pull down that ruined laundry, and rewash every stitch of it. You'll get no supper, and I don't care if you work past midnight."

Ah, motherly love.

Ruth Ann picked up the sacks and slipped out the screen door. She couldn't believe her luck—she'd somehow escaped the Belt.

The scuffed, black leather belt had belonged to Mr. Jenkins, back in the day. Back in the day when young Gertie Jenkins, to hear tell, had been almost pretty and had a deft way with pot roast and strawberry-rhubarb pie.

Ruth Ann was sure that part was a fairy tale, because Mother J could, and did, burn toast and oversalt oatmeal. She inspired peas to jump to their deaths, rather than be overboiled in one of her cauldrons. And Ruth Ann'd bet that the future of her own busted shoes lay in being drowned in Mother J's "beef" stew. She hated to cook—that's why for the most part the girls did it.

But in one of Crazy Sheila's more lucid moments, she'd told of how Mr. J was the old woman's knight in shining armor, how she'd been devastated when he died in a mining accident, along with their sixteen-year-old son. How it had changed her forever. That did make Ruth Ann feel bad. But not as bad as Mother Jenkins made all of them feel. Especially with the Belt.

Ruth Ann slung the sacks over her right shoulder, which aggravated scar tissue from the Belt under the rough wet cotton of her dress. She squelched back into the grass, toward the lines of sad, sodden laundry. Every piece looked exhausted, drunk or dead. Every item a skin that some poor soul had shed to go to a better place.

It was still raining, but not as hard. Still windy and gray, but the sky showed signs of light here and there. It was in a grumpy mood, but not throwing a black tantrum.

As Ruth Ann unpinned and wadded several pairs of long johns into the first sack, she wished she could shed her own skin and float away. Off to Heaven...or maybe not. They all wore white robes in Heaven, didn't they? Who did the laundry there? Who had to bleach, wash, dry and iron all those robes?

A vicious crack of thunder followed by lightning reminded her that she'd likely be struck down for blasphemy any moment now. No, Heaven was no place for her. She was already fallen, like her momma before her. Even if not by choice.

She unpinned a whole section of petticoats, revealing Doc Price's office in the distance. *You're the daughter of a drunken, defective, debauched...derelict.*

She didn't know exactly what the middle two words were, but they didn't sound good.

Doc was going to slice her open. Cut and tie her tubes. Fix her so she could never have another baby. And he didn't give a rat's behind that she'd said no. That she didn't want to be fixed.

She took an armload of dripping wet work dresses down and shoved them into the second sack. The first one was so full she could barely drag it a foot at a time.

How could what he was doing be right? Was there anyone she could ask for help?

Certainly not her mother. The last time she'd seen Crazy Sheila, about a week ago, she'd been in a straitjacket, spitting and cursing at anyone who came near her.

I will see you again soon at my surgery. Doc's tone had been so sure, so smug.

Will you, Doc Price? I don't think so.

Just like that, Ruth Ann made up her mind. Nobody was cutting her open. She didn't care how many degrees were on Doc's walls or how many books he'd read. It didn't give him the right to decide she couldn't have more babies.

Nobody'd asked her permission to put one in her; nobody'd asked her permission to take the child away when she'd pushed her out. She was about damn tired of being treated like the farm animal she s'posedly smelled like.

Why didn't the good doctor do something useful, like opening up Mother Jenkins and giving her a heart?

Hang 'em all.

Ruth Ann didn't know how she was getting out of here, but she was. She would get out, find little Annabel at the Dades' house and steal her back.

Three

At night, lit only by hanging lanterns, the outdoor brick laundry area resembled some forgotten corner of hell. Ruth Ann's figure created a huge shadow-ghoul on the wall behind the big iron pot, set on bricks with a fire blazing underneath. Two large tubs squatted to the right, one containing rinse water and the other thin starch made with flour.

The shadow-ghoul presided over great piles of what resembled sucked-out human hides. She sorted them, drowned them, swished them, soaped and scrubbed them, boiled them. Then she pulled them out of the iron pot with a broom handle, rinsed them, dipped them in starch and wrung them of the last of their borrowed humanity.

Lord, you did give me an overactive imagination.

But it kept her company in this dump.

The clock had long since struck midnight; Ruth Ann's arms felt like twin pillars of granite and her stomach growled and grumbled like one of Mr. Ford's new motorcars. Yet she still had mountains of laundry to process.

Outside in the distant darkness, a band of coyotes eerily howled in chorus, signaling the imminent doom of some poor creature. Closer by came the screeching, yowling and hissing of a cat fight. And closer still, the shuffling of slippers along the path to the laundry.

Had she imagined it? Who would be awake at this time of night, and who would come to the laundry? God forbid it was Mother Jenkins with the Belt.

Ruth Ann braced herself. She couldn't take much more abuse today. She might snap. Become violent like her momma. End up in a straitjacket, shrieking like a banshee at the walls of a padded cell.

The whisper of slippers stopped just outside the entrance, and Ruth Ann held her breath. *How long do it take to drown a woman in a washbasin? Stop it. Stop these thoughts! They come straight from Satan.*

The slippers belonged to Glory, who wore a long-sleeved, regulation, white-cotton nightgown exactly like the one Ruth Ann ought to be wearing at the moment. "Enjoyin' yourself?" Glory asked, her head tilted to the side.

If Ruth Ann hadn't known better, she'd have sworn those big brown eyes were filled with a compassion she wanted nothing to do with. Despite the hollering of every tendon in her neck, every muscle of her shoulders, every nerve in her arms, she hauled another sheet to the hand-cranked wringer and fed it in. "What are you doing up so late?"

Glory wrapped her thin arms about herself and stepped inside the room. "Hard to count sheep when you're terrified."

Ruth Ann started to wind the crank. "Just count 'em poppin' right into the slaughterhouse. Forget the fence." The words were out of her mouth before she could stop them.

Glory's eyes overflowed. She bent her head forward and her shoulders began to shake.

Stricken, Ruth Ann dropped the crank, hurried to her and awkwardly patted her back. "I'm sorry. I'm so sorry! Didn't mean it. Don't cry…"

"Why didn't you tell me?" the girl sobbed.

She smelled of talcum powder and innocence. Ruth Ann helplessly eyed the crooked part in her hair, the path of white, vulnerable scalp that led to her pale young forehead. "Would it have made anything better? *Shhhh, shhhh.* Don't cry."

Glory turned toward her and laid her head on Ruth Ann's breast, leaving her unable to breathe at the strange intimacy.

Slowly, unwillingly, but inevitably, she encircled the girl with her arms and rubbed her back. "*Shhhhh.* It will be okay. Everything's going to be okay."

The girl's weeping only intensified. "No, it isn't. He's going to *cut into us* with a knife!"

Ruth Ann fought down the burst of bile that image produced. She tightened her arms around Glory and closed her eyes, shook her head.

"He is, Ruth Ann. He's going to surgically remove any chance of family from our lives. No children, no grandchildren. No christenin's, no weddin's, no gatherin's on holidays. No one to care for us when we're old…Doc Price is cutting out all of that. He will surgically tie off my hope itself. Yours. It's not fair…"

Ruth Ann drew back her left foot and kicked the brick wall next to them. Her eggplant toe hit it full force, and stars exploded behind her eyes. A dry sob, driven only by pure agony, escaped her throat. No tears. Not a one.

She wanted to run from the place, from Glory's vulnerability and raw emotion. Because she might catch it, like some awful plague. She wanted to run outside, smash through the stone wall that kept them from the so-called civilized world. She'd run until there were no miles left, run to the edge of the state, the country, the very planet—and jump off.

But instead she rocked the girl, hugging her close, trying to soothe her. She held her and cared for her as she wished someone would hold and care for her.

"It's not fair," Glory wailed again.

No. It ain't fair. It ain't right. It ain't Christian. It ain't even human. And I ain't gonna let it happen.

"We're leaving here," she said to Glory. "Day after tomorrow."

"What? But—" The girl lifted her head.

"I got a plan." Ruth Ann had nothing of the sort, but the girl didn't need to know that. She was overwrought already. A mess. That was what indulging in emotion got you. Leaky eyes, sniveling, snot. Puffy face. Ruth Ann had no use for any of it.

"You do?" Hope dawned on Glory's face, and it did Ruth Ann good to see it.

"You bet," she said, dropping her aching arms from around the girl, with poorly disguised relief. She took two big, delicious steps back from the weird intimacy. "We're going over the wall, into town, making a quick stop…" She paused. What if Glory wanted to take her own baby, too? That would mess things up but good. Where would two teenaged girls and their infants go? One was hard enough.

But Glory's eyes were shining, and Ruth Ann had already opened her big mouth.

"We're gonna go get my tiny girl. What happened to your baby?" she asked for the second time.

The shine dimmed. Glory's lips trembled, and two fat tears plopped on them. "I don't know," she sobbed. And she headed back toward Ruth Ann, arms outstretched, to rekindle the hug.

Oh, no. No, no, no. That just wasn't going to happen. Ruth Ann couldn't bear any more touching, especially not from a stranger. She quite shamefully sidestepped her and grabbed an armful of wet shirts instead. She wasn't proud of herself, but she did. Their cold, lumpy dampness soothed her tired arms and frayed nerves. "What d'you mean, you don't know?"

"N-nobody tells me. Just that she's s-s-safe…"

"Well, that's something, ain't it? She's *safe*." Ruth Ann seized on that scrap of comfort. "So quit your caterwaulin'," she said, softening the words with a smile. "You'll wake up Mother Jenkins and then we'll be in the suds."

Glory shut up immediately. *Thank the good Lord.*

"What's her name, your baby?"

"Lily."

"Very pretty."

"At least they let me name her before they took her away," Glory murmured.

"Well. Maybe we can find out what happened to her once we're out."

"How are we going to get over the wall?"

I don't have the slightest notion. "Never you mind," Ruth Ann said. "I've got it figured out. It'll be a piece o' cake. You should go back to bed now," she added. "You know we need to be ready real early tomorrow, same as always. "

Glory shook her head. "No way I'll sleep." She gestured at the remaining tower of laundry. "Besides, you look like you can use another pair of hands."

Ruth Ann stared at her. She was serious! "Really?" she managed. "You'd help me?"

"Of course. Move over." Glory stepped to the wringer and took hold of the crank.

"Why?"

"What d'you mean, why?" Glory's expression was puzzled. "Two pairs of hands are better than one. And you look ready to drop."

"I'm fine." Ruth Ann's arms and legs felt heavier than lead, but she didn't particularly like that it showed.

Glory rolled her eyes and began cranking the wet sheet through the wringer.

"If Mother J catches you out here, she won't like it. And the other girls won't like you either, if they see you with me. You clearly know who my momma is."

"I do." Glory leaned into the rhythm of the wringer, ignoring the loud squeak it made at the three-quarter mark of each full turn. "As far as I can tell, you're not anything like her. Just a little cranky and standoffish and stubborn."

Ruth Ann wondered if she even had the energy to be offended by the words. She tried to muster it, failed and forced herself to the huge kettle again, fishing four shirts out of the boiling water and trying not to splash her aching hands or arms. Meanwhile, this new, unlikely friend, whom she wasn't quite sure she deserved...well, she turned her head and winked.

A corner of her own mouth turned up, unwillingly. Glory be. The girl *must* be hard up for friends if she was willing to hang out with a Riley.

They finished the washing just after the clock struck three in the morning and banked the fire. Ruth Ann took the heavy basin of starch water to a flower bed and dumped it. Then she poured the rinse water into a vegetable bed. Brought the last of the wet laundry inside to await hanging in the morning.

Finally, they crept to bed in the female dormitories, where everyone else slept like the dead. Ruth Ann did thank Glory in a whisper. She was too tired to do anything but drop her work dress on the floor, kick it under her little wooden bunk bed and crawl, clad only in her slip, under the covers. She had no energy (or need, after sweating her guts out all day in the laundry) to use the outhouse.

By that point, she had it figured out: Glory was helping her only because she wanted Ruth Ann to be true to her word and aid in her own escape. She wasn't some angel sent down by the Lord to relieve her. She had a motive, no matter how nice she seemed.

Ruth Ann was grateful for her help, but that didn't mean she should trust in the apparent goodness of Glory's heart. In her experience, people just weren't wired that way. They always wanted something from her: work (Mrs. Dade) or information they could use later (the girls who'd pretended to be her friends so that they could cull gossip about her momma) or an audience (the preacher, who loved the sound of his own voice more than Jesus) or power (Mother Jenkins, who felt free to take out her temper on those below her).

The only person whose motives she truly could not discern was her momma. Ruth Ann's thoughts turned to her as she lay under the covers. As frightening as Sheila could be, Ruth Ann was fascinated by her. And she still loved her…or loved the mother she'd once been.

There'd been lullabies, ages ago, as she was rocked to sleep. Kind, chocolate-brown eyes. A soothing hand stroking her hair. The aroma of gingerbread and cinnamon buns from the oven. Warm milk. Momma with her tummy growing large. Feeling a baby kick inside.

If only she could return to whenever that was. Before the sobbing and cursing and drunken staggering. Before the big sign on the door that Momma said meant they had to leave their cottage. Before the stern old man with the white hair and black robes and gavel had told her she had to be a good girl, then sent her to live with Mr. and Mrs. Dade.

If only she could go back and stop whatever it was that had changed things…what had it been? She needed to ask Crazy Sheila. Needed to check on her, anyway, before they left this place behind. If only Sheila was stable enough, normal enough, to come with them. Ruth Ann fell asleep trying to formulate a plan. She would *not* let Doc Price cut into her. Just the idea of it made her skin crawl.

The cock crowed, as it always did, at five a.m. She fought to stay asleep, mentally snatching the rooster by its wattles, plucking it and stuffing it into a pot. But the lanterns got lit and girls all around her stumbled from their bunks. Greta climbed down from the bed above hers, yawning and rubbing sleep from her eyes.

Ruth Ann tried to sit up, but every muscle in her body hollered in protest. She wasn't sure she could move. Finally, she swung her legs out from under the covers and staggered to her feet.

"Where's your nightgown? And what's the matter?" Greta asked her, with a hint of a smirk. "By the way, you stink something awful."

Twenty-one hours of hard labor and she didn't smell of rosewater? Imagine. Ruth Ann ignored the dig. "I worked in the laundry all night. Mother J made me rewash everything from the lines."

"Shouldn't have left it out in the rain." Greta tucked her unruly curls under a cap.

Ruth Ann shivered and reached under the bunk for her dress, aggravating every muscle and tendon. "I feel sick," she whispered, as she pulled it out and shook it. It wasn't true, but it was the only way to sneak off and see her mother. And she'd earned a day of rest.

"Ugh!" Greta recoiled. "Your dress smells worse than you do."

Ruth Ann balled it up again and lay down in a fetal position, deliberately not under the covers so her body would tremble in the crisp morning air.

"Get up, or I'll tell Mother Jenkins."

"I can't." *Now go, like the Goody Two-shoes snitch you are, and tell on me.*

"You'll regret it. Besides, someone's got to go hang up all your wet laundry from last night, and that someone is you. And because of the whole mess, we'll run behind on the ironing. That's on you, too."

Ruth Ann ignored her until she huffed and left with all the other girls. She had approximately three minutes to stick her finger down her throat before Mother Jenkins flew into the room on her broomstick.

It was actually only two minutes.

"Get up at once, you slattern!"

That word again. Ruth Ann didn't know what it meant, but it surely wasn't complimentary.

"I'm sick," she moaned. The finger treatment had produced real nausea and she could feel sweat on her brow. She convulsed.

Mother J didn't appear to care. "Get *up*, I said."

Ruth Ann did so, clutching her wadded-up work dress to her chest. She took two steps and then vomited into it before collapsing onto her bunk again.

"Ugh! Wretched girl." But Mother Jenkins couldn't argue that she wasn't ill. "Rinse that off—and yourself, you positively *reek*!—and I'll send up someone with a tea tray. Stay in bed. I don't need this making the rounds among you girls."

Ruth Ann trudged with the disgusting dress to the bathroom and took it into the bathtub with her, soaping and rinsing it and the slip along with her body. She hung them to dry over the curtain rail and then got a fresh work dress and slip from the wardrobe in the corner of the bunk room. She put them on, along with fresh undergarments, just as Irene, a girl who worked in the kitchen, brought a tray of tea and toast.

Clean and dry, with a hot cup of tea, Ruth Ann felt that she could not only escape, but take on the world. She just had to take on her formidable mother first...Nobody would check on her, she was sure, until dinner at noon.

She went to the door and peered out. The hallway was empty, so she crept from the room, slipped quietly down the stairs and outside into the gray, chilly dawn. A couple minutes' walk took her to the faded, three-story Colonial house where the "distressed" were housed apart from the feebleminded and fallen—Sheila being, quite possibly, the most distressed of them all.

Number 213, Sheila's room on the second floor, was empty. But screams and howls and cussing brought Ruth Ann to the bathroom door, which was open a crack. Wide enough for her to see her mother crouched like an animal, naked, by the wall—hurling abuse at Ruby, the dark-skinned, white-clad attendant who was trying to coax her into the bathtub.

"Sheila, honey. Won't it feel good to get clean?" Ruby tried to reason with her. She bent toward her charge and grasped her wrists to pull her to her feet.

"Leave me 'lone! I'm dirty, an' I like it that way!" Sheila's once-blond, silky hair had gone gray and wiry. It hung in her face as she kicked at Ruby, trying to get loose. "Leggo o' me! Get off!"

"Come on, now. Water's nice and warm, but it'll get cold fast."

Ruth Ann wanted to turn away but stood transfixed.

"Sheila, doll, let's get in the tub."

"Noooooo!" Her mother, unable to gain her freedom, leaned forward to bite her captor.

"Ow, dang-nabbit! You stop that, you hear?" Ruby, easily six feet in stockings and strong as an ox, lifted her mother bodily even as she twisted and kicked and fought and spit. She swung her 180 degrees and dropped her, none too gently, into the tub.

That was when Ruth Ann saw it: the long, puckered scar across Sheila's belly. She felt faint at the sight, bile gathering in her throat. Had Doc Price "fixed" her momma so Sheila couldn't have any more defective daughters like herself? It sure looked that way.

The nausea that she'd pretended to have turned real, and she dry-heaved.

"If you won't git holt of yourself," Ruby said to Sheila as she squawked, "I will! Now, we are gonna wash you. Head to toe." The attendant used one coffee-colored hand to hold Sheila in place and the other to grab a large bar of lye soap. "You want to do it? Or should I?"

Sheila took the bar of soap from Ruby, who made the mistake of sitting back on her haunches and relaxing her grip. Then Sheila bit into the cake of lye and spit it at her, erupting from the tub as she did so, splashing water everywhere.

Her freedom didn't last long, since she slipped on the wet tiles of the bathroom floor and her feet flew out from under her. She clocked her forehead on the sink and went down hard.

Dear Lord. Ruth Ann pushed the door open and knelt down to check her for injuries. "Momma! Are you okay?!"

Sheila rolled to face her, her brown eyes glassy, skin pale and waxy. One hand crept to her stomach, fingering the scar. "*You. Why are you here?*"

Her mother's words stung worse than Mother Jenkins's slap. Even though Ruth Ann knew Sheila was off her rocker, a part of her always hoped for a shred of love or affection from this woman. Sometimes she actually got one. It was surprising, a shock, even, when Sheila produced a tender smile and touched her cheek. It sent her halfway to tears. It mixed her up.

But today she didn't have to worry about that.

"Go away!" said Sheila to Ruth Ann, as an anxiously clucking Ruby risked getting close enough again to check her head.

"You want a shot or the straitjacket?" Ruby asked Momma. "You want those again? Then behave, child."

Sheila slumped into Ruby's arms as she pulled her upright, stroking her hair. *God bless Ruby.* She was the only being here who seemed to truly care about the patients. And it was hard, on a good day, to care for Momma. Most workers would just have kept her drugged to the eyeballs, rocking and drooling on herself day after day.

"*Git,*" Sheila spat at Ruth Ann. "Git outta here."

I'm plannin' on it. I'm sorry, but I can't stay.

Ruth Ann felt no anger toward her, only sadness. Pity.

"Go away," her mother repeated. "Go on. I don't want you to see me like this."

Ruth Ann didn't want to see her like that, either. She hunched her shoulders, mouthed a quick *thank you* to Ruby, and departed in search of a good story to borrow from the library shelves. An upliftin' story, one that'd take her right out of her own miserable life and into someone else's shoes.

Her tormented toe throbbed, blaring its contempt for this idea. Ruth Ann ignored it, wishing she could switch it out, too. Didn't seem likely.

Four

Ruth Ann darted from one hiding spot to the next as she made her way back toward her dormitory with a contraband title, *The Beautiful and Damned*, in her dress pocket. Seemed only fair that the beautiful, as well as the homely, be damned. She could get on board with that.

In the meantime, she called on the good Lord and her own feeble mind to enlighten her as to how to get herself and Glory off the grounds of the Colony. It was a sprawling compound outside of Lynchburg, 350 green, rolling farm acres overlooking the James River.

Visitors never saw the underbelly of the place: dormitories, kitchen, outdoor laundry, chicken coop, workhouses, outhouses and slaughterhouse. The main building, Doc Price's office and the pastures and barns looked ideal and impressive to the rich people with bleedin' hearts who paid visits in shiny motorcars and then left, beamin' with righteous pride on account of they'd written a fat check to help Doc Price keep on workin' for the greater good.

Clarence told her how, with his one hand, he scrubbed the undercarriages of their motorcars and shined the chrome headlamps while they chatted with Doc over tea and crumpets. He doffed his cap and bobbed his head when they came out, held the shiny black doors open for 'em and said, "Yes, sir, yes'm, thank you kindly," when they noted the stump where his left hand should be and told him how very lucky he was to have found a place at the Colony.

Doc Price'd smile wide, congratulate sir or madam on the magnificence of their hearts and incline his head toward any spots Clarence might have missed with his rag. Then he'd promise to send them a copy of some book on YouGenics, published by his good friend Mr. Laughlin. God only knew what YouGenics was, but Clarence strongly suspected it should be retitled MeGenics. The doc seemed real proud of it; he'd done all kinds of science for it, talked like he'd wrote the darn thing himself.

Ruth Ann thought about that as she hunted down Clarence, who, go figure, was reraking all the leaves that yesterday's storm had scattered and then dropped back down like a thousand little gifts for him. This time, he'd had the foresight to scoop them with the rake as he went along into a large wheelbarrow covered with canvas.

"*Psssst!* Clarence!" she called from behind the corner of the main manse. "*Psssst!*"

His auburn head came up. He cocked it to the side, trying to figure out who was calling him and from which direction.

"Over here. *Shhhhh.*"

He spied her, gave a nod and threw in another rake-load of leaves. Then he dropped the rake, slid his stump under one handle of the barrow, grasped the other and trundled it toward her, toward the huge pile he was all set to burn in the ash pit. It was hidden behind a brick wall a hundred yards behind the manse. His face split into a grin as he reached her. He set the barrow down and stuffed his stump into the pocket of his overalls. "Ruthie. How's things—" He cut off mid-sentence, searching her face. "What's wrong?"

She told him.

Clarence was the one person at the Colony who never made fun of her momma. And Ruth Ann was pretty much the one person at the Colony who'd never, not once, looked at him with pity because he was missing a hand. Truth to tell, she barely noticed.

"I gotta get out of here, Clarence. Doc is going to slice me open like a biscuit." She shivered. "Glory, too."

His smile vanished; his gaze dropped to her feet. "What happened to your toe, Ruthie?"

"Never mind that. I got a plan for us, but...we need your help."

His honest gray eyes met hers for a long, measured moment. Then he gave her a small nod, his broad shoulders settling a notch in resignation. "Crawl under the canvas," he said. "Quick. You'll get dirty, but I'll take us where we can talk."

She did it. The leaves were wet and smelled of oak, decay and possibility.

He trundled the wheelbarrow easily, even with her extra weight, until they were hidden from prying eyes—and ears—by the wall. "Okay to come out now," he told her.

Ruth Ann scrambled out, both grateful for his quick thinking and irritated by the humor in his eyes. He chuckled, again stuffed his left arm into his pocket, then stepped forward and picked leaves out of her hair and off her shoulders, dropping them to the ground.

She squinted at him. "What are you laughing at?"

"Nothing." He stepped back and sighed. "So, it's your turn now."

"My turn?"

"You ain't aware that Doc's been doing these operations for a while?"

She shook her head.

"He had to stop for a spell, on account of he took some man's wife and daughters while he was away making a livin' at a sawmill. Man hired a lawyer and made a big stink. Doc had to give 'em up and got real upset about it. I'm over at the office cleanin' up the plantings one morning and I hear him shoutin' at some swell about how did a damn *maggot* get himself an attorney? But then the swell tells him, calm down, find a *medical* reason to operate, and he'll be fine. So Doc says okay, and he done started up again."

Ruth Ann wrapped her arms around herself. "He didn't say there was any medical reason. I told him I was just fine, and he told me that was the problem. That my sort shouldn't breed. That he's gonna *sterilize* me." A lump grew in her throat, hard to swallow. She figured maybe it was full of tears that just got stuck there in a clog. Could go up, couldn't go down.

Clarence got real still. Just looked at her with those rainwater gray eyes, his freckles marching in solemn columns across his sunburned nose and cheeks. He said nothing for a while. Then he looked down at her toe again and blew out a breath. "Ruthie, take off that shoe and give it here."

"I don't care about the shoe! I need to get out of here, or I guess I need *me* a lawyer."

"One thing at a time. Now sit down and take off that shoe." He pulled a handkerchief from his pocket and went to a pail of water he had sitting near the wall, with a tin cup in it. He brought the cup, full of water, back to her and dipped the handkerchief into it. "Ruthie." His voice was firm.

Her face heated, and she shook her head. "My shoe...my foot...don't smell so good."

He raised his eyebrows. "And you think mine do? Take it off."

"It's fine."

"Jiminy Cricket, you are one stubborn wench." Clarence reached forward and untied the laces. "Siddown, Ruth Ann."

Reluctantly, she did. Gently, he pulled off the horrible shoe, easing the burned, torn edges from around her hideous eggplant of a toe. "Good grief. What'd'ja do to it?"

"Dropped a hot iron on it."

"Well, that were downright *feebleminded* of you." He shot her a grin full of mischief and took her foot in his hand. It was warm and firm, and the kindness of his touch made the lump in her throat grow even larger.

Clarence wrapped the wet, cool handkerchief around her toe after a brief examination of it. "It's broke. You shouldn't be walkin' around on it."

"Like I have a choice."

"You ain't gonna wanna hear this, but it needs to be lanced and drained." He found a stray brick and set her foot gently on it.

She shuddered.

"You wanna lose it?"

Ruth Ann shook her head.

"Then you'd best let me do that. After, I'll wrap it in a clean hanky. I got an idea for how to get you out of here, and when we do, I'll give you my left shoe—you can't use this one anymore."

"That's senseless, Clarence—what shoe are you gonna wear?"

"Don't you worry. I got my eye on a pair."

"A pair where?"

"There's an old man in Distressed, on the ground floor, that don't hardly get out of bed anymore. I feel bad for the fella, but he surely don't need his shoes, and his feet are 'bout my size."

"How do you know this?"

"They had me bring him a portable commode for next to his bed."

"You won't get in trouble?"

"Nah. Who's been searchin' under his bed for his shoes lately? Who remembers what they look like?"

"Well…"

"So, tomorrow, Wednesday. You and—what's her name?"

"Glory."

"Glory. You an' Glory, you meet me back here tomorrow morning just after four a.m. with anything small you want to take with you. I'll try to get you some extra bread. I'll wheelbarrow you under the canvas to the dairy barn, where they load up them five-gallon milk jugs to take to the cheese plant. Lots of times they got sacks of seed or beans laying in the wagon, too. So you crawl in right next to them, and cover up with my canvas when he gets out to fetch the jugs. Lay flat as you can. He'll likely be sleepy and won't even notice. All right?"

"That might just work."

"'Course it'll work," Clarence said, taking her foot again and peering down at it. "Just be quick, be quiet and be smart. Hide in back of the cheese plant all day, 'cause they'll look for you. Don't come out till night. Got it?"

Ruth Ann nodded as he gingerly prodded her toe. She was afraid of discovery by someone at the cheese plant, but maybe they could crawl into a tool shed or something and tell each other stories to pass the time. Then they'd make their way to the main road and follow it to the street where Mr. and Mrs. Dade lived, with baby Annabel. She knew the layout of the house like the back of her hand, and they didn't bother to lock doors.

"*There*," Clarence said with satisfaction. "It's still kinda gross, but—"

She looked down to see that her toe had wept a nasty liquid into his handkerchief and instantly shrunk to almost its normal size.

Somehow, while they'd been talking, he must have punctured it! And she hadn't felt a thing.

"*Ugh.* How did you do that?" she demanded, torn between disgust and gratitude.

"Magic," he said, slipping a pen knife back into a pocket of his overalls. He smiled at her and patted her foot. "Keep it clean and wrapped, and startin' tomorrow, in my big ol' shoe. It'll have room to heal, that way."

"I'd have kicked you if I'd known you were doin' that."

"Yeah, I know. That's why I didn't tell you." He laughed. The laughter lit his eyes, transforming his whole face and making him almost handsome.

Some emotion she couldn't name gripped her. "Smart man. Thank you. You'd make a real good doctor, Clarence."

He blushed, then snorted.

"I mean that."

"Go on. Git back in the wheelbarrow. I got only one hand and not much brain, they say. So I'll be a doctor as soon as you become first lady."

She was really going to miss Clarence.

Ruth Ann slept hardly at all, her eyes flying open in alarm at the least creak or murmur or snore in the room. Since there were twenty-three other defective, degenerate or despairing girls in the room with her, this was about every seventy-four seconds.

She yanked her scratchy woolen blanket up as far as she could and secured it under her chin. It would need to come with her. She'd instructed Glory to just put her work dress on over her nightgown, then cinch her apron tightly. They'd roll an extra pair of drawers into their blankets, along with an extra set of stockings.

The only other things Ruth Ann planned to take were a tooth-brush and a dog-eared photograph of Sheila on her wedding day. She looked impossibly young and glamorous; unrecognizable, and therefore even more precious. She was a fantasy momma, with wide eyes and a sweet smile that maybe Annabel would inherit. She couldn't wait to see her darling girl.

After this train of thought came an unrelenting procession of awful *what if*s. What if Glory didn't wake up? What if one of the other girls saw them sneak out? What if a board creaked so loudly that Mother Jenkins and all the bats in her behind awoke?

What if the milkman got sick? What if the cows stampeded overnight and there was no milk for him to deliver? What if—

Stop it. Just stop it. Count sheep.

But her own unfortunate remark to Glory haunted her, and the first fluffy little lamb she conjured jumped straight into the slaughterhouse, bleating something fierce.

At long last the infernal clock finally struck three in the morning. Ruth Ann sat up. She waited, listening for her bunkmate's breathing. It was even and deep. All clear.

She crept out of bed, pulled on her gray work dress and apron, shimmied into her stockings, eased into both her shoes. She wiggled her toe, surprised at just how much better it felt since Clarence had drained it. Then she rolled up the blanket around her few belongings and headed for the door.

Outside, a cold white moon still hung in a lilac sky streaked with sleepy clouds. It was too late for crickets, too early for even the most ambitious bird. Glory didn't come out of the opposite dorm right away. Had she gotten cold feet? Decided to report her to Mother Jenkins, instead?

Finally, the dark figure of her friend slid out, easing the door closed behind her. "Sorry," Glory whispered. "I thought one of the other girls might be awake. She sneezed. But I s'pose it must be possible to sneeze an' still be asleep."

Ruth Ann tried to quell her jitters, laid a finger across her lips and motioned toward the ash pit. They hurried around back of the manse, where Doc Price and his cheerless wife lived. *One hundred yards safe.*

They passed the little stone wishing well, the gazebo, the box hedge in the shape of a cross. *Two hundred yards safe.*

Glory panted for breath beside her as they made it past the little duck pond. Almost to the wall that hid the ash pit. *Three hundred yards safe!*

Then Ruth Ann saw a light flicker on in her peripheral vision. Top floor of the manse: servants' quarters. Someone had seen or heard them.

Ruth Ann's pulse thundered in her ears. Her heart caught in her throat; her lungs quit on her. Her knees gave out and she sank to the ground as Glory kept running, unaware. She disappeared behind the wall as a frozen Ruth Ann fixated on the light.

Who is it? What's it mean? What'll happen next?

And then, by the grace of the good Lord, the light went out again.

Ruth Ann wrapped her arms around herself and slumped forward, rocking, sick with relief.

Something rustled beside her, igniting her panic once again. But then Clarence's voice whispered, "It's okay, Ruthie. It's okay." He found her hand in the darkness and pulled her to her feet. "C'mon, now. Your chariot awaits."

God bless the man. She could have kissed him.

How Clarence, with his one hand, could possibly wheelbarrow them all the way to the dairy barn was little short of a miracle. But Clarence demonstrated daily that he could do most anything, and wheel them he did. It was some rough, bumpy going. Ruth Ann and Glory clung to each other not only out of nerves, but also so as not to knock heads.

It took a good quarter hour, Ruth Ann reckoned, and not once did Clarence stop, cuss or complain. He just made steady progress and whistled on the way. At last he set them down, and with a *shhhhhh!* he went to scout any movement on the front side of the barn. Ruth Ann huddled against Glory, heart in her throat.

Presently, they heard Clarence trudge back toward the wheelbarrow. He patted the side of it reassuringly and whispered, "Here 'e comes with the wagon."

They heard the rumble of the wheels, the steady beat of a horse's hooves, the jingling of the harness as the driver pulled up outside the barn.

"C'mon out," Clarence said, under cover of the noise.

Ruth Ann and Glory scrambled out as quietly as they could, though it was hardly a graceful process.

"Get ready," he instructed. "Once he's inside to fetch the milk jugs, you make a run for the cart. I'll be right behind you. Get flat on the grain bags right behind the seat. *Flat.* I'll cover you with the canvas and a couple o' the full bags. Move fast as you can."

At his signal, they hitched up their skirts and sprinted as if Mother Jenkins and all her bats were in hot pursuit. Clarence lifted two bags of grain and hefted them to the ground, the horse entirely uninterested in any of them. Ruth Ann threw herself bodily over the low, flat side of the wagon and burrowed down as far as she could into the remaining burlap bags of grain and seed. Glory did likewise.

Then Clarence tossed the canvas over them, tucked it in at the edges and muttered an apology as he slapped the other two bags of grain over them, squashing the girls under their heavy weight.

"You'll be fine," he murmured. "Slip off when he makes the first stop. It'll be the Russell plant. Luck of the Irish to ya, Ruth Ann. Be well, Glory." He lightly smacked the side of the wagon, and then he was gone.

Within minutes, the driver could be heard wrestling heavy, five-gallon, tin milk jugs into the wagon, as the horse stood patiently. *Thunk, scrape, grunt. Thunk, scrape, grunt.*

It was hot and suffocating under all the grain and canvas, but Ruth Ann and Glory didn't dare move. The driver, by the grace of God, didn't seem to notice anything amiss and climbed up into his seat. He took the reins, relieved himself of an impressive burp and then urged the horse forward. They were on their way to freedom.

Ruth Ann held her breath, not only against the damp, musty, yeasty odor of the wagon and its contents, but out of exultation. She was on her way to get her daughter. She could almost feel the delicious warmth and weight of little Annabel in her arms: *her* baby, not Mrs. Dade's. Hers and nobody else's.

And as for Doc Price? He wouldn't get his scalpel anywhere near her female parts. This was *her* body, not his. Hers and not the state of Virginia's.

Five

Ruth Ann's heart beat in time to the rumble of the cart's wheels, and her breath hitched with every lurch of the wagon. Her right cheek pressed against Glory's left one.

Again, the forced intimacy felt awkward and unwelcome, but she and Glory were in this together now, so it also felt right, if peculiar. They clung to each other and sweated in rhythm with the wagon's progress, bathed in the morning's humidity and the sweet-sour aroma of the milk jugs behind them. The sacks of grain piled on top of them were as heavy and unyielding as corpses.

They were on their way to freedom. Annabel. A new life.

Clip clop, clip clop, rumble, rumble, jiggle, sway, squeak. Clip, clop, clip, clop, rumble, rumble, sway, squeak. The driver cleared his throat, hacking and gurgling to free his lungs, maybe of the previous night's pipe fumes. Glory quivered silently beside her.

The journey seemed to take forever, though in reality it took perhaps half an hour. At last they made a sharp right turn, the gravel under the wheels changed to soft earth and the rumbling of the cart subsided to mere squeaking.

Ten yards? Twenty? And then the horse stopped. It expelled a grateful snort, the harness jingling as it did so.

The driver climbed down from the wagon, and they heard his

booted footsteps hit gravel again before they receded as he called out, "'Mornin', Tommy!"

"Hiya, Fred. Gonna be a scorcher."

"Sure is."

"Come on inside for the paperwork. Then we'll getcha unloaded."

"Sure thing."

Boot steps echoed on wooden planks. A door complained as it was opened and shut.

Ruth Ann wrestled with the bags of grain on top of them, succeeded in shoving them to one side and poked her head out. Fred and Tommy had gone inside a long, low wooden building silhouetted against the dawn light.

"C'mon, Glory. We got to move. Now."

They struggled against more heavy bags, shoved them aside and wriggled out. Ruth Ann tugged out Clarence's canvas, briefly wondering where he'd get another for his wheelbarrow and if anyone would notice this one was missing.

Glory leaned against the side of the wagon, disheveled and panting. They took grateful drafts of the fresh morning air as the horse eyed them, unsurprised. It smelled ripe and salty; its chest was dark with sweat and its flanks steamed. Ruth Ann ventured a hand toward its velvety, warm muzzle and stroked it. "Thank you," she whispered.

The horse blinked and tossed its head as the girls hitched up their small bundles and ran for a large woodpile, visible behind the cheese-processing plant. They collapsed behind it and panted some more. Ruth Ann shot Glory a smile of triumph, ragged at the edges with disbelief.

Had they really left behind the Virginia Colony for the Epileptic and Feebleminded?

She shifted, pulled a rock out from under her backside and wiggled her toes in Clarence's big shoe. It was an oversize slipper from a prince of a boy who had an even gaze pure as fresh rainwater. She would miss him.

Her thoughts turned to Sheila. She couldn't miss her mother. But she did feel guilty for leaving her there, all alone, with nobody but Ruby to care whether she lived or died.

Ruth Ann's heart turned over.

"We're free!" Glory marveled.

"Yes." Ruth Ann swallowed.

If only freedom weren't so terrifying.

"What the devil do you mean?" Dr. Price asked Mother Jenkins, tossing down his fountain pen and snatching off his spectacles. "The girls are gone? How? When? And where?"

"I—I'm not sure, Doctor."

"They can't have gotten far. They have neither means nor transport. They must be hidden somewhere on the grounds."

Mother Jenkins twisted her apron and shook her head.

"No, sir. I even had Clarence bring out the dogs to track them, but no luck. They're on the lam."

"Damnation!"

Mother Jenkins flinched at his curse and took a step back.

"I beg your pardon. I'm worried that the girls will come to harm."

But truth to tell, it wasn't so simple. Just as he was executing a plan to pull his name and reputation out of this intolerable obscurity...the girls had run? He didn't need bad publicity or gossip in town about runaways from the Colony.

Irritation surged in his gut, acid eddying and pooling there. How had he gone from Johns Hopkins, Harvard Medical School and Mount Sinai Hospital to the blasted Virginia Colony for the Epileptic and Feebleminded? A pox on his wife Althea's ailing mother. Why couldn't she have had a second daughter to care for her? The woman had single-handedly halted his career.

Doc stroked his beard. He couldn't allow his temper to get the better of him. It was unseemly. So were these thoughts centered on ambition. He was a better man than this. A man of medicine. He sighed and tried to gain a little perspective. He supposed he should have anticipated this escape after Ruth Ann's impertinence. The girls *were*, no doubt, afraid of the surgery. They were simple creatures, after all, with little understanding of medical procedures— even those that were ultimately for their benefit and the state's.

"You have my apologies, Doctor." Mother Jenkins stared at the floor.

"I am a busy man, Mrs. Jenkins. I cannot operate on girls who have disappeared. I suggest that you find them immediately. Indeed, if you do not find them in the next twenty-four hours, you may very well be finding yourself another post. Do I make myself clear?"

Mother Jenkins's lips flattened. A tic was visible at her left eye, above which a vein stood out, blue with rage.

She'd have to keep it bottled. He knew she took her temper out on those poor hapless girls. He didn't care for her bullying ways, but then again, one couldn't hire someone weak whom they could walk all over. So he made do with her.

"Mrs. Jenkins, you simply must take better precautions and care. Understand: these girls have neither the mental capacity nor the moral fiber with which to manage their lives. Most of them— quite sadly—should have been drowned at birth in a bucket, like so many unwanted kittens."

She nodded.

"But since they weren't, it is only Christian to provide room and board for them, see that they go to church services and work to defray the state's costs for their upkeep. And it is *imperative* that they do not breed."

"Yes, Doctor."

"We are the guardians of this little flock of black sheep, Mrs. Jenkins," he said in gentler tones. "We must protect them not only physically, but spiritually. We must not let them stray, nor sin. We must save their immortal souls."

"Yes, sir."

He steepled his hands upon his desk. "I can only pray that as we speak, those two aren't busy finding themselves a pair of drugstore cowboys and some hooch. They have no sense or judgment...Locate them, Mrs. Jenkins, and bring them back before they manage to get themselves in trouble yet *again*."

She nodded. "I'll send Clarence with the motorcar—"

"Yes, yes...I don't need the details." He retrieved his pen and gestured toward the door with it. "Thank you—that will be all. You are dismissed."

Mrs. Jenkins looked as though she'd just swallowed a fly. "Very good, sir." And with that, she left him in peace.

But it wasn't to be peace, after all. For if he wasn't mistaken, the figure of Wilfred Block, Esquire, strode down the path toward his office door. He wore a dark gray suit that had been tailored by angels, and Doc couldn't help but covet it.

Doc looked down at his middling one under the white cotton coat and sighed. Then he stood and went to greet his friend. "Good day, sir. To what do I owe this honor?"

The dapper, too handsome Block chuckled and removed his hat. "Well, to that mighty fine single malt whisky in your desk drawer, of course!"

"And I thought you were here simply for the pleasure of my company."

"A Glenlivet, I believe?"

"Glenfarclas, my man." Doc took his cue and retrieved the bottle, along with two cut-crystal double-old-fashioned tumblers. He poured two fingers of Scotch for each of them, gestured to the visitor's chair and settled back into his own behind the desk.

"To Prohibition," said Block, with a wink.

Doc raised an eyebrow along with his glass. "Indeed."

Block sighed with satisfaction once he'd swallowed. "This always aids in my interpretation of the law."

"And it's good medicine," Doc said dryly.

"The best."

Price's mood darkened further as he asked the inevitable question of Block. "So…any luck on my behalf?" He'd run afoul of the law recently, ridiculous though the case was.

"I'm afraid not. I'll file another appeal."

"Very well. But it's simply outrageous!" Doc could feel his own blood pressure rising.

Block swirled his whisky pensively. "We just need the right test case."

"Yes." Doc's agreement was heartfelt. "And I believe I've found one." If he could retrieve her.

"That would be excellent news, indeed."

Doc exchanged interminable small talk with his visitor and endured more tasteless jokes until Block had drunk yet a third tumbler of his Scotch. Doc hid his relief when the attorney hoisted himself to his feet. "See you soon at the Colony board meeting, old sport?"

Doc stood up, too. "Yes, of course."

"Then for now, I'll take my leave." Block reeled out the office door, leaving Doc alone with his thoughts.

He stared into the depths of the whisky bottle as if the spirits could provide answers to some of the questions that troubled him. *Do no harm*, stated the Hippocratic oath.

And yet two girls had fled in terror of a medical procedure that he would perform upon them. Was *that* harm?

He shook off the thought. Certainly not. They were simple creatures of the lowest order; they were of severely flawed genetics; they had both been sexually active without benefit of marriage. He was sorry for their fear—he truly was. And he'd do his best to reassure them, when the time came, that the surgery was only for their benefit.

He'd interviewed Ruth Ann's mother, Sheila, at length before tying her tubes. She was dirty, uncouth, belligerent and profane. She'd worked as a prostitute after being widowed, drank to excess and was *still* of loose morals. He'd had her examined by a psychiatrist, who'd determined that she was hysterical and mentally unstable.

Women such as Sheila Riley quite simply should not be allowed to reproduce.

Poor Ruth Ann, arriving at the Colony pregnant, was clearly a younger version of her mother...and he expected the same would come of tiny Annabel. He'd reluctantly brought her into this world when Ruth Ann had gone into labor—what choice did he have? But enough was enough. It had to stop.

He'd added the Riley women to his ongoing study. Imagine: two females alone costing the state of Virginia $132,000 over the course of their reproductive years! Now add to that the third generation: another $66,000. But those figures were, in fact, conservative.

For Sheila Riley had whelped two *other* girls besides Ruth Ann. One had died, but setting that aside for the sake of argument, each girl was capable of having a litter of four or five others. Who were, in turn, likely to deliver four or five more to the state. The costs were simply unsustainable.

But how to explain such things to a girl as simple as Ruth Ann Riley? How did one explain to a parasite that she was, through no real fault of her own, a parasite? Impossible.

One couldn't explain. One had to act. And in doing so, he'd make a name for himself—despite being stuck in this rural backwater.

Six

Ruth Ann told her fear to scram. Like any other emotion, she had no use for it. Fear made her stupid, turned her into a lump of passivity and indecision.

Though a part of her wanted to just keep hiding out behind this woodpile, a scan of their surroundings told her that it was a bad idea. There'd be several men and maybe some women working in the cheese plant as the day got under way, and there was no outhouse that she could see. That meant the woodpile *was* the outhouse, and it would have visitors.

About twenty yards yonder lay the ruins of a low brick wall that had once surrounded the property. Against it was a pile of rusted-out milk canisters. That looked like a better spot to hide for the day, until they could travel again under cover of darkness. She prayed that they wouldn't bring out the dogs to search for her and Glory. If they did, their trail would stop near the back barn where they'd slipped into the dairy wagon...and Mother Jenkins might put two and two together.

Ruth Ann nudged Glory silently and gestured toward the pile of old canisters. Glory shrugged. The girls got to their feet, listened for any sound coming out of the plant—there wasn't any—and crept toward the new hiding place. They scrambled over the wall and flattened themselves behind it, pulling Clarence's canvas up over them. They ate a quick breakfast of plain bread while undercover.

They waited and waited, as the sun rose eagerly in the east, then became bored around noon, moodily playing with clouds. It yawned and disappeared for a nap toward three o'clock...allowing rain to move in and soak Ruth Ann and Glory, despite the canvas. They were half grateful for the shower by then because of the heat. The sun returned for a couple of hours to dry them gently, and at last sank torpidly into bed in the west. Mosquitoes appeared, but the two girls didn't dare do a lot of swatting.

"Glad we moved," Glory whispered, as the fourth worker came out to use the woodpile before heading off for his supper.

Ruth Ann nodded. Every muscle in her body ached, not only from the long, awful night in the laundry two days previously, but from being jolted around in the wagon and then sitting on the hard ground all day. She pulled the rest of the bread out of her bundle and divided it between herself and Glory. That was the end of their food, so they had to make it to the Dade house tonight or go hungry.

That's when it hit her: How would they get food from then on? She and Glory had no money. And if they took food from the Dades, wasn't that stealing?

She didn't like to think about that.

But hadn't the Dades stolen her baby? Didn't they owe her a meal or two?

Okay. But then...? How did she plan to feed Annabel? Where would the three of them live?

Maybe I am *feebleminded. Wouldn't a normal person have thought this through?*

Ruth Ann slid her foot down into Clarence's shoe until her wounded toe found the leather. She pressed against it until the pain came, sharp and yet somehow sweet because it distracted her from how stupid she was. How thoughtless.

Glory chewed her bread slowly, her blond hair shining silver in the first few rays of moonlight. She looked like an angel. "Where are we going to go?"

"To get my baby, Annabel. She's in a house in town, with the couple who raised me after my momma was put in the Distressed unit at the Colony."

"But after that?"

"We'll work it out."

"So you don't know."

"No," Ruth Ann admitted. "I don't."

"I thought you said you had a plan!"

"I got us out of the Colony, didn't I? Now it's time for a new plan. But for now, we just gotta go south, toward town. And then head east 'til we find Washington Street."

"Which way is south?" Glory asked, her tone troubled.

"Well," Ruth Ann reckoned. "The sun set over there. So that's west. If I face that way, then south is to the…left. So we need to go that way until we get to town."

"If we go into town, won't somebody see us?"

"We'll stay just north of the buildings. Then we'll find Washington and cut down it to the Dades' house." Lord, did her voice sound confident! How 'bout that?

"Swell. But then…do we just knock on the door and ask for your baby? They'll say no."

Ruth Ann gently took her by the shoulders. She looked steadfastly into Glory's eyes. "We're not knocking on the door. We're going in through a window. We're not asking for Annabel. We're taking her."

"But—"

"She's my baby. I didn't say they could have her. They just took her from me, so I'm-a get her back. How is that wrong?"

Glory hunched her shoulders and shook off Ruth Ann's grip. "I don't know, but they'll make it wrong. Somehow. We're not…regular people. Why is that, Ruth Ann? Why?"

Ruth Ann shrugged. "On account of we're feebleminded, I guess."

"I don't think you are. You just figured out which way we got to go, and you remember where the house is. That seems pretty smart to me. So why aren't you regular?"

"On account of I got knocked up."

"Me, too, but I thought we was getting married. He said we would. How's I s'posed to know he was lyin'?"

Ruth Ann shook her head and sighed. "It ain't like Pinocchio. I ain't never seen a liar's nose grow, so's you can tell he's a liar."

"What about you?" Glory asked. "Did your beau promise—"

"No." Oh, he'd promised—to let her breathe again if she did what he wanted. "I don't want to talk about it." Ruth Ann turned away and folded Clarence's canvas in half, then in quarters, before rolling it up. "We need to head out."

Glory got to her feet. "Did you love him?"

"No." But she'd loved the idea of him, hadn't she? The handsome outer shell of the boy who'd come to visit the childless aunt who doted on him. She hadn't seen the stinking, rotten ooze inside until too late.

Her fault, likely, for making sheep's eyes at him.

"Then…why did you…" Glory's voice trailed off into awkwardness.

"Guess I'm just a common slut," Ruth Ann said, not knowing why it seemed easier to say that than cotton to the truth. It seemed stronger, anyways. Less whiny and pathetic and sniveling.

She wasn't going to talk about her tears or pleas or fear or humiliation or pain or the aftermath of disgust she'd felt as she lay soiled and exposed, stunned, while he straightened his clothes and turned away from her as though she were a sack of garbage.

She wasn't going to talk about his horrid smirk every time she saw him afterward, as if she were his own private joke. And she damn sure wasn't going to talk about how he'd gone still, then just shrugged his shoulders, when she told him about the baby.

How is that my problem? he'd asked.

She'd just stared at him.

Then his jaw had gone slack. *You don't think…you think I'm going to* marry *you?* And he'd laughed. A guffaw of disbelief and amusement at her expense.

She broke the juice pitcher over his head, but that brief moment of satisfaction was short-lived. Because he grabbed her by the throat and dragged her to the shed behind the house and did it to her again. Told her she was white trash and if she ever said a word to the Dades or anyone else, he'd kill her.

Would he? She didn't like to think about it.

All she knew was that he still visited the Dades. What happened when Annabel got to be twelve or thirteen? What if she was pretty?

No. It didn't bear thinking about. She was getting Annabel out of there now. It wasn't going to happen to her daughter. *No.*

"Hello? Where are you?"

Glory's hand waved in front of her face, startling Ruth Ann.

"Right here, as you can see, plain as day."

"Uh-uh. You were somewhere else. And why are you shaking?"

"I ain't." But Ruth Ann's hands trembled despite her best efforts to stop them. Perspiration had broken out under her arms and around her hairline. Her breathing had gone quick and shallow, and her pulse roared in her ears.

"Are you ill?" Glory asked, pressing her palm to Ruth Ann's forehead.

She jerked away. "I'm fine. Let's go." She realized how much she didn't want to go anywhere near the Dade home and its memories, but she had no choice if she wanted her baby. So she would.

And then she'd leave it far behind. Walk until it shrank to the size of a dollhouse, then a loaf of bread, then the head of a pin…until it vanished completely from sight and mind and ceased to exist.

The moon lit the way sporadically, flirting idly with the clouds, as the sun had. Or perhaps the clouds were dancing in front of the moon. Ruth Ann didn't really know how it all worked—she was just another ant below the heavens, casting a fearful gaze toward them when they rumbled, grateful when they cast down rays of light.

She supposed God floated above them. Was thunder His anger? Rain His tears? Lightning His fury? Sunlight and moonlight His blessing?

If that were so, then He seemed of two minds about her mission this evening. One moment, their path was lit and Ruth Ann could see the road clearly laid out before them. And yet the next moment, pitch-black wrapped them in blindness. They stumbled along, feeling their way through the dark and occasionally straying off the path because they simply couldn't see what lay before them.

She could smell clearly, though. The rich, sweet scent of tobacco filled her nostrils, chased off by the more immediate stench of things they passed: dirty, beery motor oil from the breakdown of an automobile, putrid carcass-rot from a small possum hit by its wheel, the concentrated offense of a pile of horse dung, into which she almost stepped.

She and Glory walked at least three miles, by her calculation—miles of doubt, buried fear and blisters. Ruth Ann's injured toe had plenty of space, but her foot slid back in Clarence's shoe with every step, the sweaty leather rubbing her flesh raw.

It gave her something to focus on other than dread. *Step, sting, slide, sting. Step, sting, slide, sting.*

She felt a moisture building in the shoe, probably blood. But what could she do about it? Wrap her foot in her spare pair of drawers? So Ruth Ann just kept putting one foot in front of the other, as she always did. The alternative was to crawl into the ditch and sleep…but giving up like that wasn't an option when she thought about Annabel.

"Penny for your thoughts," ventured Glory after the first mile or so.

Ruth Ann snorted. "They ain't worth that much."

"To me they are."

"Why?"

"Don't know…maybe 'cause I think you're brave. And smart."

"You got me confused with someone else, Glory-girl."

"Nope. I don't think so." Glory smiled. "So if I had a penny, I'd give it to you—let's pretend I do."

Ruth Ann shook her head. *Step, sting, slide, sting.* "Whatever you say."

"Here you go." Glory dropped an imaginary coin into her unwilling palm. "So what are your thoughts?" Her angelic face was lit with actual interest.

Ruth Ann wasn't used to anyone being interested in anything

about her except how much work she could get done and how fast. Except Mrs. Dade, who had once been kind to her, especially when she was younger. She'd patted her shoulder, ironed her frock, brushed and braided her hair.

And what was Ruth Ann fixin' to do? Steal Annabel away from her. She wasn't a good person. She was all the things Mother Jenkins said she was…but she didn't know exactly how she'd gotten this way.

"Hey, Ruth Ann. I gave you my penny," Glory teased. "Talk to me, afore I go crazy from hearing nothin' but wind."

"Okay. Here's my thoughts. I feel bad about what we're gonna do. Because I know how I felt when they took Annabel—like a giant hole got torn in me. So how can I do it to Mrs. D?"

Glory stopped and just stared at her. "Uh. Do unto others?"

"It ain't…that simple."

"Yeah, it is."

"One minute I agree with you; the next I don't. Mrs. Dade was good to me." But was she? Ruth Ann peered ahead blindly as the clouds obscured the moon and saw Mrs. D's drawn and disgusted face.

I'm so disappointed in you, Ruthie. How could you?

It wasn't like that, Mrs. D! I swear. He—

Don't you lie to me on top of it. Don't you dare.

I ain't lyin'. He made me!

Mrs. D had raised a hand as if to slap her.

Ruth Ann shrank back, sobbing.

Get out of my sight. We didn't raise you to be a slut or a liar. We've been nothing but good to you…and this is the thanks we receive? You accuse my own nephew? Get out of my sight.

The slap would have been better than the words.

Mrs. Dade, she wanted to say. *Why didn't I show you the bruises, after? The blue-black stains of shame in places no girl should have them?* My wrists, upper arms…my teats…my inner thighs. *Why did I hide them? Why didn't I know this was coming?*

The answer: *I didn't think it could get worse.*

Go! Mrs. Dade had said again. *All I can do is pray for your tarnished soul. But frankly, Ruthie, I don't want to. I will have to pray that God sends me the strength to pray for you, to forgive you.*

Ruth Ann had turned and run from the room, eyes streaming, heart shriveled above her swelling belly. She'd run into the narrow hallway, tripping on the carpet, falling forward and then failing to balance, almost tumbling backward again. She wished she had. Wished she'd cracked her skull wide open.

Glory grabbed her shoulder and shook it. "Where do you go?"

"What?"

"It's like you're gone from your own body. Nobody home in there. Where do you go?"

Away. Anywhere but here. "I dunno."

"Well, come back into yourself and listen to me. That Mrs. D, she wasn't *good* to you. She kicked you outta her house and then stole your baby."

"She *was* good. Until she wasn't."

"How was she good?"

Ruth Ann sighed. "She didn't have no daughter of her own. Couldn't. So…she chose me. Brought me to her home. Sent me off to school for a while. An' she taught me stuff around the house. Like how to clean and sew and cook."

"Uh-huh. So's you could do it for her."

Ruth Ann shrugged. "Maybe. I done it for others, too. They paid her for my time."

"That ain't bein' good to you. That's trainin' you like a dog: Sit, stay, roll over, fetch. Poop outside."

Time for a change of subject. "I was always good about that last one," Ruth Ann said drily.

Glory's laugh floated in the moonlight, which had chosen to reappear. It echoed through the branches of a massive oak tree that sheltered a bend in the road. "You're somethin', Ruthie."

Ruth Ann's breath hitched, and she stopped in her tracks. "Don't. Don't call me that."

"Sorry...?"

But she didn't answer the unspoken question. It hurt to be called Ruthie. The two women whose love she'd lost abruptly—her momma and then Mrs. D—both of them had called her that. Until they'd called her other, hateful names. She didn't want to be Ruthie. Ruthie was dead; only Ruth Ann remained.

"Okay, Miss Prickly."

She felt bad again...wanted to explain to Glory. But she didn't even know where to start. "I don't mean to hurt your feelin's," she got out.

Glory touched her shoulder. "I know that."

"How?"

"I just do."

Ruth Ann nodded and saw that they'd finally reached Washington Street. "We turn right here. Careful—nobody can see us. We need to take the alleys."

And so they did, slipping soundlessly along, with only one close call when a dog growled menace at them. "Ignore him. Keep walking," Ruth Ann instructed Glory, who clutched at her hand. "He just wants us away from his territory." Quavering, Glory tottered beside her, refusing to relinquish her death-grip on Ruth Ann's fingers.

There was something comforting in her touch, even if it initially made Ruth Ann want to pull away and keep to herself.

The hand around hers—it said she wasn't alone. If Glory wasn't quite yet a friend, she was at least a companion. And one who'd been handed some of the same injustices in life.

They reached the Dade homestead at last, and Ruth Ann stopped abruptly. There it was: the gray-painted cottage with two wide steps leading up to the front porch. Plain gray railings, black shutters and black front door. The house looked so unthreatening, so normal, so respectable.

Ruth Ann knew where the wood was spongy in the middle of the second step. She remembered the creak when Mrs. Dade opened the door. Directly inside were a wrought-iron umbrella stand and three hooks for coats. Mr. Dade's field jacket would be hanging there, as well as Mrs. Dade's dark gray woolen coat with the wide shawl collar. On the third hook would likely be the brown woolen cape they'd let her wear, still there because it wasn't hers.

Beyond the little foyer lay the formal living room with a settee, a low tea table, two wing chairs and a harpsichord. And tucked behind that was the room Ruth Ann knew the best: the kitchen, with its brick floor, scarred but still attractive farm table and the four makeshift, oft-mended wooden chairs. The cast-iron pot-bellied stove flanked by hanging vegetable baskets and a clever alcove for preserves on one side, and a pie safe on the other.

The pie safe had never protected Mrs. D's pies from either Patrick or her husband. If Mr. D found one cooling, he was likely to help himself without permission or thought that it might be for someone else. The only ones that made it to neighbors or friends unscathed were the rhubarbs. Cherry, peach, blueberry, pumpkin and pecan got half-devoured without conscience, no matter how often Mrs. D scolded him.

As long as one wasn't a pie, Mr. D was harmless, even vaguely sweet under his gruff exterior. He was mostly mustache and pipe, a pair of corduroyed knees under a newspaper. One might catch a glimpse of his bushy, graying eyebrows above the paper, but just as often they'd be obscured by a cloud of smoke.

He had never laid a hand on Ruth Ann—not in affection, not in anger, not in lust. For that, she was grateful.

"What are you staring at?" Glory whispered.

Roused from her reverie, Ruth Ann put a finger to her lips and jerked her head toward the back of the house. It was one story, thank the Lord. She wouldn't have to shimmy up a ladder to get to Annabel.

Her infant daughter would be asleep in her old bedroom directly behind the kitchen, she was sure of it. Not in the wooden sleigh bed yet—still in a crib. The Dades would be in their double brass bed in the room behind the parlor.

Her heart began to hammer now that she was actually here, though her blood seemed thick and sluggish in her veins. She moved on stiff legs around back of the house, Glory scuttling beside her. She paused outside the window of her former room, eyeing the frame, noting that the Dades had installed a new screen to keep insects away from the baby.

What are you doing, Ruth Ann? This ain't just underhanded. It's trespassing. It's prob'ly kidnapping. What if you go to jail?

Seven

Horsefeathers. It couldn't possibly be kidnapping to take back her own baby. Could it? Even if the way she was doing it wasn't exactly aboveboard.

But how aboveboard had the nurses been to simply whisk away her newborn without asking her and giving Annabel to Mrs. Dade?

Where were her rights in this situation? Didn't she have any?

Ruth Ann set down her bundle and put her hands flat on the window screen, feeling her way around its frame for a notch so that she could pull it off and get to the window itself. *There.* Notches on either side, about halfway down. She poked her thumbs into them and yanked back, hard. The screen obligingly gave way and pulled free with only a slight scrape.

She slid her fingers under the window's frame and pushed upward. Though she expected the squeak from long experience, it shredded her nerves. She kept on pushing, until the heavy frame slid up. Then she parted the lace curtains, made by Mrs. Dade's own hands, and poked her head inside.

The soft, milky scent of sleeping baby almost brought her to her knees. Ruth Ann's whole body began to tremble with longing as she hung half inside the window, supporting herself on the ledge.

Get hold o' yourself, stupid girl! Now is not the time to be mawkish. Get in, get her, then get out.

But all she could do was hang there and breathe in the essence of Annabel. She could smell the wood floor, too, and the lemon polish of the furniture, and the lavender water sprinkled on the baby's blankets. She spied a cradle in the corner and the beginnings of a dollhouse that Mr. D must be building for Annabel. A beautiful porcelain doll sat in a miniature chair, waiting for her to get old enough to play with her.

An ache grew in Ruth Ann's chest. Mr. D had never built *her* a dollhouse. But she'd been someone else's child. They must feel differently about this baby. Maybe they thought of her as their own.

"What are you doing?" Glory whispered.

Ruth Ann took a deep breath. Then she braced herself on either side of the window casing and crawled awkwardly inside her old room. She froze at a creak somewhere in the house. Once her alarm had subsided, she rose to her feet and crept over to the cradle.

Annabel lay sleeping peacefully, her pale, downy white cheeks caressed by the moonlight. Ruth Ann's eyes welled at the sight of her, at the chestnut lashes of her closed eyes against her milky soft skin. After three months, were her eyes still blue?

She reached down and touched one tiny fist, gasping softly when it opened and clutched her finger. A throbbing began deep in her womb, a primal, undeniable claim to this baby. Her baby. Not the Dades'.

Ruth Ann crouched next to the cradle and slipped her hands under Annabel's warm little body, picking her up along with the blankets that covered her. The child snuffled and cooed, her eyes opening, then closing again, as she turned her head to search for a bottle. A bottle Ruth Ann didn't have.

She rocked her in her arms and slipped a finger into the baby's mouth, hoping Annabel would find some comfort in that. She suckled it for a moment, but then turned her head again, searching. She was hungry.

Ruth Ann had known they'd have to steal milk from the icebox. She'd known it good and well, so why was her heart just about galloping out of her chest?

Stand up tall. Hold her close. Walk to the kitchen. Open the icebox and remove a bottle of milk...

Stealing. It was theft.

And the baby wouldn't drink cold milk, either. Would she? No. Ruth Ann would have to heat some. Mrs. D would surely hear her. She hadn't thought this through.

She stood frozen with the baby in her arms. Annabel began to squirm, still looking for the milk she couldn't access. Next came the gurgling. And a wail.

Shhhhhh! Don't cry, don't cry! Ruth Ann ran to the open window with the baby and crouched down. "Glory! Glory, take her, and try to keep her quiet. I got to find her some milk. Be right out."

"But—"

"Shhhhh! Here." Ruth Ann passed Annabel out the window. "Rock her."

But Annabel was wide awake now and unused to being outside at night, unfed and in strangers' arms. She opened her little rosebud mouth and howled at awesome decibels.

"No! No, no, no...shhhhhh, baby. Shhhhh!"

There was no way to go back in and get milk. They had to run.

Ruth Ann torpedoed herself through the window, landing awkwardly on the ground. She scrambled back up and ran three steps before she found herself facing the double-barrel of Mr. Dade's shotgun.

"Who are you?" he growled. "Just what in the *hell* do you think you're doing?"

Mrs. Dade came running out of the house, her hair wild and her night rail flying behind her. "My baby! What are you doing? Don't hurt my baby!"

"She's not your baby—she's mine!" Ruth Ann said, already knowing the words didn't matter. Her feelings wouldn't matter, either. Nor would the "rights" she should have, just like normal people. Her rights were all wrong.

Mrs. Dade gasped. "*What?*"

Annabel, perhaps sensing the tension, howled again, then worked herself into a series of frantic wails.

"Give the baby to my wife. You move one muscle in the other direction, and I'll blow your head off. Step into the light o'er here, so's I can see you." Mr. Dade was no longer just a pair of bushy eyebrows above or knees under a newspaper. He was defending his family, and he was deadly serious. He looked capable of anything at all.

Ruth Ann stumbled on wobbly knees and her mismatched shoes, into the light of the lantern that hung near the outhouse.

Mr. D's jaw went slack. "You! What are you doing here?"

"Ruth Ann?" Her former foster mother put a trembling hand to her throat.

The moment of horror stretched on and on.

"I wouldn't have hurt her" was all Ruth Ann said. "I just wanted—" Her voice cracked.

Mrs. Dade ignored her. "Give me my child! *At once*," she snapped at Glory.

Noooooooo! Ruth Ann shrieked silently.

Wordlessly, Glory handed over the baby, who was still wailing, despite her best efforts to soothe Annabel.

Ruth Ann didn't know whether to faint or run. But this choice, too, was made for her.

"You girls get into the house," ordered Mr. Dade. "You can't be wandering the countryside at night."

"That's all right—"

"Beg pardon?" he said, the words heavy with sarcasm. "None o' this is all right. Now get. Into. The. House."

Aghast, eye on his shotgun, Ruth Ann beckoned a shell-shocked Glory to follow her.

Mrs. Dade brought up the rear, cooing at Annabel and stroking her sweet head.

The door had been standing wide since the couple flew out in alarm. Mr. Dade closed it with a thud behind them, parked his shotgun near the dark, unlit fireplace and went about the business of lighting lanterns.

"You'd best make some sorry attempt to explain yourselves," he said. "You ran away from the Colony, I take it?"

"We—we were discharged," Ruth Ann managed.

Mr. Dade set down the last lantern on the mantel, turned and folded his arms. "Is that so?" he said. He skewered her with his gaze.

She looked away. This man had been kind to her.

"They discharged you, what, to run around alone? To rob decent folks and kidnap their babies?"

"No—"

"No, what, Ruth Ann? No, we're not decent folks? No, you didn't snatch Annabel and hand her out the window to your friend, here?"

"I—"

"What in the good Lord's name were you thinking, girl?"

"Annabel is my baby. I want her back."

"That's ridiculous. You're a child who gave birth to a child—and out of wedlock. Frankly, you and she are both lucky that Mrs. Dade and I are willing to take her in, to turn a blind eye to the circumstances of her birth. Which are deplorable, as you well know. Shameful."

"Yes, they are!" she flared back.

He flapped a dismissive hand at her.

The gesture enraged her. "It *is* shameful that I was—" She searched for the right words. "That I was *taken 'vantage of*, while under your roof."

Beside her, Glory gasped and put a hand over her mouth.

Now she knew the story. Woefully inadequate words to sum up what had happened. But there simply were none that were socially acceptable.

Mr. Dade looked uncomfortable.

"*Not another word*," Mrs. Dade said, her face darkening. "We won't entertain any more of your lies."

"They ain't—"

"Stop it! Close your mouth."

Ruth Ann did so.

"We won't wait much longer for an apology, by the way."

"An apology?! For wanting my baby back?"

"You broke into our home in the middle of the night to steal her. How can you possibly justify that?"

"*But you stole her first.*" She was just as shocked as the Dades at her words.

"How dare you!" Mrs. Dade said, while guiltily clutching Annabel like a bootlegged case of whiskey.

"How dare *you?*" Again, Ruth Ann couldn't believe the words came out of her mouth. But she'd been silent so long. "You people took her while I was sleeping! After thirty hours of labor, I woke to find her just...gone. And at first they wouldn't even tell me where. You just—you just *traded* me for my baby. Like I'm a...cow or a horse or something."

"We did nothing of the sort. Don't you put the blame on us for your immoral behavior, Ruth Ann. The Colony placed Annabel with us to give her a good home, and frankly to make reparations."

Huh? "What does that mean?"

"To make up for your being such a disappointment!"

She stood and stared at them.

Why don't you hear me? Ruth Ann closed her eyes. *Why don't you believe me?* It wouldn't do her any good to say it again. Or try to tell her truth. Nobody cared; nobody believed her. Because she was Nobody.

"Do you realize that you almost got our license revoked? Do you realize that we depend on that stipend from the state to pay our bills?"

What's a stipend? She guessed it was money.

"Where were you going to take her, Ruth Ann?" Mrs. Dade asked. "How were you going to feed her?"

Ruth Ann wordlessly shook her head. They were the same questions she'd asked herself.

"Where did you plan to live?"

Ruth Ann stared down at the shoes she wore: one her own, one Clarence's. Her feet ached, but not nearly as much as her heart. Her blisters stung, but not as much as her pride. Stupid. She was stupid. She'd convinced herself that they'd find an abandoned barn or someplace. Borrow milk from a neighboring cow. That they could maybe plant a vegetable patch...

She saw now that it had been a silly sixteen-year-old girl's dream.

"Where, Ruth Ann?"

She shook her head miserably. "I just—I just wanted a chance. To be her ma. To maybe have a normal family."

A shadow crossed Mrs. Dade's face, and she sighed. She sank down on the settee and stroked Annabel's wispy chestnut curls. "I suppose you did."

The glimmer of compassion almost undid Ruth Ann. "I just wanted to...love her."

Mr. Dade shoved his hands under his armpits and shifted from foot to foot.

Mrs. Dade gazed at Ruth Ann for a long moment and then nodded, sudden tears pooling in her eyes.

"I'm sorry, Mrs. D. I'm sorry." Was she?

Did the fact that Mrs. Dade had ached for a baby of her own and knew how Ruth Ann felt...did that make her theft of Annabel all right? Did Mrs. D's tears wash away her guilt? Or Ruth Ann's hurt and deep sense of betrayal?

No. Tears ain't holy water.

But Ruth Ann swallowed. "Can I—Can I just hold her awhile?"

"It's not wise, my dear. It will only make it harder."

"We all know I ain't wise. I'm *feebleminded*. But please, can I hold my baby girl?"

Mrs. D reluctantly nodded, just as Mr. D shook his head no. But he allowed himself to be overruled. Waving the shotgun around must've plumb wore him out.

"Sit here." Mrs. Dade patted the settee next to her. "And you— what is your name?"

"Glory," said Glory.

"Well, dear, you sit in that chair, there." Her voice hardened. "And you will both stop lying. We will have a cup of tea while Mr. Dade telephones the Colony."

"No, please!" Ruth Ann jumped to her feet.

"Don't make me pick up that shotgun again," Mr. D said wearily. "Siddown. You got to go back, and you know it. You made your bed."

I didn't make any bed! It ain't fair to make me lie in it! But Ruth Ann looked at her baby, and she sat down next to Mrs. Dade.

Glory had gone pale and clutched at the arms of her chair. She was probably wondering what Mother Jenkins would do to them. It didn't bear thinking of.

Grudgingly, Mrs. D handed Annabel to Ruth Ann, and she melted at the feel of her in her arms. At the milky baby scent. At her helplessness, her innocence, her sweetness. She never wanted to let her go.

"Thank you," she whispered. A lump as big as Shenandoah Mountain grew in her throat, impossible to swallow. She felt fused with the child, one and the same being. How could she ever let her go? "Thank you," she said again.

Mrs. D nodded quietly. She reached out a hand, almost touched it to Ruth Ann's shoulder. But she let it drop. Then she said, without further ado, "Ruth Ann, you are unwed, and you are not even of age. I'm not a monster. But you *claim* this child is related to me by blood. Whether or not that is true, she will remain in my care."

Eight

Where were the girls? *Of all the times to lose them…*
Dr. Price paced back and forth in the parquet hallway, waiting for the clock to strike three. Waiting for the appointed hour of the board meeting he'd called.

Tremont House, the executive office of the Colony, was a lovely white antebellum mansion graced by tall, fluted white columns under a portico. Its shutters and massive front door were painted a shiny black, and two polished brass lanterns on either side complemented the shiny brass latch.

It was a genteel building, perfect for administration and fund-raising. Dark, dignified portraits of do-gooders hung framed in gold against forest-green, flocked wallpaper. Potted plants in Chinese vases preened near the tall windows.

Inside what had once been a dining room that seated thirty, a vast oriental rug stretched under what had become the Colony's boardroom table. Price forced himself to sit down at the head of it to wait.

The long walnut table gave ample camouflage to his jiggling leg. Nervous and annoyed as he was, he still projected an air of imperturbability—he had to, as superintendent of the Colony and its chief medical officer.

Mrs. Parsons, the Colony's receptionist, fluttered about with pressed, embroidered napkins, silver trays, tea and finger sand-wiches. Eventually the other board members began to arrive, and Price put on his most genial expression.

They greeted him, accepted refreshments and took their seats. Wilfred Block lounged elegantly to his left, while Anselm Stringer, a former member of the Virginia legislature and the Colony's legal counsel, sat to his right. Stringer would help Price make his case today.

Other members included regional doctors, professors, business-men and a pastor who all made charitable contributions to the cause. At each man's place at the table lay a copy of Dr. Harry Laughlin's 1922 book, *Eugenical Sterilization in the United States*.

Dr. Price formally opened the meeting while Mrs. Parsons settled herself in a corner with a Smith Corona typewriter to write up the minutes for the secretary…and steal admiring glances at that dandy Block.

"Thank you for your presence today, gentlemen," said Price. "I'll do a brief review from our last meeting for the three members who were not present. To start with, I will assume that you are familiar with the term *eugenics*, or the science of good breeding?"

Block rolled his eyes. "Who isn't? Every newspaper and maga-zine is awash in the topic. The state fairs are now hosting Better Breeding competitions for American families, as well as cattle."

"Yes, indeed." Dr. Price aimed a genial smile at him before turning back to the group. "The term *eugenics* was coined by Sir Francis Galton—Charles Darwin's cousin—when he examined the studies of Gregor Mendel on pea plants about six decades ago. Mendel was able to breed out the weaker, disease-prone strains of the plants through his experiments on dominant and recessive genes. This is *scientific proof* that we can also breed out—in fact *eliminate*—the traits of feeblemindedness, deformity, drunkenness, criminality and moral degeneracy that are threatening our society."

Block raised his eyebrows. "You trying to close the Colony and put yourself out of a job, Doc?"

Mrs. Parsons giggled in the corner like a schoolgirl, though the question didn't merit such a display of mirth.

Dr. Price produced an obligatory chuckle, then took a sip of water. "This science," he continued, "has been researched, proven and documented extensively. And we have all agreed unanimously that the feebleminded should not propagate, because of the future burden on this Colony, the state of Virginia and indeed the entire nation. We simply do not have the capacity to house these degenerates for their entire reproductive years— the cost is staggering."

Nods of assent traveled around the table.

"While of course there is nothing to be done about some, what we need to seriously consider is a permanent solution to allowing the most capable to be released to fulfill specific roles in society— as laborers, domestic help, farmhands, and so forth. They can lead relatively normal and productive lives, good lives in the service of God and country—as long as we curtail their ability to breed more of their kind.

"Therefore, we propose to adopt the sterilization program we discussed at our last meeting—shocking and distasteful as it may be to those encountering the concept for the first time. Sterilization is far kinder and more compassionate than the alternatives, which frankly include"—Price paused for effect—"euthanasia."

Both Mrs. Parsons and the elderly Baptist pastor gasped. "Euthanasia?" he repeated, clearly horrified.

"It has been suggested as a solution," Dr. Price affirmed.

"However, it is not one that we advocate here at the Colony. We must be *progressive*," he said, "but not pernicious. Those who treat the feebleminded have a strong commitment to moral treatment and compassionate care, and it is my conviction that we can do a great deal to help our patients. However, we *cannot*, under any circumstances, let them multiply."

The old pastor shook his head. "Seems to me that none of this should be decided by us. It's all up to God."

Wilfred Block raised a lazy eyebrow at him. "You weed your garden, don't you, Pastor?" he asked. "This is no different. These people are crabgrass, dandelions, nettles, poison ivy! If you don't stop them, they overrun everything and choke your tomatoes, your lettuces, your cucumbers and beans."

The pastor still demurred.

Block leaned forward and clasped his hands on the table. "Perhaps it's a little cruel on the surface, but ultimately for the greater good."

Price nodded. "And it's much kinder than an actual castration, you'll agree."

Mrs. Parsons froze, aghast, over her typewriter, forcing Price to apologize as several men, including the pastor, flushed and crossed their legs under the table.

The pastor looked horrified. "That is against the laws of God."

"I personally shudder to think of such a procedure," Stringer said.

"Indeed, don't we all," Block said in amused tones.

Dr. Price nodded. "And yet castrations have been performed at other facilities such as ours, not to mention at mental hospitals across the country."

Heads shook around the table, while Mrs. Parsons turned fuchsia in her corner.

"I agree that it's quite cruel and distasteful," said Dr. Price. "Of course," he continued, "it is the females who are the majority of our problem, gentlemen. Women of *any* intellect are a temptation to males. Women of feeble intellect are unable to remember their morals or repress their sexual impulses, and they become little better than rabbits, multiplying uncontrollably and spreading disease, not to mention their degenerate germ plasm."

"Compulsory sterilization still seems…wrong," argued the pastor. "Against nature."

Block waded into the argument. "Is it *right* for this country to be overrun by degenerates and imbeciles who either won't or can't support themselves? The undesirables feed and breed upon us like maggots—we must put a stop to it."

Dr. Price redirected. "We must carefully cultivate thorough-breds instead."

Murmurs of assent rippled around the table.

"So," the good doctor emphasized, "let us look at the possibility of giving as many patients as possible their freedom—which sterilization allows. Once they have been trained to be useful and productive, once we are assured that they will not be able to propagate more of their type, they can be released and assimilated back into society, where they can lead happy, relatively normal lives. Thus, far from being barbaric, sterilization is actually a kind and compassionate choice."

Heads nodded.

"Furthermore, compulsory sterilization is not so far removed from compulsory vaccination for the public good." Price nodded at his partner.

Stringer took over. "So we ask you, gentlemen, to review the model sterilization law created by Dr. Harry Laughlin. We ask that you peruse, on your own time and of course at your convenience, the volume in front of you. For now, suffice it to say that Dr. Laughlin's model law is of great assistance in creating similar statutes to the ones passed by Indiana, California, Nevada, Kansas, and many other states.

"But to accomplish this here in Virginia, gentlemen," he announced, "we've got to create an airtight case to get the law on our side, as Indiana did in 1907. All prisons and state hospitals there are authorized to sterilize mental defectives, criminals, moral degenerates and sexual perverts. We here in Virginia are lagging behind."

Stringer looked around the table, meeting each man's gaze in turn. "Every reasonable-minded, educated person—doctors, scientists, reformers, charity workers, and socially prominent, concerned citizens such as yourselves—must be a proponent of eugenics. Gentlemen, it is up to *us* to create and pass a sterilization law here in Virginia."

Dr. Price took his cue. "Which brings us to the primary reason we are here today. I believe I have found the perfect test case," he said. "She is a sixteen-year-old resident of the Colony who has already given birth to one illegitimate child. Her mother is also a patient. Both may be categorized as morons, according to Mr. Goddard's chart of the hierarchy of feeblemindedness. So there is little doubt that her baby, Annabel, will develop abnormally, given her genetics."

"Is there a way to tell definitively?" Block asked.

"The baby's measurements and weight are normal, but there's something not quite right about the eyes—and her reactions to stimuli are delayed. I would judge her to be of low IQ. I can ask her foster mother to bring her here for an exam. My nurse and I, as well as the social worker who facilitated the adoption of baby Annabel, will be able to testify regarding her mental state."

The men continued the conversation, noting that Sheila, the grandmother, was a lunatic and spent a good deal of time in a straitjacket.

Then Price got to the point. "In order to move forward, the girl, Ruth Ann Riley, will need some sort of guardian to challenge my proposed surgery, and she will also need a lawyer. Someone who, of course...has the Colony's best interests at heart."

"My, my." Block smiled like an alligator about to close in on an unwitting duck. "I'm known for my excellent defense work, you know. Perhaps I'm available."

Something in Dr. Price's stomach slid, greasy and guilty. "Perhaps you are, Wilfred." He certainly was the perfect candidate for the job. "The question is how to present all of this to Miss Riley."

"She's a moron," Block reminded them all. "She won't be hard to convince. She has absolutely no understanding of the law or what's at stake. And she trusts you as a doctor."

Dr. Price stroked his beard. The greasy, guilty thing in his gut slid again. "Just so. As a matter of fact, I've already told her about the procedure, and she seemed none too happy about it."

"At the Vineland Training School in New Jersey, I believe they just tell them that they're undergoing an appendectomy," another physician at the table ventured.

"As we've done here," Price admitted, with a sidelong glance at Block. "But I was...challenged...recently."

"Most of them don't need to know, nor are they even capable of comprehending the implications of the procedure," Block said impatiently. "But in this case, we *want* the girl to object. And since she has, Dr. Price shall find himself honor bound to request the state to appoint a guardian to look after her interests. Her father is presumed dead and her mother is a lunatic."

The good doctor's queasiness persisted. *Honor bound.*

"You tricky old fox." Block displayed his teeth again, the vile crocodile. He seemed to positively enjoy the idea of this deception.

Dr. Price didn't particularly want to think about it. As the probable producer of more degenerate offspring, Ruth Ann needed to be sterilized anyhow, and the ruse was a means to an end. *It's merely a white lie, when all is said and done...perfectly justified.*

But still. His conscience niggled at him.

"Win or lose, the other side shall appeal," Stringer said, looking directly at Block. "We will take this case all the way to the Supreme Court of these United States."

Block fingered his gold pocket watch. "And in the process, we shall make legal history." He nodded at Stringer, then leveled his gaze upon Price. "And medical history." He turned back to the group at large. "We shall also be lauded as the greatest of patriots."

Price formally closed the meeting, seconded by Stringer. As the other gentlemen lingered to socialize afterward, he found himself wanting a drink, quite badly. To celebrate, of course. He'd won. Hadn't he? As long as Ruth Ann Riley could be quickly found.

Nine

Ruth Ann writhed internally. It was true that Mrs. Dade was no monster. But it felt monstrous, just the same, when she took Annabel back, looked at her husband and quietly said, "Elijah."

It felt monstrous when Mr. Dade, with a quick nod, trudged to the wooden box telephone that hung on the wall and turned the crank on the right side to ring the operator. It felt monstrous when he spoke into the mouthpiece and asked to be connected to the Colony.

"No!" pleaded Ruth Ann. Before she even knew what she was about, she'd rushed to the telephone and ripped the earpiece out of Mr. Dade's astonished hand. She hung it up as he sputtered. She ducked, expecting him to smack her.

"What in tarnation—"

"Please! Listen to me. Listen to me and Glory 'fore you make the call. Please don't send us back to the Colony. They're going to do something awful to us—an operation!"

"An operation?" Mr. Dade repeated. "What sort of operation?"

"Doc Price says he's going to fix it so we can't have babies."

Mr. Dade's mouth went slack. He exchanged a glance with Mrs. Dade, who looked equally shocked. "How…how would he do that?"

Ruth Ann's face flamed. "Slice us open at the belly and tie our tubes, like—like string on a parcel, I guess. I don't rightly understand it, but that's what he says."

Silence.

"Why?" Mr. Dade asked, at last.

"Why? He says we shouldn't have babies, that's why...that my momma is...de-botched and, and...degenerous? I think that's what Doc said. And that I'm-a same. That people like us shouldn't breed."

More silence. Some weird kind of struggle took place on Mr. Dade's face as he looked from the photograph of his nephew Patrick to his wife. Then Mr. Dade said heavily, "Ruth Ann, Doc Price wouldn't do this unless he had good reason. You been liftin' your skirts again."

"*What?* No!"

"You must be."

"I ain't!"

He shook his head.

Mrs. Dade compressed her lips, avoided Ruth Ann's gaze and stroked Annabel's cheek.

"I swear it. You got to believe me, Mr. Dade. I'm not like that!"

"And yet my wife is raising your child." He put up a hand as she once again began to protest her innocence. But as usual it was futile.

Annabel slept, blessedly unaware of the aspersions being cast upon her biological mother's character.

Mrs. Dade got up. "Girls," she said in brisk tones, "nobody from the Colony is going to drive here to get you at this hour of the night. Let's make up the spare bed in the baby's room for you. She'll sleep with us, and we'll ring the Colony in the morning."

Oh, swell. But Ruth Ann nodded. She was too tired and low-spirited to do anything else. And it was, frankly, a miracle that the couple wasn't sweeping them out onto the road, given why she'd come here.

"It won't do you any good to run," Mr. Dade said brusquely. "You've got no money, no food, nowhere to go."

She nodded again. No sense arguing—it was all true. Funny how fear, a bit of bread and a pipe dream about her baby had given her such wings of possibility…but now, once again, they'd been clipped.

Defeated, she and Glory followed Mrs. Dade into Annabel's room, her former room. "You know where the linens are," Mrs. D said, retrieving another blanket from the baby's cradle and swaddling her in it.

"Yes, ma'am." They were stored in a cedar hope chest in the hallway. Ruth Ann had been fascinated with its treasures when she was younger; she herself had never had a hope chest or any spare time to sew or embroider anything to go in one.

"Make sure you tuck the corners, hospital-style, or your feet will get cold." Mrs. Dade turned, and it was then that she noticed Ruth Ann's bloodied, mismatched man's shoe. "Dear heavens, child. Wherever did you get that shoe, and how have you hurt yourself?"

Clarence. She knew a moment of panic. *Don't get Clarence in trouble!* She had to ditch the shoe before morning, in case Mother Jenkins were to recognize it. Because there would be no avoiding Mother Jenkins tomorrow. Or her belt. She shivered.

"It's nothing, Mrs. D. Dropped an iron on my toe, and it got all swole up, so's I found a bigger shoe."

"That's a *gentleman's* shoe," Mrs. Dade said, in tones of disapproval.

"Couln't fit in my regular one. And the iron burned clear through the leather, anyways."

"But where did you get a man's shoe?"

"I—um. There was extras in a closet, ma'am."

Mrs. Dade eyed her dubiously. "I doubt that."

Ruth Ann remained silent. What could she say?

"You need to get right with God, Ruth Ann. And you, too, Glory."

Amen to that. But how? How is it me an' Him got so sideways to begin with? What is it I'm bein' punished for? Lyin' about how I got a shoe? Tryin' to get back my baby? Stuff I ain't done yet?

Her daddy had left them, her momma'd gone around the bend, her sister and brother'd been taken and put somewhere's else— all by the time she was five. Why? Why had God got so mad at a little girl like her?

She didn't understand. She doubted Glory did, either. Why didn't anybody tell the boy who'd promised to marry her to "get right" with God? Why hadn't anyone told *Patrick* to do that? Why hadn't anyone sent *him* away to some colony for the...the violently depraved? Why was his "truth" more believable than hers? Why couldn't *men* get knocked up and push a baby out o' their behinds?

Why, why, why?

But when Mrs. Dade left the room, closing the door behind her, Glory unquestioningly, obediently, sank down to her knees, bent forward and clasped her hands.

Our Father, who art in Heaven, hallowed be thy name...

"Criminy. That'll do us a lot o' good," said Ruth Ann sullenly, but flopped down on the bed next to her. "Our Father's never been walloped with Mother Jenkins's belt. Has He?"

It was sacrilege. Glory opened her eyes. "Don't say such things."

"Why not? You gonna tell me that we're to learn something from all of this? Some valuable life lesson?"

Glory sighed. "Maybe."

"Well, then what on earth is it?"

"Beats the daylights outta me."

"Huh, just you wait. Mother Jenkins will be happy to do that."

Ruth Ann tumbled into a sleep that was like a black pit of nothing. She awoke with a start when the back door thudded shut: Mr. Dade, no doubt, on his way to use the outhouse.

This would be her only chance to appeal again to Mrs. Dade, to make her understand. She slipped out of bed, leaving Glory ever-so-faintly snoring with her cheek pillowed by her hand.

She felt horrid that she'd brought her on this ill-advised adventure. Glory had an innocence about her that Ruth Ann barely remembered in her own self. And the last thing she wanted was to watch it wither on the vine, drop rotten into the dust like her own.

She'd wanted to whisk Glory away before that could happen, protect that shining, trusting quality. Why? Because she was drawn to it, and hoping to be warmed by its rays? Be blessed by the shimmer? Catch it and treasure it, like a lightning bug in a jar?

She didn't know. But she would try her best to explain it to Mrs. D.

She hoped that Mr. D had been avoiding his greens as usual and would have an extra-long commune with nature.

She slipped down the short hallway and knocked softly on Mrs. Dade's bedroom door.

"Yes?"

Ruth Ann gingerly opened it. "Mrs. D?"

Her former foster mother was propped against her white pillows, with Annabel resting against her breast, her tiny body curled peacefully into her curves. The sight made Ruth Ann ache in a way she hadn't known she could. She felt the void not only in her womb but in her heart, in her very soul.

There was something divine about the peace that radiated between them; they were Madonna and Child. But Ruth Ann had been whited out of this picture, painted over. She'd been subtracted from the equation that equaled this sacred love.

She was yet again the outsider. She wasn't a person. She was an ache. Would she ever be anything else?

"Come in, child. But, *shhhh*. Annabel just fell back asleep. She was a bit fitful during the night. Did you hear her?"

Ashamed, Ruth Ann shook her head. *See what kind of mother I'd make? One who sleeps through her own child's cries. This is for the best, at least for now. For the bitter best.* She steeled herself to say so. If she said the words out loud, then Mrs. Dade might be…grateful. In an odd sort of way.

But the words stuck in her craw when she opened her mouth. "How long does she sleep, between feedings?"

"About two hours. If I'm lucky, three. But this past night, she woke up almost every hour. Tummy troubles, poor mite."

"How…how can you tell? That it's her tummy, and not something else?"

Mrs. Dade looked at her with something like pity. "By the way she cries. The way she squirms. And the way she relaxes when I rub her tiny belly to soothe her."

Ruth Ann nodded silently. She inhaled as much oxygen and courage as she possibly could. "Mrs. Dade…I know that you…that God didn't give you no babies of your own."

Mrs. Dade's nostrils flared, and her arms tightened almost imperceptibly around Annabel. Otherwise she was perfectly still.

"And I know that I have no right, especially after last night, to ask anything of you. But please, won't you help us? Glory and me? Please don't let Doc Price slice us open and take away…" She couldn't get it out. Her mouth worked.

"Glory, especially. She don't deserve that. Her beau—he said they were gettin' married, promised her it didn't matter—"

"The more fool she." The rising sun toyed cruelly with the lines around Mrs. Dade's mouth. Found and exposed the silver in her hair. "Free milk. The oldest story in the book."

"She ain't a cow. She's a good person, Mrs. D. She deserves a better life than this. She deserves a second chance… Maybe I don't. Maybe Annabel is b-b-better off here with you. But Glory—"

Mrs. Dade moved her feet restlessly under the covers, as if she were trying to step away. "What do you think I can do about anything? I don't decide such matters. I'm a housewife, Ruth Ann."

"Please. You know people in town. Folks look up to you. They listen to what you got to say."

Mrs. Dade's mouth tightened. "Not since my former ward disgraced my good name."

Ouch.

Ruth Ann sucked in a breath and focused on the specks of dust illuminated by the sunlight streaming through the window. They drifted without purpose, eventually settling on the floor and other surfaces, so someone like her would have to mop them up.

Sticks and stones… The words hurt, despite the old adage, but Ruth Ann was past caring about that kind of pain; she reverted to numbness.

It wasn't sticks or stones or judgment she feared: it was a

scalpel. A gleaming, wicked, sterile, silver scalpel in the hands of a man with an M.D.

"I never meant to hurt you, Mrs. D. You been good to me. You looked after me, when I was small. Maybe—" Her voice cracked. "Maybe you even loved me a little."

Mrs. Dade averted her gaze, then drew her knees up under the covers and shifted the baby. "And this is the thanks I get."

"*Yes.*" Ruth Ann said it urgently. "Annabel, this little *angel*…She is the precious thanks that you get. Maybe you feel I done you wrong, Mrs. D. But *she* came from it. Two wrongs— me and, and…" She couldn't bring herself to say Patrick's name. "Me and him. We *did* make a right. She's a gift from God, a tiny miracle, and that's a fact."

Mrs. Dade didn't utter a word, but her face said it all: the tenderness in her eyes, in the index finger she used to trace Annabel's cheek, in the softening of her lips as she bent forward to kiss her downy head.

"And now she's yours," Ruth Ann whispered.

Two tears, followed by a third, rolled down Mrs. Dade's cheeks and then fell onto the flannel of her night rail, soaking into the fabric.

"Now," said Ruth Ann. "Imagine if Doc Price had 'fixed' me afore I ever came to you. Annabel would never have been born."

The back door thudded heavily as Mr. Dade returned from his call to nature.

"Please, Mrs. D." Ruth Ann put a hand on her arm. "*Please* help us."

Mrs. Dade slid her legs to the side and out from under the covers. She didn't shake off Ruth Ann's hand; it fell away naturally as she found her slippers and got to her feet. "I need to put the kettle on for coffee and start the biscuits and bacon."

It wasn't a yes, but it wasn't a no, either. Ruth Ann nodded.

"You want to hold her, while I do that?"

Annabel's dark blue eyes fluttered open, and the baby stared right into Ruth Ann's soul. She saw it all: the longing, the pain, the fear, the desperation, the raw wound of love that was afraid to blossom. How was that possible?

Last night, she'd broken into this house fully intending to steal back her baby and run off with her. She'd thought of Annabel as a human doll, an extension of herself. But Annabel was a little being in her own right, and she deserved the comfort and security of a better life than Ruth Ann could give her.

"Here," Mrs. Dade said, holding out the baby.

Ruth Ann's breath hitched. "I…I can't. If I hold her again, I won't be able to give her back. And she's better off with you, I know that. You just make me one promise, Mrs. D."

Her foster mother's eyebrows rose in question.

"You swear to me you'll never leave her alone with him. With *Patrick*." She spat the name.

It was only then, at long last, that the unwelcome truth dawned in Mrs. Dade's eyes, breaking the surface of her denial and creating eddies of shock. She tucked Annabel into the crook of her arm and put a hand over her mouth. Took a trembling breath through her fingers.

Sensing the tension, Annabel began to wail.

"Swear it." Ruth Ann's voice was hard and fierce to her own ears. "If you are gonna be her mother, you make me that promise."

She got the barest nod. But it was all she needed. Someone had at last acknowledged her truth…and would protect her daughter.

Ten

I t was Clarence who drove Mother Jenkins to the Dades' home, in the Colony's gleaming black Model T. Clarence helped the old witch out of the automobile, then stood outside and waited, leaning up against the automobile, hand and stump in his pockets. He wore a tweed cap over his neatly clipped, coppery hair and no expression at all, save for a tiny furrow in his brow.

Ruth Ann lit up at the sight of him, but carefully masked her expression as the old toad came inside, shot her a scathing glance and seemed on the verge of spitting on Glory. Ruth Ann's stomach flip-flopped, and her heart slammed against her rib cage. *What will she do to us later? Once Clarence delivers us back to the Colony?*

The urge to run again almost overwhelmed her, a primal flight instinct. But she had nowhere to go, nobody to turn to and no money or skills to earn any—unless she let men like Patrick have their way with her. Just the thought had her almost retching onto Mrs. D's braided parlor rug.

Mother Jenkins may have wanted to beat the stuffing out of them upon sight, but she restrained herself. After the single acidic glance, she ignored them and took tea on Mrs. D's settee. She stiffly apologized for Ruth Ann and Glory's "abhorrent" intrusion. Not that Ruth Ann knew exactly what that meant. It surely didn't sound good, though, especially the "whore" part.

At least Mrs. Dade finally accepted that she was no whore. Ruth Ann didn't kid herself that she'd share that news with anyone else, however. Better to have a disgrace of a ward than a rapist nephew—who wanted *that* noted in the family Bible? Best to leave the blame on the outsider, that ungrateful serpent in the bosom.

Ruth Ann had a brief, uncomfortable fantasy that, like a serpent, she had a forked tongue and could stick it out and hiss at Mother Jenkins. Sink her teeth into her. But she hated snakes more than she hated Mother J, so she shook it off with disgust and focused on counting the planks in the parlor floor.

"You can be sure these two reprobates will be punished," promised her tormentor.

"They're just young girls," Mrs. Dade said mildly. To Ruth Ann's astonishment and huge gratitude, she said nothing at all about them trying to steal Annabel. Glory looked as though she might kiss her.

"They are old enough to know better," Mother Jenkins said, with a severe glance in their direction. "And they could have been molested—or worse—on the road!"

Don't take no road for that to happen. But Ruth Ann kept her mouth shut.

"Don't be too hard on them," Mrs. D said in soothing tones. "I believe Ruth Ann just needed to see for herself that her little one is in good hands."

"She'd already been told so." Mother J shot her another venomous glare.

Ruth Ann tried not to wither under it. She wiggled the toes of her right foot, clad now only in a stocking. She'd gone to the outhouse after speaking with Mrs. Dade and parted sadly with Clarence's shoe, her only shot in a lifetime at Cinderella's slipper.

Clarence's shoe deserved a better fate than to fester in the muck, but Mother Jenkins could never, ever know he'd helped them escape, and that shoe would have been a dead giveaway.

So Ruth Ann slipped it off regretfully and blew it a kiss. She wished it bon voyage and sent it spiraling down under her bum. It sank without a trace.

"Where is your shoe, child?" Mrs. Dade asked now, setting down her teacup with a frown. "The—"

But she broke off when Ruth Ann widened her eyes and shook her head silently.

"Wretched girl," Mother Jenkins said. "Do you think they grow on trees?"

Glory stifled a giggle, while Ruth Ann conjured such an image in her head. Button-up boots on the lower limbs, perhaps. Dancin' shoes blooming in the middle. Bedroom slippers sprouting from the higher, wispy branches. Maybe a few stockings waving festively among them all.

Did normal folks think about silly things like this? Or just the feebleminded? She didn't know.

Mother Jenkins set her cup down, too, a little less than graciously. "Where *is* your shoe?"

Ruth Ann thought fast. "It busted clean through and fell off a-cause of walkin' all this way. Already had the hole, ma'am. From where the iron burned it through."

"That could have been repaired. So not only have you defied the rules, alarmed everyone, shirked your chores and forced me to come and get you—now you're costing us extra money that is not budgeted."

Ruth Ann looked down at the floor and mumbled an apology.

"Well, Mrs. Dade. I don't want to take up any more of your time…"

Please take up more of her time. Oh, please.

Ruth Ann's scar tissue began to itch. She knew the Belt was coming, as soon as they got back to the Colony. Beside her, Glory nervously picked at her cuticles. She'd chewed a white-rimmed, swollen sore on her bottom lip. It looked painful.

"Oh, no, not at all," Mrs. Dade fibbed. "It's a pleasure to see you, Mrs. Jenkins, as always."

"Likewise. I only wish the circumstances were happier. These girls have caused a great deal of trouble for everyone."

Trouble follows me like a mangy dog—one with fleas.

"They've been no inconvenience. Just a…a surprise."

"Well. It's time to get them out of the way of decent folk and back where they belong."

I'll never belong at the Colony, not as long as I live.

If only she could turn back time to before Patrick had arrived. Then she could stay here again, in her snug little bed and in her own room. She could do laundry and cook for one couple instead of three hundred stray misfits, a few of whom wore diapers.

She almost opened her mouth and begged to stay. But Patrick would of course visit here again…which didn't bear thinking of. And where would that leave Glory? To face Mother Jenkins and the Belt alone, when none of this had been poor Glory's idea.

Cain't do it.

So she stood up dutifully and smoothed her gray dress, locking her knees so they wouldn't shake. She ran over and pressed a kiss to Annabel's forehead. And then she moved to the door.

"I'm quite sure you have something to say to Mrs. Dade before you leave, the both of you," Mother Jenkins snapped.

"Sorry, ma'am," Glory said quickly.

"I'm sorry, Mrs. D." Ruth Ann locked eyes with her.

Mrs. Dade fidgeted, seemed to want to say something. Her eyes were troubled; she opened her mouth but then closed it again. She cast a glance at Mother Jenkins. "Be well, child. All right? You take good care of yourself."

Ruth Ann's mouth twisted wryly and she nodded. She didn't really have a choice, now did she? Nobody else would take care of her.

Out the door they went and down the steps, propelled by Mother Jenkins's beefy palms, heavy between their shoulders.

Clarence doffed his tweed cap and moved to open the rear door for them.

"Don't be silly," Mother J snapped. "You don't need to extend such courtesies to these little sluts."

"Yes, ma'am," said Clarence, but continued to hold open the door all the same. He handed Glory in first and then Ruth Ann, squeezing her fingers as he did so. Placing a gentle hand at the small of her back as she climbed in.

She treasured his kindness in much the same way as she'd treasured his shoe.

Mother Jenkins didn't bother to wait for him to open the front passenger door. Puffing, she hoisted herself in and pulled it closed with a bang that caused Clarence to wince.

"I am mortified," she scolded them. "Simply mortified. How dare you? You have caused me trouble, inconvenience, embarrassment and possibly my position at the Colony! You have worried Dr. Price and thrown his surgery schedule into disarray. And you have burdened the other girls with your work during the time you've been missing."

Ruth Ann remained silent. So did Glory.

"Well? What do you have to say for yourselves?"

They exchanged a glance. Glory's hands were trembling.

Ruth Ann took a page out of Clarence's book and squeezed her fingers.

He started the engine, bracing his stump on the wheel, and put the Model T into first gear. His other hand and his feet moved smoothly in coordination so that they felt barely a lurch even as he changed to second and then third as they picked up speed.

Ruth Ann had only ever taken two other automobile rides in her life: one to the judge's chambers when she was assigned to the Dades and one to the Colony. She inhaled the smells of the engine exhaust, the heated rubber of the tires, the rich loamy leather of the seats.

She imagined briefly that she was not a disgraced runaway, but some great lady, draped in fur and riding in luxury to a ball. What must that be like? Perhaps she'd wear a headband with a feather and smoke a cigarette in a long holder. She'd seen the pictures of such women on the covers of old issues of *Vogue* and *Harper's Bazaar* and *Life* magazine when they were donated to the Colony.

She imagined wearing silk stockings with the seams straightened on the backs of her legs and white leather pumps with no scuffs. A lovely handbag to match…she would use words like *darling* and direct gentlemen to "be a love and just fetch my coat."

"I asked you a question!" Mother Jenkins thundered, utterly ruining her daydream.

Glory squeaked and shrank back in alarm.

"What?" Ruth Ann asked blankly.

"What do you have to say for yourselves?"

"Um…"

"Um? Um? That's all you can produce?"

"Yes, ma'am. Sorry, ma'am."

"*What were you thinking?* Of course, I'm clearly giving an imbecile far too much credit. You *don't* think, do you?"

Ruth Ann felt so blue that it was hard to come up with even a feeble fib. So she ripped pieces of the truth off the tale and waved them in surrender, like a white flag. "I...I talked Glory into comin' with me to see my baby. Jest wanted to see her, is all. Weren't Glory's fault, ma'am. I was mighty persuasive. A-cause I didn't want to go alone."

"And then? Then what were you going to do afterward?"

"We was comin' back, Mother Jenkins. We was. We just wanted to see if we could find Glory's baby, too. Check in on her."

"Ridiculous. Irresponsible. Dangerous. Improper."

"It's hard, not knowin', when it's your flesh an' blood," ventured Glory. "An' nobody will tell you a thing."

"Did I give you permission to speak?" Mother Jenkins growled.

"No, ma'am."

"Then don't."

"Yes, ma'am."

"I said: Do not speak! The two of you have been away for more than twenty-four hours with no chaperone. God alone knows what you've been doing."

"We ain't done nothing wrong—"

"Nothing wrong! I beg your pardon!" Mother Jenkins's head seemed to spin on her body, and in a feat of acrobatics, she was suddenly facing them, reaching over the seat to grab Ruth Ann by the ear.

"Not like that—*oww!*"

"Nothing wrong," Mother J repeated incredulously. Her hot breath stank of coffee and liver; her bosom pressed ominously into Ruth Ann's face when she yanked her forward. Strapped into an industrial-strength brassiere, it was boned and unyielding as the armor of a tank. It reeked of body odor and kitchen grease, thinly disguised by a sprinkle of eau de toilette.

Ruth Ann wanted to vomit, but she was so scared that the bile stuck in her throat.

"You just wait until we get back!" Mother J rasped. "And see what happens to you." With that, she shoved Ruth Ann backward and, still clamping viciously to her ear with her left hand, whacked her face but good with the right hand as Glory cowered in the opposite corner.

The velocity of the blow unbalanced Mother Jenkins, tipping her forward. She let loose of Ruth Ann's ear and grabbed at her shoulders instead, to balance herself. She hung there panting for a moment, trapped over the seat like a beetle, with her enormous bum in the air.

That was when a hyperventilating Glory spilled into hysterical, and then horrified, giggles. She was unable to stop herself. Ruth Ann could see that, as Mother J let go of her shoulders and then lunged at the poor girl.

Glory screeched, her teeth chattering, as Mother J's hands encircled her neck.

Clarence swerved to the side of the road and stomped on the brakes, which caused Mother Jenkins to hurtle backward, her bum bouncing off the glove box and her chin off the top of the seat. She bit her own tongue almost clean through at the tip and blood ran into her mouth, coating her teeth. She looked like something out of the worst kind of nightmare.

What followed was incoherent shrieking, followed by a petrified Clarence whipping out his handkerchief and holding it to Mother J's mouth. This stemmed the flow of blood and muffled what Ruth Ann felt sure were curses.

"Ahwahbuuhtyouwinaninthofwahwife!" Mother Jenkins roared through the handkerchief.

I will beat you within an inch of your life, Ruth Ann interpreted. She and Glory clung to each other, horrified. They simply stared at her.

"Youthithlebithes! Youwihpayfohthith!" Then the old toad turned on Clarence. "Anthyou! Whahthuhhehithwrohwihyou?"

He shook his head wordlessly.

"Whahhahyouthoothayfohyohthef? *Mohon!*"

This last word Ruth Ann discerned to be *moron*. It wasn't as difficult to translate as the rest of them, even with Mother J's freshly flapping tip o' the tongue.

"I were afraid we was gonna have an accident," Clarence managed. "I 'pologize, Mother Jenkins. I'm real sorry, ma'am. Are you okay?"

"Duhahwookokay? Dwoothing ithiot!"

If anyone sounded like a drooling idiot, it was their keeper. In fact, she sounded more feebleminded than anybody at the Colony.

"Lemme look at it," Clarence said. "At your, ah…injury." He stretched out his hand to take possession of the cloth at her mouth.

Mother Jenkins swatted his hand, then hauled off and smacked *him* one.

Clarence winced.

Ruth Ann flinched. She knew what that felt like.

"Gehawahfwuhme—thithithyohfaulth. Donthuthme! Thutht *thwive*."

Drive.

Clarence seemed to translate this just fine, for he nodded, ignoring the scarlet handprint blooming on his cheek.

And so they all set off again for the Colony. They made a right odd foursome, they did: one-handed Clarence with Mother

Jenkins spitting blood in the front; and poor hysterical, throttled, quivering Glory with one-shoed Ruth Ann in the back.

Ruth Ann squeezed Glory's hand again, and then took herself off into a fresh daydream of a banquet with white linen tablecloths and gleaming silver, sparkling crystal and hothouse flowers everywhere. There'd be music playing, maybe Al Jolson…and she and Glory'd be decked out to the nines in loads of pearls and sparkling gowns. Clarence'd be there, too—why not? And he'd be wearing a three-piece suit with a necktie knotted just so. His hair would be slicked back from his forehead and he'd ask Ruth Ann to dance.

They would all sip champagne—or maybe just lemonade, on account of she'd heard champagne made ladies silly and gentlemen bold. He and the other gentlemen would whirl her and twirl her like a sparkling top all over the shining parquet of the ballroom floor. They'd spin her like glass and treat her as if she were just as fragile. Precious.

They'd be respectful and not paw at her. They wouldn't palm the back of her head and push her face into the wall while spewing horrid things into her ear.

That was the end of her daydream. It coincided with the turnoff to the gravel road that led to the Colony.

Glory began to mumble the Lord's Prayer, and Ruth Ann echoed it in her head.

And deliver us from evil…

Clarence caught her eye in the rearview mirror and winked at her.

Ruth Ann tried to wink back, but she wasn't very good at it. And there was nothing the least bit winky 'bout their situation. She knew it was just his way of reassuring her.

But what could a boy with one hand do to protect her and Glory from a furious witch with an army of bats in her behind? And what could he do to rescue them from a doctor wielding a scalpel?

Eleven

I wuhdeahwithouater," promised Mother Jenkins, fit to be tied as Clarence helped her out of the passenger seat of the Model T.

Ruth Ann interpreted this to mean "I will deal with you later."

"IhahgotheeDocPwithe." She had to go see Doc Price. Clearly about her tongue.

Ruth Ann allowed herself the brief fantasy that Doc Price would cut out Mother J's tongue altogether, but such good fortune was unlikely to befall her and Glory. She settled for hoping, then, that he'd have to stitch her licker back together with a big needle and that it would hurt something fierce.

"Gethawok!" ordered Mother Jenkins, pointing savagely toward the kitchens.

Get to work. Ruth Ann nodded obediently and asked God's forgiveness for her terrible thoughts. *Sorry, Lord, but I'm right tired of turnin' the other cheek.*

She also couldn't help yet another wish—that Mother J had lost so much blood from her tongue that she'd be weak and would sleep for a week, leaving them in peace. Maybe she'd have sweet dreams, too, and forget about punishing them.

Fat chance o' that.

When she and Glory entered the kitchens via the mudroom, all chatter and clatter stopped. Fourteen other girls turned to stare at them, eyes wide and avid.

"M-mornin'," ventured Glory with a weak, tepid smile.

Nobody said a word. They just exchanged glances with one another and drew their skirts away from Ruth Ann and Glory when they passed them on the way to wash their hands in the big farmhouse sink. Treating them like they was germs, or viruses.

Ruth Ann was used to this, being Crazy Sheila's daughter, and therefore the subject of gossip and ostracism. But Glory wasn't. Her lips trembled with hurt and humiliation. It made Ruth Ann mad on her account.

"Afraid we'll infect you?" she asked the room in general.

Elbowing and snickering were her only responses.

Big surprise.

"Afraid we got cooties?" Ruth Ann shook her skirts at them, turning in a circle so's to spread the imaginary body lice evenly among them all. "Go, boys! Boot-scoot, ya coots. Get 'em all. Jump into their drawers. Crawl up in their armpits."

Glory gasped and then giggled.

Ruth Ann winked at her, just as Clarence had winked.

Where she found the nerve to get up to such tricks, she didn't know. She supposed it was on account of she knew she was gonna get walloped within an inch of her life anyways, so she had nothing to lose. It was a good feeling, sorta.

The girls' expressions were comically horrified. They clucked and scratched like a bunch of hens. But they still wouldn't address her to her face—not even hours later, when the last potato had been peeled, the last onion sliced, the last pea shelled, and all the pots and pans had been scrubbed, dried and put away.

Ruth Ann's arms, hands, back, legs and feet ached, and she longed something desperate for a shower.

That, of course, was Mother Jenkins's cue to reappear and frog-march her and Glory from the sink, where they'd been working apart from the others, to the large kitchen butcher-block. She told them to put their hands flat on its surface. Then she took her time selecting just the right heavy wooden cooking spoon, while the other girls watched, tense and round-eyed.

Glory was quite literally shaking in her shoes.

Ruth Ann gritted her teeth and took her mind somewhere else.

Whack! Glory screamed with the pain. *Whack, whack, whack. Whack, Whack.*

Ruth Ann closed her eyes.

"Thah," Mother Jenkins said with another *whack*, "wih teath you"—*whack!*—"to stheel Cowony properthy"—*whack*—"anth ruh away!" *Whack.*

Poor Glory shrieked with each blow to her knuckles. Tears coursed down her cheeks.

And then it was Ruth Ann's turn. *Whack! Whack, whack, whack. Whack-whack.*

She didn't make a sound, just braced herself for each excruciating blow that set her knuckles on fire. It seemed to her that Mother J put extra force into her punishment: she was panting like a hound in summer, and when Ruth Ann opened her eyes she could indeed see black thread stitching at the end of the woman's tongue.

Mother FrankenJenkins.

There were sweat circles under her arms, her hair—the part not confined to its bun—was matted to her head, and perspiration dotted her forehead. Her eyes were dark pools of venom. She looked like a madwoman. And the person she was maddest at was Ruth Ann.

Try as she might, she couldn't get one tear out of her victim, which seemed to make her even angrier.

When the agony could get no worse and Ruth Ann's hands had been reduced to bloody meat, Mother Jenkins stopped. She marched to the sink and tossed the cooking spoon into it.

"Thoomowoh," she announced, "youwihgehthebehwt."

Tomorrow, they would get the Belt.

And with those glad tidings, Mother J departed the kitchens.

For a long time, nobody moved.

Then it was Greta, Ruth Ann's bunkmate, who without a word, ran and got wet cloths for each of them. She and another girl, Doris, helped to wrap their hands. Who knew Greta had a heart?

"I'm sorry," Ruth Ann whispered later, after they'd bathed and painfully washed their hair and brushed their teeth. She'd snuck over to the opposite dormitory, where Glory had already gotten into bed. "I got you in a whole heap o' trouble. I sure am sorry, Glory."

The girl was quiet for a moment. Then she said, "You ain't got no call to be sorry. I wanted to go with you. I wanted a different life. So I'm just as guilty as you."

"My plan weren't a real good one," Ruth Ann said.

"Better'n mine, to be stuck here for forever and a day."

"It did feel pretty swell to get outa here for a while."

"I just wish...that we'da seen my baby, too. Someone's got to know who has her."

Ruth Ann nodded. "Must be some file somewheres, with the name in it. Maybe we can look for that."

"Would Doc Price have it in his desk?"

"Maybe."

"D'you think she got fostered out or adopted?"

"We're feebleminded," Ruth Ann said bitterly. "So nobody'd

want to adopt our babies. It's bound to be a foster family and just until she's old enough to work."

"Shhhhhhh!" a girl hissed. "Some of us are tryin' to sleep around here."

Glory sighed.

Ruth Ann slipped back to her own dormitory and her own bed, wondering how on earth to access Doc's office. Volunteer to clean down there? Trade off with whoever did? She might not be so smart, but she knew how to open a door and a file cabinet drawer. She knew how to read well enough to find a name in one. And she had hands—no matter how bruised they were at the moment—that could open the file so she could read the rest of it. So there.

There was no comfortable position, with her damaged knuckles, except for flat on her stomach with her hands palm down, above her pillow. And the pain was still excruciating, making it impossible to sleep.

In the morning, her hands hurt worse than they did the night before. The knuckles were raw and red, the skin split open. It was painful to wash her face, brush her hair and teeth, put on her clothes and shoes.

It was painful, too, to carry the metal tray in the dining hall, to grip the spoon for her oatmeal or the tin mug for her coffee.

To Ruth Ann's shock, Greta gave her the honey she was allotted for her own oatmeal.

"You can have this. I'm gettin' round anyway."

Ruth Ann squinted at her. "Why're you bein' nice to me?"

Greta shrugged. "You want it, or not?"

Ruth Ann nodded, stirring it in with a wince. She took a bite. The oatmeal tasted like Heaven in a bowl. "Thanks." But she was still mystified.

Greta tugged at her cap. "You were brave," she said after a while.

"Stupid, more like."

Greta smirked. "Both."

Ruth Ann half smiled.

"Well," her bunkmate said. "At least you smell better today."

Ruth Ann lifted an eyebrow, then took another bite of the sweet oatmeal.

"See ya later." Greta shimmied out from behind the wooden bench and took her own tray back to the service bin, just as a Colony nurse entered the dining hall with a clipboard.

"Glory Southwick?" she called.

Next to Ruth Ann, Glory froze with her coffee cup to her lips. "That's me," she managed.

"I'll need you to come with me, please."

Ruth Ann swallowed her bite of oatmeal and stared at Glory, who remained rooted to her seat. "What's this about?" she asked.

Glory's face was blank. She shook her head.

The nurse tapped her pen on the clipboard. "It's a small administrative matter. Now, Miss Southwick, just put your tray away and come with me."

Ruth Ann wanted to stop her, but Glory nodded. She stuffed the last corner of her toast into her mouth and washed it down with her remaining coffee. Then she tidied up her breakfast things while Ruth Ann's sense of foreboding built.

Where was the nurse taking her? For what?

For nothing good, that was certain.

But Glory had no choice, and she went like a dutiful lamb to the slaughter.

Ruth Ann *knew* when Glory didn't return to work on the

ironing. She knew when she didn't appear at supper and she never saw her return to go to bed in the opposite dormitory.

Glory had been taken to Doc Price, and he'd done the surgery on her. Ruth Ann felt sick at the thought.

How could anyone do that to another human being unless the situation was desperate? Maybe they called it medicine, but it sure seemed like violence to Ruth Ann.

Do unto others as you would have them do unto you. The Golden Rule she'd been taught in school. 'Cept it sure didn't seem to apply to everyone. Leastways, a whole lot o' people seemed to make up their own rules. 'Specially men with lots of fancy letters after their names.

Do unto others...

So how would Doc like it if they bonked him over the head, stretched him out on the kitchen butcher block and carved him open with the big bread knife? How'd he take it if they was to yank out a few of his intestines or part of his liver? And then knit him back together with kitchen string?

He wouldn't like it one bit, 'specially if he said no, and they was to do it anyways. Just decide for him that it was for the "greater good" that he not have that part of his liver or those few inches of his intestines.

The more she thought about it, the angrier she got. Poor, sweet, innocent Glory would have a big red scar like Sheila, and she'd never be able to have another baby. What had Glory ever done to deserve that? She was quiet and respectful and said her prayers. She was the type to help out a strange girl stuck in the laundry all night—for no other reason than that the help was sore needed.

And what had it got her? It'd got her gutted like a fish.

She must be recovering in the infirmary—that had to be where they'd stashed her. Ruth Ann made up her mind to go see her as soon as she could slip away.

But before she could do much plottin' as to how, Mother

Jenkins appeared in the dining hall and after a quick scan, fixed her hairy glare upon none other than Ruth Ann. "You!" she said. "Geth oveh heah."

All eyes turned on Ruth Ann. Her stomach clenched, her palms went damp and her scar tissue itched. Clearly it was time for the Belt. She wiped her hands on her skirt, finished her coffee and stood. Her heart pounded triple time as she walked her tray to the bin and then trudged reluctantly toward Mother Jenkins.

Another frog-march, this time from the dining hall to the mudroom outside the kitchens. At least she wouldn't take the whupping in front of everyone. The humiliation of yesterday was almost as bad as the pain. Almost.

Left, right, left, right, left, right.

Something squeaked with each step. Was it Mother J's shoes, her overburdened brassiere, or the bats in her behind fighting to swarm out?

Once again, Ruth Ann thought mighty hard about tearing out of her grasp and making a run for it. But Mother J would only hunt her down, and then it would be even worse once she got caught again. So she allowed herself to be propelled toward her fate.

"Gethinthide," her tormentor ordered.

She opened the door and went in. The mudroom smelled of must, soil and ripe feet. Several umbrellas stood upright in a wooden tub in one corner. There were hooks with slickers, coats and shawls hung on them. And on the far right, from the last hook, swung the Belt. Brown leather, an inch and a half wide, heavy brass buckle on one end.

Ruth Ann got brave enough to look over at it, just as Mother Jenkins drew in a sharp breath of surprise. "Where...?"

Ruth Ann couldn't believe her eyes—or her good fortune.

The Belt was gone. It had simply vanished. But who had taken it?

Twelve

Evidently Mother Jenkins didn't feel that an umbrella made the right instrument for a flogging. After a search of the mudroom failed to turn up her favorite torture device, she was stymied. The Belt, after all, was a memento of her dead husband. Maybe Mother J fondly remembered beatings he'd given *her* with it?

Ruth Ann couldn't say. But she was greatly relieved when the old toad ordered her to get to work in the laundry, so off she went.

As she hauled buckets of water to boil, her thoughts returned to Glory. What if Doc Price slipped with the scalpel? What if he couldn't stop the bleeding? What if Glory just didn't wake up after the surgery?

She'd lit the fire and hauled more water for the starch basin when Clarence appeared, whistling jauntily. He stopped once he caught sight of her hands.

"Lord love you, Ruth Ann—what did that old sow do to you?"

"Nothin'," she said, trying to hide them in the folds of her skirt.

He stepped forward and nabbed her left wrist, bringing her fingers out of hiding. He swore under his breath.

Every time a scab tried to form on her knuckles, it got split open again whenever she did something as simple as brush her teeth or wrap her fingers around the handle of the water pump. Then the wound would weep again, and repeat the whole sorry process.

"Cooking spoon," she said by way of explanation.

"Dang it. Thought you girls'd be aw right after I disappeared Mr. J's belt."

Ruth Ann's mouth dropped open. "*You* stole it?"

Clarence smiled. "Dunno. Might've needed some extra leather for a horse's harness."

She laughed, the sound odd to her own ears, since she didn't have a whole heap o' things to laugh about and hadn't in a while. "You're a peach, Clarence."

He turned pink, starting with the tips of his ears. "Nah. More of a banana." Then he seemed to find something indecent about that, because his flush darkened to raspberry. Raspberry with cinnamon freckles.

She pretended not to notice. "D'you know where Glory's at?"

Clarence stilled. He kicked at a charred lump of wood at the edge of the fire. Then he nodded. "Infirmary."

"Did Doc Price—"

"Yeah." Clarence's rainwater-gray eyes went flinty. "Bastard."

"Is…is she all right?"

"Well. She's alive, anyways. But looks like she'd rather not be."

Ruth Ann's heart squeezed. "So you've seen her?"

He nodded. "Doc had me come in yesterday to plane a door that was sticking and fix a broke lock on a file cabinet. So I sees her lying there, pale as death. Same color as the sheets. Ignorin' the food the nurses give 'er."

Poor Glory. "Did you say hello?"

"Yeah. Not so sure she could place me. She's in a world all her own, a world o' hurt."

"Probably a morphine kinda world."

Clarence compressed his lips and nodded.

"Mother Jenkins will be watchin' me. I don't think I can get down to the infirmary to see her...not 'til after supper, anyways. If I get any." Ruth Ann thought hard about any way she could cheer Glory up. "Clarence? You said you had to fix a broke lock on a file cabinet—can you pick a lock on one, too?"

His blush returned. He shifted from one foot to the other under her gaze. "Yep," he said, with obvious discomfort at the disclosure.

Ruth Ann brightened. "We're trying to figure out where her baby's gone. Glory's. Name of Lily. Lily Southwick. Doc's got to have it in his medical files somewhere. Think you can look?"

Clarence took a deep breath and looked around furtively. "If it was anyone else but you askin' me, Ruth Ann, I'd say heck no. But it is you, so...I'll try. Won't be easy, though."

"You're a peach!" she told him again.

"Apple," he said this time, the raspberry color returning to his ears and neck, then blooming in his cheeks.

"So you think you can give Glory a message for me, Clarence?"

He nodded. "Sure thing."

"You tell her..." Ruth Ann was stumped. What could she say to make Glory feel better? Make her smile? "Tell her the Belt is gone. And that there's no more cause to be blue. That she don't need to have more babies, on account of we are gonna hunt down the one she's already got."

Clarence smiled at her. "You're a good friend, Ruth Ann."

"Huh?" She was honestly taken aback. "I don't have any friends."

He blinked. Then he raised his eyebrows quizzically. "What am I, then? 'Sides a peach?"

She went to punch him in the arm, but stopped short—

given the condition of her knuckles. "You're...I dunno. You're just...Clarence."

He nodded. "You tell me if that changes, you hear?" Humor lit his eyes.

Ruth Ann stared at him. "You're a goof."

"Maybe so." He took her hand and inspected her injuries with a frown. "How you gonna do laundry like this?"

Ruth Ann shook her head. "I just got to do it. No two ways about it." She pulled her hand away.

He gave her that level gray stare of his, then said, "I'll be right back."

He returned in ten minutes with a gift even better than his shoe: a pair of work gloves, some cotton rags and some Rawleigh Antiseptic Salve in a brown, yellow and red tin.

Ruth Ann had the water boiling in the huge laundry cauldron by then and was fixing to drop several shirts into it with the long stick she'd use to stir them.

"Ruthie, put those down and give me your hands," Clarence said. "This'll make 'em feel better."

Why did a lump grow in her throat? Why did sudden tears sting her eyes? "You don't got to—"

"You're right, I don't got to do it. But I'm here anyways, so you may's well cooperate." He smiled at her, and her heart rolled over like a dog doing a trick. She did her best to swallow the lump, without much success. And then she extended her hands.

Clarence used one clean rag to apply the salve, which stung a little at first, but that subsided quickly. He coated each wound and wrapped another clean cloth around her four fingers, then one around her thumb. Finally, he slipped on a work glove. Then he did her other hand the same way.

Ruth Ann blinked furiously to keep the tears from escaping and streaming down her cheeks. She couldn't show such vulnerability. She hadn't felt cared for like this in years…well, except for the last time Clarence had tended to her, lancing her toe so gently.

"You're like an angel," she whispered.

"Nah. I cain't be a peach and an angel at the same time," he reasoned. "And a flying peach with a halo—well, that would look awful strange."

Ruth Ann laughed.

"Besides, angels have big white wings, not…" He gestured toward his stump.

Ruth Ann hesitated. "So—how did it happen?"

Clarence was silent.

"Sorry. Hope you don't mind me askin'. Guess it's rude."

"It ain't rude. It would be, if that was the first thing outta your mouth when we first met. But you can ask now. It wasn't from no accident with farm equipment or nothin'—I was born with only one hand." He shrugged.

"So…?"

"So my old man thought it was some sign of the devil or whatnot. Made him less of a man to have a baby with only one hand, and he was shamed by it. Needed sons with two hands to do farmwork. So he took me right away to the orphanage."

"That's awful, Clarence."

His expression was carefully blank. "What're you gonna do?"

"You can do most everything a—" She stopped. She'd been about to say a "regular" boy. Clarence wasn't irregular.

He shot her a knowing glance. "Yeah, I know. I work at it. I don't let nothin' stop me."

She wanted to wrap her arms around him and give him a hug. But she didn't want him, or anyone else, to think she was "abwhorrent," or loose with men, like her momma. So Ruth Ann did nothing of the kind. She didn't even punch his arm, even though she now had salve, a bandage and a glove on her knuckles, all thanks to him. Better than a gold bracelet or a diamond ring.

"You sure don't" was all she said. There was a pause, during which she looked down at her man's gloves and he looked down at his pilfered shoes. She gestured toward them. "So nobody said nothin' about them shoes?"

He gave a wry smile and shook his head. "Nobody 't all. Not even the gentleman I borrowed 'em from. To hear tell, he was a right miser most of his life. But now he's off his rocker, so he's unaccountably generous."

"Imagine that."

"Wonders never cease. The good Lord works in mysterious ways, don't He? Though sometimes we truly do have to be His hands and feet. So He's gotta provide us with gloves and extra shoes, don't He?"

This time Ruth Ann did punch him in the arm. "You gonna get struck by lightnin', you keep talkin' that way."

"That may be. I think He understands, though. Like how'd I realize that poor horse was lackin' a piece of harness if He didn't show me the light and lead me to old Mr. J's belt?" Laughter spilled from Clarence's gray eyes like sunshine, splitting open a rainy sky by surprise.

She punched him again. "You'd best be careful, Mr. Smarty-Pants."

"They says my pants is the smartest thing about me, here at the Virginia Colony for the Epileptic and Feebleminded."

"I mean it! Be careful."

"Always. A fellow with one hand—he can't take no unnecessary risks. Wouldn't be prudent." Rows of even white teeth—only one in the front slightly snaggled—accompanied this whopper.

Why did this make her want to kiss him? Ruth Ann took a step back, so as not to. She was nothin' like her momma and never would be.

"If you're so bent on bein' prudent," she said mock-severely, "then you probably shouldn't go pickin' any locks."

"Nope, I shouldn't." His eyes danced. "Might lose my, what's it? Oh yeah: moral compass. I mean, a fellow with one hand—how's he gonna pick hisself a lock and hang on to that sucker at the same time? It's for sure he's gonna drop it. So he'd best not take it along on the journey, know what I mean? He'd best leave it under his pillow."

"He'd best," she agreed, the corners of her mouth tugging up.

This time it was Clarence who—lightly—punched her in the arm. He started whistling again as he walked away.

Ruth Ann missed him instantly. She also missed Glory's comforting presence, that pure golden innocence that wrapped her in a Glory-cloud. Part of it was that she gave without seeming to want anything back. It was a rare quality, that. And that was the kind of gal Doc Price didn't want making more babies?

She missed Glory, but as she worked she hung on to the sweetness of her that lingered from the night they'd labored together here in the laundry, sweating and groaning along with her as she fed the starch-dipped clothes into the wringer.

In Glory's absence, Ruth Ann entertained herself by imagining that each shirt, pair of drawers and trousers she drowned savagely in the boiling water was, in fact, Doc Price. And each slip, work dress, brassiere and pair of bloomers became Mother Jenkins.

She stabbed them up with the stick, flung them toward the huge iron pot as they hollered and screeched and poked them down, down, down until, spewing bubbles, they hit bottom and struggled back upward only to be submerged by Justice Ruth Ann Riley yet again.

Do you repent? she asked them.

We don't answer to the likes of you: feebleminded, de-botched moron.

Oh, but this here's my domain. I'm the Dark Queen of the Livin' Laundry. So I'm sorry to say that you do *answer to me. Take this! And that! And yet another! Ha.*

Glug, glug, glug. Gasp.

Do you repent?

Never.

Then down you go again...ha ha. That'll take the starch outta you and your smug attitude.

Oh, please!

That's the ticket. You beg me. But to no avail. This here's for what you done to my momma, Doc. And this here's for Glory.

She supposed she did get a little carried away.

And this, this is for my busted-up knuckles, you old biddy with the bat-infested behind—

"Ruth Ann?" Clarence's voice intruded on her dark doings.

She reared back, blinking into what had somehow become the sunshine of high noon, and half-blinded by it. His silhouette was visible at the entrance to the laundry walls.

"Who you talkin' to?" he asked, peering inside.

"Nobody." It wasn't possible for her face to heat any more than it already had, because of the fire under the huge cauldron. Next to it, she really must look and smell like a witch.

"You must hate Nobody somethin' fierce," he teased.

"That I do." She pushed her hair back out of her face and wished that the bodice of her dress wasn't soaked through.

"What did Nobody do to you? You seem to be stabbing and drowning him—"

"Clarence," she interrupted. "You got a reason to be here asides makin' me feel foolish?"

"Well, yeah. I want my shoe back." He sounded dead serious. "Trade you the gloves for my shoe." He walked inside, the sun now illuminating his unsmiling face and level gray gaze.

Stricken, she looked down at the replacement shoes Mother J had tossed at her the night before. "I—I—uh," she stammered. How to tell him the sorry fate of his first gift? This was awful. She couldn't. "It, ah…"

"I'm kiddin' around, Ruthie. You couldn't tell?" He grinned.

Her mouth worked. She stamped her foot, then bent over and rummaged for a dirty sock to throw at him. He ducked, hooting with laughter.

"Your shoe got drowned in an outhouse," she informed him, no longer feeling so bad about it.

"That's just plain *wrong*, Ruth Ann." He shook his head sadly.

"Where else was I s'posed to hide it from Mother Jenkins when y'all came around? In the baby's cradle? She couldn't know you helped me."

"And here I was, plannin' to have it bronzed on account of you wore it."

"That is a big load o' horsefeathers, Clarence, and you know it," she said severely.

"You filled my shoe with poo to save my hide, huh?" He was still chuckling.

"Yes. Yes, I did. And I'm-a startin' to think you're full of it, too—you know that?"

He just smiled at her.

It did something funny to her insides, something that she didn't like one bit. In fact, it came real close to giving her a gas pain.

His smile faded as she scowled and shook her long stick at

him. What if he was doin' all these things for her so she'd let him under her skirt? Softening her up like butter?

Patrick had acted all nice at first, too.

"So what's it you came back here for, Clarence? Huh?"

He shoved his stump and his hand into the pockets of his overalls. "To tell you I didn't have no luck with the first file cabinet."

"You already tried?!"

He nodded. "But there's somethin' else." He took off his cap, clamped it under his arm and scrubbed his fingers through his damp copper hair. His mouth was flat, his expression grim.

"What?"

His gaze poured over her like cool water with an intent to soothe. For that very reason, it made her shiver instead.

"Sweet baby Jesus, Clarence. What is it? Is it Glory? Is she all right?"

He nodded. "She's holdin' steady."

"Is it her baby? Did the baby die?"

"I don't know anything yet about the baby."

"Then what is makin' you look like the Grim Reaper his own self?"

"Ruthie...you're on Doc's list. For surgery."

Thirteen

She was back on Doc's list? This soon? Ruth Ann stared at Clarence blankly for a long moment before her nerves and her stomach took over. It began with more sweat all around her hairline, then extra saliva in her mouth. Then she ran past Clarence, out behind the wall of the laundry, and was sick.

He followed her, to her chagrin. Offered her his handkerchief. Rubbed her between the shoulders.

"Please, Clarence. For pity's sake, just go away."

"Ruth Ann, I'm sorry—I just wanted to warn you. I didn't know what else to do. I didn't want you to be taken unawares."

"I know. Thank you." She had braced her hands, in his gloves, against the stone wall, and her head now hung down between them as she spit the last of the sick out of her mouth. She wanted to upchuck a second time when she thought about Doc Price slicing his steel scalpel into her. She didn't want to be naked around any man, ever again—and especially not unconscious, like a cut of beef laid out for a stew. The idea horrified her.

Clarence waved his hankie near her cheek again, but she shook her head. She stood up, wiped her mouth with her hand and then marched around the corner and into the laundry again. She rooted around until she found a shirt that she was positive was Doc Price's. She pulled it to her face, recognizing his fancy aftershave, and mopped her mouth, forehead and neck with it. Then she dropped it in the dirt.

"I could use that for somethin' even worse," suggested Clarence.

She gave a weak laugh. "You'd just get in trouble. And so would I, if they found out."

"Yeah." He set a comforting hand on her shoulder.

Even though she knew instinctively that he was only being kind, she moved out from under it. She felt dragged down by a heavy, sodden blanket of fatigue and hopelessness.

Still, she thought of Mrs. Dade's face when she'd begged her to keep Patrick away from Annabel. The dawning of belief there. The reluctant acceptance of Ruth Ann's truth. The realization of the injustice that had been done to her ward.

It gave her hope—though maybe hope was a curse.

"I got to finish up here," she said to Clarence. "And then I got to write a letter. I know you've already done more than enough for me, more than anyone could ask...but can you find a way to get it to Mrs. Dade? The lady at the house where you came to get us?"

Clarence nodded. "Yeah. I'll figure somethin' out."

She almost threw herself into his arms. She had a weird feeling he could sense that. And he could also sense just how uncomfortable it would make her if she did.

So he stepped back. "I'll hoof it to her on one condition: you stop callin' me any kind of fruit, you hear? Nor anything with feathers, neither." He shook a finger at her, but the crinkles around his eyes belied the gesture.

She nodded, her throat clogged with gratitude. "You're the bee's knees, Clarence. You truly are."

March 4, 1924

Dear Mrs. Dade,

I hope this letter finds you and Mr. Dade and little Annabel in good health.

Thank you for your kindness during my recent visit.

I write you now on account of what I told you, ma'am— that there is an operation planned for me—and real soon. I'm sorry to trouble you again, but I do not know who else to ask for help.

Doc Price already done Glory's surgery. Wants to do mine on Tuesday.

Please, do not let them do this to me, if you ever cared for me at all, please help. I want to set my life right. I want to leave here one day and have a family of my own. You trained me your ownself to run a household...you know I ain't so feebleminded that I cain't do it. Please, Mrs. Dade, please help.

Yours truly,
Ruth Ann Riley

Ruth Ann wrote the letter quickly with pencil and paper she borrowed from Mother Jenkins's kitchen desk. She wrote it in back of the outhouse, away from prying eyes. She reread it and crossed out *ain't*, changing it to *am not*. She struck out the *i* in *cain't*. Then she folded the letter into a small square that she tucked into the pocket of her dress.

She prayed that Clarence would remember to come and get it from her, since she never knew exactly where the Colony would have him working, and she could hardly march up to the men's dormitories and knock on the door to ask for him—that'd make them think she was ab-whorrent for sure.

She finished the washing, rinsing and starching assigned to her hours later. She was left with three massive baskets of wet clothing and sheets that weighed more, it seemed to her, than a whole quarry of boulders. Ruth Ann looked up at the sky before she even attempted to move them to the clotheslines.

The sun peeked coyly from between a pack of puffy clouds, then disappeared again, casting an eerie, dirty-yellow light through them. She decided that maybe today, it was better to hang the clothes on lines in the lean-to. That way they wouldn't get rained on, 'cept maybe a bit at the edges, and Mother Jenkins wouldn't make her rewash the whole stinkin' lot o' them—totally unnecessary, if you asked Ruth Ann, since fresh rain had to be purer than collected rainwater in a barrel, and just as pure as well water. But nobody never did ask her opinion, on that or anything else.

She hefted up one of the baskets of laundry-boulders and trudged with it down to the lean-to that sometimes sheltered animals from the wind, only to discover that it was chock-full of boys with hammers, planers, sanders and sawhorses with projects laid across them. They weren't going to be displaced by something as unimportant as her wet laundry. Dismayed, she turned around and trudged back to the outdoor lines. She'd have to risk pinning the laundry again in the open air.

The sun, truly fickle today, popped out again laughing, like a child playing hide-and-seek.

"You sure think you're cute, don'tcha?" Ruth Ann muttered at it.

It scattered illusory gold coins through the trees and diamonds on the lawn, daring the likes of her to try to collect them, much less spend them.

If she had a real bushel of gold and diamonds, the very first thing Ruth Ann would buy was one of them big Lamneck Laundry Dryers she'd seen advertised in last year's *Life* magazine. The size of a shed, it had dozens of metal bars for hanging clothes and sheets upon, and it was heated! Imagine that. So it wouldn't matter if there was a doggone hurricane outside: the laundry would be nice and toasty and Mr. Sunshine could play all the games he wanted. Wouldn't that be sheer heaven?

That would be a gift to the poor girls like her at the Colony, before she'd bribe the board to let her go. Why they called them folks a board did not make the least bit of sense to her, unless they were just real *bored* when they sat around listening to the Colony's problems and voting on what to do about 'em.

The second thing Ruth Ann would buy was her very own cottage, with a garden she could grow flowers in—and she'd paint the front door and the shutters blueberry blue. She'd get some window boxes and paint them the same color and put flowers in them, too. She'd put a rocking chair on the porch and sit in it every evening looking at the sunset and the flowers.

Maybe she'd invite Glory over, or Clarence, and they could drink iced tea with her. She'd have Mrs. Dade and baby Annabel come for supper. Maybe she'd even invite Sheila, if she was behavin' and promised not to screech vile things at Ruth Ann or try to burn the place down.

What else would she buy? A motorcar! If Clarence would teach her to drive it. It didn't look to be all that difficult…

"Head in the clouds agin, I see," Clarence's voice teased her, as he came along trundling wood in his wheelbarrow.

She blinked back to reality. "Well, if they'd just decide whether they's goin' or stayin', my head wouldn't need to be up in 'em," she retorted. "They don't make it easy on wash day."

"Want to set that basket on top o' the wood?"

She was sorely tempted. "Now, how's that fair? To make you push the firewood *and* the soggy washin'? Thank you, but no thank you, kind sir."

"I don't mind."

"Well, *I* mind on your behalf."

"Anybody ever tell you that you're stubborn?"

Her lips twitched. "Now, why'd they tell me a thing like that?"

"No reason. So you got something for me?"

Ruth Ann nodded. She looked to the right, the left and behind them to make sure nobody saw, and then she slipped the letter out of her pocket and tucked it into one of Clarence's. "Cain't thank you enough."

"It's nothin', Ruth Ann."

She stopped. "It's everything."

Wilfred Block, Esquire, raised his eyebrows, blinked and adjusted his pince-nez when a slight, gray-haired woman with a baby stepped into his office. She was clearly uncomfortable, and as unused to seeking the counsel of a solicitor as he was unused to swaddling an infant.

Block stood up, as a gentleman should do in the presence of a lady—though she wasn't precisely a lady. Her clothing was worn, threadbare and not at all fashionable. Her shoes had seen better days. Her hair wasn't cropped, it was coiled in a knot and secured with pins. This was no flapper; he pegged her as perhaps a factory foreman's wife. She wore a thin gold wedding band that she twisted nervously as she gently bounced the baby.

"G-good day," she mumbled, taking in his own appearance and flushing slightly.

Block took it as his due. He was used to making ladies overheat.

"And a good day to you, madam. How may I help you?" he inquired. "Please, sit down." He gestured toward the visitor's chair in front of his imposing Chippendale desk. It was an excellent set piece for deposing witnesses. It loomed and they shrank.

The woman paled in the face of its regal, legal magnificence, but she sat in front of it, settling the baby awkwardly in her lap. The infant, swathed in a pink blanket, aimed her myopic blue gaze at Block and blew a spit bubble.

Charming.

"What a lovely little daughter you have there, Mrs....?" Truth to tell, she looked too old to be the mother of an infant.

"Dade," she said, seeming unable to look away from his eyes. It took her a moment to recover. "And thank you, Mr. Block. You're very kind to say so."

"A bit young to require an attorney-at-law, though, eh?" he said jovially.

"I beg your pardon? Oh! You're only joking—"

"Yes, yes. Apologies. I'm hopeless, a card-carrying card."

She smiled uncertainly and plucked at the baby's blanket.

"May I offer you assistance on some matter, Mrs. Dade?"

She raised her troubled gaze to his. "Well, perhaps. I hope so. Everything I tell you is in confidence, correct?"

"Indeed it is, madam. You may rest assured on that score."

"All right. Thank you. I hardly know where to begin...I had a ward, Mr. Block, for around a decade. She was placed with us at the age of five, and she recently left us at age sixteen after finding herself in a...troubled condition." Color tinged Mrs. Dade's pale cheeks at the mention of this. "We could not tolerate such immoral behavior under our roof."

"Oh, dear. Of course not. I understand."

"So we had to send her away. But frankly, we were reluctant

to lose the stipend we received from the state in exchange for looking after Ruth Ann—"

Block jolted. "I beg your pardon? Did you say *Ruth Ann?*"

"Yes. Why?"

"What is her last name?"

"Riley." Mrs. Dade blinked at him, while Annabel gurgled and blew another spit bubble.

Block sat back in his chair, unable to believe it. Then again, his shingle was the most prominent in town, hard to miss.

"Why, sir?"

"Oh, nothing important. You were saying?"

"Well, sir, she was of great help to me around the house as she got older. So arrangements were made for me to care for her baby, once she gave birth to her."

"Ah," Block said, wondering where this was going. "So you wish to adopt the infant, then?"

"No. Well, yes, perhaps eventually...but that's not why I'm here. Ruth Ann paid me a visit recently—to say hello and to...to check on little Annabel. Ruth Ann was very disturbed because she's been told that she will have to have an operation of a delicate nature. One that will prevent her from, ah, having any more babies."

"I see."

"Ruth Ann does not wish this surgery to be performed upon her. But it has been scheduled for Tuesday, nonetheless. She is quite upset and has asked for my help in preventing this medical procedure."

Block marveled at the delicious irony of this situation.

"Does she not have the right to refuse it?"

To think that he'd just been debating ways to approach the girl...and here God was dropping her right into his lap.

"Where does Ruth Ann reside now?" he asked, playing dumb. "Is she in a home for unwed mothers?"

"She's at the Virginia Colony for the Epileptic and Feeble-minded."

"You don't say."

"Yes, it's where Ruth Ann's mother is, as well. She's unstable and—well, she has a number of issues."

"What sorts of issues?"

Mrs. Dade plucked at the baby's blanket again, then re-tucked it around her. "She's prone to emotional outbursts, she's a drunk, she's rated a moron in terms of IQ, she doesn't maintain proper hygiene—and before she was processed by the state into the Colony, she was given to…certain unsavory and immoral proclivities."

Block easily read between the lines: Ruth Ann's mother had been a prostitute. "Good gracious. Well, then. You are to be doubly commended for first taking on this woman's daughter and now her granddaughter. That's a rather pernicious set of genetics."

Mrs. Dade sighed and nodded. "I'm afraid that's probably what the doctor at the Colony is thinking, as well. But Ruth Ann was always a sweet girl and not at all stupid. She learned to read and write and do basic figuring."

"That's as may be. But she clearly seems to take after the mother in terms of her moral code."

Mrs. Dade was silent. She wound the corner of the baby's blanket tightly around her index finger, then removed it and did it again. "I don't know," she said at last. "She says—"

After a long, uncomfortable pause, Block gallantly filled in the gap in conversation. "My dear lady, don't they all claim either immaculate conception or force? What else can these girls say? I wouldn't give it a second thought, considering her background.

People of a certain class—and by that, I mean low—learn to lie, cheat and quite often steal at their mothers' apron strings. They're ignorant, debauched, lazy, shameless."

"Ruth Ann—she wasn't like that."

"*Wasn't* being the operative word, it seems, Madam."

Mrs. Dade sighed again. "I promised to try to help her, Mr. Block. That's why I'm here. Is there anything you can do on her behalf to put a stop to this surgery?"

"Possibly. But I'm concerned that your good nature, your soft heart, not be taken advantage of. Not to mention your wallet."

"Oh, dear. I—I can't pay you, Mr. Block."

Swell. No dough. He'd figured as much, but it had been worth a try.

"Well, sometimes I do take cases gratis." If they had the potential to make a name for him in legal circles, he did. And allow him to collude with his friend Dr. Price, not to mention a legal luminary like Anselm Stringer. "Is Ruth Ann still a minor, Mrs. Dade?"

"Yes. She's sixteen."

"And her legal guardian is now the state of Virginia, which has placed her in the Colony's care?"

"I believe so."

"All right. Let me look into the legal statutes involved, and I will contact you again shortly."

"It's Ruth Ann you should contact. She wrote me a letter. I—my husband doesn't know I'm here. Frankly, I'd rather he didn't. He wouldn't want me to be involved in any of this."

"I see. Do you have the letter with you, Mrs. Dade?"

"Yes, I do." She pulled a tightly folded, rather grimy piece of notepaper from her pocketbook and handed it to him.

"May I retain this for my files?"

"Yes, I suppose so. I have no reason to keep it."

"Thank you. It's clear to me that you care very much for your former foster daughter, and that you did the best you could with her. I commend you for that. But blood always tells, dear lady. We cannot escape our breeding. A weed will never become a prize orchid or a rose, eh? A mule can never become a thoroughbred."

Mrs. Dade nodded uncertainly as she stood up.

He took her free hand in his, patting it. "Everything will work out fine, Mrs. Dade. I'll see to that."

Her eyes widened; her breath hitched.

He enjoyed the effect he had on women, he truly did.

She seemed to recover her senses. She pulled her hand away and settled the baby into the crook of her other arm. Annabel was a beautiful child, he had to admit that. It was a shame that she, too, the poor innocent, would grow up to be mentally and morally lacking.

But it simply couldn't be helped: it was in her genes.

Fourteen

R uth Ann replaced one of the heavy black irons on the back of the stove and hefted yet another so that she could finish pressing the sheet she had over her board. Why it was necessary to iron dad-blasted sheets, she couldn't for the life of her figure out. As soon as a body laid down on the bottom one, the darn thing'd be wrinkled again. As soon as the top one got squashed under that same person's arm, it'd be wrinkled, too.

But either God or *Good Housekeeping* had determined that women's energy be spent in this futile pursuit, so here she was, with seven other girls, squashed into the back of the kitchens like so many overgrown, perspirin' sardines in a can. Or maybe oysters. She'd rather be an oyster, come to think of it, since at least they got to make pearls afore they were scooped out of their shells and robbed of them.

How glamorous, to create a pearl! Imagine that...hunching over a grain of sand for months and forming something so beautiful from it. Was a pearl an oyster's baby?

She ran the iron back and forth over the sheet, her thoughts darkening. Oysters didn't have to get married to make pearls, now did they? And nobody fussed at them or treated them like shabby barnacles when they did.

But they did get harvested, shucked, robbed, eaten, digested and pooped out, their shells tossed aside. So maybe she wasn't doing too badly, in the great scheme of things. She'd only been harvested, shucked and robbed so far. Not eaten, nor all the rest.

Ruth Ann adjusted the sheet on the board and finished ironing it. What was wrong with her, comparing her life to an oyster's? She was plumb crazy. She set the iron back on the stove with a heavy clank and proceeded to neatly fold the sheet into halves, then quarters, eighths and so on.

"Ruth Ann Riley?" called a familiar voice.

She looked up and saw Clarence in the doorway.

"Is Ruth Ann back there?" he asked.

"Yes, I'm here." She laid the sheet on the ironing board and elbowed past the other girls. "You need somethin', Clarence?"

"There's a gentleman asking to see you."

She was puzzled. She didn't know any gentlemen.

Clucks and whistles came from the other girls. "A gentleman caller, she has? Well, well, Ruth Ann…What have you been up to?"

She shook her head. "Are you sure he means me?"

"Yep. He's waitin' on you in the front parlor."

Who could it be? Clarence gave no sign.

She wiped her sweaty face with her palms, wiped those on her dress. Then she attempted to smooth her hair, though she was sure it was hopeless—like trying to coif a mop. She wished she didn't smell like a carthorse after ironing for most of the morning.

"For crying out loud, lookit 'er primping…"

Ruth Ann did her best to ignore the whispers and jeers. She followed Clarence outside, trying to glean any information from his expression. He just jerked his head toward the main house, the Colonial near the gates, where the reception area, the parlor and the intake office were.

"Who is this gentleman?"

"Name of Block. Wilfred Block, *Esquire*." Clarence drawled the last word in an exaggerated fashion that suggested he didn't think much of the man in the parlor.

"What's that mean?" Ruth Ann asked.

He shrugged. "Means he's awful impressed with hisself, you ask me. He's quite the billboard. A high hat."

She didn't know what to make of this. "Why's he here to see *me*?"

"You'll have to ask him. See ya later, Ruthie. I got to go polish his flivver."

Ruth Ann walked up the path to the house. She hadn't been here since she'd been processed through the intake office, where they asked her a load of questions and tested her IQ and put all the answers in an official-looking file that got locked away in a tower of other ones.

The door opened as she climbed the three steps up to it. Mrs. Parsons waved her in. In her mid-sixties, Mrs. Parsons wore navy or moss-green or burgundy dresses with white lace collars, and was the receptionist at the Colony.

"Heavens, child, come in. Don't keep Mr. Block waiting any longer. He's an important man."

"Sorry," Ruth Ann said. "I was workin' on the—"

"Never you mind that. Come along."

Ruth Ann followed her to the parlor door, where she stopped short at the sight of the gentleman inside. He looked as though he'd stepped out of a magazine advertisement. He was tall, with chestnut hair and narrow green eyes set in an angular, fine-boned face. He had a nose a man could hang a hat on.

He wore a three-piece suit nicer than Doc Price's and a snowy shirt with a silk necktie. He had on polished black shoes she could see her hand's reflection in, when she finally extended it to shake his. She felt unworthy to touch his manicured fingers, but he'd extended them toward her first.

"Hello, Miss Riley," he said, with a blinding smile. "Wilfred Block, Esquire."

Miss Riley? Nobody called her Miss Riley. It made her feel strange and grown-up and sophisticated. "Hello...?" She stood staring at him.

He seemed to realize the effect he had on her, for his smile widened a smidge.

Her face heated as she realized that, like some kind of booby, she'd left her hand in his warm, firm one for far too long, and quickly pulled it away.

Mrs. Parsons fingered her lace collar and watched the by-play avidly.

"I'm an attorney, Miss Riley."

She had no idea what that was, and it must have shown on her face.

"A lawyer."

"Oh." She still could come up with no reason why a man of the law would want to say boo to the likes of her. She breathed in the scent of his cologne, though. It smelled of heather, leather and privilege. It smelled of college and European travel and house parties and champagne...she wanted to drift off on a cloud of it and float around the world.

Judging by her moony look, Mrs. Parsons was on her own cloud of his cologne. She seemed about to crash through it, fall to her knees and beg Mr. Block to marry her on the spot.

"Mrs. Parsons, will you excuse us, please?" Block asked serenely. "I have something of a private nature to discuss with Miss Riley."

Mrs. Parsons's face fell. "Of course," she said, but took her sweet time walking to the door and closing it behind her. If Ruth Ann had to guess, she'd bet that her ear was pressed flat against it and would be for the duration of the chat.

"Now, won't you sit down, Ruth Ann?" Block gestured to the sage-green velvet upholstered settee in the middle of the parlor. "Is it all right if I call you by your given name?"

She nodded.

She eyed the settee dubiously, then cast a glance at her own behind, afraid she might have brushed up against something dirty or sooty in the kitchen. She'd never been invited by anyone to occupy the settee before. But slowly, awkwardly, she sank down upon it. Ohhhh. Goosedown pillows. Jiminy Cricket, it felt as though she were leaning back into soft butter.

He settled into an armchair next to the settee and crossed one long, well-tailored leg over the other. Even his socks were beautiful. There were tiny clocks embroidered on them. Ruth Ann wondered how long it had taken someone to stitch twenty or thirty clocks on each sock.

She then returned her gaze to those mirrorlike shoes. She could not picture Wilfred Block, Esquire, giving one of them to a de-botched "slattern" with an eggplant-sized toe—or anyone else, for that matter.

"What's a slattern?" she blurted, before she could stop her silly mouth from asking.

His pale winged eyebrows shot up into his hair. "I beg your pardon?"

"Do you know what it means? The word *slattern*?"

He fought a losing battle not to smile. "Ah…it means a dirty, untidy female."

"Oh." She supposed that she was one, after all. The idea depressed her.

"Why?"

"You just—you just look like a person who would know."

This time he outright chuckled. "I look as though I know dirty, untidy females?"

Horror. "No!" Ruth Ann squirmed. "No, that's not what I meant...I 'pologize, Mr. Block. Really, I do. I meant you look like someone who knows what words mean."

"Thank you. Law school is certainly no picnic in the park."

She had no idea what to say to that. So she took another whiff of his cologne and wondered how much a pair of shoes like his cost. She was certain that it would be rude to ask.

"Miss Riley—Ruth Ann—shall I tell you why I'm here to see you?" Block inquired.

"Yes, please."

"Yesterday a lady by the name of Mrs. Dade paid me a visit."

Ruth Ann's pulse quickened. *Lord bless her!* Mrs. Dade had come through for her.

"I presume you know why?"

"Yes, sir. Dr. Price, the gentleman what's—I mean, *who's*—in charge of the Colony, wants to do a surgery on me—"

"And you would rather he did not."

"No, sir. I'm downright scared of it. He just did it to my momma and to my—my friend. Her name is Glory. She's real down and out 'bout it. She can't never have no—I mean, *any*—more babies, and they took away her one baby she did have. They took mine, too."

"I would like to help you, Ruth Ann. If you'll allow me to."

"Yes, please. But how can you help?"

"I would represent you in a legal proceeding."

"What does that mean?"

"We would file a petition to challenge the right of Dr. Price and the state of Virginia to make this medical decision for you, against your will."

"A petition?"

"A piece of paper that asks the court to stop the surgery until we can argue this in front of a judge."

"Oh."

"I would do the arguing, but I'd do it on your behalf. And the surgery would, at the very least, be delayed until the judge makes a decision."

"Oh."

"Would you like me to do that for you, Miss Riley?"

"Yes!" she said, feeling dazed. "Yes, please, I would."

"All right. Then you will need to formally retain my services."

She didn't like the sound of that. "Retain?"

"You need to hire me."

"Like, with money?" Her heart sank. "I don't have no money, Mr. Block. *Any*," she amended.

"I anticipated that." He smiled his dazzling smile again. "So here's what's going to happen, Ruth Ann." He dropped a bill in a denomination bigger than she'd ever seen before. Dropped it right there on the rug in front of her, where it sat, folded like a greenish, headless bird with its wings spread.

She stared at it, wide-eyed.

"Now, Ruth Ann, you pick that up."

"But—"

"Go on. Just pick it up," he instructed, while drawing a leather satchel up onto his knees.

She debated it. If she reached forward and took it, wasn't that stealing? If he was giving her the money, why didn't the man just hand it to her? Why throw it on the floor? Was this a trick?

"But it's not—"

"It's fine, Miss Riley. Trust me." He nodded reassuringly.

Finally, half expecting Mother Jenkins to fly out from behind the drapes and whack her senseless, Ruth Ann got up, bent down and took the bill between her fingers. The paper was different, finer, than regular notepaper or brown parcel paper. It looked to be woven, and in the center of it was a blunt-featured, kindly looking gentleman with shoulder-length hair.

She'd never seen so much money before in her life—and it all boiled down to one slip of fancy paper. Amazing. And so was his casual disregard for it. Imagine flicking it onto a rug, like a bit of cigar ash onto a porch.

Meanwhile, Mr. Block opened his satchel and withdrew some papers. He flipped through the pages and handed one of them to her, along with a fountain pen. At the bottom of the paper was her name, typed out, and a space for her signature beneath it.

She sank back down onto the settee, into the soft-butter pillows, and tried to read the document, but every other word may as well have been in Latin.

"This document says that I am your representative in a court of law, and that we are asking the court to intervene on your behalf as regards the surgery. If you agree, then just sign your name at the bottom and give me back the banknote in consideration of my services."

Now she understood why he'd wanted her to take the money. Because he'd always intended on getting it right back from her.

He raised his eyebrows, waiting expectantly. "Miss Riley?"

She inhaled his scent yet again, and, unable to help herself, looked for a ring on the fourth finger of his left hand. There was none.

She blushed fire as he followed her gaze with his own, his chiseled mouth quirking up at the right corner. *Stupid, stupid,*

stupid, Ruth Ann! He'd sooner court a billy goat than you. Girls like
you don't end up with men like him.

"Trust me," he repeated.

She pressed the paper to the coffee table in front of the settee
and signed her name with mortified, trembling fingers. Then she
handed it back to him, along with the pen and the banknote.

He put the lot back into his satchel. "Thank you, Miss Riley,"
Block said, and stood to leave.

She scrambled to her feet as well and took the cool, dry, firm
hand he proffered again.

This time, he drew it up to his mouth and kissed it—her hand!
Kissed. It. Electricity shot through her, streaking along every
nerve in her body.

She pulled away as if scorched and simply stared at him, mute.
She wanted to plunge her hand into ice water, but there was none
at hand. So she thrust it behind her back, instead.

"I'm honored to be at your service," he said, something disqui-
eting lurking in his green eyes. "This is a cause dear to my heart."
He lifted an eyebrow at her continued silence. "Ruth Ann?"

"Y-yes, sir?"

"Have a lovely afternoon. I'll be in touch."

Fifteen

T hrice in one week, my dear fellow!" Doc Price exclaimed, as Wilfred Block darkened his office door again. "How marvelous." Inwardly he groaned. His expensive bottle of Scotch was now as good as gone.

And get an eyeful of the man's Joe Brooks attire. Doc coveted this suit even more than the other. It was made of a charcoal-gray superfine, the tailoring so sublime that Price wanted to weep. It had been cut by a maestro and stitched by an artist. Then there was the gold watch he ostentatiously examined before jauntily tucking it away again in its pocket.

"You won't believe it when I tell you why I'm here," Block said. "Spot of giggle water, old sport? Lawyering is thirsty work."

"Of course, of course." Doc leaned forward and opened his bottom desk drawer. He retrieved the precious Glenfarclas and caressed the bottle mournfully before setting it down and fetching two crystal tumblers. He poured a grudging inch into both and nudged one toward his unwelcome guest.

Block nodded his thanks, took a swallow and then said expansively, "Now, don't get in a lather, but I'm here on behalf of my client."

The suggestion that he might be anything other than calm and even-tempered annoyed Dr. Price. "Your client?"

"Yes, old man, a client." Block chuckled. "Ruth Ann Riley."

Doc paused with his glass midway to his mouth and set it down again. "How did you manage this so soon?"

"I am creative, wily and excellent at my job. Thus, I represent her, as of ten minutes ago."

Dr. Price opened and then closed his mouth. "Quick work, Block. You do realize, however, that she doesn't have a wooden nickel to pay for your services."

"She must have been the recipient of a windfall," Block said airily, "which allowed her to put down a basic retainer fee. Besides which, I'm offering her quite a good rate. I'm an extraordinarily kind man. Heart of gold." His eyes glinted.

Like your watch. But Doc didn't say it aloud. He picked up his Scotch again and tossed some back, eyeing the lawyer askance over the crystal rim of the glass.

"I understand that you have told Ruth Ann of the proposed surgery?"

"You are correct," Doc said evenly. "I informed you of that at the board meeting."

"The young lady has made clear to me that she does not wish the operation to be performed. I will request, therefore, a stay of…execution…as we bring suit." With a flourish, Block tossed back the rest of his Scotch.

"The *young lady*," Price said, playing the game, "is a ward of the state of Virginia, and in the absence of a parent, the state decides what is best for her. I am the state's representative here at the Virginia Colony for the Epileptic and *Feebleminded*. Need I emphasize that last word?"

"Ah. But I understand that there *is* in fact a parent? And that she, too, resides on the premises."

"Sheila Riley? Oh, yes, a charming individual," Doc said

drily. "Morally bankrupt, used to prostitute herself. And equally feebleminded—in fact, more so, since she struggles with mental illness. Shall I present you to her?"

"Please. I'd like to make her acquaintance."

"Be very careful what you wish for."

"I'm careful in all my dealings, Dr. Price. That's why I'm here. Listen to what I'm saying and read between the lines." Block nudged his empty glass across the desk, eyeing it significantly.

Doc cursed him roundly but silently as he again poured an inch of liquor into his glass. "Which lines?"

"Bear with me, dear fellow. To have a guardian other than yourself appointed for Ruth Ann, I must meet the mother myself and determine that, in my legal opinion, she is an unfit parent. Are you following me, Dr. Price?" A smile played on the lips of the attorney.

Doc poured himself another inch of Scotch. "I am," he said.

"Are there any other progeny of Sheila Riley's who can be located?"

"Yes. Though one is deceased, there are two other children, a boy and a younger girl, I believe."

"Are they similarly afflicted by Mrs. Riley's polluted proto-plasm?"

"We would have to find them first, then examine them."

"We will do so. My friend, there is now an end in sight to the legal troubles you've encountered recently, while attempting to do your duty to society and stop these—these *people* (I use the term loosely) from breeding. From further contaminating the gene pool of this great country, these United States of America. We can now move forward with the board's plan to change the law."

"Excellent," Doc said. "But don't you have a conflict of interest, here, Block? If Ruth Ann Riley is now your client?"

"Yes. Therefore, as of this moment, you have just fired me from your other case. I'll recommend someone to take my place."

"What would the bar association say about this?"

"The bar won't care a whit. Do you think a girl like Ruth Ann merits their attention? And she wouldn't even grasp the concept of conflict of interest. Besides, let's define her 'interest,' *per se*. How is it possibly in her *interest* to have more illegitimate children that she has no means to support? How is it in the state's or the country's interest to support them for her, and for those offspring to continue to breed even more genetically flawed and disastrous generations to come?"

"I can't say that it is. My ongoing research proves it."

"Exactly. By subsidizing entire 'colonies' of these flawed and degenerate beings, we foster an underclass of people who drag the rest of us down—economically, intellectually, morally, socially. So let us have no more talk of conflict of interest. We have a very good case for not breeding more miserable inmates."

Block set down his tumbler and leaned forward, his eyes bright. "You, my good fellow, will have a veritable pulpit for proclaiming the results of your research. It will be in all the newspapers! It may even get national coverage, since we are so close to Washington."

Doc swirled the Scotch in his tumbler. He would make a name for himself, even trapped in this rural backwater. He'd put into practice decades of unassailable and progressive scientific theory.

Block continued. "Between Stringer and me…this is a strategy that will vindicate you, Doctor, and free you to do your very important work. And it will bring *me* into the legal spotlight, give me a platform from which to run for the Virginia state senate. Following that, the U.S. Senate. I will position myself as a champion of the common man—or woman, as the case may be. A defender of constitutional rights."

"Be still my heart," Doc Price murmured, though that greasy thing was back to sliding around in his gut. He ignored it, palmed the Glenfarclas and unscrewed the cap. "Another drink, old boy?"

"Don't mind if I do," answered Block. He pushed his glass toward Doc, who poured long and generously. "Cheers, my man. To strategy!"

Doc nodded. "To Wilfred Block, Esquire: white knight. And to the science of good breeding."

Sixteen

Ruth Ann had floated, bemused, out of the parlor and somehow down the steps and onto the lawn without feeling her own feet or legs. She had a lawyer! A handsome big timer, who was going to protect her from Doc Price and his scalpel.

And he'd kissed her hand. Like he was some kind of prince.

She pulled it from behind her back and stared down at it, the red, raw, mottled, mangled and blistered hand that had been so honored. It was hideous, because of Mother Jenkins and also from months of hard labor: endless loads of laundry, mountains of ironing, miles of floor-scrubbing and acres of potato-peeling and pea-shelling.

Her hands hadn't always looked this way. But the burns from boiling water and hot irons, the irritation from bleach and lye and the nicks and cuts from paring knives had all taken their toll.

What must Mr. Block have thought? How could he have brushed something so unsightly with his lips?

She wished she could go to a beauty salon, like those rich ladies in town with their fur coats and their own automobiles, and get a manicure. Or at the very least buy some lotion at the five and dime. What she wouldn't give for some Thurston's Hand Cream. Mrs. Dade had some near her dressing mirror, along with a fine antique hairbrush and comb set that had been her grandmother's.

Clarence caught up with Ruth Ann on her way back to the kitchens. "Hey, Ruthie. What did that swell want with you?"

"Clarence! You'll never believe it. He's my *attorney-at-law*," she said proudly. "Me! I have me a lawyer. And he's going to stop Doc Price from cuttin' me open. He's going to file a *petition*—strange word, sounds like a cross between *petticoat* and *competition*. Anyways, it's a paper that goes to the courthouse. And Mr. Block will talk to a judge for me and ask the judge not to let Doc Price do the operation, since I don't want it."

"Hmmm" was all Clarence said.

"Ain't this a marvel!"

"Yep."

What's wrong with the boy? Why isn't he excited for me? "I'll bet Doc Price is going to be mighty annoyed." The thought gave her satisfaction. The idea that she, all of a sudden, had the power to resist his God-like edicts—it almost made her giddy.

Clarence tugged on his earlobe. "Well, I hate to tell you this, but it sure didn't look like he was annoyed, Ruth Ann, when I saw him with Mr. Block just shy of an hour ago. Them two was flappin' their gums, tippin' back coffin varnish and gettin' splifficated, if you must know."

"Coffin varnish?" Ruth Ann was mystified. "Whatever are you talkin' about, Clarence?"

He shot her a glance full of significance. "You know—panther sweat."

She goggled at him, uncomprehending.

"Bootlegged *whiskey*, Ruth Ann."

"Oh!"

"Yeah. Anyways, the Doc and your fancy-pants lawyer-fella was just jawin' away, gettin' along like a house on fire, an' becomin' right ossified. *Esquire* couldn't hardly stagger 'round, in them glad rags o' his, by the time I helped him into his freshly polished motorcar and sent him on his way."

"Clarence, you seem out of sorts."

"Do I, now?"

"Yes, you do. Aren't you happy for me?"

"I'm-a tryin' to be. But there's somethin' I cain't put my finger on. Somethin' that ain't right."

She waved this away. "Applesauce! Did you know that Mr. Block had thought of downright everything? He even brought a hundred-dollar bill, so's I could give it back to him to hire his services."

"He brought a what? A *C-note*?"

"Yes! I ain't never seen one before. You?"

Clarence shook his head. Then he snorted. "Well, ain't he an egg. Fella's chargin' that kind o' kale, I'd like to see him workin' for it and not chin-waggin' with the doc what's tryin' to slice you open."

"Well, Clarence, he prob'ly's got to 'chin-wag' with Doc, or how's Doc gonna know that he now can't do no such thing? He's gonna write him a letter, when he's but two hundred yards away on the same patch of land?"

"All I'm sayin', Ruthie, is that somethin' don't smell right to me."

Ruth Ann thought of Mr. Block's cologne. It sure had smelled right to her. But she didn't reply.

"It's one thing for Esquire to ankle on over to Doc's office to have a word. It's another thing altogether for them two to kick their feet up on the desk and polish off a bottle—whiles I polish away on Esquire's hayburner, by the bye."

"Well." Ruth Ann thought about it. "Maybe they started by havin' words, but then wanted to make things right? So they shook hands and sealed the deal with a wee bit o' firewater."

"Hokum."

"You callin' me stupid, Clarence?"

"No, Ruth Ann. But you just don't know the ways of men—'specially college men who get handed a ticket to the good life and can't spare a thought or a nickel for people like us, who wash their drawers, their dishes and their motorcars. People who only got one parent in life—or one hand."

The hostility in his voice shocked her. He'd always been easy-going, whistling, uncomplainin' Clarence. A twinkle in his eye and sterling in his soul. But maybe she didn't really know all that much about him.

"But he *is* sparin' a thought for me. And Mrs. Dade sent him to me, you know."

"Right. The lady what's stolen your baby."

"She didn't—" Ruth Ann struggled with her emotions. "Annabel's better off with her than with me. What can *I* give Annabel?"

Clarence lifted an eyebrow and screwed up his mouth, and her irritation with him grew. Why was he stomping on her hope? Trying to squelch her salvation? What right did he have? What real knowledge of the lawyer-man did he possess? All he had was some weird hunch.

"Mr. Block is tryin' to help. He even gave me the money to pay him. Seems to me that's the way of a *good* man."

"Ruthie. He don't know you from Adam or Eve. What reason does he have for doin' this on your behalf?"

"Why does he need one?"

"He ain't a pastor, Ruthie! He's a lawyer. What if he asks you to earn back that money later?"

She felt kicked in the stomach, breathless with outrage. "What are you suggestin'?"

He just looked at her. "Do I really need to spell it out?"

"How dare you, Clarence!"

"Have you thought about it? What would you do?"

"Bite your tongue. He won't! He's not that kind. He is a *gentleman*. He even kissed my hand!"

"Is that right." Clarence's cinnamon freckles faded into a sea of brick red, and his normally calm, rainwater-gray eyes grew stormy. "Well. That's just ducky." His tone was scathing. "So what would you do?"

"I am not ab-whorrent!"

"Then where'd your baby come from?"

"*Oh!*" She raised her hand as if to slap him, and then, shocked at herself, clamped it under her arm so that it couldn't escape and do the deed by itself. "How can you ask me that, Clarence? How?"

He averted his gaze, shamefaced.

"You ain't never asked me that before. Why now?"

He stared at the ground, swallowed, shook his head.

"Not that it's any of your beeswax! But I didn't have a choice. Do you hear me? I got my neck wrung like a chicken, my head slammed into a wall, my skirts drug up and my bloomers pulled down. I got laughed at, and I got forced—"

Shock and naked pain had bloomed on his face. "*Stop.*"

"You asked me, Clarence, and now you're gonna hear it!" Hot tears streamed down her face, surprising her. She went to wipe them away with her sleeve.

"No—I cain't. Please." To her own shock, he slipped his arms around her and pulled her to him, his dry cheek sliding along the moisture of hers. He was solid muscle; he smelled of freshly mown hay, of coffee, of wood shavings. Of simple emotions in a complicated boy.

She shook in his embrace, not like a leaf but like a whole pile of them, not attached to any twig or branch or tree in the whole world. Just fragmented and forlorn and fallen.

"I'm so sorry, Ruthie," he said. "God, I'm sorry."

She didn't know how to react to the simple affection. Immediately her mind jumped to how it would look to anyone who might glimpse them. "Clarence, someone will see. Let go of me."

He did. He stepped back, but only so far. He brushed her tears away, tenderly, with his own sleeves. To her astonishment, she saw some moisture in his eyes, too.

He blinked it away, compressed his lips and said, "I'm-a *kill the sonovabitch.*"

"Clarence!" She'd never heard him swear. "You're not killing nobody. It ain't worth goin' to jail for, and at least Annabel came of it all…and…" She ran out of words.

"Who did it?" He stood there, ramming the stump of his left hand into the palm of his right, over and over again. It was downright alarming.

"It don't matter," she said neutrally.

"It does." His eyes were like gunmetal. Hard. Cold.

"Clarence, what is eating you? You are not yourself."

"What's eating me?" He gave a short bark of laughter that wasn't really laughter. Far from it. "I dunno, Ruth Ann. An' I prob'ly couldn't spell it, even if I could name it."

"Why do you despise Mr. Block?" She put her hands on her hips. Maybe he'd apologized, and she could feel that he cared about her, and that made her feel warm inside, but she still wanted to set him straight. "Is it just on account of he's got nice clothes and a motorcar?"

"You're all wet, Ruth Ann."

"Says you! Ish kabibble. Maybe you need to take a look inside yourself: do you hate him 'cause you want those things, and he's got 'em? That ain't right."

Clarence glared at her. "Mayhap *you* like him 'cause you want those things, and he's got 'em."

What a hateful thing to say! Her head filled with steam, like a kettle a-boil. Any moment it would whistle, and twin puffs of smoke would pour out her ears. "Well, I never! Now you're callin' me a gold digger, after you called me a whore? Nice, Clarence, real nice."

He stomped his foot. "I didn't call you either of those things! An' I don't wanna fight with you. Maybe you're right, and I ain't bein' fair to this cake-eater. Maybe I just wanna be the one to solve your problems, not him. So put that in your pipe and smoke it, Ruthie."

Her mouth dropped open. What exactly was he saying?

Clarence had gone from his former brick red to beet red. "You want to see Esquire as a hero? I can't stop you. But I will tell you this: I seen his type before. I ain't book smart, but I sure am people smart, and that fella—he may look spiffy, but you mark my words, he is a weasel and a windsucker."

"Aw, tell it to Sweeney, Clarence." But there was no heat in her words.

"We're done, here." He shoved his stump and his hand into his pockets, turned and walked away.

"Yeah, go chase yourself," she called after him. Then she folded her arms across her chest and kicked a perfectly innocent tree that just happened to have the misfortune to be nearby. It didn't yelp, lash her with a branch or even so much as drop an acorn on her noggin in return. "I'm sorry," she told it belligerently. Then she kicked it again, just for being there and for being silent.

"Why am I always 'pologizin' to people? To doctors? To baby

thieves? To God? To trees? Whyever am I such a sorry girl? Whatever have I done to be so blasted *sorry*?!"

But the tree didn't seem to be speaking to her, not that she could blame it. She wondered if Clarence would, after he got over his tantrum.

After Ruth Ann had got back to the kitchens and ironed several more dang-blasted sheets while enduring nosy questions and digs from the other girls, she crept down to the infirmary, stopping to pluck some yellow roses on the way. She stuck them in a jelly jar that she filled at an outside water pump and managed not to slop too much water on herself as she walked over.

The infirmary was a two-story, redbrick building with shrubs planted in a neat row on either side of its black front door, just as the patients were arranged in neat rows of beds inside the twenty-six-person wards.

Ruth Ann was waved in apathetically by the nurse on duty behind the reception desk. She was smoking a cigarette and painting her nails at the same time, something that struck Ruth Ann as dangerous. She was pretty sure nail polish was flammable, but she didn't say anything. The nurse wouldn't be interested in her opinion, anyways.

She slipped into the ward, which was less than half full. There was an old lady in the farthest bed, her white hair askew and her eyes wide and wild. "Help me, help me, help me…" she moaned, over and over again. Ruth Ann's heart clenched with pity as she saw that the poor woman was tied to the bed.

A middle-aged man with yellowish skin and huge hollows under his eyes lay in another bed, snoring and drooling steadily onto his pillow. She resisted the urge to stop and wipe his mouth.

A young girl of ten, maybe, huddled under her blankets, shivering so much that her teeth chattered. "I want my mommy," she said plaintively as Ruth Ann approached. "I want my ma."

Poor little mite. "Is she here in the building? Do you want me to get her for you? Do you want another blanket?"

"No. She's in Heaven, miss," the little girl said, her dark eyes as big and bruised as plums. "I want her back."

"Oh, sweetheart. I'm so sorry. She's…she's in a better place now."

"But why'd she leave me in this one?"

"She didn't mean to, honey. God just called her to His side."

"Well, I think He's mean, then!"

Ruth Ann stared helplessly at her. "Sometimes, I guess He seems that way. But He loves you…"

"Why? And how do you know?"

Oh, dear. "Because you're beautiful, and smart, and sweet—"

"I'm not sweet. Nurse Schuyler says I'm willful and I got a wicked tongue."

"Well," Ruth Ann said, trying to hide a smile. "Do you want to be sweet?"

"No."

"All right, then. Don't be. God gave you your wicked tongue, so you just make sure you use it for something good—like makin' folks laugh. Not making 'em cry. Okay?"

The girl pondered that. "I s'pose."

Ruth Ann finally spotted Glory in the opposite row of beds, lying pale and listless. Staring at nothing. Ruth Ann waved, but got no reaction.

"Can I hit someone, if I want to make 'em cry?" asked the little girl.

"What?" Ruth Ann had been midstride to go see Glory, but she stopped and turned back. "No! No, you may not. On account of they'll just hit you right back, and then you'll get sore and hit 'em again, and they'll hit you back again, and on and on it goes. That's why you don't even get it started—'cause it never, ever ends."

"Oh."

"Why would you want to make somebody cry, anyways?" Ruth Ann asked her.

"Because I wanna cry, but I can't anymore—I'm all dried up. So I'm just mad. I'm mad enough to hit somebody so they cry instead."

"Listen," said Ruth Ann, moved by the little girl's honesty and odd logic. "That makes sense. You're sad and mad that your ma isn't here. But other people got enough to cry about without you piling on. So you got to work it out a different way."

"What's your name?" the little girl asked. "I'm Izzie."

"Pleased to meet you, Izzie. I'm Ruth Ann."

"Why are you here?"

"To see my friend Glory, over there." Ruth Ann hesitated, finding herself unable to just walk away and leave the small girl alone. "D'you want to come meet her? She's sad, too."

"How come?"

"She…had to have an operation. Now she can't never have no more babies. So that makes her feel like cryin'. But I'm pretty sure, lookin' at her, that she's all cried out, too. Come on. Let's get you an extra blanket to stop those shivers, and you come over to meet her."

Bundled in two white wool blankets, Izzie resembled a small ghost. Ruth Ann took her by the hand and they walked across the middle aisle of the ward and down to Glory's bed.

"Hi, there," Ruth Ann said. "How are you feelin', Glory-girl?"

No answer. Just a blank stare.

Ruth Ann held up the jelly jar of yellow roses. "I brought you these. Aren't they pretty? Like sunshine, bloomed into velvet."

Glory at least did her the courtesy of rolling her eyes in their direction.

Emboldened, Ruth Ann took her hand and brushed one of her friend's fingers across a petal. "See?"

"I'm Izzie," said Izzie. "Are you going to die?"

A furrow settled between Glory's eyes. She rolled them in question toward Ruth Ann.

"Izzie! You can't say—"

"Because if you are, will you find my ma in Heaven and tell her that I miss her real bad, and that she should come back, because God does *not* need her more than I do?"

"—things like that," Ruth Ann trailed off, horrified.

Glory regarded Izzie with something like dark amusement. "I'm sorry to disappoint you, cutie, but I am not going to die. But I surely would find your ma for you if I was. I want you to know that."

"Oh. Thank you." Izzie looked crestfallen, and Ruth Ann struggled not to laugh at the sheer innocent awfulness of it all.

Then Izzie brightened. "Is anyone *else* here going to die soon?" she asked, craning her neck and scanning the beds.

Ruth Ann met Glory's gaze; their lips twitched simultaneously, and before they could stop themselves, they were hooting.

"What's funny?" Izzie demanded. "I just need one person to die! How else can I get a message to my ma?"

Once Ruth Ann had caught her breath, she tried to explain. "You got to pray, Izzie. It's like that. You can talk to your ma through God, and you can listen to see if she answers you in your head. But it's not at all nice to wish that somebody else will die just so's you can get a message to her."

"Oh." Izzie pulled the blanket more closely around her narrow shoulders. "Well, all right, then."

Glory struggled upright, wincing. "How old are you, Izzie?"

"Nine."

"Why are you here in the infirmary?"

Izzie put a hand to her abdomen. "Dr. Price took out my appendix."

A wave of nausea hit Ruth Ann. She blinked rapidly and avoided Glory's eyes.

"It hurts."

"I'm sorry, cutie," said Glory. "My tummy hurts, too."

"An appendix must be awful big," Izzie mused. "It left a big scar."

Acid shot up Ruth Ann's esophagus. "Where…where's your scar, honey?"

Izzie unwrapped the blankets and pointed at her lower abdomen, moving her finger from left to right. "Want to see?" She grasped the hem of her hospital gown and flipped it up, baring her midriff.

Ruth Ann gasped at the sight of the angry, puckered red scar with black stitching; it marred the child's smooth, pale flesh almost from hipbone to hipbone.

Glory shut her eyes tightly, her lips moving in prayer.

Oh, dear Lord. Doc Price has sterilized—no, mutilated—a child.

Seventeen

As she unpinned several lines of clean, dry laundry, Ruth Ann wondered how Glory was feeling, when she'd get out of the infirmary and if she and Izzie were keeping each other company.

Ruth Ann felt a little guilty that everything was going her way—aside from Clarence's odd behavior. She buried her face in a crisp white sheet before removing it and folding it. What luck!

Her knuckles were healing, thanks to the salve, bandages and gloves. Mrs. Dade had got her a lawyer, and Mr. Block was even meeting her at Doc Price's office later today to explain to him that he was not *allowed* to do the operation, on account of they were goin' to court. Imagine anyone tellin' Doc, the superintendent of the whole Colony, that he couldn't do something!

It made her feel downright giddy, so much so that when she moved on down the line to unpin a pair of bloomers, she made them dance the Charleston on the way to her laundry basket. She'd seen a picture of them flappers in *Life* magazine, all short hair and short skirts with painted lips and yards of pearls…dancing as if they hadn't a care in the world.

Come to think of it, all the bloomers on the line were much too long to go under a flapper dress. What on earth did they wear under those tiny skirts? Couldn't be hardly anything at all. Ruth Ann blushed just thinking about it.

As she moved down what had to be miles of shimmying, fluttering fabric, her thoughts also turned to Sheila. She unpinned entire chorus lines of bloomers and chemises and petticoats; shirtwaists and skirts and dresses; undershorts, trousers, shirts and handkerchiefs; sheets, curtains, tablecloths, napkins, aprons. Basket after basket.

The laundry smelled so much better at this end of the process: like mountain breeze and pine and sunshine—unsoiled, bright and forgiven. It smelled of a new morning, a fresh start.

Did Sheila ever feel this way after one of her forced baths? Ruth Ann knew it was a good possibility that Ruby was cleaning up her momma right this very moment, since Mr. Block wanted to meet her for some reason. She hoped Sheila would be civil. She also hoped the lump on her momma's forehead had receded and that she wouldn't be chompin' and spittin' any soap at poor Ruby.

There were many times when Ruth Ann had felt sorry for herself, what with the way her life had gone and the chores she had to do. But what she dealt with was nothing compared to what Ruby had to do. Ruby wrestled with the crazies, fed the infirm who couldn't feed themselves, changed adult diapers and wiped bums, bathed the elderly and incapacitated. She scrubbed bedpans and cleaned up vomit. Ruby deserved a medal of honor, a tiara and most likely a halo. Not that she was likely to get any of those in this lifetime.

Ruby's dogs must be barkin' something fierce by day's end, especially after walking the three miles back to her house in the colored section of town. The very last thing Ruby must want to do when she arrived home was cook for her family. So Ruth Ann decided that when she got her own cottage with the window boxes and rocking chair on the porch, she'd invite Ruby for supper, too.

She passed the time with more visions like this, barely register-ing what her hands did with the laundry. She'd been washing, rinsing, starching, pinning, unpinning and ironing laundry since she was eleven years old. *If Mother Jenkins ever cuts my hands clean off, then they'll just keep on workin' by their ownselves. Kind of like a chicken keeps runnin' circles even without a head.*

Ruth Ann finished her lines with only a few minutes left to spare. She stacked the baskets neatly in the mudroom. Then, feel-ing more than foolish, she checked her reflection in the window outside, smoothing her hair back, pinching her cheeks and biting her lips.

You ain't the ugliest female alive, Ruth Ann, she said to it. *But you ain't no flapper with a perfect marcelled bob and a truckload of pearls, neither.* Someday, though, she was getting out of here, and long afore she got herself a cottage or a rockin' chair, she was gonna buy herself a pot of lip rouge, a tiny brush for it and even a mirrored compact with pressed powder and a puff. What treasure! She'd seen them in the magazines, and in the window of the five and dime. Truth to tell, it was the first time—even afore baby Annabel and the milk—that she'd ever in her life been tempted to steal something.

It was a big fat ugly sin to covet these beauty accessories: true. But they were such dainty, mysterious items. The magical keys to some kind of divine feminine power.

What if she had a pocketbook to put them in? Along with a pack of cigs, an ebony cigarette holder, a silver lighter...even some cash.

She must've lost track of the time and got quite a moony look on her face, for next thing she was aware of, Clarence was snappin' his fingers in her face.

"You on this planet, or some other, Ruthie?" he asked. No wink.

"Oh" was all she could come up with. "Hi, Clarence."

"Heya. Your high hat, *Esquire*, is coolin' his heels outside o' Doc's office. You aware o' that?"

"Oh! I'm late!" She shook off her silly daydreams, gathered her skirts and commenced to gallop toward Price's office. "Thanks—meanin' you no disrespect," she called back to him, over her shoulder.

He made no response, just watched her go.

She arrived, out of breath, to find Mr. Block already seated in Doc Price's visitor's chair, and the two of them seeming quite civil, as if there was no disagreement at all about her surgery. In fact, there were two crystal tumblers on either side of Doc's massive desk, with some brown liquid the color of strong iced tea in them.

When they saw her through the window, they both stood, and Doc even opened the door for her, instead of calling, "Come in," as he usually did, without moving.

"Good afternoon, Ruth Ann," Doc said with a smile.

"Afternoon, sir." She nodded. Then she felt herself flush as she glanced in Mr. Block's direction. Lord, the man's eyes were green—almost the same green as the spring peas that she shelled by the hundreds. "Afternoon, Mr. Block." Would he kiss her hand again?

"How nice to see you again, Miss Riley." He made no move to take her hand at all. He produced a smile that seemed just a little greasy at the edges and gazed pointedly at the one visitor's chair.

"Oh, ah, right. Yes," said Doc. He dragged the library ladder near his bookshelves forward and placed it next to the chair. "Please, have a seat. Both of you."

Ruth Ann moved toward the ladder—there was no question who would sit on it. The de-botched and ab-whorrent one among 'em, for sure.

But Esquire—a pox on Clarence, she shouldn't think of him by that name—stepped toward it first. "No, no," he said gallantly. "I'll take the bookish perch. You shall have the chair, Miss Riley."

Doc Price raised an eyebrow.

Her blush deepened. "It don't seem right—"

"I insist." Block gestured toward it.

Such a kind soul, such a gentleman. And that cologne…Ruth Ann sank into the chair and smoothed her skirt. "Thank you."

"Ah, would you care for some refreshment, Miss Riley?" Doc asked. There was something in his voice she couldn't quite read. And he'd certainly never called her Miss Riley or offered her anything to drink. Had her hirin' a lawyer won his respect? Or was it for Mr. Block's benefit?

She eyed the two tumblers. She might be feebleminded, but she was 90 percent certain that she'd caught the scent of whiskey punctuating Esquire's cologne.

Dad burn it! Mr. Block's cologne, that is. Well, not my beeswax. I sure ain't gonna tell the Temperance League.

The two men stared at her expectantly until she remembered that Doc had asked her a question. "Oh. No, thank you, sir."

They exchanged a glance pregnant with meaning—she couldn't say as to what.

"Miss Riley," Doc began. "It has been brought to my attention by your attorney, here, Mr. Block, that you are fearful of the surgery that I discussed with you. Before your…adventure." He eyed her from behind his cold, silver-rimmed spectacles.

Ruth Ann squirmed in the chair. "It weren't meant to be an adv—"

"Yes, yes. I've been told that you merely wanted to check on your baby. That indicates a commendable instinct toward responsibility."

Having little idea what that meant, she simply looked at him.

"That's a compliment, Ruth Ann," Mr. Block said.

"Oh." Ruth Ann picked at her cuticles. "Thank you?"

"Yes, yes." Doc pulled off his spectacles and polished the lenses with his handkerchief. "I wish to inform you, my dear girl, of several things."

Since when am I Doc's "dear girl"?

"First of all, the operation in question is very simple and quite safe. There is absolutely no reason to be alarmed."

Right, Doc. You just gonna cut a big cheery smile into my belly, so's I can look down and wave to it on grummy days. Just how dad-gum feebleminded do you think I am?

"So I want to reassure you upon that score. Now, second, I realize in hindsight that I didn't present to you all of the pertinent facts about your case."

As 'posed to the impertinent ones?

"As an unwed female with no stable home, it is the Colony's—and therefore my—responsibility to society to ensure that you do not find yourself, ah, shall we say…at…*loose* ends."

Mr. Block fell into a coughing fit.

Doc replaced his spectacles and eyed him severely. "Are you quite all right, Wilfred?"

"Yes. Pardon me, Doctor."

"So we find ourselves in something of a dilemma. You are the probable producer of degenerate offspring, Ruth Ann."

Dill Emma? Offspring? Is that like a handspring? She hadn't the faintest idea what he was talking about.

"It's not your fault. You are not responsible for your genes, or, given your mental state, for your…ah…inability to control your baser impulses."

Doc was spewing Greek. But he seemed to be waiting for her to nod, so she did.

"My dear, we can either keep you here for the next thirty-odd years, or we can give you your freedom almost immediately, and the opportunity to work and marry and lead a normal life outside the Colony. Would that appeal to you, Miss Riley?" Genuine kindness shone from his eyes.

Freedom? Life outside? Those were concepts she understood. "Why, yes, sir. Of course, sir." Hope dawned within her. But then she remembered her recent, disastrous experience with the outside world. The sinking realization that she had made a mistake to leave and hadn't thought things through.

If she left the Colony, wherever would she go? Where would she live? What would she do? How would she eat?

But Doc was still talking. "And there is also the distinct possibility, my dear, that the Dade family would take you back in, thereby allowing you to be part of your infant daughter's life. You could help raise her, under Mrs. Dade's supervision."

Oh! To have a home again. It was a dream. She'd fulfill the promise she'd made to her daughter—that she herself would raise her. Hope bloomed within her.

To hold Annabel. Feed her. Bathe her. Rock her. Soothe her cries. Watch her grow up…the unimaginable joy of that…is he for real?

"Would you like that, Ruth Ann?"

Lost in the possibilities, she didn't even hear him.

"Ruth Ann?" Doc's voice intruded. "Would you like that?" He cast another significant glance at Esquire.

"Yes! Oh, yes, I most certainly would, sir." She couldn't keep from beaming. "Yes!"

She glanced at Mr. Block. Had the lawyer worked this magic? He was worth his weight in gold. He lounged gracefully on the library ladder, looking like he'd stepped out of *Life* magazine, his chestnut hair escaping its pomade and falling over his forehead. He nodded at her.

This was incredible. She grinned like a jack-o'-lantern—she couldn't help it.

Doc smiled back, forming a steeple with his hands on the desk in front of him. Far from threatening her with a scalpel, he now looked benevolent and cozy, like someone's grandpa. "I'm very pleased to hear you say so, Ruth Ann. It is my greatest wish and highest calling to ensure the safety, well-being and happiness of my patients here at the Colony. I do hope you know that."

She nodded. "Yes, sir."

Maybe Mrs. Dade will let me sleep with Annabel in my old room at the house. After all, she needs her rest—she could do with some help. Newborns ain't easy. Angels, yes. But demanding ones.

"Good girl."

Good girl. Words she longed to hear, especially from an adult. How long had it been since someone, anyone, had called her that? *Good girl.* She swallowed a lump in her throat the size of Clarence's shoe. Blinked away the sudden sting in her eyes.

Doc Price went on talking, but to her it was some mumbo jumbo. Then they nattered on 'bout some movement—the one Clarence had heard him tell of—called YouGenics.

Ruth Ann stopped paying attention after a while—none of it had anything to do with her. Look at that: Mr. Block's socks had tiny pine trees embroidered on them today. Wouldn't it be a lark to knit little pink tulips or yellow ducks into a baby blanket? She would ask Mrs. Dade to teach her how to knit. So she could make not only blankets, but hats and booties and mittens for baby Annabel.

The trouble with so many men o' learnin' is somethin' they never learn: that not every poor soul wants to be as learned as they are. Most folks just want to go about their business without a lot of nonsense rattlin' to and fro in their skulls.

Ruth Ann sat still, brimming with thankfulness at the possibility of a new life with Annabel, while them two suits flapped and flapped their gums some more. Lord love 'em, they gibbered until they got thirsty again. *If that's tea and not whiskey, then I'm Mrs. Calvin Coolidge.*

But she didn't give a rat's behind what they drank—as long as they kept their word about sending her back to live with her baby. The specter of Patrick briefly crossed her mind, but she dismissed it. She could care for little Annabel just fine—with a knife in her brassiere.

Finally, the two gentlemen ran out of words, thank the good Lord. Mr. Block's green eyes were a touch glassy when he got to his feet and suggested that Ruth Ann take him to meet her momma. Oh, dear. She cast a questioning glance at Doc Price.

"It's just fine, Ruth Ann," he said.

"Well…" Her face heated, then her neck. The simple truth was that she was embarrassed. She didn't want this Magazine Man to think less of her because her momma was dirty, or foul-mouthed, or blotto. "She's prob'ly busy."

"Busy?" Doc removed his spectacles again and rubbed at his eyes. "Sheila Riley hasn't been busy since the constable picked her up for—" He had the grace to break off. "She won't be busy," he said.

Ruth Ann's face now felt sunburned. She must be the color of a ripe tomato. "I—"

I don't want to do this? My momma ain't someone you should meet? How could she say either of those things?

"Go on, now, Ruth Ann. Be a good girl and show Mr. Block, here, to the Distressed unit. Find Sheila and make the introduction."

A good girl...one who could live in a normal home again and mind her baby.

"He needs to meet her for the court case," Doc explained.

Ruth Ann supposed that made sense. So, resigned, she cast about for a way to warn Mr. Block. "My momma...She can be, um, unpredictable. And downright fractious."

"I'm sure she's charming," Mr. Block said. "I look forward to making Mrs. Riley's acquaintance." He offered Ruth Ann his arm. "Shall we?"

She was dumbfounded. He wanted her to lay her calloused, blistered, broken mitts on his fine woolen sleeve? No. She couldn't.

And yet she wanted to, with every fiber of her being. Just as someone else. As an elegant debutante maybe. Not Ruth Ann Riley.

Wilfred Block raised his eyebrows and exchanged another one of those glances with Doc, who compressed his lips, got to his feet and opened the door for them.

Ruth Ann realized that her mouth was hanging open. She closed it and got to her feet. But she did not place her hand upon Mr. Block's arm. She moistened her dry lips and linked her fingers together behind her back, before ankling on out of Doc's office.

"I'm very pleased for you, Ruth Ann," Doc told her as she left. "You're going to be free and happy. And you'll help us make history."

She would? And how was that, exactly? But she smiled politely. "If you say so, Doc."

Eighteen

Mr. Wilfred Block, Esquire, did not find Sheila Riley charming in the least. She was scrawny, shifty-eyed and unkempt. Several of her teeth were missing, and the ones she did have were the color of ripe cheddar.

"Well, ain't you a big six," Sheila said, eyeing him from head to toe, her glance lingering far too long just south of his waistband. "Cash or check, daddy-o?"

His color rose. She was the coarsest, most common woman he'd ever encountered.

"Momma," said Ruth Ann, "this here's Mr. Block. He's my lawyer."

"That right?" Sheila half-blew, half-spat out a lungful of cigarette smoke, like a human exhaust pipe. "I got better uses for 'im. What in tarnation d'you need a lawyer for?"

"On account of I don't want the same operation Doc Price did on you. So I wrote to Mrs. Dade, and she found Mr. Block, here."

"You got a lawyer to tangle with Doc Price? He won't take kindly to that. It's a big mistake."

"It's not," Ruth Ann said. "Doc knows. We just had a meetin', the three of us. He's bein' real civil 'bout things."

"Hooey. Somethin' ain't right, then." Sheila turned her gaze to

Block again, though she still addressed her daughter. "How you payin' your fancy lawyer's fees?"

"I am handling Ruth Ann's case gratis," Wilfred said. But he realized the woman would have no knowledge of Latin. "In other words, for free."

Sheila blew out another toxic cloud of smoke. "Oooh, *gratis*, he says. Thankee, kind sir, for 'splainin' to poor white trash such as myself."

Her daughter winced. "Momma…"

"What else you handlin' of Ruth Ann's?" Sheila asked Block, taking a drag on her cigarette and squinting at him through a pair of eyes that looked like raisins.

"*Momma!*"

Block goggled at her. "I *beg* your pardon, madam?"

"You heard me, Mr. Block." She drew her lips back in a sneer. "What's a lawyer want with my girl? 'Specially if you ain't makin' any dough off 'er."

"I occasionally take on cases for the, ah, less privileged members of socie—"

"We don't need your charity, Block-head," she spat, then picked a tobacco particle off her lower lip and dropped it to the floor.

Lovely. "I believe Ruth Ann has decided she does."

"Ruth Ann is not of age, and I'm her mother. *I* decide what she needs."

"I'm afraid that isn't true," Block said. "Your daughter is a ward of the state. She no longer answers to you."

Sheila shot him a look to kill; Ruth Ann looked as though she might kiss him. He took a step back from them both. If he'd had any lingering question about his role in all of this, it was quickly evaporating.

"You listen to me, you big palooka," Sheila said, advancing

upon him with her cigarette. The ash at the tip glowed orange with ill intent.

"Lord ha' mercy," a large colored woman said, entering the room and looking from one to the other.

"This is Ruby," said Ruth Ann. "Ruby, Mr. Block."

He nodded at her. She nodded back.

"My daughter don't need no fancy-pants lawyer," Sheila declared. "Last thing I need is for Doc Price to kick me to the curb on account of you and Ruth Ann. I weren't pleased to be brought here, but they treat me all right. I get three squares a day and a roof over my head. Unless I need a little somethin' extra, I don't have to suck no co—"

"MOMMA!"

"Shut it, Sheila!" Ruby roared.

Block had seen all he needed to. Sheila Riley was a scourge upon humanity, a disgusting specimen. And it was alarming that she'd had more than one child. His research had disclosed that there was, indeed, another daughter out there. She must be found immediately, before she, too, could breed.

He was finished, here, but evidently Sheila was not. "I don' know what you up to, mister, but I can smell that it ain't good. So you prance on back wherever you came from, and you stay away from Ruth Ann. I catch you 'round her again, I will take an' shove the scales of justice right up your tight ass."

"How dare you, madam?"

"Woof, woof."

"I don't take orders—or threats—from the likes of you," Block informed her.

"Aw, you don't? Too bad. How 'bout you take this, then?" Sheila struck, quick as a snake. She ground the glowing tip of her cigarette into the costly wool of his suit.

He knocked it to the floor as she cackled maniacally. "What the—are you *mad*?!"

A black hole smoldered, right above the breast pocket.

Ruby grabbed Sheila, kicking and screaming, and hauled her away as he stood there, looking down at the hole in shock. It was a miracle the cigarette hadn't burned through his waistcoat and shirt, too.

"It's the straitjacket for you, Miz Sheila," Ruby scolded. "You behavin' like some evil hag from a nightmare, you is…"

Ruth Ann had gone white, her hands over her mouth. At last she dropped them and whispered, "I'm so very sorry, Mr. Block. I didn't want to bring you here…Are you all right? Did it burn right down to the skin?"

Wordlessly, he shook his head.

"Mr. Block, I 'pologize from the bottom of my heart."

He felt sorry for the girl. She was clearly mortified. But no matter what her feelings, the degenerate line of Riley had to end, and as God was his witness, end it would.

Not a week had gone by when yet again, Ruth Ann was summoned away from the kitchens to the main administrative building. Was Esquire—Mr. Block—here for another talk? She made a sorry attempt to smooth her hair in the reflection of a kettle on the stove. She pinched her cheeks and bit her lips as she hustled up the hill and across the green lawn that spread like a giant lie in front of the house.

Mrs. Parsons ushered her into the same parlor, where she sat on the same settee and marveled all over again at the softness of the down pillows behind her back. And then sure enough, Mr. Block came in. Along with a little wisp of a girl, her blond hair braided tightly into two pigtails, her blue eyes pink-rimmed from crying.

Ruth Ann stared at her. She looked familiar somehow, but... Then she saw the stuffed bear the girl clutched.

If Ruth Ann hadn't been sitting, she'd have fallen to the floor. "*Bonnie?*"

The little girl didn't say a word.

Mr. Block pushed her forward. "Say hello to your sister, sweetheart."

Ruth Ann flung herself toward the little sister she hadn't seen since she was seven, and Bonnie just under two. Since the horrible afternoon when Sheila had been hauled away, spitting and shrieking, and they'd all been separated.

Bonnie shrank back, clearly terrified by the stranger lunging at her. She seemed small and young for her age. Had she been badly treated? Malnourished?

Though Ruth Ann wanted nothing more than to take the little girl into her arms, she pulled up short. "Bonnie, do you remember me? Woothie." She chuckled. "You used to call me Woothie."

Bonnie tilted her head slightly, her lips silently forming the silly name.

"I used to carry you around like a baby doll. You and Calico Bear."

Bonnie slowly held up the bear for inspection. It was faded, it had been mended and patched with many different fabrics and thread, it had lost an eye—but it still had two ears and a button nose.

Ruth Ann nodded. "Calico Bear lives!"

Bonnie smiled. It was a shy smile, just as ragged and worn as the old bear, a smile far too weary for a child's face, and it split Ruth Ann's heart wide open.

"Oh, Bonnie. Oh, honey." She couldn't *not* take her into her arms now, though her sister, like her, didn't seem to know what to do with this show of affection. She allowed it, though, standing awkwardly in Ruth Ann's embrace.

She smelled of rose soap and sunshine and little girl. She smelled of the innocence Glory had just lost. She smelled like love and family. Ruth Ann had never inhaled such a heavenly scent. Her throat tightened and her eyes stung.

At last she released Bonnie, but kept a hand on her shoulder as she turned to Mr. Block. "I can't ever thank you enough. Not ever." She swiped at her eyes.

For once, he had nothing fancy to say. He stood silent and nodded, though he wore an odd expression. He looked...abashed? Was that it?

She didn't ponder it much. Because after nine long years, she was standing next to the dearest, most precious thing on earth besides Annabel—her baby sister.

Mrs. Parsons and her lace collar flew back into the room with a tray that had coffee, cream, sugar and a biscuit on it. As well as a single, red, perfect strawberry. She set the tray down in front of Mr. Block and made a fuss about what he wanted in the coffee.

The strawberry looked like the red, freckled nose of some sad creature, cut off its face and set on a plate. Ruth Ann shook off the weird sensation it produced in her; shook off the odd doubts that Block's expression called up within her.

He thanked "Mrs. Parker" quite graciously and begged her pardon when she informed him a bit snippily that her name was Mrs. Parsons. He lifted that coffee cup as if it contained holy water and absolution and gulped from it without looking at any of the women.

Then Mrs. Parsons banished her and Bonnie from the parlor. "Ruth Ann, you'll want to get your sister settled into the dorm. Greta has been moved to another bunk. Bonnie will have her spot

above you. All right? Move along. And then you'll report with
Bonnie to Mother Jenkins. She'll set up her schedule of chores."

Bonnie edged a little closer to Ruth Ann, hugging Calico Bear
to her chest.

"Yes, ma'am." Ruth Ann didn't want to take her anywhere
near that old toad Mother Jenkins. But she reached out and
took her sister's hand, gave it a squeeze. "Does she have a
suitcase?"

"She has a crate. It's by the kitchen door. You girls go out that
way—we've got visitors coming for the board meeting."

*Of course. The board won't want to see the likes of us on that big
green lawn. That's for croquet, so they won't be so bored.*

"You want to see where we sleep, Bonnie?" Ruth Ann smiled
at her sister. Sister…she couldn't quite believe she had one again,
after all these years apart. After all this time alone except for the
once-a-week visit with Crazy Sheila.

Bonnie hesitated, then nodded. *Cain't she speak? Is the poor
girl mute?*

And what would happen when she took her to meet Momma?
Would Sheila treat her any better than she did Ruth Ann?

They took three steps toward the door to exit the parlor.

"What is that dirty bundle of cloth you've got there, child?"
Mrs. Parsons advanced upon them.

Bonnie shrank back against Ruth Ann and tried to clamp
Calico Bear under her armpit.

"It's a bear," Ruth Ann said. "She's had it since she was a baby."

"Well, that's quite long enough. You're a big girl now, Bonnie.
Give it here, to me."

Bonnie hid behind Ruth Ann, shaking her head *no, no, no*.

It struck Ruth Ann again that her sister seemed immature for
her age. *Feebleminded? Or just traumatized?* And she was tiny.

"She refused to leave it behind with the Wallaces," Mr. Block said. "They informed me that she's very attached to it."

"It looks filthy," said Mrs. Parsons. "And she's eleven years old. Far too old for a teddy bear."

"Please, Mrs. P, can she keep it? This all's a lotta changes for her."

Mrs. Parsons sighed. "Fine. But I'll tell you right now that Mrs. Jenkins won't like it. That bear is doubtless infested with fleas." She stepped back from them, as if one might leap up her skirt.

Ruth Ann squeezed Bonnie's shoulder and they took another two steps toward the parlor door.

"Don't you have something to say to Mr. Block, Bonnie?" Mrs. Parsons cast a slightly moony look toward him and fingered her lace collar.

Bonnie shrank against Ruth Ann and just stared at the woman, then at Esquire.

"Something along the lines of *thank you*? Come on, girl, what's wrong with you?"

Bonnie nodded, twisting Calico Bear's paw.

"Well, then say it. Say the words."

The little girl opened, then closed her mouth. She cast a glance of mute appeal at Ruth Ann.

Esquire—darn it, Mr. Block!—set down his coffee cup and raised his pale eyebrows, waiting along with Mrs. Parsons and her lace for Bonnie to respond.

The moment stretched on and on.

Two tears escaped from Bonnie's pink-rimmed eyes and rolled down her face, pooling at the corners of her Cupid's bow mouth.

"Bonnie, sweetheart?" Ruth Ann ventured.

Mr. Block picked up his coffee cup again and drained it. "I don't know that she speaks," he said, and then replaced it in its saucer. He picked up the biscuit and took a bite, while the straw-berry nose continued to squat, lonely, on the plate. "She hasn't said one word since I collected her from her foster parents."

Mrs. Parsons clucked. "What impertinence."

"I'll say thank you," Ruth Ann interjected quickly. "For both of us. You've made me so very happy, Mr. Block. I never thought I'd see our little Bonnie again. Thank you. You are such a *good* man." She let go of Bonnie's hand and rushed forward to take his.

Startled, he tried to pull it away, but she hung on and brought it to her mouth. She kissed it, just as he had kissed hers the other day.

He turned scarlet and blew biscuit crumbs out of his mouth.

"Ruth Ann," snapped Mrs. Parsons, "what impudence! What are you thinking?!"

What had she done wrong? She'd just wanted to show her gratitude. "I—"

"Leave. Out the back. Go on, and take your rag-mannered sister with you. I never!" Mrs. Parsons turned to Mr. Block. "You have my most sincere apologies, sir. These girls—they're not brought up correctly. More coffee?"

"No need, Mrs. Parklin. And it's very kind of you, but no thank you…"

"Bonnie," said Ruth Ann as they walked down the path behind the main building, skirting the lawn. "Bonnie, I can't believe you're here!"

Her sister just nodded. Not a hair escaped her tight braids, as they slid one inch down, then one inch back up with the motion of her head.

"Are you happy that Mr. Block found you? Brought you to us?"

The little girl looked down at her shoes. They were nice ones, with few scuffs and no holes. Her dress was pale blue and clean, as were her nails. Her small hands were free of blisters or scars. Whoever the Wallaces were, they seemed to have cared for her well. Maybe they'd even loved her; treated her as their own child.

Maybe Bonnie wasn't at all happy to have left them. Perhaps she was a blessing to Ruth Ann, but Ruth Ann and Sheila and the Colony were all a nightmare to her.

That was a horrid thought. A painful one.

"I'm over the moon to see you," Ruth Ann said, doing her best to disregard these doubts. "And Sheila—Momma—she will be, too. Do you remember Momma?"

Bonnie stopped in her tracks and cast a sidelong glance at Ruth Ann. She fiddled with Calico Bear and swallowed, hard.

"Do you remember, sweetie? I know you weren't even quite two…"

No reaction.

"She used to make oatmeal for us, with butter and milk and honey. At the old black potbellied stove. You ate it with your fingers, even though we tried to get you to use a spoon. And one time I gave it to you way too hot…you howled and threw it on our brother Wally's back. Momma got real mad at me, on account of your little tiny hand was all red and we had to scrape the gunk off Wally's shirt and rewash it."

No reaction.

Where was Wally? Did he still have that spark of mischief? Did he still look trapped in his pants by those sober suspenders? Ruth Ann hadn't allowed herself to miss him in a long time.

"Another time," she said to Bonnie, "you tried to feed Calico Bear your oatmeal. Didn't work so well…"

There! A curve of those Cupid's bow lips, a dimple appearing in Bonnie's cheek.

"You remember that?"

A nod. The braids raised and lowered an inch. The part in Bonnie's hair was so neat it might have been made with a ruler. It bisected her sweet head in two, as her life had been bisected. Before and after. But what now?

"Momma...she used to smell like apples. On the good days, anyways." Before Daddy had died and she started smelling of sweat and gin and other, unmentionable things. Of something crazed and desperate and the musk of strange men.

Bonnie nodded. She remembered! Ruth Ann's heart leaped and swung forward in her chest, like a man on a trapeze. Eager to please an audience.

Her words came faster, tumbling out. "We had the apple tree out front, and the two cows out back: Patches and Nellie. Wally had to milk 'em every morning before school. He was so gentle with them. They loved him."

She didn't bring up the last time she'd seen Wally, lying bloodied in the dirt beside the house. She didn't bring up some of the words he'd shouted at Momma...*Whore!*...or the words she'd screeched back...She didn't want to remember them, or the way the big, smelly, mustached man who'd been in Momma's bedroom spat on Wally after he'd come out the house and beat the tarnation out of him. She didn't care to think of Wally groaning in the dirt, cussin' at her to keep away from him and not let Bonnie near him like that.

Mostly, she didn't want to think about how they'd never seen him again. Had Mustache killed 'im? Had Wally killed Mustache and gone off to jail for it? Or had their brother just upped and left 'em all high and dry? Run off somewheres?

She didn't know. Neither did Sheila—leastways, she didn't even allow anybody to say his name aloud. Who knew what secrets Momma kept inside that hard, malicious head o' hers, under that stringy, gray-blond mop of hair.

Should she even take Bonnie near Sheila? Ruth Ann didn't want her baby sister traumatized even more than she clearly was. She wanted to know everything about her, but it sure was hard to figure how to start, what with the poor thing not speaking a word.

"Bonnie," she ventured. "Did you used to talk?"

Hesitation. Then a nod.

"How long's it been, then, since you did?"

A shrug.

"Did you talk at the Wallaces' house, sweetie?"

A shake of the braids.

"Were they mean to you?"

Another shake.

Ruth Ann reached out to touch one of the silky, pale braids. Bonnie shrank back.

"I won't hurt you, honey. Ever." She paused. "Did somebody else hurt you?"

Hesitation.

Oh, dear God. Had someone beaten Bonnie, or worse?

A slow shake of her sister's head had Ruth Ann almost sobbing in relief. "Okay. I'm very glad about that. Maybe one day you'll tell me why you stopped speaking. Maybe."

Hesitation, and then the briefest of nods.

If only Ruth Ann could just hug her, wrap her in warmth and safety and never let her go. If only Ruth Ann could make whatever had gone wrong all better. But this silence of Bonnie's was about more than a skinned knee.

They walked along in silence for a few moments more, and then Ruth Ann spied a familiar coppery head around the bend of the path.

"Clarence!" she called, running toward him with Bonnie in tow. "Clarence, look here! That nice Mr. Block found my sister! Can you believe it? He went and found her and brought her here to me!"

Clarence stilled, with his good hand gripping the handle of a rake. He shoved his stump into his pocket and waited for them, smiling down at Bonnie. The sun shone through the trees, lighting up his hair, a beacon of good nature. "Hi, sweetheart," he said. "And what might your name be?"

Bonnie eyed him curiously for a moment before she gave him an answering smile.

"Her name is Bonnie," Ruth Ann told him. "I ain't seen her since she's under two years old. I can't believe Mr. Block tracked her down! And here she is, after all this time. It's a miracle. Mr. Block is like an angel, I'm tellin' you."

Clarence lifted a skeptical eyebrow. "Sure. Maybe his halo's in the shop for repairs."

"Clarence!"

He shrugged, shut his mouth and made no further comment about the possible divinity of Esquire. "So, Bonnie, what do you think about all this? Is it pretty swell to see your big sister Ruth Ann again?"

The little girl clutched Calico Bear to her chest and nodded.

"Who's your friend, there?"

Bonnie held out her bear without hesitation.

Clarence had to lean the rake handle against his shoulder, but he accepted the toy for inspection. "He's right handsome, even though he's missin' an eye. Does he have a name?"

She compressed her perfect little doll's lips.

"Is it Pirate?"

Bonnie shook her head, the corner of her mouth tugging up.

"Is it Cyclops?"

The little girl's brow knit. Another head shake.

"Cyclops were mythical critters with one eye. A teacher told me about 'em. Okay, then, is his name Button, and is he smiling on account of he's dressed so funny? His bear suit is all kind of colors."

Ruth Ann laughed. "His name is Calico Bear."

"Right, why didn't I think of that? Calico Bear is a right perfect name for this little guy."

Bonnie nodded. Then, to Ruth Ann's discomfort, her little sister stepped forward and tugged Clarence's stump right out of his pocket. And he let her.

She inspected it carefully, running her fingers over the small, smooth end where his hand should have been. All the while, Clarence stood stock still, bemused.

At last, Bonnie nodded, smiled and took her bear back from him. She touched the paw of the bear to his stump, then guided it back to its pocket.

As Ruth Ann stood with her heart in her throat, Clarence somehow found his voice.

"Well, I'm right glad to meet Calico Bear, too. And you, Miss Bonnie. It's a pleasure."

Nineteen

The rows upon rows of wooden bunk beds loomed like a man-made forest in the dormitory. Ruth Ann felt like a wicked witch leading little Bonnie into the room, where her sister clearly saw monsters under and behind every structure and ghosts under every white sheet. This was evident in her reluctant gait, in the way she startled at every sound, tucked her chin and clutched Calico Bear, as if expecting a blow.

Ruth Ann herself was used to it, but she tried to see the place through Bonnie's eyes: vast, cold, institutional. No rugs, no pictures on the walls, only clothing and towels hanging from pegs. No books except a large Bible on its stand. A girl named Carlotta was taxed with reading it aloud to them by lantern light on Sunday evenings. Ruth Ann actually liked it, though she was often frustrated by the big, old-fashioned biblical words. But the sighs and snores of many girls punctuated each verse Carlotta read.

Ruth Ann's very first action, upon their arrival, was to set down Bonnie's crate at the foot of her bed, climb up to the bunk above hers and show her sister how to hide Calico Bear inside her pillowcase and under the pillow.

Mrs. Parsons was correct: Mother Jenkins would not take kindly to the "flea-ridden" teddy, even though it smelled to Ruth

Ann of lye soap and a little bleach. Perhaps Mrs. Wallace had washed and disinfected it for Bonnie.

"This is where we sleep," she told her. "I'll be in the bed right below this one, okay? So if you need anything, you know where to find me."

Bonnie clung to the railing of the bunk as if it were a ship and they were about to sail away from here. Ruth Ann wished they could. Her sister had the slight build of their mother, but the wide blue eyes of their father, along with his dimples. What if they could sail this bed right up to Heaven and find him? When folks went away up there, did they ever come back to check on their loved ones? Did they ever help out? Or did God keep 'em busy, doin' angel work for other people? Had Daddy sent Mr. Block to bring Bonnie?

Ruth Ann took comfort in that thought.

Then it was time to face reality—meaning Sheila, in the Distressed unit.

"Would you like to go see Momma?" she asked Bonnie, stroking the silk of her braids, grateful she was allowed to this time.

Her sister nodded.

"All right, we'll do that. I have to tell you, though, that Momma is..." Momma is what? Deranged? Full of poison? A chain-smoking hag full of hatred and spite?

How did she explain any of that to an eleven-year-old girl who'd just been ripped out of whatever home she'd previously known? How could she prepare Bonnie for the...Anti-Momma?

Bonnie gazed at her expectantly.

"Momma isn't well. Not healthy or strong. And sometimes she says stuff...yells stuff...that she don't mean. That's all. I just want you to know that before we go see her."

Bonnie brought the tip of one braid to her mouth, clamped it between her teeth and sucked on it.

Gently, Ruth Ann pulled the little girl's hand away and tugged the pigtail out of her mouth. "You don't have to be afraid." *Liar. Liar, liar, pants on fire. Liar, liar, on a tightwire.*

She'd call for Ruby, make sure she was in the room when Bonnie met Sheila. If their mother turned into a she-devil, Ruby would sedate her. And Ruth Ann would just step into Sheila's shoes. *She'd* be the momma.

It brought her a sense of peace, that idea. If she couldn't be a real ma to Annabel, at least she had another chance, now, to be one to Bonnie. She would belong to someone, and someone would belong to her.

But first they needed to get this meeting over with—as unpleasant as it might be.

Ruth Ann led Bonnie outside, then around the box hedge in the shape of a cross and down the pathway that led to the Distressed unit. The building's faded pink bricks seemed exhausted from holding each other up, and its four self-conscious columns, there to evoke grace and justice, looked ironic, not Ionic.

The great black door swallowed them like a mouth, and they followed a tongue of carpet into the hallway. No attendant appeared to guide or harass them; Ruth Ann caught a glimpse of three figures outside on a small terrace, smoking.

So they climbed the stairs and Ruth Ann, her pulse loud in her own ears, led Bonnie to room 213—lair of the gorgon, den of the demented.

Ruby heard their footsteps and came out of an adjoining room. She waved to Ruth Ann, then came over.

"Ruby, this is my little sister, Bonnie! Come back to us after all these years."

"Well, hello there." Ruby beamed at her.

Bonnie looked up at her with wide, frightened eyes. She took a step backward, toward Ruth Ann.

"What's a matter, child? Ain't you never seen a colored woman before?" Ruby laughed, only a little bitterly. "We don' bite. I promise you. We's good people."

"Ruby's the very best," Ruth Ann agreed. But the atmosphere remained a little awkward.

"Well, you go on in, then, and see your momma. She's heard through the grapevine that little Bonnie's here, an' she's been waitin' for the both of you." Ruby turned on her heel and walked away, disappearing back into the room she'd come out of.

It was a pleasant surprise to find that Sheila was bathed and in a fresh nightgown and robe. Her hair and nails were clean. She looked bright-eyed, almost normal. She looked up when the two girls entered the room, and her jaw slackened, her thin lips parting in something like wonder as she gazed at Bonnie's face.

"Come here, child," she said, in tones full of butter and jam. She stretched out her hands. "Let me look at you, my dear. Oh! My baby Bonnie, my sweet girl, you're... you're so *beautiful*!"

Ruth Ann gaped.

Sheila utterly ignored her.

As Bonnie advanced toward the serpent-woman, Ruth Ann wanted to call her back. Jerk her away, tell her that this creature was not their mother. That she was a demon who'd shucked her scales and retracted her fangs and claws, wrapped herself in the skin of some other poor woman. She was poised to bite off Bonnie's head and suck out her guts.

"Do you remember your momma, doll baby?" Sheila asked in honeyed tones. "You remember me, don't you?" And she began to *sing*, of all things.

> Hush little baby, don't you cry;
> Mama's gonna sing you a lullaby
> And if that song, it don't get heard,
> Papa's gonna get you a mockin'bird...

Sheila had always taken liberties with the verses; made up her own to suit herself.

An ache began just below Ruth Ann's diaphragm, slowly filling her with longing.

> And if that silly bird fly away,
> Mama's gonna call it a brand-new day.
> Down to the market you'll go in a pram,
> And Mama's gonna get you a can o' Spam...

Under Ruth Ann's fascinated, horrified, stunned gaze, Bonnie laughed.

And then Sheila did, too.

And Bonnie ran to her, pigtails flying.

Ran right into the mother-monster's arms, as if she belonged there. As if she'd been waiting years for this very moment. As if she *loved* her.

Sheila wrapped her evil, skinny arms around Bonnie and squeezed her tightly. "Oh, my darlin'. Oh, how I have *dreamed* of this moment! I was so afraid I'd never see you again." Her voice shook.

Then Ruth Ann herself began to tremble. It started in that same place the ache had, at her diaphragm, and then eddied out along her spine. It dropped down to her knees, then shot up to her lungs, where it emerged in shallow, short breaths and then gasps. What was wrong with her?

She stood rooted to the floor, wavering like a dandelion in a strong wind.

Why was she a weed, while Bonnie was a flower?

Why had Sheila never once, in her recent memory, hugged her—Ruth Ann—the way she was hugging her sister? As if she were precious, as if she couldn't get enough of her. As if she were the only person who mattered to Sheila in the whole, wide world.

The ache in Ruth Ann bled into a bitter rending and twisting of every organ in her body. She couldn't breathe, couldn't move her feet, couldn't think.

She simply hurt.

She felt one with pain. One with loneliness. One with rejection.

She stood there, dry-eyed and speechless and numb, until Ruby's warm, heavy hand slid around her waist, turned her and walked her out into the hallway.

It was Ruby who hugged her to her massive bosom and rubbed her back and made soothing noises. She hummed gently. "Everything's gonna be all right, child."

Ruth Ann stood in her embrace like a petrified tree.

"Breathe now, honey. Deep breath in, deep breath out."

She shook her head. It hurt to breathe. It hurt to see. It hurt to think.

"C'mon, now, Ruthie. Breathe for me. I'm-a tellin' you, there is stuff in this world that don't make no sense and never will. Stuff there is no explainin'. But you a good girl, Ruthie. You the best kinda girl. An' if that ol'—" Ruby took in some air. "If that *mmmmm-hmmmm* in there cain't see it, that is *her* problem. It ain't yours. You hear me? She crazy. She not all bad, but she plumb crazy. You knows it and I knows it and so does everybody 'cept her and maybe Li'l Pigtails, there. But she'll find out on her own."

Ruth Ann stood silent, still trembling, as Ruby rubbed her arms, up and down, with her big, strong, kind hands.

From Sheila's room came the sound of more lullabies and more of Bonnie's sweet laughter. Then her first word, a glad one, in answer to whether she was happy to see her momma again.

"Yes!"

A fresh wave of pain had Ruth Ann doubling over, almost knocked her off her feet. And with it came utter self-loathing. How could she be bitter and jealous over such a lovely, joyful reunion? What kind of person was she? Certainly not a nice one, curdling and souring with envy of her little sister.

Ruby took her arm. "Come on, Ruthie. You and me, we gonna go get a nice cuppa tea. And a biscuit or two. Will you keep an old woman company?"

The tea and sympathy did little to banish the ache inside Ruth Ann. The biscuits stuck in her craw; the tea was as bitter as her emotions toward her mother.

"Why?" she asked Ruby. "Why doesn't she love me, too?"

Her friend reached across the scarred wooden kitchen table and took her hand. She squeezed it. "Mayhap she does, in her own way."

Ruth Ann shook her head. "She used to. I remember her loving me. But she doesn't now. Why?"

Ruby rubbed her thumb over the back of Ruth Ann's hand. "I don' have the answer to that question. Maybe you should ask her sometime."

"How do I ask her that?"

Ruby pursed her lips and shook her head.

"Do I walk in with some tea and toast one morning and drop the question like...some kind of bomb? Or do I sit there with her until she starts railin' at me on account of somethin' and then ask her why she hates me so much? Do I write her a letter that she hardly cain't read, anyways?"

"More tea?" Ruby asked, getting up.

"No." Ruth Ann felt like hurling the cupful she already had against the wall. "Thank you," she added sullenly.

"I love you, Ruth Ann," said Ruby, out of the blue.

The statement was so unexpected that it hit her like a brick on the head. She sat there blinking, like a frog on a very unstable lily pad.

Ruby put her hands on her hips and stared at her, eyebrows raised, a smile playing around her mouth.

Ruth Ann found her voice. "I—I love you, too, Ruby. I really do. You're always so good to everybody, even if you don't suffer fools gladly."

Ruby chuckled. "Well, you ain't no fool. So you listen to me. I love you, and little Bonnie will, too. She'll come to remember you better. But the most important thing is this: God loves you. So you put that in your pipe an' smoke it."

Ruth Ann hid a smile at those words. "I don't have a pipe, Ruby."

Ruby flapped her apron. "Lord save us, you know 'zackly what I mean, Ruthie! Now git on out here," she said, her tone more affectionate than the words, "and go get your sister, afore Mrs. Jekyll turns into Mrs. Hyde and scares the bejeezus out that little cutie."

"Yes, ma'am."

"I got to get back to work. It don't never stop, 'round here."

No, poor Ruby's work was never, ever done. That was for sure.

Ruth Ann put her cup, saucer and plate into the big iron sink and headed for the stairs, her friend's words echoing through her mind. *Why don't you ask her sometime?*

She reached the landing, and then took the right turn for the second set of stairs. Up she trudged. Could her deepest personal mystery really be solved by doing something so simple? Just asking a question?

She made her way to room 213, forcing one foot in front of the other, her chin up and her shoulders back like a soldier. If only she had armor to protect her from her mother.

No sound came from the room. No lullabies and no tinkle of Bonnie's laughter. It made her nervous as a cat in a rocking chair—she didn't know why. It wasn't as if Sheila would physically harm her own child, and especially after such an outpouring of affection—would she? Ruth Ann quickened her steps and all but burst around the doorway.

Sheila sat there alone in her worn, pale green armchair. Her bony feet, clad in terrycloth slippers, rested on the matching ottoman. She turned her head and skewered Ruth Ann with a glance.

Why did it even hurt anymore? Silly. "Where's Bonnie?"

"Takin' a tinkle. Why?"

"Just…asking."

"We're fine. You can buzz off."

Anger sizzled through Ruth Ann like a spark of Mr. Franklin's famous electricity. And before she even knew it, she asked the question. "Why do you hate me so much, Momma? I'm your daughter, too!"

Sheila's eyes narrowed on her. "Why do you even need to ask me this?"

"*Why?* What did I ever do to deserve it?" she blurted. "What's wrong with me? Why don't you love me like you love Bonnie? Why are you so mean to me all the time?"

Sheila went purple in the face, a vein bulging at her temple and her nostrils flaring. "You know good and damn well why I cain't stand the sight of you!"

Ruth Ann stared at her. "I don't! I don't! *I don't!*"

"You little wart. You little weasel. You—"

"Tell me why the hell you hate me so much!"

"You ran and got people. *YOU.* You brought people to our house. *You're* the whole sorry reason I *lost my kids* and I'm locked up here like a goddamned monkey in a cage!"

Twenty

W h-what?" Ruth Ann managed.

"So don't you play dumb with me, you little bitch," Sheila spat.

As Ruth Ann stared at her, uncomprehending, that day came back to her.

The day she'd scampered inside to ask Momma something, and the door to her bedroom was closed. Ruthie had opened it, without thinking, without knocking, to find a big naked man on top of Momma, choking her and making noises. Momma was moaning, saying *please* ... begging for her life.

Ruth Ann had stood, rooted to the spot, for too long. Paralyzed by the sight of the biggest, ugliest white butt she'd ever seen and just below the dark, evil crack of it, the Thing—like a plucked chicken neck—ramming into her mother. Horrible, the scene. Something out of a nightmare. Something cooked up by the Devil straight out of Hell.

Ruth Ann instinctively covered her eyes. Then she'd spun and run...to find help. Wally was nowhere to be found, long since gone; Bonnie was standing in her crib on the front porch, clinging to the bars and howling.

Ruth Ann had run all the way down the packed-dirt drive to the road and, still screaming, flagged down a neighbor taking his turnips to market. *Mr. Petrie! Mr. Petrie! Come quick! A man is killing Momma! Oh, please, come quick. He's killing her.*

Mr. Petrie done turned his horse and cart right into the drive, grabbed his shotgun from behind the seat and gone scramblin' into the house, hollerin' and wavin' the gun, while Ruth Ann grabbed little Bonnie off the porch and hid, hyperventilating, behind old Petrie's cart.

Prolonged cussing and growling came from the house. But no shots.

Please get the bad man. Please don't let Momma die...

Ruth Ann got tiny Bonnie quieted down and tried not to think about what was going on inside the house. She waited, heart in her throat, for what seemed like ages.

She stared at the turnips; at their pale, exposed bodies, their gangly, hairy little root-beards and their bright green shoots. The ones that gave 'em away and got 'em yanked, naked, out from the ground.

The turnips stared back at her, smudged and white. Embarrassed, judging by their purple-stained cheeks. They lay all topsy-turvy, sprawled and helpless to avoid bein' dragged off to be boiled and sliced and chewed on by people.

Ruth Ann heard the springs of the back door creak, and then it snapped shut. Heavy boot steps stomped across the porch. Something or someone rustled through the fields behind the small barn out back.

And then Old Petrie threw open the front door and slammed it closed behind him. His gun pointed down at the ground and his face was as red-purple as pickled beets. The hand not holding the gun was opening and closing again into a fist.

Ruth Ann sprinted toward Petrie. "Momma? Is my momma aw right?"

He nodded, dragging a big rough paw down his face. "Your momma is just fine."

"But—"

"She's fine, Ruth Ann."

Ruth Ann stared at him, uncomprehending. "But where is the bad man? Did you chase him out the back door? Can we still git him? Where's my momma?"

Old Petrie's eyes got all hard and squinty; his mouth screwed up like a wad of chewing gum. He looked like he'd just got a whiff of dead carcass. "Your ma's inside, gettin' dr—uh, gettin' herself together. What—how much did you see, Ruth Ann?"

What she'd seen was horrible, disgusting, awful beyond awful. She didn't even want to *think* about it, ever again. But she knew she needed to tell the truth and nothin' but the truth. She swallowed the icky, sick feeling creeping up her throat. "I saw that man's big, white, pimply, hairy butt. And, and, and I saw a ugly *chicken neck thing*—"

Mr. Petrie stuck his palm out. "That's enough."

"He was on top of my ma, and he was doin' somethin' real *bad* to her!"

"Yes, indeed he was," said Mr. Petrie, who'd gotten—not that it seemed possible—even more beety in the face. "Little darlin', let's you and me and tiny Bonnie there take a ride with my turnips."

Ride? Why? "But my momma—the man—what if he comes back?"

"He ain't comin' back."

"How do you know he won't?"

"I just know. I tole him if he did, he was gonna get his dirty, horny head blowed off. I ain't puttin' up with this filth around here."

"He had horns? I didn't see no horns. Is he the Devil?"

Mr. Petrie dragged his hand down his face again. He seemed

to need a moment to get his thoughts together. "Let's get you and little Bonnie up onto the seat, here. C'mon. I'll give you a boost."

"Where are we goin'?"

"We're going into town to meet the constable."

Constable. Sounded like a cross between constipated and able. Ready, willin', an' able to swallow castor oil? "Who's that?"

"He's a very nice gentleman who has your best interests at heart, darlin'. You don't need to be afraid of him. You just tell him what you tol' me. Well, 'cept no need to mention that, uh, chicken neck thing. That ain't really talk for decent folk."

She was indecent? "Sorry, Mr. Petrie."

His lips quivered. "That's aw right."

Bonnie began to fuss again in Ruth Ann's arms. She rocked her, trying to soothe her. And the familiar lullaby came right out of her mouth.

> Hush little baby, don't you cry
> Ruthie's gonna sing you a lullaby
> An' if that song, it don't get heard,
> Ruthie's gonna buy you a mockin'bird...

Beside her, Mr. Petrie blew out a breath, just like the one his horse did as he shook the reins and got the cranky animal to rumble the cart forward again.

> And if that mockin'bird don't sing,
> You don't worry about no-thing...

Ruth Ann broke off when she glimpsed Mr. Petrie's grim expression. "Did I do somethin' wrong? Are you mad, Mr. Petrie? You mad at me?"

"Lord, no, Ruth Ann. You done everything right. You done saved your momma. You gonna talk to the constable, and I am gonna talk to the priest. And we are gonna keep on savin' Sheila Riley, just in case she needs a little extra help, okeydokey? You done the right thing. It's all gonna be just fine, sweetpea."

She'd thought Mr. Petrie was such a nice old man.

But he was a big ol' lyin' sack of root-beard turnips, that's what Mr. Petrie was.

The constable was indeed a right fine gentleman. He got his wife to look after Bonnie and give her a bath and some porridge while he took Ruth Ann into his study to have a chat with her. That's what he called it: a chat.

They had a chat with his cat and his hat.

The fancy hat that said he was Somebody Important sat high on a hook near the door, and his long black coat hung under it.

The cat was curled up on the hearth, warming its backside near the fire. Ruth Ann didn't know anybody who kept a cat inside the house. Cats were supposed to live outside or in barns, catching mice. "What's his name?" she asked the constable, who didn't look at all constipated. He did look able, though. Tall and lean and bespectacled, dressed in a snowy-white, starched shirt. It matched his snowy white hair.

He chuckled. "His name is Justice."

He had to be kidding around. The cats she knew were called Snowball, or Tiger, or Hoss. *Justice?*

The black-and-white cat squinted lazily at Ruth Ann through demonic yellow eyes and then yawned, exposing the inside of an unexpectedly cavernous cat-snout, carpeted in pink and rimmed with dozens of sharp, white, nasty teeth. The animal seemed bored, unimpressed by her presence.

She usually liked animals. Ruth Ann didn't like Justice one bit. She also didn't care for the way he licked every inch of his body while she told her story yet again to the constable—omitting the big hairy butt and so on, of course. She wanted to be decent, after all.

He asked a few questions that didn't seem to have anything to do with anything, but then adults were nosy and oftentimes not as smart as they thought they were. Every kid knew that. It was why they had to be treated with extra respect and called "Mister" and "Missus" and "Miss." And "sir" and "ma'am." So's they wouldn't get upset and catch on that the kids were aware of their tricks and their pretenses of knowin' it all.

So when the constable asked her if she had a lot of uncles, she said no, sir. And when he asked her if Momma took in as much washing and mending as she done used to, she said no, sir. And when he asked her did Momma make stuff in the bathtub that smelled like turpentine, she said beg pardon, sir, but it smelled more like paint thinner.

When the constable asked her if her and Bonnie and Momma had enough food to eat, she said mostly, sir. But when they didn't, one of Momma's friends would come over for a spell.

The constable got a mighty peculiar look on his face when she said that. He asked were they gentlemen friends?

Ruth Ann told him exactly what she thought: no, sir. They hardly seemed like gentlemen. They didn't have nice, snowy-white shirts like his own or wear polished shoes. They didn't seem like they bathed much. They were rough.

And did they have supper with the family? Or were they there for private business?

No, sir—she was right glad they never stayed for supper. Momma told her to go take Bonnie somewhere's else while they had adult conversation. And she wasn't to interrupt. Or come back to the house until Momma called.

The constable looked down and made some notes with his fancy pen. Then he asked where she, Bonnie and Momma bathed if there was smelly paint-thinner stuff in the bathtub? So she came right out with the truth: they used the water pump outside, and yes, sir, it was freezing cold in the winter.

The last strange questions the constable asked her were about Momma's housekeeping and were there any vermin? And also about whether Momma drank the stinky stuff in the bathtub—yes, sir, sometimes she did. And whether she talked or walked funny after she drank it?

Well, sir. Ruth Ann didn't like talkin' trash about Momma.

The constable said it was just fine, that he was gonna help her. Help her and little Bonnie, too. So Ruth Ann 'fessed up that yes, after drinkin' that stuff, Momma did talk like a *reaaaally* slowed-down gramophone recording. And she swayed back and forth and had to hang on to the furniture to get herself off to bed.

The constable thanked her very much and told Ruth Ann that she was a good girl.

She smiled at him, and he gave her a sweet that she divided in half and let Bonnie suck on part of, long as she held it tight between her thumb and forefinger, so the little girl wouldn't get it stuck in her throat and choke.

After that, she sat by herself in the constable's study, watching Justice lick its paws, then its belly all over, and then some right nasty parts.

She looked at all the leather-bound books with gold writing on their spines. She wondered what they were about. She wondered just how many pages were in each one; how many words were on each page; how many letters made up every word. So many gazillions of little tiny black marks, each with its own sound and meaning.

Justice sneezed twice. Then it crouched down and began to cough and hack.

"Are you aw right?" she asked the cat.

It lashed its tail.

"Fine. I won't ask again."

Justice gasped and hacked some more. And then it hurled a big, nasty hairball right out onto the constable's hearth. It shook its head, licked its chops, then turned around and stalked off, leaving the mess there for someone else to clean up.

That was all Ruth Ann remembered about Justice.

Twenty-One

Ruth Ann returned to the present, to reality and to her mother's loathing of her.

Even as she stood there, seared by Sheila's vicious gaze, she retreated emotionally to a safe distance. As an observer on this different and unreachable planet, Ruth Ann felt pity for her. She examined each harsh, unforgiving, bitter line in her mother's waxy forehead, her drawn, bunched, spittle-flecked lips, the brackets that grief, hardship and betrayal had carved around them.

Here, then, was the answer, the key to her misery. She'd pried open the door and shrunk back as the reason for her mother's malevolence bludgeoned its way out.

But the long-buried anxiety and devastation within Ruth Ann escaped with it, and at least the confusion bled away. The wound remained, but at least there was at last a reason for it.

"I was a *child*," she said quietly. "Younger than Bonnie. I thought that man was killing you. I ran to get help."

"You set my life on fire," Sheila hissed. "Then you helped your ownself. Never a thought for me or for your sister—"

"That's not true! I didn't understand what would happen—that they'd take you away, that they'd split us all up! I didn't know how you were making money. I didn't know exactly what that stuff was in the tub. I ain't never heard tell, back then, of Prohibition or prostitution!"

"What's Prohibition?" Bonnie's voice came from the hallway. "Why are you fighting?"

Sheila's face underwent a transformation before Ruth Ann's very eyes. The wrinkles smoothed out, her lips plumped, and her eyes shone with love. It was unnerving…and it was strangely reassuring. There was goodness and light in her mother.

"We're not fighting, angel." The acid faded from Sheila's tone. "So you found the potty?"

Bonnie nodded. "Yes, ma'am. Just down the hall, like you said."

"Good girl. You come in here again and give Momma a kiss." She pointed to her cheek.

Bonnie did as she was told, then settled comfortably into the armchair next to Sheila and laid her head on her mother's shoulder.

Ruth Ann stared at this scene of domestic bliss and swallowed the lump that began to build in her throat. She fought the urge to crawl into the chair, too—or even to sit at the foot of it, just to be part of it in some small way. But it was clear that wasn't ever going to happen. Sheila would never allow it.

She took herself out of the equation and dug deep for the love she felt for Bonnie, for the gratitude that, thanks to Mr. Block, she'd found her sister and mother at long last.

And that Sheila had found Bonnie. Their mother was softening around the edges; the contours of her bitterness blurring into light as well as shadow. Ruth Ann could see vestiges of her prettiness coming alive as the long-buried love within her was rekindled.

It was a downright miracle.

The grandfather clock downstairs in the hall chimed four times, startling Ruth Ann. "We have to go," she said. "I have to take Bonnie to meet Dr. Price. And then Mother Jenkins." She barely restrained a shudder. Perish the thought.

Sheila's face fell, and she cast Ruth Ann a look of annoyance.

"I'm sorry, Momma. But it won't do to keep Doc Price waiting."

The lines around her mother's mouth returned, along with the wrinkles in her forehead. "No. We can't waste the fine doctor's time. He's got patients to mutilate, don't he?"

A rare moment of synchronized panic hit both Sheila and Ruth Ann. She could see the flash of it in her mother's eyes, where it froze.

"Bonnie, my little doll, will you run and tell Ruby it was real nice to meet her?" Sheila said, giving her another kiss.

Bonnie nodded and obediently scrambled down from the armchair. "Where is she?"

"She'll be here, in one of the rooms. Maybe snipping old Mr. Daughtry's whiskers in 219."

"Okay."

Once Bonnie was gone, Sheila clutched the armrests of her chair until her fingers went white. "Promise me, Ruth Ann. You promise me that you won't ever let Bonnie see that butcher alone. You know what I'm talkin' about. You seen my scar."

"Yeah. I seen it. And I won't. Doc Price lays a finger on one hair o' her head, I will make him sorry he ever been born."

Sheila relaxed her death grip on the chair arms and sat back, shrewdly evaluating Ruth Ann. "I believe you mean that."

"Never meant nothing more in my life."

"He gotten to you, yet? The doc?"

Ruth Ann shook her head. "No, but he wants to. I told you. That's why I have me that lawyer, remember? Mr. Block. The one got the hole in 'is suit, now, thanks to you. He's the one who went off an' found us Bonnie, even though you were right 'rageous awful to 'im."

"The Block-head found our Bonnie?" Sheila frowned. "There's somethin' not right about all this. And agin, how is you payin' this fancy lawyer man? You goin' off behind the barn with 'im? You gotta be."

"Momma! I told you, I'm not like that."

"Miss High and Mighty, ain't you? Lemme tell you somethin': any and every woman alive is 'like that,' if it comes down to feeding her kids or not. Yes, even *you*. A good God-fearin' *preacher's wife* is *like that*, if her husband is dead and her children is hungry and cryin' and don't got no place to go. If she got to blow the man what works at the bank—"

"Momma! Stop it."

"—so's she don't lose the house, she gonna blow 'im! If she got to screw the dry-goods clerk for a pair of shoes for her boy, 'cause he cain't go barefoot through snow three miles to school, then by gum, she gonna hike her skirts and bend it over right next the dang cash register!"

Ruth Ann was horrified. "Momma—"

"So don't you give me none of your guff, your *I'm not like that*. You think you're better than me? Huh? Well, you ain't! What kind of brat calls the constable on her own ma, the woman tryin' to keep food in her belly and clothes on her back and a roof over her dang head?!"

"I didn't call the constable on you. All's I did was take a ride from Mr. Petrie into town. I didn't know what a constable was, nor any better than to talk to him!"

"What's a constable?" asked Bonnie, popping back into the room. "Why are you yelling at each other?"

"We wasn't yelling, sweet girl," Sheila told her. "We was just raising our voices."

"Oh." Bonnie frowned.

"And I don't think I'm better than anybody," Ruth Ann told her.

"Okay." Her little sister looked uncertainly from one of them to the other.

"Are you ready to go meet Dr. Price?"

Sheila met Ruth Ann's eyes fiercely. Ruth Ann gave a single nod. On this, they were in 100 percent agreement. Another miracle.

"I'm not sick," Bonnie said. "But I guess so."

"Not at all, sweetheart." Ruth Ann took her hand. "Doc Price is a nice man who wants to do a simple 'wellness' exam on you. Just take some notes on your age, height, weight and so on. Is that all right with you?"

Bonnie shrugged. "I'd rather stay here with Momma."

That makes one of us.

"I'd rather you stay with me, too, darlin'," Sheila said. "But we got to follow the rules 'round here."

"Who makes them?"

"People like Doc Price and Mother Jenkins. So come along, now, Bonnie. You can come back to see Momma tomorrow."

"Please do, baby girl." Sheila hugged her tightly yet again and pressed a kiss to Bonnie's forehead. "I love you."

The shock of those words, again. Ruth Ann felt kicked in the gut. Sheila had never said them to her, not ever. Though mayhap she'd said them when she was a baby.

"I love you, too." Bonnie wriggled out of her embrace and skipped to the door where Ruth Ann waited. She took her hand again, looking up in puzzlement at her expression. "Don't you love Momma, too? Doesn't she love you?"

A pregnant pause ensued. "Of course," Ruth Ann and Sheila said in unison. "Of course."

Mother Jenkins hated Bonnie's blond braids upon sight. Hands on her hips, she looked her up and then down again. "Turn around," she ordered, and glared as a confused Bonnie did so. "You think you're right precious, don't you? A little Swiss Miss. With your big blue eyes and all that hair."

Ruth Ann stood appalled. How could Mother J be envious of an eleven-year-old?

You are. Why not her? The thought was unwelcome and vile. She didn't want to be anything like Mother Jenkins, not ever.

Frightened of the old bat, Bonnie said nothing; just gripped Ruth Ann's hand more tightly. Ruth Ann gave hers a squeeze.

"It's got to go," Mother Jenkins declared. "That much hair will attract lice from miles around. Carlotta! Get the scissors at once."

Bonnie shrank into Ruth Ann's skirts. "But…I don't want them cut off."

"Did I give you permission to speak? Do you think I care about your opinion, you little slut? What hovel or tavern did Block scrape you out of? What cathouse? Bet they sell you as a virgin every night," she spat.

Bonnie shot her a bewildered look as Ruth Ann clapped her hands over her sister's ears. "Mother Jenkins!"

The woman had the grace to flush.

"Mother J, please. She's only eleven years old and innocent as an Easter chick."

"Spare me," muttered the old bat. But she was abashed enough to look away and get busy with folding some kitchen towels.

"Please, ma'am, don't cut off all her hair. I'll make sure it's clean and we'll keep it up off her neck and plaited tight. I promise."

Carlotta returned with the scissors, handed them to Mother J and cast a pitying glance at them as she left. Bonnie hid behind Ruth Ann.

That irritated the witch. "Come out from behind your worthless sister," Mother Jenkins demanded.

Bonnie peeked under Ruth Ann's arm.

"Out, I said!"

Trembling, she skittered in front of her sister, but pressed back against her. Ruth Ann set her hands protectively on Bonnie's shoulders.

"M-m-my momma likes my braids," the little girl said. "She'll be mad if you cut them off."

Mother Jenkins stared incredulously at her and then laughed. It wasn't a nice sound. "I should worry about the likes of Sheila Riley?"

Ruth Ann took a deep breath. "I would worry, if I was you, Mother J. You know how Momma gets, and Bonnie's her baby. She's likely to—"

"Did I give you permission to speak?"

"No, but—"

"Then shut your silly piehole!"

"Mother Jenkins, all's I'm sayin' is Sheila's mean as a snake, tricky as a fox and vicious as a rabid coyote. You really wanna tangle with that?"

Ruth Ann got backhanded for this bit of unsolicited advice.

Bonnie squeaked, turned right around and ran—her offending braids flying out behind her like twin battle flags.

"How dare you?" thundered Mother J. "And get back here, you little brat!"

Ruth Ann pressed a hand to her cheek and willed Bonnie to keep running, though the consequences later didn't bear thinking of.

"Momma!" Bonnie shouted as she ran. "Momma!"

Ruth Ann sighed. Now Mother J would know exactly where to track her down.

Sure enough, the old battle-ax surged through the kitchen door in hot pursuit, huffing and puffing.

Ruth Ann followed, dreading the scene about to unfold.

Clarence appeared from around back, to see what the ruckus was about.

Ruth Ann grabbed his good arm. "Clarence! Quick, run get Doc Price. This ain't gonna go nowhere good…no tellin' what my momma will do if Mother J drags Bonnie outta there to cut off her hair."

"Huh?"

"Just run! Get Doc!"

Clarence hoofed it down the hill toward Doc Price's office.

Ruth Ann took off after Mother J again. She could see Bonnie in the distance, braids still streaming behind her, her little white-stockinged legs pumping madly as she ran toward the Distressed unit.

Mother Jenkins looked like a cross between a charging rhino and an armored tank.

Ruth Ann didn't care what she had to do, as long as she got between Bonnie and the ferocious house mother. House mother—she was more like a house crocodile.

And how would Sheila react to this little party? To this threat to her newfound baby?

Ruth Ann hoped Clarence would run real fast. They were all about to find out.

Bonnie beat Mother Jenkins and Ruth Ann by at least a quarter mile. She pounded on the door until a mystified attendant in white opened it and let her in. From there she ran up the stairs and to room 213.

By the time Ruth Ann galumphed up the last stair, right behind the monstrous gray-clad behind of Mother Jenkins, Sheila was stalking down the hallway in her bathrobe and slippers, arms akimbo. Aside from those few details, she was in a Mood. Lethal.

Her venom, in the form of the most colorful and obscene language Ruth Ann had ever hoped to hear, spewed before her. It was a marvel.

Sheila insulted Mother Jenkins's parentage, her status as a human being, her face, her body, her IQ and her right to life. And that was just for starters.

Mother J was a bastard whelped by a diseased bitch in heat. She had a face that belonged in her drawers, a body bigger than a continent, the intelligence of a maggot—and Sheila was gonna rip her limb from limb.

Now that she wasn't the target, Ruth Ann stood back to admire it all. Sheila was a downright poet of gutter-filth.

Mother Jenkins stood there, mouth agape, trying to process the words Sheila hurled at her. She'd never heard anything like them before—that was clear. And she got redder and redder and huffier and puffier. She looked ready to explode.

But it got even better.

Wiry Sheila stalked forward until she was eyeball to massive bosom with Mother J. And she poked a bony finger right into her chest, spittle flying all over. "You touch one hair of my Bonnie's head, you piece of shite, and I will make you sorry your momma ever got reamed by a chimney sweep an' his broom! I will creep into your bedroom while you sleep and I will violate you seventeen different ways. Then I will slit your throat. Do you hear me?"

Mother Jenkins goggled at her, clearly in shock at both her murderous tone and intent.

"I said, DO YOU HEAR ME?!"

She'd heard her. Because Mother Jenkins's reaction was to thrust out her meaty, sausagelike fingers and throttle Momma.

Bad idea.

Ruth Ann didn't like to think about it, but over the years, Sheila must have had to defend herself against various horrid men who wished to do things to her that she didn't agree with. So Mother Jenkins? She was no match for Crazy Sheila.

Her mother half hissed, half laughed. And then she did the thing Mother J least expected. She didn't lurch backward. She didn't try to pry the hands off her throat. Instead, she sprang upward and *headbutted* Mother Jenkins, smashing her nose.

And when Mother J released her, rearing back and shrieking, Sheila hauled off and punched her, once in each monstrous breast. A right hook, *bam!* And a left one, *bam!*

Mother J sagged back against the wall, clutching her nose and whimpering, arms braced protectively across her boobs.

"*Holy smokes!*" said Clarence from behind Ruth Ann. He bent to brace himself on his knees, panting from the run to get there.

"Wanna go agin?" Sheila taunted. "C'mon, Gertie Jenkins! Pull up your saggy bloomers and come git some more o' this. You sad sack of mule shite!"

"Oh, my stars," Ruby murmured. She emerged unhurriedly from room 217.

If Ruth Ann didn't know better, she'd think Ruby'd been stallin' afore she stepped in. Everybody hated Mother Jenkins. Even the kindest, most Christian souls at the Colony. Maybe Ruby had discovered another meaning to "turn the other cheek." Maybe sometimes turning your cheek meant your eye got turned away with it and didn't see the necessity of steppin' in to interfere right away?

Sheila hollered at Mother J, "You ever frighten my little Bonnie agin—"

"WHAT IS GOING ON HERE?" thundered the voice of

none other than Doc Price. He appeared directly behind Clarence. "I WILL NOT HAVE THIS IN MY ESTABLISHMENT!"

"That…that termagant!" Shouted Mother Jenkins, pointing a now bloody sausage finger at Sheila. "She assaulted me! She must be tied up, locked up! Never to be allowed out of a cage again!"

Ruby looked at Sheila.

Sheila looked at Ruth Ann.

Ruth Ann looked at Clarence.

Clarence looked at Doc Price.

"That's surely not what I saw," Clarence said to the doctor.

"Nor I!" Ruth Ann jumped in.

"Me, neither," Ruby put in.

"She choked my momma!" cried Bonnie, who finally crept out of Sheila's room. Bonnie pointed at Mother Jenkins. "She put her hands 'round Momma's neck and started squeezing. She lifted her clean off the floor!"

"Why, you little liar!" bellowed Mother Jenkins.

"I saw it myself," Ruth Ann said.

"Plain as daylight," Ruby said.

"Me, too." Clarence backed them all up.

Mother Jenkins used the wall to help her stand up again. "This is all egregious nonsense! *Look at my face*, Dr. Price! Sheila Riley attacked me! After spewing the most vile language—"

"Silence, Mrs. Jenkins! Be quiet at once." Doc Price turned to Clarence. "These women are all hysterical and bound to be unreliable. Now, you tell me what you saw, young Clarence."

"Yes, sir. I come runnin' up the stairs, there, an' I round the corner and I see Mother J with her hands wrapped 'round poor Sheila's skinny little neck."

Doc Price narrowed his eyes upon Mother Jenkins, who began to protest. "Quiet. Let the boy speak."

"Mother J's three times as big as Miz Riley, but somehow's Miz Riley sorta bounces off 'er toes and bonks her head into Mother J's nose—just so's she can get a breath, sir, on account of she's bein' choked, you understand."

"Yes, indeed. A perfectly natural response."

"An' then I seen Mother Jenkins let go o' Miz Riley."

"But," hollered Mother J, "she punched me in the—"

"Silence, woman!" Doc Price bellowed.

Clarence nodded. "I ain't gonna lie. Miz Riley did hit her, sir, but it seems to me that she was still very frightened, fighting for her life. Seems a clear case of self-defense."

"Thank you, Clarence. What I don't understand, Mrs. Jenkins, is what you are doing away from the kitchens and laundry. You do not belong here. What is your explanation?"

"She chased me, sir." Bonnie fixed her big, blue, innocent eyes upon Doc. "She said horrid things to me and my sister and she wanted to cut off my braids. She walloped Ruth Ann in the face and she got scissors, and I ran. I ran here to Momma, on account of I was real scared."

Doc Price turned to Ruth Ann. "She hit you?"

Wordlessly, she pointed to her cheek, which still stung.

"And she chased you here," he said to Bonnie. "An eleven-year-old child."

"Yes, sir."

"I see." A severe expression had settled on Doc Price's face. "Ruby. Please assist Sheila in getting cleaned up and then I will examine the injury to her neck and throat. I see the marks clearly."

"Doctor, you don't understand!" Mother Jenkins broke in.

"Not another word, Gertrude Jenkins. You have terrorized a young girl, abused one patient, overstepped the bounds of your authority and then physically assaulted another patient, one known to be mentally unstable. You are done here at the Colony. You may pack your things. You're relieved of your duties."

"But—"

"*Fired*, Mrs. Jenkins. Go! Pack your belongings and *leave the premises at once.*"

"Doctor—"

"Which part of *GO* do you not understand, woman?! I'll not have the likes of you here, mistreating my patients. This is a place of refuge and kindness—"

It's a what? If Ruth Ann hadn't been so taken aback, she'd have laughed.

"—for the less fortunate in our community. How dare you behave as you have?"

To everyone's utter incredulity, Mother Jenkins burst into tears.

"You have not had an easy life," Doc Price said. "I'll give you that. But there is simply no excuse for pouring out your misery upon the hapless heads of these poor souls. It's not right. It's not proper. It's not Christian. Now go. When you are packed, Clarence will take you into town and drop you wherever you wish."

Ruth Ann found herself feeling sorry for Mother Jenkins. But then that made her angry. How could she feel anything at all for the old witch? Besides, she had all them bats in her behind to keep her company. And if she got real hungry in the future, she could always eat one.

Twenty-Two

Once Mother Jenkins and Clarence had left the Distressed unit, Ruby took Sheila down the hall to the lavatory to clean the blood out of her hair and get her changed into a clean nightgown and bathrobe and slippers.

Doc Price looked at the scarlet-spattered wall—it hadn't escaped the carnage either—and removed his spectacles to clean them. Once he'd replaced them, he gestured for Ruth Ann and Bonnie to follow him into Sheila's bedroom and have a seat.

"Nobody," he said to the younger girl, "will be cutting off your braids, sweetheart. And if anyone should try, you let me know about it. All right?"

Bonnie nodded. "Yes, sir. Thank you, sir."

Doc looked at Ruth Ann. "Is that the first time Mrs. Jenkins has slapped you?"

"No, sir."

"Was it a regular occurrence?"

Ruth Ann shrugged.

"Did she physically harm other inmates or patients?"

"Well, sir. There was the Belt."

Doc Price's lips tightened. "The belt? You mean she was beating you girls?"

"Yes, sir."

"Was it for just cause?"

Ruth Ann hesitated. "Sometimes. But usually just if she felt like it. She got good at comin' up with reasons."

"Can you provide me with an example?"

This was all very irregular. Ruth Ann wasn't sure she could trust this new, kindlier side of Doc Price. But then again, he'd downright gone and fired Mother J. She wouldn't be 'round no more. So why not give instances of her doings?

"Well, sir...there was the time I got the Belt because it rained."

"I beg your pardon?"

"All the laundry? It was hangin' out to dry? But a squall came out the clear blue yonder an' soaked it all agin. Mother Jenkins held out, sir, that it were—I mean, was—my fault that it got ruint and needed rewashin'. So she took the Belt to me."

"Good Lord."

He might be good, but He sure ain't shown Himself 'round the Colony lately.

Ruth Ann wished she could shoot that thought out of her head, like a pigeon out of the sky. She was gonna get struck by lightnin' for sure. Any day now.

Doc scanned Ruth Ann's face as though searching for germs. "Ruth Ann, when you ran away, was it to escape Mrs. Jenkins?"

"No, sir."

He squinted at her, and she began to fidget.

"Sure, an' I din' like Mother Jenkins, sir. But I truly wanted to go an' see my Annabel. I wanted to see for myself that she was all right. Safe an' healthy an' cared for. That is the truth."

She omitted that she'd planned to steal her back, that she'd planned to run with her far away and make a life for them somehow. Doc already had all that knowledge in his books; he didn't need that extra little bit of information, did he? It was hers and hers alone. Well...hers and Glory's and Mrs. Dade's.

Doc nodded and sighed. "I'm not condoning it, my dear."

Whatever that meant.

"But I do understand. It's nature. Even a cow in a pasture will mourn and low for her lost calf."

Ah. She was back to bein' no better than a farm animal.

But she didn't have time to think about it too hard or get offended. Because Ruby brought Sheila back in, and Bonnie ran to hug her. Then she pulled out of her arms and, when Sheila sank into her chair, the girl gently touched the marks around her throat.

"See what that bad lady did to my momma?" Bonnie said to Doc Price.

"Yes, my dear. I do. I'm very sorry. That's why the bad lady is going away." He got up and went over to Sheila, who had adopted a fragile, helpless demeanor. She looked up at them all and made big doe eyes.

Ruth Ann once again marveled at her mother's ability to adapt to any situation. She found herself firmly quashing a giggle. But the giggle was rattlin' around her insides and doin' its best to bust out her mouth and right into the room.

She couldn't allow that. Because what she was witnessing was a strange kind of power. It was the kind of power that people with no power created. The type certain women used all the time around men.

Sheila couldn't headbutt Doc Price to get what she wanted. But she could mess with his head...get him to feel like an important doctor and a protective man. Someone she needed.

The giggle got downright squirrely inside Ruth Ann.

Because she might be feebleminded...

But she knew deep down inside that Sheila Riley didn't need anyone or anything at all. Sheila was her own kingdom inside that scrawny, bony little body.

In the end, Ruth Ann sorta had to respect that.

"Does it hurt, Sheila?" Doc asked.

She thrives on hurt. She massages it and tucks it away for a rainy day.

"Oh, yes, Doc. It does."

"Let me see. Is it painful to swallow?"

Best keep your distance, Doc. Lest she swallow you.

"Yes, sir."

"Why did Mrs. Jenkins throttle you?"

"I just tried to protect my sweet Bonnie. That's all, Doc."

Bonnie nodded, made her blue eyes even wider and chewed on one of her braids.

Oh, my.

The giggle inside Ruth Ann turned into a tornado of hilarity.

Young Bonnie is smarter than I will ever be. She's already learning from a pro.

"Poor child," Doc murmured. "Poor child. All right, Sheila, my dear. It's soup for you, and hot tea as well, for a week. Ruby will bring it to you on a tray."

Hooray for Ruby.

But all Ruby said was "Yes, Doctor."

"And, Ruby, will you clean up that mess on the wall, please."

"Yes, Doctor. Right away."

Sheila gave him a grateful smile. "The tea an' soup'll surely make my throat feel better, Doc. Thank you."

"Of course. I must say, Sheila, you seem to be making great progress here at the Colony. Most wonderful progress."

A twinkle of malice sparked in Sheila's eyes, quickly hidden by downcast lashes.

Behind him, Ruby rolled her eyes at Ruth Ann.

The giggle tornado touched down in her stomach, then took off again and whirled up toward her heart. Soon, she wouldn't be able to stop it bursting forth.

Then Sheila laid on her shite, laid it on extra thick. "Doc," she said. "I know I got downright hysterical when I was fightin' for my life with Mother Jenkins. I do feel bad. Maybe—maybe you ought to check on her poor nose? I was plumb out o' my mind with fear. I think maybe I done broke it—purely by accident, you understand."

"Why, that's very thoughtful of you, Sheila Riley. I'll be sure to examine her before she leaves the Colony."

"Thank you, Doc," Sheila said in those honey tones she kept stored somewhere in the recesses of her raspy, demon throat. "I sure would feel more at peace with things if you did."

Once Doc had left the building, Ruby emitted a great snort before she went and got a bucket and some rags to clean the spray of blood off the wall.

Ruth Ann could no longer hold in her mirth. The tornado giggle twisted right up her gullet and burst out in uncontrollable laughter.

"What you laughin' at?" asked Sheila, the honey gone from her tone and her eyes shrunk back to raisins again.

Ruth Ann hooted some more. "You," she gasped at last, wiping her eyes with her sleeve.

"What's so goddamned hilarious 'bout me?"

"That diamond-cut filth what spewed out your mouth at Mother J, for one thing. Ain't never heard nothin' like it. It was so dang horrible that it was beautiful."

Sheila grinned. "'Twas, warn't it."

"The chimney sweep *and* his broom...where'd you learn to talk so vile? Sailors an' stevedores?"

Sheila went still and her eyes went far off and vacant. Then she brought herself back and gave Ruth Ann a wink. She chuckled, looking downright pleased with herself. "Never you mind."

"I ain't never seen no expression like that on *any* human face before. Mother Jenkins looked like you'd run a billy goat down her throat, an' it was kickin' her from inside."

"Good. Nasty old sow. I'd a kept goin' if she hadn't grabbed me by the neck when she did." Sheila put a hand to the bruises as if to brush them away. Her mouth tightened.

"It's long past time that someone gave her a lickin'," Ruth Ann said. "Put her in her place."

Sheila gave a snort that turned into a bark, and the bark into a guffaw. "Yeah, no foolin'. 'Twas a right pleasure."

Before either of them knew it, they were laughing...*together*. And Bonnie joined in. For a moment, they were a family—a mother and her two daughters, sharing a moment. It warmed Ruth Ann, wrapped her in an unfamiliar glow of happiness. But—

Bonnie! The poor child had heard it all. Ruth Ann turned to her, appalled. "Bonnie? Did you, um, understand the words what Momma said to Mother Jenkins?"

Sheila put a hand to her mouth, then smirked and let it drop with a shrug. "She'll learn 'em soon enough."

"Bonnie?"

Her sister shook her head a little too quickly, eyes downcast. "Well...I did like the part about how Mother Jenkins's face belongs in her drawers." When she raised her face, those blue eyes were full of mischief.

"Ha!" crowed Sheila. "That's my girl."

Ruth Ann tried, but failed, not to laugh again. Even though

they really shouldn't be teaching the child to make fun of adults. "Bonnie," she said, her voice quivering, "why don't you see if Ruby will find you a biscuit and maybe even some jam for it?"

"Okay!" She scampered off.

Ruth Ann turned to Sheila. "Momma..."

"What." Her tone was fierce now. All humor had vanished.

"Are you all right? Really?"

"I'm *fine*."

Sheila would never be fine. Not in any sense of the word.

"Took you long enough to ask, though."

Ruth Ann sighed. "I'm sorry. There was a lot goin' on. And Doc looked you over."

"Old butcher."

"Yeah—why was he so nice? To any of us?"

"Don't make sense. I'm tellin' you, somethin' 'round here stinks."

They sat in silence for a while, before Ruth Ann ventured a next question.

"Momma. How'd you know how to do that? Headbutt Mother J?"

Every line on Sheila's face converged and deepened. She closed her eyes, rubbed the hollows underneath them with her thumbs. "I just did."

"Nobody taught you?"

Sheila's eyes flew open. "Oh, sure, Ruthie! You bet. I went to a fancy chokin' school, where we learned cotillion dancin' and chokin' each other out. That's where I learned to knee gentlemen callers in the balls, too, darlin'!"

Ruth Ann withered under the sarcasm.

"It's where I got taught that if some asshole's got you by the hair and is slammin' your head into the dresser while he tries to get your knickers pulled down, you spray him right in the eyes with the perfume you pilfered from the five 'n' dime. Let's see, what else did I learn at the Chokin' Academy?

"You see, my girl, *I didn't need your help* that day you rode the turnips inta town! I taught my ownself. Afore I met your daddy, I had me a nice job keepin' house for an older couple whose son had gone off to the big city, got married and stayed there. Well, he come home for a visit, he seen me, and he decided he'd like to get under my skirt. He waits for his ma and pa to go to market, and he wrestles me down on a bed. And you know what I did, little darlin'?"

Ruth Ann wasn't sure she wanted to hear more. But she kept quiet. Her mother never talked about the past.

"What I did was wait 'til he's unbuckling his belt. And then I gets both o' my feet free and I kicks him so hard in the gut that he flies backward, clear through the window and down to the ground two stories below. *That's* what I done, and damn, did it feel fine."

"What happened to him? Did he die?"

"Naw, he didn't die. He wished he did, though. Got hisself quite a bruising. Had to stay there in bed for weeks."

"What happened to you?"

"I got my ass fired. Even though his ma and pa believed me over him. They couldn't have anything like that goin' on in their household."

That sounded all too familiar to Ruth Ann.

"When you's in a bad way, Ruthie, you either lie down and take it—or you invent a way not to. I'd rather dish it than take it—if I got a choice. Learn from that. Aw right? Learn and don't never forget it."

Ruth Ann sat there for a spell. And then she admitted, "I didn't have a choice. When I got knocked up with Annabel."

Sheila closed her eyes again. She sat so still that Ruth Ann was afraid that like Lot's wife, she'd turned to a pillar of salt. The room got so quiet that they could hear Mr. Daughtry breathing, a couple rooms over. They listened to the wind in the trees outside, the caws of a blue jay and his mate.

"I'm so sorry, baby."

Baby?

"I'm so very sorry. I know I ain't always real sweet to you, Ruthie. I been mad at you a long time. I haven't always liked you much, nor you me. But I wouldn't wish *that* on even a nasty old sow like Gertie Jenkins."

Ruth Ann released a breath she hadn't been aware she'd been holding. "Thank you, Momma."

Sheila opened her eyes. Though they still reminded Ruth Ann of raisins, they now glowed with an unholy light. "Never you mind thankin' me. You tell me the name of the sum bitch who done it to you. He gonna pay for it—I promise you. We gonna make sure o' that."

Twenty-Three

Sheila's statement both warmed and alarmed Ruth Ann. While part of her couldn't help cheering and wanting to plot out some deeply satisfying vengeance upon Patrick, any such action could very well damage her court case to stop Dr. Price from doing his surgery on her.

"Momma," she said now.

"What?"

Ruth Ann hesitated. She had just, at very long last, come to some sort of truce with her mother. She felt, if not her love, then her desire to at least have her daughter's back and work to punish the man who had hurt her. Powerful stuff. Promising. Addictive.

But what if Ruth Ann could win her case? And in the process, save other girls here from having to undergo that same operation?

Look at what the good Mr. Block had done already: he'd found Bonnie and brought her here; he'd reunited their family—odd and damaged though it may be.

"Momma, I don't want to do anything bad to Patr—to the boy who forced me. I don't want to get in trouble, or Mr. Block might not want to help us anymore. You know, if he thinks we're bad people, crazy or violent."

"Let me tell you somethin', girl. Your Mr. Block-head is a slippery character."

"He ain't! He brought us Bonnie! How can you say that?"

"Oooh, right. He brought Bonnie *here to the Colony*. Why? Out the goodness of his fine-tailored heart? I think not."

Ruth Ann waved a hand.

"You tell me: Why does he want all of us here all together, of a sudden?"

"Because…because she's a young girl, and she needs—"

"Bonnie was a young girl last month and last year, too. Why's it now that she needs us? Huh?"

"I didn't have a lawyer last month or last year. I just hired him!"

"Listen to you: *I just hired him*," Sheila mocked. "Did you really? Or did he hire you?"

Ruth Ann thought back to the afternoon when he'd casually dropped a C-note on the carpet in front of her and told her to pick it up. She thought about him kissing her hand—but then recoiling when she'd kissed his. What was all of that about? She didn't know.

Sheila scoffed. "So anyways, you swear you ain't screwin' him—"

"I'm not! I told you."

"So what's he want from the likes of you, Ruth Ann? You ain't that much to look at. You don't understand half the words he uses. He drops into your lap like some man-manna outta Heaven…"

"Mrs. Dade got him to come see me. There's nothing suspicious. It was Mrs. Dade. I asked her to help. So she did."

"Mrs. Dade, what took your baby away from you? And farmed you out to work for the neighbors for money? Right. She wants to help you like she wants to help a fox into her henhouse."

"Momma, you don't understand."

"Oh, I understand, all right. You got a thing for the fancy lawyer man and his viper-green eyes. I seen the way you look at him, an' it made me puke. Your Block-head ain't the hero you think he is. You been around as long as I have, you'll understand that men want one o' three things: food, sex or fortune. We know you ain't feedin' him, or he'd drop dead o' poisoning. You say you ain't screwin' him, so what's that leave?"

Sheila had clearly gone around the bend, again. Ruth Ann got up to leave. She was exhausted, she was confused, and now that Mother Jenkins wasn't around to threaten her hide, all she wanted to do was sneak off to her bunk, fall into it and take a nap.

"What's that leave?" Sheila demanded again.

"Fortune," Ruth Ann said wearily. "But that don't make any sense. Ain't got no money to pay him—he's the one gave me the hunnert dollars for his fee—"

Sheila bolted upright in her chair. "He done *what*?"

Ruth Ann filled her in on what had happened when he came to see her the first time.

Sheila lit a cheroot and took a long drag on it, drumming the fingers of her other hand on the grungy arm of her chair. "*Gratis*, my bony ass," she said. "That feller has himself somethin' up his snotty sleeve."

Ruth Ann put a hand up to her aching neck. "What, Momma? What can he possibly hope to gain from workin' with me?"

"I dunno. I'll bet it's got to do with lawyering, though."

"Of course it does. He's a lawyer."

"Fortune, girl. Food, sex or fortune. Somethin' about your case is gonna *gratis* hisself with the court or a judge or the John Q. Public. You mark my words, Ruth Ann, and you wake up! You smell the coffee. Then you throw the whole dang pot—*gratis*—at his pomaded head."

When Ruth Ann startled awake from her nap, she cringed and braced herself for the blow that would come from Mother Jenkins, who was screechin' at her in a dream. Chasin' her with a rollin' pin.

But Mother Jenkins was, unbelievably, gone from this place. And as Ruth Ann stretched and yawned in her bunk, she felt like a whole new person. She stretched some more, and then swung her legs out from under the covers and onto the floor, which felt cold but solid under her stockinged feet.

Had anyone noticed her prolonged absence? Or were all the girls clucking and gossiping about the downfall and banishment of Mother J? Who'd be put in charge of them, now that the old harridan was gone? Please the Lord it wasn't somebody worse.

She went to the lavatory and splashed water on her face, then put on her dress and shoes and wandered out for a look-see. She snuck over to the outdoor laundry, but not a soul was there and the fire under the massive iron pot had clean gone out.

In the kitchens, it was a different story. All the girls were there, heads together, gums a-flappin'. Hoots and shrieks of laughter punctuated the most lurid speculation.

"…heard tell she went right to the poorhouse!"

"…sold her extra dress and apron right on the street."

"…knocked on the Stringers' door to see if they needed a housekeeper, and when Mrs. Stringer said no, then she asked if they be needin' a *parlor maid*."

"What a whopper, Doreen—"

"I swear it's true! I had it from Jimbo, old lady Stringer's gardener's son."

"What're you doin' steppin' out with *him* again?"

"Well, he 'pologized…"

"Puh-lease, Doreen, you ninny…"

Mother Jenkins, begging for work as a parlor maid? Ruth Ann couldn't believe it.

"The Stringers said 'no, thank you,'" said Clarence, interrupting her eavesdropping.

She squeaked and jumped at least a foot into the air. "You scared the bejeezus outta me, Clarence!"

"Sorry," he said, smiling. "How you doin', Ruthie?"

"Okay, I guess."

"That ma of yours is somethin' else." He scratched his nose absently.

"Ain't she, though."

"I never seen nor heard anything like that in my lifetime." He laughed.

"Most people haven't."

"It's gone around, Ruthie. You know it has."

"Yeah, I'm sure." She jerked her head toward the kitchens.

"Funny thing is, your momma's now a hero."

Ruth Ann blinked. Then blinked again. "She's a *what?*"

"She took on—and took down—Mother J! The girls were cheerin'," Clarence said, "when I stuffed her in the flivver and drove her out the gates. *"Cheerin'."*

Ruth Ann broke into a smile. "They were?"

"No foolin'."

Her smile faded. "But Clarence, where'd you end up takin' that old buzzard?"

He sighed. "Lotsa places. She were bawlin'. I'd never imagined I could feel sorry for that woman, but I did. So we tried the Whistlers and the Stringers. We tried Old Lady Trotter's boardinghouse, but she cain't afford it. An' so finally I done took her to the First United Methodist Church. Pastor took her in, says he'll help her find some kind o' job somewheres."

"Oh. Good to know, I s'pose."

Clarence regarded her with one eyebrow lifted. "But you're as glad she's gone as anyone, ain't that the truth."

"Yeah. It is." She fidgeted under his gaze. "I never did thank you for runnin' to get Doc Price. Lord only knows what woulda happened if you hadn't. I think Sheila'd have killed Mother J, and that's the truth."

Clarence chuckled. "I'm with ya on that. Your momma may be skinny, but she's a right truckload of mean."

Ruth Ann felt that same powerful giggle rising in her again, pushing to get out. "I'll put that on her headstone, when she passes: 'Here lies a Mother, a Grandmother, a Truckload of Mean.'"

Clarence whooped. "Cain't imagine her ever restin' in peace."

"No. She'll haunt this place forever an' a day."

They laughed together, his hearty baritone wrapping around her soprano and sharing in the joy of pure irreverence.

"Are we awful, Clarence?" Ruth Ann said, when their mirth subsided.

"Yep." He grinned at her, his freckles dancing down his nose and over his cheeks. "We are one-hunnert-percent terrible, awful, no-good people."

"De-botched and de-generous," she agreed.

"You betcha." Clarence leaned forward and planted a kiss right on her lips. Then he walked away, whistling.

Clarence had *kissed* her. Ruth Ann stared after him, her fingers involuntarily touching the spot where his mouth had been, right there on hers.

And then he'd turned his back on her, before she could even react.

That was hardly fair.

His coppery head, his broad shoulders, his trim waist, his long legs, slowly receded and disappeared from view, and still she stared after him, fingers to her lips.

The renegade giggle within her receded right along with him.

She didn't know what or how to think. But she felt oddly light, as if she could lift, rise high into the blue sky and drift away on the breeze, like one of them kites at the seashore; look a robin in the eye, smell a cloud...spin silver out of raindrops.

That was how she felt.

Because Clarence had kissed her, and he'd smelled of hay, sunshine and laughter.

She'd liked it.

Ruth Ann didn't know what to make of this. She didn't *like* liking it. The kiss brought with it electricity, got things going in her body that shouldn't get going. It scared her, made her feel things she shouldn't feel. Think things she shouldn't think.

Like what Clarence might look like without his shirt on.

Ruth Ann's face flamed.

The good Lord would surely strike her now. She had cheered on her wicked mother, she'd found glee in another's misfortune and now she was in danger of becoming like the wrong Mary if she kept this up.

She was in danger of becoming her momma.

Blood will tell, folks liked to say.

The very idea of becoming the spittin' image of Sheila plain horrified her.

She wouldn't allow it. She would never be anything like Sheila Riley. Not ever.

And Clarence—he couldn't just go around kissing girls. The nerve of him!

She knew she wasn't much to look at. So did he kiss Greta, too? And Carlotta? Or even Glory? Who else might he kiss? Did he kiss a different gal every day of the week? Was it Meryl on Monday, Tabitha on Tuesday, Wendy on Wednesday?

A small voice somewhere in the back of Ruth Ann's head told her she was bein' irrational, thinkin' a mountain out of a molehill. And she told the voice where to go, on account of she refused to have voices in her head like Crazy Sheila. She didn't attack people, neither. Nor march up to people, like Clarence, and *kiss* them.

How dare he?

The next time she saw Clarence, she'd smack his face good and proper. Why, she'd knock those freckles into next year.

Twenty-Four

The Colony was full of surprises these days. Thursday afternoon the following week, Mr. Block's fine motorcar came purring through the gates with none other than Mrs. Dade sittin' in the rear seat. Ruth Ann saw her through the kitchen windows, plain as daylight, and almost dropped the pot she was scrubbing.

Whatever was Mrs. Dade doing here, in this place for the Epileptic and Feebleminded? She appeared to be occupied with something in her lap. Perhaps that something was baby Annabel!

The motorcar headed downhill toward Doc Price's office.

Ruth Ann excused herself to the outhouse—Carlotta had been put in charge of the girls for the time bein' and was far easier goin' than Mother J—and ran breathless in the same direction as the car. If she could catch one glimpse of her baby...

Had she grown much? Gained a few ounces or even another pound? Had her hair got any longer? Did she still coo like a little dove?

Ruth Ann had to see her.

But what if Doc Price got mad that she was there?

She decided she didn't care. She crept closer to his office and caught the wail of a child. Annabel was inside! What were they doin' in there to make her cry?

A primal, protective anger arose and clawed in her belly. Ruth

Ann flew to the door of Doc's office, turned the handle as if she had any authority to do so and marched inside.

Mrs. Dade sat in the reception area, her hands clasped to her mouth, evidently feeling the same way that Ruth Ann was feeling.

"What are you doing here?" they said to each other simultaneously.

Ruth Ann grasped her shoulder. "Where's Annabel?"

"Doc Price asked us to come here so he could do some tests on her."

Ruth Ann went cold inside. "Tests? What kind of tests?"

"I don't rightly know. He just said he needed to measure some things. Her head, her height, her responses to…stimuli?"

"What's stimuli?"

"I'm not sure."

"He ain't doin' no operation on her, is he?" Ruth Ann put a hand on the door frame to steady herself. She gripped it tightly. "No kind of surgery?"

Mrs. Dade shook her head. "He didn't mention anything like that."

Ruth Ann went weak in the knees. "Oh, thank the good Lord."

But Annabel was still wailing audibly behind the closed door of Doc's surgery. She wanted to charge it like a bull, trample it down and snatch her baby away. The protective instinct was so strong it frightened her. She'd do anything she had to do to keep Annabel safe. Anything at all.

Sheila's words came back to her, disturbing in their truth.

Lemme tell you somethin': any and every woman alive is "like that," if it comes down to feeding her kids or not. Yes, even you. A good, God-fearin' preacher's wife is like that, if her husband is dead and her children is hungry and cryin'…

Another howl came from behind the door, and Ruth Ann couldn't stand it any longer. She turned that handle, too. She barged in. "What are you doin' to my baby, Doc?!"

Annabel was naked and lying on a cold, metal scale. Other than that, the baby was fine. There were no needles or hoses anywhere close to her. Just a nurse in white from head to toe, and Doc, with a clipboard and a healthy dose of outrage at her behavior.

"What do you think you're doing, Ruth Ann Riley?!"

"I—I—was afraid for my baby—"

"How are you even aware she's here?"

"I saw Mrs. Dade in Mr. Block's car. Oh, please, cover her up, Nurse. She's cold!"

"We just had to get her weight," the woman said, wrapping Annabel in a blanket without further delay.

"Then why was she hollerin' so fierce, just before?"

"We had to take her temperature, Ruth Ann," Doc Price said. "Most babies don't enjoy that, you know."

Heat flushed her neck and face.

Doc finished making a note on his clipboard and tossed it aside. He gentled his tone, but he still conveyed his displeasure. "You have no business being down here."

"I just wanted to see her, Doc." She hated the note of begging in her voice.

"You are quite obsessed with Annabel," he said. "It's not at all healthy."

Not healthy? For a mother to love her own baby? Mayhap, Doc, you should have your own head examined by another doctor. "I'm sorry," she said, not meaning it at all. "I just...love her."

Doc sighed. "You gave birth to her, and that is all."

She simply stared at him.

"A cat births a litter of kittens, but she doesn't *love* them. A bitch whelps her puppies, but she doesn't *love* them. A mare drops her foal, but doesn't—"

"How do you know?" Ruth Ann blurted.

The nurse gasped, while Doc went ramrod-straight. "I beg your pardon?"

"How do you know what cats and dogs and horses feel, Doc? It ain't like you can ask 'em. It ain't like they can answer you back and you can write it all down on your clipboard."

Doc went purple in the face behind his steel-rimmed spectacles. "Ruth Ann. You are a Riley, none of whom has ever passed the fifth grade. Yet you question my medical knowledge? I have degrees from Johns Hopkins and Harvard! And you—"

"*Sixth* grade." Ruth Ann said it quietly.

"What?"

"I passed the sixth grade. Top of the class. You can ask Mrs. Dade, out there."

Doc spluttered and grew even more purple in the face.

And then Ruth Ann asked the question that she and Sheila couldn't seem to answer: "If you think so poorly of us Rileys, then why are you helping us out, Doc?"

"I don't think poorly of you. I pity you…"

Pity? She didn't want or need Doc's pity.

"I've explained to you compassionately that your mental state, your gene pool, is in no way your fault…I'm trying to *help* you."

"Why? And how come you entertain my lawyer Mr. Block in your office and have him bring my sister and my baby here to the Colony?"

Doc Price goggled at her for a moment. "Because it's my duty as an American, my duty as the director of this establishment and my duty as a Christian to do so," he informed her, weakly. "Now I ask you to leave my office."

His word was law.

Ruth Ann took a last, longing look at Annabel. She had indeed grown, and so had her hair. She was so beautiful.

"Leave," Doc ordered, again.

The nurse stood silent.

Mrs. Dade, still sitting in the reception area, wrung her hands.

Ruth Ann trudged to the door she'd flung open so urgently and didn't let it hit her on her way out. She was more confused than ever. Doc had been kind to Momma, examined her bruises, ordered tea and soup to be sent to her all week. He'd fired Mother Jenkins for her cruelty to the girls. And yet, he looked down upon them as...*animals*? Pitied them?

She didn't know what to make of it all.

Good thing she ran smack into Mr. Block outside Doc's office. He was smoking a fancy cigar and just about choked on it when she ankled out.

"Miss Riley!" he exclaimed.

"Don't you Miss Riley me." She folded her arms and raised her chin. "Were you even gonna tell me you was—*were*—here with my baby? With Annabel?"

He stared at her, his cigar smoke curling into the air and then evaporating like a poor excuse. "Well, now, I, ah—"

"So you weren't gonna tell me."

"It was merely a doctor's appointment for the child," he said weakly.

"It was a chance for me to see her."

"I should think that only causes you pain, Miss Riley."

"It does. But I want to see her anyways."

He sucked on the cigar and then blew out more smoke. "I don't understand..."

"You're not a mother."

"No, and there's little chance I'll ever be one," he joked, trying to lighten the atmosphere.

She just stared at him. "You're my lawyer, right?"

"Yes…?"

"Then I'd like you to ask Doc and Mrs. Dade in there if Sheila and Bonnie an' me can spend an hour with my daughter. We're family."

"Miss Riley, that's highly irregular—"

"I don't care."

"I'm not quite sure I can prevail upon—"

"Pre-vail? What does that mean? Can you just talk plain English to me, Mr. Block?"

"My apologies, Miss Riley. I'm not sure I can talk Dr. Price into allowing this."

"Please try, Mr. Block? Please? Just an hour. My momma's never even seen her granddaughter. Never met her."

Esquire hesitated, then nodded. He ground the tip of his cigar against the drainpipe at the corner of Doc's office. "I'll do my best."

"Thank you."

"In the meantime, I should tell you that we have a court date. We will be arguing your case in front of a judge here in Amherst County, and you will need to go there with me to answer some questions. All right?"

"What kind of questions?"

"I'll come again next week, Ruth Ann, to discuss them with you and prepare you."

She should be nicer to Mr. Block if she wanted him to stay her lawyer. "All right."

It brought an ache to Ruth Ann's heart to see Sheila cooing to little Annabel, holding her in her arms, rocking her. Bonnie stood behind the chair, bending to marvel over the baby's tiny fingers and gasping in delight when Annabel closed her fist around one of Bonnie's and held on.

Mr. Block had prevailed. Gotten his way—which was really Ruth Ann's way.

He and Doc had some words about it, though. Loud ones. Doc had thundered things like "irregular" and "unhealthy attachment" and "impudence." Esquire had bellowed back stuff like "immaculate legal precedent" and "judicial proceedings" and "three generations" and "keep her pliable."

She had little idea what most of the words meant, but she was grateful that her lawyer was fighting on her behalf. It was about time someone did.

Bonnie had Sheila to fight for her. Annabel had her, Ruth Ann. But Ruth Ann had nobody, except for Block. He wasn't family, but he would have to do.

Sheila began to sing her strange, made-up-on-the-fly lullaby verses.

> Hush little baby, don't you cry
> Grannie's gonna make you a nice big pie
> An' if that pie don't feed you good,
> Grannie's gonna ask the neighborhood
> For milk 'n' honey and a chocolate cake
> They'll bring 'em all for your own sweet sake...

Ruth Ann bit her lip to suppress a smile. "Grannie" had used that same mouth to spew filth at Mother Jenkins only weeks ago, but Annabel had no idea. She blew a spit bubble in appreciation of her grandmother's musical talents.

"You're an auntie," Ruth Ann said to Bonnie. "How does that feel?"

"Kinda old," Bonnie said.

Whereupon Sheila reached up and tugged one of her braids. "Oh, yeah, quite the wizened crone, you is, darlin'."

Bonnie laughed, the baby gurgled with delight, and the three of them basked in the sunshine of three generations of love.

What Ruth Ann wouldn't have given for a camera in that instant. Or an artist. She wished she could capture the scene somehow, and hold it tight against her heart. It was that rare, that pure, that magical.

But she was on the outside—always on the outside. Why? Why couldn't she ever belong? Why couldn't *she* ever be accepted or cherished? She seemed doomed to look at her own family through a pane of glass, her hands and forehead pressed against its cold surface. They were there, visible but unreachable.

Sheila must have sensed her thoughts. She cast a glance over at Ruth Ann. Her lips flattened, but softened again as she turned back to the baby.

Well, nobody could look at Annabel and not melt. It wasn't possible.

She squirmed and cooed and gurgled in her grandmother's lap, wriggling her feet in their little booties, shaking her tiny fists and joyously happy to be alive. Ruth Ann didn't want her ever to lose that joy...

She swallowed hard and brushed her sleeve against her nose.

Sheila turned her way again. "Oh, quit lookin' all hungry," she snapped, but without heat. "Like you could eat the moon and fart out a cloud. Git on over here, girl."

Always a poet, was Sheila.

Ruth Ann gaped at her.

"You heard me. Annabel is *your* baby."

Ruth Ann's eyes burned. *She is, and yet she ain't...*

Sheila cocked her head. She swung her feet, in their terrycloth slippers, down to the floor. She patted the place where they'd rested. "C'mon over here, Ruthie, and siddown with us on the otterman."

Blinded by the sudden tears in her eyes, Ruth Ann did as she was told.

Twenty-Five

Glory returned to work after her recuperation in the infirmary hospital. She was still pale and listless, and Ruth Ann's heart ached for her. She went to see Carlotta, the new temporary house mother, with the seed of a plan.

Carlotta was a mild-mannered, pragmatic, plump girl with mouse-colored hair who talked to the Lord more than she talked to anybody else and seemed to like it that way. Yes, she agreed, nine-year-old Izzie was a handful and needed an older sister or mother figure to take her under her wing. And yes, Glory would fit the bill right nicely. She needed a larger purpose to pull her out of the blues.

And yes, they could all do their rotation in the laundry together with young Bonnie, so that the girls got trained properly by their older mentors. Then they could do their rotation in the gardens and back to the kitchens for canning.

Ruth Ann could have kissed Carlotta. Instead, she thanked her profusely and promised that they'd all work hard and teach the younger girls to value the power of contributing to their community. Then she ran to find Glory and Izzie and Bonnie.

Glory shook her head in wonder at the news. Her blond hair seemed faded; the shadows under her eyes reached all the way to her cheekbones. "How'd you pull this off, Ruth Ann?"

"I asked." She shrugged. "And we done received," she said with an impish grin.

Izzie was less enthusiastic. "But I don' *wanna* 'tribute to my community.' I want to play dolls."

Glory bit her lip in an effort not to smile. "I understand, cutie. But we all have to earn our keep. You can put your doll in your pocket, though, and she can learn how to wash the clothes, too. How's that?"

"She can't see through a pocket, silly," Izzie said.

Now it was Ruth Ann's turn to bite her lip.

"Well, I s'pose she can sit on top the wall, then, and watch us from there. How would that be?"

"She'll get cold!" There was no pleasin' Izzie.

"Then we'll make her a coat after dinner. How would you like to do that?"

"Can I help?" asked Bonnie.

"Of course you can!" Glory said, at the same time Izzie knit her brow and said, "No."

The best-laid plans... Ruth Ann put her hands on her hips. "Why not? Why cain't Bonnie help make the coat, too?"

"'Cause she ain't invited."

Bonnie's face fell. "But I wanna learn to sew."

"Glory is *my* friend, not yours," Izzie announced.

Glory laughed. "You are both my friends."

"No. I found you first! An' anyways, Bonnie's got a ma. I don't."

Ruth Ann sighed. "Friends are to be shared, Izzie, like food and laughter and wisdom, darlin'. Not that we have a whole lot o' that here at the Colony for the Feebleminded, but even a fool's canny at times. Anyways. You girls are gonna have to learn to work together and get along."

"I don' want to work. An' I don' want to get 'long with nobody," Izzie said mulishly.

"Well, you gotta work, or you get no supper. As for gettin' along with other people, I cain't make you, but I'd surely advise it."

"Why?"

Ruth Ann bit her lip again to stop it from quivering. "On account of if you don't, they're likely to pull your hair, spit on you and maybe even steal your doll. Do you want any of that to happen?"

"No."

"All righty, then. Get along with others. Be nice to them, an' they'll likely be nice to you."

Izzie turned to Glory. "Is that right?"

"Yes, cutie, it is."

"Huh." She thought about it for a bit, then turned to Ruth Ann. "What's *canny* mean?"

"It means clever. Now, canny we all be friends and get to work?" Ruth Ann winked at the little girl, and Glory laughed.

"I s'pose so," Izzie said gloomily.

"Can I bring Calico Bear to sit on the wall with her doll?" Bonnie asked.

"Sure thing. They can supervise us all."

"What's that mean?"

"They'll look on and make sure we wash the clothes right."

"Who's Calico Bear?" Izzie wanted to know.

"My stuffed animal," Bonnie said. "What's your doll's name?"

"Louisa. It was Susie, but then I changed it to my ma's name..."

Glory raised her face to the sunshine and inhaled the fresh, crisp air as Ruth Ann piled the wood to get the fire started under the huge cast-iron pot. She stacked the logs carefully to create an air pocket in the middle, since the flames needed oxygen to do their job, just like people did.

Glory brushed her hands against her lower belly and leaned

against the wall with her eyes closed. Her hair stirred softly in the breeze and played along her cheeks. Her eyes fluttered open as a ladybug, of all things, landed on her nose. She put up a hand to brush it off.

"Don't!" said Ruth Ann. "She's good luck."

Glory gazed down cross-eyed at the tiny red spotted creature. "Good luck don't fly into a place like this. And it's got nothin' to do with me."

"She's good luck," Ruth Ann insisted. "You'll see."

"She's got nine spots!" Bonnie said.

Izzie frowned. "I only see seven."

The two girls counted again while Ruth Ann lit the fire and fanned it to a cheery blaze.

"Okay, nine," Izzie conceded. "I wonder if Mr. Phelps sent her?"

Ruth Ann straightened. "Who?"

"Mr. Phelps, the old man in the infirmary. Before he went to Heaven, he promised me he'd find my ma. And he said he'd send her down to see me."

"I'll bet you're right!" Glory smiled, still cross-eyed, at the ladybug. It raised and dipped its wings, as if to agree.

Izzie rushed forward to peer at Glory's nose some more. "Hi, Ma!" Her childish, but very real, bad attitude and anger slipped away in the face of this possibility. "You look so pretty! What's it like to fly?"

Glory and Ruth Ann exchanged a glance. Was this sacrilege? Should they correct her? Or was this God's simple way of comforting a child who'd endured bitter loss?

"What's it like to be good luck?" Izzie pressed on. "Why do you have to be good luck for other people? I miss you...I miss you so much, Ma."

The ladybug fluttered its wings.

Bonnie stared at Izzie, moving closer to Ruth Ann, who slipped an arm around her.

Then doubt seemed to creep into Izzie's mind. "Wait. This is silly. Nurse said my ma's an *angel* now. Not a ladybug." She turned to Ruth Ann and then kicked the wall. "What's the truth? Was Nurse lying?"

Ruth Ann remembered kicking that same wall, to make her toe hurt so that she could feel something. "Nobody's lying, sweetie. Who's to say exactly what an angel looks like? Why can't an angel have ladybug wings instead of big feathery ones?"

Izzie peered at her, her gaze uncertain.

"None of us has ever seen an angel," Glory chimed in. "So maybe they can put on a ladybug dress every now and then. Who knows?"

Ruth Ann smiled and nodded. She wished she could give the child all the answers she didn't have herself. But surely, lacking those, it wasn't wrong to give her hope? To give her the possibility that her ma did love her still from beyond, and had come to visit her upon Glory's nose? How could that be so wrong?

Izzie turned back to the ladybug on Glory's face. "Nine spots," she said, with a sidelong glance at Bonnie. "You were right. Nine spots for nine years old."

Bonnie smiled.

"Maybe Ma wants me to be your friend," Izzie speculated dubiously.

The ladybug fluttered its wings energetically.

"She does," Bonnie said, pointing.

Izzie nodded. "Well, okay then."

Glory and Ruth Ann exchanged another glance over the girls' heads.

Both God and children work in mysterious ways, an' that's the truth.

* * *

Whistling came from beyond the laundry's walls, announcing the arrival of Clarence. He rounded the wall, and Ruth Ann felt her face getting hot immediately. She snuggled Bonnie closer to her.

"Mornin', girls," he called. "You pretendin' to be statues?"

"No," said Izzie. "We're talkin' to my ma, who is now a ladybug on Glory's nose."

A pause ensued while Clarence worked this out. "Is that right?" he asked, keeping a straight face.

"Yes, it is. She came to say hello and see if I'm all right."

"Can I meet her?"

Izzie nodded. "I s'pose so. Ma, this here's Clarence."

He joined them in the laundry. "How do you do?"

The ladybug lifted a wing, and Clarence doffed his cap in reply.

"She likes you," said Izzie.

Clarence grinned. "Well, what's not to like?"

Ruth Ann no longer wanted to knock his freckles into next year. Was there no creature—insect, animal, child or adult—that he wasn't kind toward? How could she smack a fellow like him, even if he'd taken a liberty with her?

The ladybug confirmed her opinion by fluttering off Glory's nose and landing on the bill of Clarence's cap.

"Look!" Izzie pointed. "She wants me to be friends with Clarence, too."

Clarence's grin got broader. "Well, of course she does. Your ma doesn't want you to be alone. She wants us all to take care of one another, don't you think?"

Izzie's hazel eyes lit up, and she nodded. "We're gonna make my doll a coat so she won't be cold sittin' on the laundry wall. Want to help?"

Clarence tugged on his earlobe as he considered this. "Well, I don't rightly know how to sew," he said, "but I think I can hunt you girls down some fabric for this coat."

"Calico Bear might get cold, too," ventured Bonnie. "Could we make him a coat, too?"

Ruth Ann nodded. "Sure we can. Can you find enough cloth for two?"

"I bet I can." Clarence put his good hand on Bonnie's shoulder. "You girls give me until tomorrow, aw right? I'll start lookin' 'round about for it."

Ruth Ann didn't know whether to meet his eyes or look away.

He made the decision for her. "Hiya, Ruthie. I hear you and Bonnie and Sheila got to see little Annabel for a spell." His rainwater gray eyes held compassion and concern.

Somehow, he got it. He got how wonderful it had been and also how very difficult it had been to hand her back to Mrs. Dade. She didn't know how he understood, but he did.

Ruth Ann nodded.

Before he could say anything else, Bonnie broke in. "I'm an auntie!"

"Yes, indeed, you are," Clarence said gravely. "That is quite an achievement. Congratulations."

Bonnie beamed. "Thank you."

"I want to be an aunt," Izzie exclaimed. "How can I be an aunt?"

Glory chuckled. "Well, do you have an older sister?"

"I think so."

"You're not sure?"

Izzie shook her head.

Ruth Ann stepped in. "What's your surname, Izzie? And is Izzie short for Isabel?"

"Yes. It's Isabel Emmons."

"How do you spell that?"

Izzie blinked. "Dunno."

"Well, we'll figure it. Clarence, here, is going to do a bit of…research…for Glory. So he may be able to help find out if you're an aunt, too."

She shot him a glance. "Aren't you workin' on that, Clarence?"

He nodded. "It just takes a bit o' timin' and fiddlin', if you take my meaning. Plus leavin' that, uh, compass we talked 'bout behind." He winked at her.

Compass?

Oh, right. The moral compass that he needed to lose. Well, nobody thought the de-botched and de-generous had those, now did they?

"Come to think of it, I may need your help, Ruthie," Clarence said, alarming her. He leaned down close, and she ducked away.

"Ruthie," he said patiently, "I ain't gonna bite you."

He meant "kiss," and she knew it, and he knew she knew it.

"I need to tell you somethin' private. So gimme your ear."

Reluctantly, she allowed him to get close enough to whisper, while Glory distracted the two girls. Ruth Ann could smell the sweet hay on him, and the sunshine, and a scent that made him uniquely Clarence.

His breath tickled her ear and sent a shiver over her skin, raising goosebumps. Making her nervous as all get-out. "I'm-a need your help real late one night, Ruth Ann, as a lookout."

"At night? Someone might hear me sneak out."

"You done it before, remember? An' nobody heard."

"But it was awful when we got caught, Clarence. Just plain awful."

"Ain't no Mother Jenkins here now, Ruthie."

"No, but if they catch us up at the main buildin' in the files, they might call the police!"

"Shhhh. We ain't gonna get caught, Ruth Ann."

"But—"

"You need my help, and I need yours. That's the simple truth. So just trust me. It's gonna be aw right."

She wanted to believe him. But would it be? And was it wise for her to help break into the Colony's files when she had so much at stake with the court case looming?

Twenty-Six

I t was three nights later that Ruth Ann crept out of her bed at two a.m. to meet Clarence up at the main building. It wasn't wise of her at all, but she was determined to bring back the color to Glory's cheeks and the hope to her eyes. The innocence was long gone; it would never waft around Glory again. That still made Ruth Ann angry, but it was one thing—like virginity—that nobody could ever steal back.

Bonnie slept peacefully in the bunk above hers with Calico Bear clutched to her heart under the covers. Ruth Ann checked on her and paused to cover up one of her feet again; she'd kicked off the blanket. Then she stood in her chemise in the dark, listening and shivering in the night air.

Around her there came the sounds of deep even breathing from the other bunks, an occasional whimper from a nightmare, a gentle snore. And...what was that? Soft weeping. She was pretty sure it wasn't possible for a body to cry in her sleep, so that meant someone in the room was awake. Which meant Ruth Ann couldn't leave.

The sobbing seemed to be coming from the far left corner, where a new girl had been placed in a lower bunk. Should Ruth Ann go and see if she could comfort her? Not that she was good with that sort of thing...Or should she crawl back into her bunk and wait out the grief?

After a brief debate with herself, Ruth Ann decided that it was unkind to ignore her. That if she were in the same situation, she'd want someone to comfort her, *un*comfortable as that might be— sympathy from a stranger.

So she felt her way through the forest of bunks until she got to the right one. It was definitely the new girl. "What's wrong?" she whispered.

Sniff. "I hate it here," the other girl whispered back.

"You'll get used to it."

"Never."

"What's your name?"

"Jenny. Yours?"

"Ruth Ann." Great, now she could be identified by a witness if anything went wrong up at the main house. "Jenny, can I sit down?"

"I guess so."

Ruth Ann did. "It's gonna be okay, but it'll take a while. The girls here aren't bad. A little gossipy, maybe. A couple mean ones. But you're lucky that you didn't come while Mother Jenkins was here…"

"Who's that?"

"The old house mother. She was a wicked witch with bats in her behind."

Jenny giggled. "But she's not here anymore?"

"No…" Ruth Ann told her stories about Mother J and made her laugh about "boiled-shoe" stew and the day the old woman came back from the outhouse with a corner of her skirt tucked into her bloomers, and how nobody told her; they'd just let her go about her business like that. That they all cheered when she left…until Jenny's breathing slowed again and became deep and even.

Then, as the clock struck three a.m., Ruth Ann crept back to her bunk and dressed hurriedly in the dark, hoping she didn't have a similar wardrobe malfunction to Mother J's while doing so. She listened carefully again, and then, shoes in hand, made for the door. Before she could ease it open, Bonnie climbed down from her bunk with Calico Bear in tow. "Where are you goin', Ruthie?"

Applesauce! This was not working out at all as they'd planned. Not even a little bit.

"Just to meet a friend, Bonnie."

"Can I come?"

"No, sweetie. Go back to bed, and I'll see you in the morning."

"But we're not s'posed to leave this room at night. You're breaking the rules."

Ruth Ann sighed inwardly. "You're right, darlin'. I am. But sometimes—" She broke off, because she couldn't in good conscience teach a nine-year-old girl that it was okay to wander around anywhere in the dark by herself. "You know what, Bon? You're right. Let's both of us go back to sleep."

She helped her little sister back to her bunk, and then crawled into her own, praying that Clarence would understand when she saw him later. It took about forty minutes for Bonnie to fall back asleep. As quickly as she could, Ruth Ann crept to the door with her shoes yet again. Nobody'd bothered to lock it since Mother Jenkins's inglorious departure, so she eased it open and shimmied out into the night.

The moon flirted with some night clouds in an inky sky; the stars winked down at her as if to dare her onward toward the dangerous errand up at the main building. A light breeze stirred the branches of the cherry and dogwood trees, and chilly dew had gathered in the grass to chill her naked feet.

Ruth Ann sprinted for a ways without her shoes on, then

paused behind a hedge to slip them on and lace them. So far, so good. Not even an owl had hooted.

She slipped past the boxwood hedge in the shape of a cross, then the pretty little wishing well that was as big a lie as the lawn—no resident of the Colony ever bothered to wish on it— and finally the gazebo that perched near the curving drive that led up to the administrative building.

Clarence had told her to meet him in back, so she skirted the edge and snuck around. There was no sign of him. She peered into the indigo darkness, wishing she could part it with her hands like a curtain. There were no streetlamps here, nothing to light the way.

Ruth Ann felt her way along the ledges of the windows. His plan had been to leave one unlatched during the day so that they could enter through it. She counted down…one, two, three, four and then reached the back door. Then one, two, three—the third was open a slight crack. Clarence must have gotten tired of waiting for her and was already inside.

Ruth Ann's hands shook as she pushed open the window. She was breaking and entering like a thief. They *were* thieves, if she thought about it. They were there to steal information that didn't belong to them. What she was doing was almost certain to be de-botched and de-generous.

Then she waved away the thought. The information might not belong to her and Clarence, but it most certainly *did* belong to poor Glory. It wasn't fair for her to wonder every night of her life what had happened to her baby. It wasn't right.

And Ruth Ann was now an old pro. She'd gone through the window at the Dades' house, after all. She could go through this window, too. So she did, though the sill was higher and made of brick. It took some very undignified scrambling and waving of body parts in the air that ought not to be waved in the air.

She landed in a heap on the floor. "Clarence?" she whispered.

There was no answer.

He'd said that he'd located the files in an office on the second floor. So Ruth Ann kept fumbling around in the dark like an earthworm. She felt her way past the settee with the feather pillows that felt like leaning back into butter. She banged her knee on the console table behind it. "Ow, dangnabbit!"

She made her way into the grand foyer and crouched to avoid being illuminated by the gas lanterns that hung on either side of the big, black-painted front door—they shone light through twin glass panels on either side.

Then Ruth Ann sprinted up the stairs. "Pssst, Clarence?"

"Over here" came an answering whisper. "What took you so long?"

She followed the sound of his voice down a pitch-black hallway.

"In here," he prompted her.

And at last, there he was, on his knees beside a four-drawer file cabinet, his face ghoulish in the light of an oil lamp. He looked as frustrated as she'd ever seen Clarence look.

"I done found the files a half hour ago. Got tired of waitin' for you. What happened?"

Ruth Ann filled him in. "Seems like you didn' need my help at all."

"Yeah, Ruth Ann, I do." His tone was surly.

She was puzzled. "Whatever for?"

He didn't answer. Just handed her a file with a tab that said, "Southwick, G."

She sank down next to him, and there it was again: his scent of hay, sunshine and Clarence. She breathed it in, then took in a second lungful, hoping he didn't notice. He sat silent next to her.

"You gonna open it?"

"Yes. Why do you sound mad?"

"I ain't mad."

"You sure seem like you are—"

"Holy Moses, Ruth Ann, just open the dang file and let's find out where Glory's baby is. For Pete's sake…"

She did what he asked, and he held the lantern up so she could see better. Even mad, he was thoughtful.

SOUTHWICK, GLORY ANN, read the sheet on top.

AGE: 15 BIRTH DATE: April 6, 1910

REASON FOR ADMITTANCE:

Removed from family home; physical abuse.

MOTHER: Shaughnessy, Mary Jane   DECEASED

FATHER: Southwick, Peter John   WHEREABOUTS: Unknown

SIBLINGS: Brother, James. Age: 18   WHEREABOUTS: Unknown

Brother, Paul. Age: 20   WHEREABOUTS: Unknown

PHYSICAL DESCRIPTION:

Female.   Weight: 118 lbs   Height: 5' 3"

Anglo Saxon.   Hair: Blond   Eyes: Brown

MENTAL EVALUATION:

Moron, Low Grade

Ruth Ann stopped and quivered with outrage. *Glory sure don't seem like a low-grade moron to me.*

Reading comprehension: Grade Level One

Mathematics skills: Grade Level One, basic arithmetic

Able to perform basic household duties

PHYSICAL EVALUATION:

In general good health.

Scar above left ear upon admittance; bruises on upper arms; facial lacerations.

Gave birth to healthy female, 7 lbs. 3 oz., on September 3, 1924.

NAME OF CHILD: Lily Southwick.

Salpingectomy performed by Dr. E. Price on October 13, 1924 due to infection.

Ruth Ann gasped. "She didn't have no infection. None at all!"

"What are you talking about?" Clarence asked.

"Says here that Doc did a, a, salpin-whatever—his evil surgery—on Glory on account of she had some infection in there. She didn't."

"How do you know?"

"On account of she never said nothin' about it."

"Well, those things are kinda private, after all, Ruth Ann."

"Well…" Maybe he was right. "But she hadn't even seen Doc Price at all since she had the baby."

"So maybe he wanted to check her, and then he found the infection. He's a doctor. He ain't gonna be doin' surgeries that people don't need, is he?"

"He sure as shootin' wants to do one on *me* that I don't need."

"But…there's a reason. He says you shouldn't have more babies."

"On account of how the Rileys are de-botched, de-generous and whatnot. Fine, if he says so. But he never said that 'bout Glory's family. Not so's she heard, anyways."

"Well…keep readin'."

Ruth Ann kept scanning the pages in the file until she got to the excitin' part:

CHILD PLACED INTO FOSTER CARE on September 10, 1924
with Carl and Elizabeth Fawley at 37 Willow Bend
Road, Richmond, Virginia.

"Got it!"

"What's it say?" Clarence asked eagerly.

She turned the paper toward him, so he could read it for
himself.

He waved it away. "Yeah—read it aloud, so's I can hear
you say it."

And suddenly she knew. "Clarence?"

He hunched his shoulders.

"You can't read, can you?"

"I can read just fine." He sounded mad all over again.

And she got mad, too. He was lyin' to her, and she knew it.
"Then *you* read it aloud."

He refused to meet her gaze. He folded his arms across his
chest and said nothing.

"Clarence, you don't have to be embarrassed that you cain't
read. It ain't a crime."

"I don't wanna talk about it," he said flatly.

"They didn't send you to school, here at the Colony? On
account of..." She gestured toward his stump.

"I said I don't want to talk about it!" he blazed.

"I'm sorry. We won't, then." Clarence's face, lit by the lamp, had settled into hard angles that she'd never seen before. A hostile pulse beat
under his jaw. His lips were compressed into a straight, bitter line.

"So Glory's baby," she switched the subject, "is with a family
called Fawley. They live in Richmond, on Willow Bend Road."

"That ain't exactly close by," Clarence said. "It'd take hours to
drive there from here. A full twenty-four-hour day to walk it."

"At least we know where she is now. And we can tell Glory."

"Yeah."

They sat in silence for a moment, and she inhaled his scent again. She was tempted to put her hand on his arm, or her arm around his shoulders, just to let him know she didn't think less of him for not bein' able to read.

But she was afraid to touch him because of what the physical contact had done to her the other day. She didn't want to be Sheila. So she tried to comfort him with words.

"Clarence, it's okay. It's no shame that...you know, that you cain't—"

"It *is* a shame. They wouldn't send me to school on account of this." He pointed to the stump. "Why should a cripple like me get any book learnin'? I was never gonna amount to nothin' anyway."

Oh, Clarence...

She could feel his raw pain, and she couldn't stand it. "Fine. You're right. It *is* a shame—"

He reared back as if she'd slapped him.

"—a shame *on them*. Ain't nothin' wrong with you! And ain't nobody on this earth who's born perfect, does perfect or dies perfect. You're smart as they come, Clarence. And kind. And generous. And handsome. You want to know what I think? I think it was your *father* who was feebleminded, for givin' a treasure of a boy like you away."

He sat there, just starin' at her as if she'd hit him in the head with a brick. It was hard to tell, in the dim light of the oil lamp, but she could have sworn she saw tears gather in his eyes— quickly blinked away. Then he took her hand in his good one.

"I think you're the most beautiful girl I ever seen, Ruth Ann Riley."

She could feel a blush climbing her cheeks. "Banana oil. I ain't much to look at, everybody knows that."

"You're beautiful," he said again, squeezing her hand.

The warmth and strength of his touch seeped into hers, and it felt so good that it was impossible for her to pull away. "You need you some spectacles, Clarence."

"No, I do not need me any spectacles. You got skin like fresh milk, and lips like raspberries, and—"

"Raspberries has little hairs all over 'em, Clarence. You sayin' I have hairy lips?"

"No! Would you listen to—"

"And I have an upturned nose like a pig's—"

"—what I'm tryin' to—"

"—and eyes like—"

"—say?"

"—raisins, just like my—"

Clarence yanked her forward and stopped her words with his own mouth. Firm and yet gentle on hers. Insistent and yet respectful, somehow.

Her lips parted under his and she yielded to the kiss, electricity racing through her nervous system and raising a warning that she chose, for the moment, to ignore. How could anything feel so good as to meld into this man, feel his heartbeat thudding under her left palm as she slid it, in wonder, over his chest?

He let go of her right hand and cupped her cheek with his, stroked her ear, sent shivers throughout her entire body.

It felt so good that it brought tears to her eyes. To be touched like this…she'd never known such magic. Or such yearning for it never to stop. Such a desire for more.

He clasped the back of her neck and deepened his kiss, tenderly exploring her mouth.

And the unmentionable things began to happen in her body again as she responded.

This was temptation. This was the Devil. This would, no doubt, result in something like what Patrick had done to her—maybe not as violent, but no less humiliating and no less wrong.

Ruth Ann tore her mouth away from his, pushed at Clarence's chest and scrambled backward.

"What?" he asked raggedly. "What's wrong?"

"This." She wiped her mouth on her sleeve.

"No, it ain't."

"It's a whole lotta wrong, and you know it."

"It's natural to feel this way."

"I don't feel nothin'," she said.

"Liar."

"Don't you call me a liar!"

"Then don't lie to me," he said matter-of-factly.

"You quit kissin' me, Clarence. Quit it."

"Why? I didn' do nothin' you didn' want me to do, and you know it."

"I do not want you to kiss me!"

He stared at her, shaking his head. "Aw right. I get it. You can't get past this." He shook his stump at her.

"What? No! That has nothin' 'bout anythin' to do with it, you dumb ox!"

"Oh, now I'm a dumb ox. That's just swell, Ruth Ann. Fine an' dandy." Clarence got to his feet and set the oil lamp on top of the file cabinet. "We got to get out of here. It's comin' up on five o'clock in the mornin'. Folks 'll be gettin' outta bed, soon."

"Clarence, you are as wrong as you can be—"

"You done with that file, yet? You need to copy down the address? 'Cause the ox, here, surely won't remember it. Just like he couldn't remember the string of letters that spelled out S-o-u-t-h-w-i-c-k, so's he could locate the darn thing."

Ruth Ann wanted to smack his freckles into next year again, but she wouldn't. Because Clarence was clearly just as smart as any man, and because she'd hurt him without intending to, and because…"Clarence, I don't even think about you not havin' a left hand, and that's the honest truth. You always stuff it in your pocket an' hide it from me, anyways."

"Wouldn't you? Would *you* want folks gaspin' and gogglin' at somethin' freakish like this? Would *you* wanna listen to kids tauntin' you and askin' why don't you get a hook on the end?"

"Clarence—"

"So you got the address, Ruthie? Or not?"

"I got it."

"Then let's go, before somebody catches us…"

From downstairs, there came a squeak and a creak as the big black door opened, and a thud as it closed.

"Quick! Put the file back!"

With shaking fingers, Ruth Ann grabbed it, rifled through the other files to find its correct spot, and shoved it in. She slid the drawer home.

Clarence put a finger to his lips and then extinguished the oil lamp. "Back stairs," he whispered. "Follow me."

Twenty-Seven

Clarence took Ruth Ann's hand again, and she didn't protest because she was scared witless and blind as a mole in the darkness, to boot. "Take the oil lamp," he whispered, and she did. They crept to the doorway and peered around it. There was a flicker and then the slightest glow of dirty yellow seeping up onto the landing from below, as if someone on the ground floor had lit a lamp. Then a creak, and another, as the person started up the stairs.

Ruth Ann and Clarence crept down the gloomy hallway to the servants' stairs as quickly as possible. The oil lamp in her left hand shook, the glass top quivering against its metal collar.

There was no banister to guide them or to hang on to. "Squat and bump down on your keister," he whispered, letting go of her hand. "Otherwise, we're likely to trip and fall."

She did as instructed, and they bumped down together with little grace, crouching at the bottom of the staircase. She'd have bruises later for sure—but nothing compared to the ones she'd have if they were caught.

"Who's there?" called a female voice. Was it Mrs. Parsons? Ruth Ann couldn't tell. Whatever was she doing there at this hour of the morning?

They froze and remained silent.

Footsteps and accompanying floorboard creaks echoed along

the upstairs hallway. The dirty yellow glow from the lamp followed them. "Is anyone there?"

They hardly dared to breathe.

Eventually, the footsteps receded again, heading into one of the rooms.

"C'mon," Clarence whispered, taking her hand again. They kept low and skittered like crabs through the hallway door, back into the parlor with the settee and feather pillows, around them and all the way to the unlatched window.

He eased it open, swung his legs over the sill, and dropped easily to the ground below. "Give me the lamp."

She handed it over, and he set it on the ground. Then he held out his hand to help her down.

She put her leg over the sill, swung her other one over as well, and hesitated.

"Put your hands on my shoulders, Ruthie." Clarence waited patiently.

She braced against him, and he slid his right arm around her, lifting her down and depositing her gently on the grass. He was all hard muscle; even the arm with no hand was rock solid. She remembered marveling that he could wheelbarrow her and Glory all the way to the dairy barn.

Clarence then brushed past her, pulled the curtains together again and tugged closed the window. "Let's go!"

They made it back to the female dormitories without any incident, and she realized that Clarence had gone out of his way to see her home safely—the men's dorms were clear on the other side of the lake.

"Thank you," she said. "Clarence, I want you to know that you're wrong. About me not wantin' to be with you on account of—"

"Good night Ruth Ann," he said. "Sleep well—for the next half hour." He turned and walked away.

Dadburnit! Stubborn man. "Clarence!" she called as softly as she could. "Please don't be that way…"

He kept walking.

Ruth Ann slipped back into her dormitory and snuck to her bunk, checking to see that Bonnie still slept peacefully with Calico Bear.

She shucked off her dress, kicked off her shoes and then slipped into her night rail. She had half an hour to lie lazily under her blanket before everyone around her began to stir, and then it would be time to get up again for breakfast and go back to the laundry with Glory and the girls for the next few days.

She couldn't wait to tell Glory that they'd found out where her baby was…see the sparkle come back to her eyes and the color back to her cheeks. See the life bloom again in her friend.

Her thoughts drifted back to Clarence and how he hid his flaws from her. His lack of a hand. His inability to read. His sensitivity about that—and his deep hurt at how he'd been treated all his life. Like he was a circus freak or an idiot, simply because God had withheld one of his hands.

She closed her left fist and imagined she didn't have the use of her fingers on that hand. What would that be like? It would be impossible to cut meat with a knife and a fork. Difficult to fold laundry. She'd be unable to put up her own hair.

And if she'd been born a boy? What a challenge to wrestle with other boys. To button a shirt. To bait a fishing hook or scale a fish.

But easy to open a book, to learn to read and write the alphabet, to quantify figures and do arithmetic. Whyever would the Colony deny a boy like Clarence basic schooling? It made no sense at all.

She thought of his cover-up, his shame, the grim lines of his face and the flattening of his lips. Lord knew she'd only been schooled through the sixth grade herself, but she could teach Clarence to read. And teach him she would—whether he liked it or not. *So there, you big, not-dumb ox.* They would start with Mr. Mark Twain. He was quite wonderfully funny and wise, not at all highfalutin. Clarence would prob'ly like him a lot.

"We found out where baby Lily is," Ruth Ann told Glory as she made up the fire for the washing kettle. Glory was separating garments and colors. They'd sent Izzie and Bonnie to fetch more water.

"You did?" Glory dropped a white petticoat into a pile of men's black trousers.

"Yes. She's—"

"Tell me everything! Who's she with, how's her health, was there any pictures in the files?"

"No pictures. But far's I know, she's in good health and she's with a couple in Richmond, name of Fawley."

"How far is Richmond? Can we go see her? Oh! I want to see her, Ruth Ann!"

Oh, dear. "I don't think we can get there, or that they'd let you, but at least you know the name o' the people. Maybe…maybe you could write them a letter?"

"I ain't good at writin'. I want to see her sweet little face."

It was prob'ly a good thing that Glory didn't want to write. Ruth Ann realized belatedly that any letter sent from the Colony would reveal that someone had broken in to the files. And that would mean big trouble.

"I don't think it's possible," Ruth Ann said.

Glory burst into tears.

Oh, no. What have I done? All's I wanted was to bring joy to her.
Ruth Ann stared at her in dismay. "I'm right sorry, Glory, an' that's
the truth. I just wanted to bring you news of Lily, that's all."

Glory wiped her face with her apron. A good thing, since
Bonnie and Izzie were now visible a hundred yards away, lugging
their buckets of water from the pump.

"I know, Ruthie. You're a good soul. You are. It's just hard to
know my baby's out there, bein' cared for by some other woman,
and not even know what she looks like. Not be able to see her or
touch her or hold her."

Ruth Ann swallowed, thinking of Annabel and the hour they'd
been able to spend together with Sheila and Bonnie as a family.
"Glory, that may be a blessing."

"How can you say that? You at least got to see your baby,
hold her."

"But then I had to give her back," Ruth Ann said gently. "It
hurt something fierce. You'd have to say goodbye all over again,
too. And it only tears a fresh wound in your heart."

"I don't care," Glory said, pasting a fake smile onto her face as
Bonnie and Izzie got close. "I'm-a find a way to see her."

Ruth Ann nodded and said nothing. But she had a bad feeling in the pit of her stomach. Maybe she should have left the
files alone.

"Thank you," Glory added. "Don't mean to be ungrateful."

"I know."

"So will you go with me?" Glory asked.

Oh, no. Oh, no, no, no…

Ruth Ann turned to take the buckets from the girls as they
came into the laundry, panting. She sloshed the water into the

rinse tub and handed back the empty pails. "Off you go again for two more."

They skipped away, happy in their newfound friendship.

Ruth Ann turned back to Glory. "That ain't a wise thing to do."

"It weren't a wise thing to do when I went with you to find Annabel, neither. But I done it anyways." Glory put her hand on her hips, pursed her lips and waited.

What to say? "We got in so much trouble. You really want more?"

"Mother Jenkins is gone now. Doc Price already done his worst to me. So who cares?"

I care. I got a court case about to happen. I don' wanna lose my lawyer. Ruth Ann hesitated. "Things are different now, Glory…We were stupid. We didn't think 'bout how we'd live on our own with two babies. How we'd make money or get food."

"What's different, Ruth Ann Riley, is that you're all high an' mighty now with your lawyer and you won't help me like I helped you."

The injustice of this statement—and the kernel of truth in it—stung. "That's not fair! That's not how it is."

"It is fair. Besides, I didn' say I wanted to steal Lily. I just want to see her."

Ruth Ann said nothing.

"Why else would you go diggin' up the name and address for me? Did you do this just to be mean? What is wrong with you? I thought you were my friend!"

"I am your friend. Sometimes a friend's job is to tell you the truth: that trying to go see Lily is a bad idea. That it will only lead to heartbreak."

"You ain't no friend. You just don't feel like doin' for me what I done for you. Well, guess what, Ruth Ann? I all a sudden's got a real bad stomachache. I don't feel like doin' no washin' with you. Guess you'll have to do it all alone. Just lookin' at your face makes me sick. See ya."

As Ruth Ann gaped at her, Glory turned on her heel and marched off.

So much for putting the sparkle back into her friend's eyes and the color back into her cheeks. So much for good intentions.

Ruth Ann found the very spot where Izzie had kicked the wall a few days ago, and she kicked it hard herself. Now both Glory and Clarence were mad at her. The only friends she had in this godforsaken place seemed to no longer be her friends.

After she finished all the laundry, Ruth Ann sank to the ground, drew up her knees, and folded her arms upon them. She put her head down and closed her eyes. She inhaled the starch of her own apron, then the rich, loamy scent of the dirt under her and the grass that took root in it. *Lord, why didn't you just make me a blade of grass? They don't care whether the blades next to 'em are friend or foe.* How much simpler her life would be. She'd just grow upward toward the sun and pray for enough rain to survive.

But she was neither vegetable nor animal. She was reluctantly human. So she got up off her behind and dusted it off. She went to find a book, a pencil and some paper. Then she set about findin' Clarence.

She had to go all the way to the stables to locate him, where he was brushin' and groomin' the horses.

She inhaled the smell of the old wooden structure, the sweetness of the hay, the clean straw spread in the stalls and the sharp ammonia emanating from one stall where a piebald had relieved itself.

A friendly chestnut mare with a white star on her forehead

nickered softly as Ruth Ann approached. She wished she had a carrot or a bit of apple for her, but she didn't.

Clarence peered out from the stall where he was working, his brush resting on the rump of a big bay gelding. "What brings you to the stables, Ruth Ann?"

"You. You got it all wrong, last night."

"Dumb ox me," he said, and picked up the brush again. He swept it through the bay's coal-black tail. The bay didn't seem to notice, just kept on munching his bale of hay.

"You ain't an ox, and you ain't dumb, neither." Ruth Ann unlatched the stall and slipped inside with him. The bay rolled one eye in her direction, then ignored her.

Clarence raised his ginger eyebrows. "What're you—"

She took the brush from him and set it on top of the stall gate. Then she put the book in his hand: *The Adventures of Tom Sawyer*.

"What's this?" He shot her a look of pure aggravation. "Why're you givin' me a book when I can't read?"

She smiled at him. "On account of we're goin' to change that."

After a brief back an' forth verbal tussle, Clarence finally led her to the tack room, where they sat down at an old, scarred wooden table with the book and pencil and paper. Ruth Ann introduced him to Tom Sawyer, and after some scowlin' and growlin' 'cause he felt stupid, Clarence an' Tom got along like a house on fire.

He laughed like crazy when Tom snookered all the other boys into whitewashing Aunt Polly's fence. "I'm-a try that with the polishin' of the flivvers when them rich people come to visit the Colony—though not for no dead rat or string to swing it with."

"You'd rather have the firecrackers," she guessed.

"Of course."

"Want to try writin' a little?"

Clarence cracked his neck and ducked her challenging gaze. "I'm real bad at it."

"So you've tried it before. That means you want to."

He shrugged.

"What's the matter?"

"I don't like lookin' a fool in front of you."

"You don't. The only way that'll happen is if you give up afore you even start. So here." She handed him the pencil and placed the paper on the table in front of him. "You don't have to fill the whole page. Let's just write us out two sentences from Mr. Twain's book. Which were your favorites from the chapter we read?"

Clarence thought for a moment, then grinned. "The part about how Tom had a nice, good, idle time, an' if he hadn't of run out of whitewash, he'd of bankrupted all the other boys."

"Okay, perfect." Ruth Ann found the two sentences. "So your first word to write is *he*. That's *h* and *e*. Huh-ee." She pointed to the word. "So you copy them two letters. Easy."

Clarence did as she told him. His letters were by no means perfect, but he did fine.

"Good job!" Ruth Ann told him. "Now the next word is *had*. That's huh—aa—duh. So copy that out, too."

Before long, Clarence had written out the two sentences on his piece of paper. He sat staring at them in bemusement.

Ruth Ann had him read them aloud, twice. And then she clapped her hands and, surprising them both, gave him a kiss.

He blushed like a red-headed beet.

"We are gonna keep workin' at this, Clarence!" she informed him, skittering away when he made as if to kiss her back. "Pretty soon, you'll out-read every boy in the dorm who's made fun of you. And out-write 'em, too. You keep the book for now—just hide it out here. You're gonna love Tom. He'll be your friend forever." Unlike Glory. Her smile slipped away.

"What's the matter?"

She told him about it.

"Oh, good Lord. I didn't think o' that, neither. But it makes sense that she'd want to see her baby, right? We'll come up with somethin' and she'll take back her words, Ruthie."

She wanted to believe Clarence.

But Glory had changed so much since her surgery. Did she care enough about Ruth Ann to stay her friend? And would she ever reclaim the same sweet soul that had been surgically removed?

Twenty-Eight

On a dreary, bitterly cold day in November, Mr. Block's shiny black motorcar pulled into the circular drive of the main building at the Colony. Ruth Ann had been summoned there by Mrs. Parsons to meet him so that they could drive to the Amherst County Circuit Courthouse. They would stay at a boardinghouse in town for the duration of the trial.

Mr. Block looked dapper in a new three-piece suit and his gold pocket watch. His hat sat at a sober, lawyerly angle that also set off his fine green eyes. Ruth Ann felt extra-shabby in her plain shirtwaist and skirt and ugly brown coat.

She shivered at the prospect of going to a courthouse. What did a courthouse even look like? And the state (what did the State look like?) had appointed her a guardian to look after her "interests." Whatever those were.

The courthouse was a two-story building: white with black shutters, like so many at the Colony. It looked pristine and disapproving, just as they did. As if it would rather people like her didn't enter. A redbrick walkway led up to the main door, and a tall, skinny monument that Mr. Block said was put there by the Daughters of the American Revolution stood in the center of it.

Ruth Ann followed Block to the left of the statue and asked what it was for.

"To remember the sons of this county who died fighting in the civil war," said Mr. Block, "and not so very long ago."

She wondered who remembered the daughters of the county, but didn't say so aloud. She also didn't quite understand why any war was called civil, when killin' your countrymen, it seemed to her, was downright *un*civil. Seemed to her that it was the state that was feebleminded, not her. But nobody never asked her opinion, so she'd best keep her mouth shut.

A man waited for them outside of the double doors. Mr. Block introduced him as Mr. Shaw, her state appointed guardian, who had filed a legal petition for her against Doc Price and the board of the Colony.

"A what?" asked Ruth Ann.

"It's a request to the judge. It asks him to stop Dr. Price from doing the salpingectomy operation on you."

She shivered. The *s* word. Sounded like a cross between a scalping and somethin' worse.

"That's why we're all here today," Block continued. "Mr. Stringer will argue that Dr. Price should be allowed to do the surgery. I will argue that he should not. And then the judge will decide."

She nodded. "All right."

Inside the courthouse, which smelled of books and scrolls and philosophy, sat a clerk who asked their business and directed them to a room paneled with rich wood and filled with benches made of the same. In the middle of the room was a gate, and behind it were two long tables for lawyers. At the front was an elevated platform with a massive desk on it. Mounted behind it were the state flag of Virginia and the U.S. flag. It was all very official-looking. And it made Ruth Ann nervous.

Mr. Block instructed Mr. Shaw and her to sit at one of the long tables, and he sat there, too, placing a pile of books and papers in front of him.

Ruth Ann sat awkwardly in the wooden chair and wondered what she should do with her hands in a court of law. Clasp them in her lap? Place them flat on the table? Hide them in her skirts? Steeple them and pray?

The doors at the rear opened and Doc Price came in, along with Mr. Stringer. They nodded at Mr. Block but barely gave her a glance.

A group of young men entered next and sat on the benches.

"Law students," Mr. Block told her.

"Interested in *my* case? Why?"

"They just like to watch the law being created. This is like a classroom to them."

"I see." But she didn't.

The next to arrive was a group of three journalists. Block, Stringer and Doc Price all went over and shook their hands. But Block didn't offer to introduce her, so she sat glued to her chair, looking at nothing in particular while her hindquarters got heavy and then drifted off to sleep. She shifted her weight, to no avail. The carpenter had built extra discomfort into the seats.

When Mr. Block returned, he had some advice for her. "Now, there may be things said today that hurt your feelings or that you do not agree with. But under no circumstances should you open your mouth. Trust the lawyers—me and Mr. Stringer—to do the talking. Understood?"

"I guess so."

"Otherwise the judge will get angry. Don't make the judge angry, Ruth Ann."

"All right." She didn't want to make anyone angry. Seemed

like God an' everyone else had been angry at her all her life; she wasn't sure why. An' now even Glory was mad.

At last a door in the front of the room opened, and a clerk leaped to his feet. "All rise. The honorable Judge Peter B. Watkins, presiding."

Everyone in the court got to their feet while the judge, in his funereal black robes, made himself comfortable. "You may be seated."

Rustles and creaks and whispers ensued, and then there was silence.

Judge Watkins ordered the two lawyers to proceed, and they were off to the races. Ruth Ann learned a lot of stuff she hadn't known she didn't know.

"Very recently," Mr. Stringer announced, "the Commonwealth of Virginia passed a law authorizing the compulsory sterilization of the intellectually disabled. This progressive and ultimately compassionate statute is based on sound legal precedent: similar laws were adopted by Indiana in 1907, California in 1909, Nevada in 1911, Kansas in 1913. Several other states are in the process of enacting them."

What a load of mumbo jumbo. She sure would love to get her some of that commonwealth. She didn't have a penny to her name.

"In September of this year, Dr. Eugene Price filed a petition to his board at the Virginia State Colony for Epileptics and Feeble-minded. This petition was to perform a salpingectomy upon one Ruth Ann Riley. Your honor, Miss Riley is seated at the plaintiff's table in front of you, along with her state-appointed guardian, William Shaw, and her attorney, Mr. Wilfred Block, Esquire.

"The reasons for the petition and the decision to sterilize Miss Riley are manifold. Miss Riley is the daughter of one Sheila Riley, also a resident of the Colony, who is both mentally and morally defective. Dr. Price estimates that she has the mental capacity of an eight-year-old, is prone to violent verbal and physical altercations, and has a liking for strong spirits and foul language. Moreover, she has a record of prostitution and has given birth to three children without sound knowledge of their paternity."

Ruth Ann's mouth dropped open. *That's a lie! Our daddy was Cullen Riley. And he died, an' left Momma and the rest of us without any money...* She poked Mr. Block in the ribs, wanting to tell him so. But he put a finger over his lips and shook his head.

"The eldest of these children is a boy of twenty. He might, in a decent family, have stood in for his father as its head and provider. But he is nowhere to be found. The second eldest is seventeen-year-old Miss Riley, who is estimated to have the mental capacity of a nine-year-old—"

Nine? Then how in blazes did I pass the fifth and sixth grade?

"—and who has been removed from a respectable foster home due to incorrigibility and immoral behavior."

What's incorrigible *mean? How was I immoral? These are lies!* Ruth Ann poked Mr. Block again. And again, he shook his head and put his finger over his lips.

"Miss Riley was admitted to the Colony recently, unmarried and pregnant. She has, in turn, given birth to an illegitimate daughter, Annabel Riley, who represents a third generation of mental defectives. She has been described as 'not quite right' by the social worker who placed her with her foster parents, and according to the esteemed Dr. Arthur Estabrook of the Eugenics Record Office in New York, she displays 'backwardness.'"

Horsefeathers! Nothin' at all is wrong with my Annabel. She's as bright and beautiful as any child can be. Bring her right into this courtroom and let the judge see her.

But Ruth Ann knew better than to poke Mr. Block again. And the judge had frowned at her the second time she did so.

"So there can be no doubt," Mr. Stringer continued, "that in the case of the Riley family, we have not one, not two, but *three* generations of mental and moral defectives, women who have a high probability of continuing to breed in this strain, producing more and more unfortunate creatures who cannot or will not care properly for themselves or their progeny, pollute the gene pool of the great state of Virginia, and endanger the public welfare. The Rileys, like the Kallikaks, the Jukes and the Tribe of Ishmael, are manifestly unfit to live in decent society. Shall we turn a blind eye while they continue to breed? Shall we let their offspring continue to live in state-funded colonies, off the taxpayers, while they provide nothing of value in return?"

Ruth Ann wanted to throw one of Mr. Block's law books at Mr. Stringer's head.

Livin' off the taxpayers? Providin' nothin' of value? Hadn't she just washed Doc Price's shirts and drawers the other day? Darned his socks? What was she, a boil or a pustule?

"Your honor, I submit to you that we should *not* turn a blind eye. We should put a stop to the breeding of this sort of person. But Mr. Shaw has filed a petition with the court to object to the salpingectomy, on the grounds that it denies Miss Riley due process and equal protection under the law. Where is the *people's* due process in this case, your Honor? Where is the equal protection for *society*?"

Mr. Stringer, having spewed his lies and distortions, smugly went back to his chair.

Ruth Ann had to content herself with the fantasy of Sheila headbutting *his* nose, and spilling his blood all over his papers. Momma wouldn't stand for this nonsense.

Now it seemed to be Mr. Block's turn. "Your Honor, may it please the court, I will submit that the aspersions cast upon Miss Riley's mother are hearsay, as well as the aspersions cast upon her own character. Furthermore, Miss Riley's daughter is not of the age to be asked questions or answer them. She is an infant.

"I will now demonstrate exactly how this operation would violate the rights of Miss Riley to due process under the Constitution of the United States of America and to fair treatment under the Equal Protection Clause of the Fourteenth Amendment.

"The Constitution declares that all men are created equal. This extends to women of this country as well. It is a basic and fundamental right for an adult to marry and have children, to create a family unit. The salpingectomy, so ordered by Dr. Price and the board of the Virginia Colony for Epileptics and Feebleminded, curtails Miss Riley's ability to have children and thus reduces her chances of making a marriage and living outside the Colony.

"The proposed surgery would also treat Miss Riley inequitably in terms of the Fourteenth Amendment, since not every inhabitant of every institution similar to the Colony is forcibly sterilized. Nor is every woman living *outside* of such institutions.

"I would further argue that while this country does indeed strive to uphold the ideal that all men are created equally, God himself does not create each man, or woman, equally. Ruth Ann Riley has never been blessed with above-average intelligence, a stable home, adequate nutrition or proper parenting. I submit that to take away her right to create a family of her own is cruel and unusual."

There was a rustle among the law students at this. *He isn't making her shine*, one of them whispered. *Whose side is he on?*

"Thank you, Your Honor," Mr. Block said. And he sat down.

Ruth Ann was dumbfounded. That was all he had to say on

her behalf? She couldn't help it. She poked him again and leaned forward to whisper into his ear. "But Mr. Block—we do know who my daddy is. And I finished the sixth grade, and—"

"That's not really the issue here, Ruth Ann. It's about whether your constitutional rights are being violated."

"Order in the court!" Judge Watkins thundered. He pounded his gavel for good measure.

Ruth Ann was confused. Didn't it violate her rights for a man like Mr. Stringer to tell lies about her and her family? "Forget about the Constitution," she said. "*I* was violated. By Mrs. Dade's nephew…I *wasn't* immoral. I told him no, but he didn't care."

"Silence. Order in this court," the judge said again, with a stern look right at Ruth Ann.

I cain't even talk to my lawyer? What kind of justice is this?

"Mr. Stringer, do you wish to produce any witnesses to buttress your arguments?" the judge asked.

"I do, Your Honor. I wish to call Mr. Gilbert Trench."

Block looked down at his papers and squared them, as the bailiff went to get Mr. Trench, whoever he might be.

Gilbert Trench was not an aromatic individual, nor was he a natty dresser. His hair, though combed, lay in strings upon his scalp, and he did not seem to be a regular user of tooth powder, judging by the grayish-blue hue of his remaining teeth and the angry color of the gums that'd been divorced by the missing ones.

Ruth Ann wished that she didn't recognize him. But she did.

Judge Watkins grew ruddy as he gazed upon the man. His eyes bulged in their sockets. "Mr. Stringer, what is the meaning of this?"

"One moment, Your Honor. Mr. Trench, do you solemnly swear to tell the truth, the whole truth, and nothing but the truth, so help you God?"

"Yeah."

Please don't tell the truth. Please lie.

"And is it your testimony that on the afternoon of May 17, 1914, you visited the home of Mrs. Sheila Riley?"

Ruth Ann swallowed, hard. *Yes. Among other things, to knock my brother, Wally, into the dirt...leave him lying there all bloody.*

"Yeah," said the witness.

"And what was the purpose of that visit, Mr. Trench?"

It was the awful man's turn to flush. He sent a sideways glance toward the judge. "You promise I won't get in no trouble, Mr. Stringer?"

"You have paid your debt to society, Mr. Trench. Now, why did you visit Sheila Riley?"

Trench ran a finger around the inside of his collar. He looked quickly at Ruth Ann, and then away. "I, ah, purchased her, ah, services."

"And were those services sexual in nature, Mr. Trench?"

He poked his tongue into his cheek. "You might say that."

"But do *you* say that, Mr. Trench?"

"Yeah."

"And do you know of other men such as yourself who regularly visited Mrs. Sheila Riley for similar purposes?"

"Yeah."

"Would you care to expound?"

"Huh?"

"Details, Mr. Trench. Who were these men?"

"I promised I wouldn't name no names."

"How many were there?"

"'Bout eight. Ten, mebbe."

"And you personally saw them coming and going from Sheila Riley's home?"

"Yeah."

"Thank you, Mr. Trench. That will be all."

Judge Watkins looked like he had gas. "Mr. Block? Do you wish to cross-examine the witness?"

Block shifted in his seat. He made a show of squaring his papers again. "No, Your Honor."

Good. Ruth Ann agreed with him this time. She didn't want to know any more. And she didn't want anyone in the court to know more, either. This was humiliating and shameful.

Trench was led back out of the court by the bailiff. The judge glanced at Mr. Stringer. "You have another witness?"

"Yes, Your Honor. I wish to call Mrs. Gertrude Jenkins."

Ruth Ann shrank back in her seat. *Why is Mother Jenkins here?*

The bailiff brought her in, looking thinner and older and even meaner than she used to, what with her nose now being crooked.

After she swore the oath to tell the truth, Stringer led her through his series of questions.

"Mrs. Jenkins, you were formerly the house mother at the Virginia Colony for the Epileptic and Feebleminded, were you not?"

"Yes, sir."

"And were you familiar with Sheila Riley and Ruth Ann Riley while you worked there?"

"Indeed I was."

"And what was Sheila Riley like, in your experience?"

"Crazy and violent and...loose."

"Can you give some examples of what you mean, Mrs. Jenkins?"

"Well. I found her in flagrante delicto with the junior gardener, at one time. She traded for cigarettes and gin."

Ruth Ann didn't know the Latin, but she could imagine what it meant. She cringed, sliding lower in her chair.

"Ah. Go on."

"The last time I was in her presence, she said things of such a vile nature, in such foul language, that I cannot repeat them in this court."

"And?"

"She was also physically violent. She smashed my nose. Broke it."

Let's talk about why, *you old battle-ax!*

Mr. Block said nothing.

Ruth Ann kicked him in the ankle, tried to get his ear, but he shushed her. And the judge glared.

You tried to choke the life outta Momma! Tell that *to the court.*

She was sorely tempted to stand up and explain the nature of the last encounter between her mother and Mrs. Jenkins. But she didn't want to make the judge angry. So she sat there mute and boiled inside.

"Was Sheila Riley often restrained because of violence, Mrs. Jenkins?"

"Yes. Constantly. She had to be put in a straitjacket, lest she hurt others or herself."

"And what was your impression of Ruth Ann Riley, while you were employed at the Colony?"

Mother Jenkins turned her crabby eyeballs toward Ruth Ann. "She'll turn out just like Sheila."

Banana oil, I will! How dare you?

"And upon what do you base that assessment?"

"She's dumb as a brick—"

Oh!

"—and about as motivated. She was infernally slow at any task given to her. Oftentimes she'd do idiotic things, like leaving laundry hung out in a rainstorm…"

How can you blame me for a sudden squall that blew in? Ruth Ann almost flew out of her chair and punched the old witch.

"And she arrived at the Colony pregnant—big as a house. We all know what causes that condition, and she most definitely was not married. So she is following in her mother's footsteps, you mark my words. The apple doesn't fall far from the tree."

I'm-a throttle her, see if I don't... I'm-a shove that apple up there with the bats!

"That will be all, Mrs. Jenkins. Thank you."

"Your witness," said Judge Watkins to Block, who was scribbling something in the margins of one of his papers. He didn't appear to be listening.

"Eh? Oh. No questions."

No questions? Was he deaf and dumb? Ruth Ann kicked him again. How could he not give her the chance to tell her side of the story?

He glared at her and shook his head.

Don't make the judge mad, Ruth Ann. He had the power to sign off on the surgery, or even put her in jail if he wanted.

"Mr. Stringer? Any further witnesses?"

"Yes, Your Honor. I'd like to call Mrs. Betty Lou Parsons."

What on earth is Mrs. Parsons doing here?

The receptionist and her lace collar marched in, all prim and proper, and sat down.

"Mrs. Parsons, you work as a receptionist and administrator at the Virginia Colony for the Epileptic and Feebleminded, is that right?"

"Correct."

"And in your position there, have you had occasion to be in the presence of Ruth Ann Riley?"

"Yes, sir. On more than one occasion."

"And it was on a recent occasion that she was in the room with you and Mr. Block, her lawyer."

Ruth Ann, startled, glanced at Block. He kept his gaze on the witness.

"Yes, sir."

"And what did you see her do?"

"Miss Riley threw herself at Mr. Block and…she *kissed his hand*." She said it in a low stage-whisper, full of drama and insinuation.

Ruth Ann could no longer contain herself. "It wasn't like that! I was expressin' my gratitude—"

"Silence!" Judge Watkins pounded his gavel and stared her down with such contempt and disgust that she wished the floor would open up and swallow her. "*Order in the court.*"

Mr. Stringer smirked at her. "And what did Mr. Block do, Mrs. Parsons?"

"He reacted very properly, sir. He pulled his hand away and discouraged her advances."

"I should hope so," Mr. Stringer said. "And why, Mrs. Parsons, do you think Ruth Ann Riley was, ah, trying to be…affectionate…with Mr. Block?"

"I couldn't say, sir. But it may have been that she wanted him to work extra hard on her behalf."

"Objection," said Mr. Block. "Speculation."

The proceedings went on and on, like some drawn-out nightmare that Ruth Ann couldn't seem to awaken from. She couldn't understand all the complex language and legal terms, nor the scientific charts about "traits" and "genes" and "heredity." She didn't know most of them "witnesses" Mr. Stringer called in to flap their gums 'bout this an' that. For goodness' sake, whyever was some gentleman natterin' on about pea plants in a foreign country called More-of-ya? Whatever did *peas*—foreign or domestic—have to do with her and Momma?

She'd never heard of the families called Kallikak and Juke and Tribe of Ishmael that hers was bein' compared with, but she did comprehend that she and Momma were bein' right vilified in a court of law. The Riley name, the Riley bloodline, the Riley smarts—they was all bein' plum assassinated. They was even callin' Annabel, not even a year-old baby, stupid.

All them folks in the courthouse rustled and bustled and oohed and aahed and seemed to think they'd just purchased a five-cent bag o' popcorn outside and was watchin' a silver screen motion picture, starrin' herself as the mustache-twirlin' villain.

The two lawyers strutted back an' forth like two bantam cocks, spewin' rattle-trap 'bout the 8th and 14th Amendments to the Constitution.

And yet nobody would let her speak up for herself or for her momma. She wished she could put Sheila on the stand to give her speech about how even a preacher's wife would be "that kind of woman" if her children were starvin'.

She wished she her ownself could tell them that it was Patrick who was violent and immoral—not her. And that Mother Jenkins'd had her a score to settle.

She wished she could tell them all that she'd passed the sixth grade and about the book she was readin' at night by oil lamp: *Little Women* by Louisa May Alcott.

But nobody would let her open her mouth.

As for Judge Watkins, he continued to look as if he had some awful bad gas.

So feebleminded or not, Ruth Ann figured she and her family had about as much chance in this fight in the Amherst County Circuit Court as the Christians of yore had with the lions in Rome.

Twenty-Nine

The trial took the better part of a week. When the judge got to wanting his supper and got tired of it all, he'd pound his gavel and send 'em off to the boardinghouse for the night, which served a nice chicken pie and where Ruth Ann marveled over the actual goosedown duvet on her bed. She'd never slept under anything like it.

That cock-of-the-walk lawyer Stringer, he just kept on callin' people in to swear on that Bible and hold forth in court. He called a nurse who said Momma was the worst sort of riffraff who let her children run wild and live on the streets.

Mr. Block didn't ask her a single question.

Stringer called the social worker who'd brought Ruth Ann to the Colony to get all them tests and then have her baby. Miss Celeste Wilson, who'd been kind back then, appeared now to think Ruth Ann was a sewer rat.

Yes, she agreed, Ruth Ann was likely to become a parent of "deficient offspring" if she was allowed to leave the Colony and go live on her own. She had an immoral tendency, just like her momma. She was inclined to get into trouble, and she was feeble-minded, and "these girls so often went 'wrong.'" And look out! She'd already had a baby out of wedlock—a baby who wasn't "quite right."

Ruth Ann couldn't help it: she stuck her tongue out at Miss Wilson.

The judge pointed right at Ruth Ann and pounded his gavel.

A fancy gentleman from the Carnegie Institution hopped up there and talked about how he'd studied Momma and her and baby Annabel. That wasn't rightly true. He compared them to some other families in books. Families who were de-botched and de-generous and diseased and downright daft.

And finally, Mr. Stringer called Doc Price.

He asked him why he'd ordered a sterilization procedure on her. Doc Price said that it was on account of if he didn't, she would need to stay at the Colony for upward of thirty whole years—until she couldn't have babies no more.

But if she had the surgery, then she could leave the Colony and get married and lead her own life and be happy. And she wouldn't keep on costin' the state so much money.

Ruth Ann hadn't realized that she cost the state money. After all, she worked hard. She cooked and cleaned and did laundry and ironed and gardened and…

But to hear them gentlemen tell it, livin' at the Colony cost about as much as livin' at the Ritz-Carlton Hotel. So the state did want her to leave and not stay there for the next dad-gummed thirty years.

Mr. Block did get up to "cross-examine" Doc Price. And he asked Doc, wasn't the surgery "cruel and unusual"? But Doc said no, and he chuckled. He said all 'twas involved was a simple cut to some tubes, an' that nothin' was removed.

Mr. Block then asked Doc if it was true that if Ruth Ann did have the operation, that the Dades wanted her back?

Did they? Would they let her come home and take care of Annabel?

And Doc said yes, absolutely. That was his understanding.

She could be with her baby again. She couldn't wait!

Mr. Stringer's last "witness" was a big pile of paper from yet another fellow at the Carnegie Institution, some bigwig who traveled a lot and gave speeches—even in Europe.

Ruth Ann fell asleep during the dronin' on as these papers were read aloud to the court. Judge Watkins sure noticed, and he banged his gavel at her again, so's she jumped in her seat. He glared at her. But how was a body to help bein' so bored and sleepy?

She smothered another yawn as the two lawyers got up one final time and proceeded to repeat stuff they'd each said on the very first day of the trial. These were the closing arguments. Ruth Ann was glad. The lawyers could close the arguments, and then maybe she could go close her eyes for a spell.

At last, it all appeared to be over and done with. But she stood, bewildered, as the judge left the courtroom and the lawyers got their papers together and shook hands.

"But…he never opined one way or the other!" Ruth Ann said to Mr. Block.

He gazed down at her from his superior height, his green eyes reflecting amusement at her expense. "My dear girl, he must take some time to think about his ruling."

"How long do we have to stay here while he does that?"

"We don't. We all go home and wait."

"He's not going to tell us today?"

"No, Ruth Ann. Most certainly not. This is a legal matter of great importance and must be considered carefully."

"How long does he have to think about it?"

"As long as he likes. Days, weeks, months."

Ruth Ann wanted to stomp her foot right there in the

courtroom. Judge Watkins was no longer there to squint at her and pound his gavel, after all. But she knew that it wouldn't do any good at all. And she'd already poked and kicked her own lawyer a number of times.

"Can I tell him now that a lot of that stuff wasn't true? Especially that part what Mrs. Parsons said?" Her face flamed. "Because that's not how it was!"

"No, Ruth Ann. You can't talk to the judge. The trial is over."

"But those people spouted off a bunch of lies about me and Momma and Annabel."

"Mr. Stringer was making his case for Dr. Price. So he brought in witnesses to bolster his arguments."

"But I didn't get to argue about his arguments and say they were wrong!"

"No, Ruth Ann. Because that's not how it works."

"Why not?"

"That's not how the court operates."

"But then why didn't *you* stand up and say they were lies?"

"Because they are *opinions*, Ruth Ann. The witnesses stated their opinions. Opinions are not lies."

"But they're *wrong* opinions."

"Opinions are neither right nor wrong. They're just what somebody *thinks* about something."

"I don't understand…"

"I know."

Good-lookin' or not, she wanted to smack the man. "Why couldn't I talk? Why couldn't I say those folks were lyin'? That man from the Carnegie place—he didn't spend no time at all with me, nor Momma. He talked to us each for mebbe fifteen minutes! And I'm much smarter than a nine-year-old…"

Mr. Block sighed. "Ruth Ann, if I had put you on the witness stand, Mr. Stringer would have asked you a lot of questions that would have made you look like a loose woman, a prostitute just like your mother."

"Momma wasn't no prostitute...not really...she needed money to feed her children."

"If she ever exchanged her, ah, favors for money, then in the eyes of the law she was most certainly a prostitute."

"But—I could have explained to everyone."

"No, you couldn't have. Mr. Stringer would have twisted your words against you. He would have made you look immoral and stupid. He'd have made you look like an imbecile..."

"A what?"

"Or worse, an idiot."

"What's an imbecile?"

Mr. Block paused and shook his head. "Do you remember the big chart that Mr. Stringer put up in the court? The one showing mental defectives in three categories?"

"I didn't rightly understand it."

"Morons are at the top. Imbeciles are in the middle. And idiots are at the bottom. You are at the top of that chart, Ruth Ann. But by the time Mr. Stringer got through with you on the witness stand, he would have reduced you to the very bottom, and made you look like the Whore of Babylon, to boot."

"But—"

"And he would have tricked you into saying it yourself. Mr. Stringer is a very clever man and an excellent lawyer."

"But so are you, aren't you, Mr. Block?"

He preened a bit, at that. "Well, yes. I am."

"So you could have got the better of him, surely?"

"My dear Ruth Ann, in a court of law things aren't always

so simple." He patted her shoulder. Then, leaving her with even more questions, he went to get his coat and hat.

She was quiet on the drive back to the Colony. She pondered it all while Mr. Block whistled as he drove. Her head spun faster than the wheels of the motorcar turned. She had more questions than there were leaves on the trees.

When at last they turned into the tall, wrought-iron gates of the Colony, she turned to him. "Do you think we'll win, Mr. Block?"

He wore a peculiar expression and didn't meet her eyes. "I don't know, Ruth Ann. It's up to the judge. But if we don't win, we will appeal the decision to a higher court."

"All right. And if we don't win there?"

"I will take your case all the way to the Supreme Court of these United States."

"You'll do that for me?"

Mr. Block nodded. "I most certainly will."

She fidgeted, plucking at the fabric of her skirt. "What if— what if I don't want to win? What if I don't want to stay here at the Colony for thirty years? What if I just want to go back to the Dades place an' take care of my sweet Annabel?"

Mr. Block pulled up at the doors of the main building and idled the car. He got out, rounded the hood and opened her door to hand her out. "It's in the hands of the law, now, my dear. Everything's going to work out fine. You'll see."

Ruth Ann most certainly did not want to see Mrs. Parsons after what she'd said in court. So she turned her back on the main building and deliberately walked over the expanse of green lawn toward the female dormitories, instead of skirting it and taking the stone path. Marching over the lawn was the most direct route to them and the kitchens, and she dearly wanted to see little Bonnie after bein' away for so many days.

But Bonnie wasn't in the kitchen. She wasn't out in the laundry, either. Nor was she in the garden or the dairy barn, where Izzie was learning how to milk the cows.

"Have you seen Bonnie?" Ruth Ann asked her.

"No. She got called to Doc's office yesterday, an' she didn't come back for supper, nor afterward, neither."

Black, winged fear flew into Ruth Ann's throat and lodged there. *Oh, no. Oh, no, no, no.*

Without a word, she turned and ran. She ran out of the dairy barn, through the pasture, past the stables and the henhouse. She ran all the way to the main house, right over the lyin' lawn again, up the hill where the house loomed and then right back down it. She arrived breathless at the infirmary with her lungs on fire and burst through the door.

"Where is she?" she demanded of the nurse at the reception desk. "Where's Bonnie Riley?"

"You can't just come barging in here, young lady—"

"Where is my sister?!"

"You need to calm down, this instant."

"You need to—" But Ruth Ann didn't finish the sentence. She just flew past the desk and into the main hall of the infirmary, searching among the twenty-six white-sheeted beds. She found Bonnie about halfway down on the left, looking paler and even more drawn than Glory had, if that were possible.

"Oh, Bonnie, darlin', what did they do to you?!"

"It hurts, Ruthie..." Bonnie whispered. "It hurts."

"Oh, sweetheart, I know it does. I'm sorry. I'm so sorry." She took Bonnie's hand, squeezed it and kissed her on the forehead.

She kept her voice gentle and sweet, even while rage built within her. A violent fury that would not be channeled or controlled.

"Where were you? I kept calling for you, Ruthie."

"Oh, Bonnie...remember? I had to go to town for a while, to be in court."

"Are you back now? I'm sleepy..."

"Yes, I'm back now." Ruth Ann smoothed her sister's hair and stroked her braids.

"Why are you shaking, Ruthie?"

On account of I'm-a murder Doc Price, you see if I don't. "I'm just a little chilly, sweetie. You go on back to sleep, you hear?"

"All right. But it hurts."

"Go to sleep, darlin', and you won't feel it so much." Ruth Ann stayed by Bonnie's side until her breathing slowed and evened out. Then she got to her feet and made her way out of the infirmary, walking past the nurse at reception without a word.

She marched straight over to Doc Price's office. It no longer intimidated her. She turned the handle of the door and threw it right into the wall. And then she threw open the door of his examination room, where she found him peering into a patient's ear.

The patient took one look at Ruth Ann's face, jumped off the examination table and flattened herself against the wall.

"Ruth Ann! What in the name of God do you think you're—"

"What did you do to my sister, you son of a bitch?!"

"—doing? How dare you? Get out of this room at once!"

"What did you do to Bonnie?"

"Get out. Get out! I am with a patient, as you can see—"

"You sliced her open, didn't you, Doc?"

"You are violating her privacy—"

"You violated my sister!"

"I did nothing of the sort, young lady. How dare you insinuate such a—"

"You did the salpin—salpin-thing, didn't you? She's eleven years old, Doc. *Eleven*. How could you do that to her?"

"She had an infection, Ruth Ann. She needed the operation—"

"I think you're a no-good, rotten liar!" she shouted.

"Christina," he said to his patient. "I do apologize. But can you give us the room, please? I will be with you as soon as I resolve this situation."

Christina fled, running smack into the attending nurse.

"What on earth is going on here?" she asked.

Ruth Ann slammed the door in her face. She whirled on Doc Price, whose own face had mottled with temper.

"Eleven years old! How can you possibly justify it? Do it to me, if you got to, but my baby sister? You're a fiend. A fiend! How could you?"

"I'm nothing of the sort. You need to get a hold of yourself, Ruth Ann Riley."

"No, Doc. I need to get a hold of *you*." Her tone had gone low and vicious. "So does a judge. You should be locked up and never allowed to 'practice' medicine again. 'Cause we are the unfortunates you practice on. And that's just plain wrong."

"You have clearly lost your mind, young lady. And you'd best shut your filthy, insolent mouth. The only thing a judge is going to decide is if you should be committed to the Distressed unit, like your lunatic whore of a mother—"

"She ain't a lunatic, Doc! She's just furious at how she's been treated. And she wouldn't-a been no whore if our daddy hadn't of died! You ever had to worry where your next meal's comin' from, Doc? Huh? Ever had to worry 'bout how to feed your hungry kids? Oh, that's right—you ain't got any kids. And you get paid a lot o' money to 'care' for us…"

"You're out of your mind," Doc Price said. "I am going to give you a sedative, Ruth Ann." He walked toward the wooden cabinet that stood against the wall and opened it, withdrawing a syringe and a vial. He removed the cap from the syringe, tapped the barrel of it and then inserted the needle into the vial.

"You're not giving me anything, Doc."

"Sit down." He drew several cc's of fluid into the syringe, then withdrew the needle and put the vial back into the cabinet. Then he calmly advanced upon her.

"Get away from me," Ruth Ann warned him.

"Sit down, I tell you. No? Have it your way. I'll administer it with you standing." He grasped her arm.

Ruth Ann spit in his face. Then she snatched the needle out of his hand and stabbed it into his shoulder, depressing the plunger.

While he wiped his face and opened and closed his mouth in shock, staring at the syringe, she lunged toward the cabinet and grabbed the first weapon she saw: a scalpel.

"Help!" Doc Price shouted. "Help me, somebody!" He pulled the syringe out of his meaty shoulder.

She brandished the scalpel at him while he shrank into the corner. "You stay away from me, Doc. And you stay away from my sister. You ever touch her again, Momma and I will get you. Don't think we won't."

"Help!" yelled Doc Price.

The door flew open, and the nurse on duty ran in, quickly taking in the situation. She clamped down on Ruth Ann's right wrist with an iron grip and hung on with all her might while calling for another nurse.

Doc came out of the corner, wobbling now from the medicine, but still strong enough to grab Ruth Ann's left wrist. The second nurse came in to help.

They pushed Ruth Ann's face into the wall. Then they yanked her wrists together, slammed her to the floor still kicking and screaming, and one nurse sat on her while Doc staggered over to his chair like a drunk and collapsed. The other nurse ran to the cabinet and found bandages.

They secured her wrists. Then they gave her a shot of whatever was impairing Doc.

"Gether to tha Distwessed uny," he ordered. Then he pitched forward onto his desk.

Thirty

Ruth Ann awoke blearily, muzzily. Her head had been stuffed full of cotton wool and hurt like the dickens. She tried to put her hand up to it but couldn't. She couldn't move her feet, either. She was tied to the bed she lay in. It was dark and smelled of must and body odor. She had no idea where she was, and she had to pee.

"What…where…?" she mumbled.

"Well, butter my butt an' call me a biscuit. Sleepin' Beauty's awake," said Momma. Her voice came from somewhere to the right. Ruth Ann turned her head and made out her slight form in a bed next to hers.

"Welcome to the Distressed unit, darlin'. You was droolin' on yourself when they broughtcha in, so you prob'ly don't remember much."

"No," said Ruth Ann. "Can't say as I do."

"Well, the word is you attacked Doc with a syringe and his own scalpel." Sheila cackled. "I'm right proud of you, girl. But what I'd like to know is why."

Momma's proud of me, after all these years. Ain't that rich. "He did the operation on Bonnie while I was in court," she said.

Sheila lay there silent for a long moment. "If I ever get me the chance, I'm-a operate on *him*."

Ruth Ann believed her.

"I swear it: I will chop somethin' right off that man."

"I'll help you."

They lay together in silence for a few moments.

"He said it was on account of infection," Ruth Ann told her.

"He's a lyin' sack of shite."

"I know."

"An' just how was court? Have a ball, there, with your fancy-pants lawyer-man?"

"No. It was days an' days of sittin' ramrod straight in an awful wooden chair with a snooty judge glarin' at me and a whole lotta folks tellin' lies 'bout all of us Rileys. An' I wasn't allowed to say a single word."

"I told you it warn't no lucky break. I told you that Esquire fella warn't on your side. He got somethin' up his sleeve, he does."

"But what? He ain't gettin' money. He ain't gettin' 'free milk.'"

"I seen the way you look at him, Ruthie. You'd give it to 'im if'n he asked."

"I would not!"

Sheila grunted her contempt.

He was right handsome. But she didn't need to feed no starvin' children, and she was nothing like her momma. Never would be.

No. She'd just screamed and cursed and spat and attacked a man...but she was nothin' like Sheila Riley at all.

Oh dear Lord, please do not let me turn into my momma. Anythin', Lord, but that.

Dawn was creeping through the windows along with the irony.

"So what'd it get you, all this court nonsense?" Sheila asked.

"Dunno. Judge ain't made up his mind, yet."

Momma snorted. Then she said, "I got it. I know why Esquire

is helpin' you. I'd bet you anything he is somehow makin' a name for himself with your case."

Ruth Ann thought about it. "There was law students and newspaper reporters in the courtroom," she said.

"Oh, was there, now? So your Mr. Fancy-Pants is gettin' notoriety out of this. An' next thing you know, he'll maybe run himself for office. The Senate or some such thing."

Ruth Ann thought about that, too. And about morons and imbeciles and idiots.

She *wasn't* at the top of that chart—she was at the bottom. She'd been so stupid. She was a right droolin' idiot.

Her man-manna from Heaven ... with that C-note he'd dropped all casual-like on the floor. *Pick it up* ... And she had. Given it back to him along with her misplaced trust. She'd been snookered.

"What happens next, Ruthie?" Momma asked.

"Well, Mr. Block said if we don't win this time, he will take my case all the way up to the Supreme Court."

"Oh, he did, did he? That's the big-time. So that's what Esquire wants. To meet up with a whole pocketful of judges. There's a bunch of 'em there. Seven, I reckon."

"Nine," Ruth Ann said. "I remember from school. Nine judges on the Supreme Court to decide the law of the land. Oh, dear Lord, Momma. I didn't understand. They're gonna make it a *law* that people like us can't have babies."

Ruby came in presently to untie them and take them to the outhouse, one at a time. Ruth Ann got to go first.

"Did you really attack Doc Price?" Ruby asked, her eyes wide and shocked.

Ruth Ann sighed and rubbed at the ligature marks on her wrists. "He done that surgery on Bonnie. She's *my baby sister*,

Ruby. She's so young, and she's in pain. I couldn't stand it. He did it behind my back, while I was gone."

Ruby's lips flattened, and she shook her head.

"I didn't set out to attack him. I did go down to his office to holler at him. And then he says he's gonna sedate me…" Ruth Ann told her the story.

"But now you're stuck here, child. All you did was hurt your ownself, in the end. And don't think that Doc won't put all this stuff in your files."

She walked Ruth Ann back down the hallway. "I don' wanna tie you again, child. But I got to. Them's the rules."

Ruth Ann lay wearily back on the bed, and Ruby did her best not to make the ligatures too tight. Her touch was gentle; her kindness once again made Ruth Ann's eyes sting.

Then it was Sheila's turn to visit the bathroom.

Almost immediately after they left, there was a knock on the frame of the open door.

"Ruth Ann?" Clarence stood there in a clean flannel shirt and denim trousers, with a bunch of yellow daisies in a jar. He was a sight for sore eyes.

"C'mon in. I'd get up, but…" She gestured with her chin toward her bonds.

"Oh, Lord have mercy, Ruthie. What—why—here, let me untie you."

"No, Clarence. Thank you, but you'll just get into a whole heap of trouble."

"What happened? People are sayin' you attacked Doc Price…"

She told the story yet again, while Clarence listened in disbelief. "So, like they say, you gave the doc a dose of his own medicine."

She nodded. "You shoulda seen his face, when I done it, Clarence! He looked right gob-smacked. He looked like…I dunno, like…one of his shoes started talkin' to him. And then he passed out on his desk like a street bum."

Clarence began to laugh.

And then she did, too, though there was really nothing funny about her situation.

"When can you go back to your regular schedule?" he asked.

"Don' know."

"Doc won't leave you here forever, will he?"

Ruth Ann shrugged. "Ruby says he'll put all o' this in my file."

"Huh. Good thing we know where those are."

She smiled at him. "Good thing."

"Well, did you win your court case, Ruthie?"

"Won't know for a spell. Judge is thinkin' about it all."

He nodded.

"Clarence, I…I feel dumb as a brick, but I think you and my momma were right about Mr. Block."

"Esquire," he said, with a twist of his mouth. But he didn't say *I told you so*.

"O' course we was right," Sheila said, coming back into the room with Ruby. "I ain't never wrong. Who's this?"

"Clarence, Momma. Momma, Clarence. Clarence, be afraid. She bites."

Sheila hooted. "Only on occasion, young sir."

He looked uncertainly from Ruth Ann to her mother and back again. Then he grinned and shook his head.

"And this is Ruby, who takes care of us 'violent lunatics.' Ain't she lucky?" Ruth Ann rolled her eyes.

"Hi, there, Ruby." Clarence put out his hand.

Ruby was clearly taken aback—not used to white folks wanting to shake with her. But she finally smiled and stuck out her hand. "Nice to meet you, Clarence."

"Likewise."

"Well," said Ruby. "I got to get on with tyin' Miz Sheila to her bed agin."

"Right," said Clarence, as if this was totally normal. He hesitated, then put the jar of daisies on Ruth Ann's nightstand. "These are for you."

"Thank you." She wished she could get up and kiss him—on the cheek, of course. Her thoughts tried to wander back to that night by the file cabinet, but she blocked them.

They locked eyes.

"Will you—"

"D'you want me to—"

"—come visit again?" they said simultaneously.

They smiled at each other.

"Yes," they said in unison.

"All right, then." Clarence walked to the door.

"I'm glad you came," Ruth Ann said.

"So am I." Clarence left, whistling.

"That boy is sweet on you," Sheila said once his footsteps had faded.

Ruth Ann didn't respond. She didn't want to talk about Clarence with Sheila. He was…private…to Ruth Ann. He wasn't an object for gossip.

"What a shame 'bout that hand of his. He'd be a right handsome fella if not for that—what'd'ya call it—stump. But that there is off-puttin'."

"I don't even notice it," said Ruth Ann, through gritted teeth.

"Well, I sure do. Even with his wrist stuffed down in his pocket, I can tell there's no hand there. He could save himself the trouble of hidin' it."

Ruth Ann's pulse kicked up and beat hard at her temple. "Can't you understand he'd be self-conscious 'bout it?"

"Things is what they is," Sheila said flatly. "Cain't change 'em."

So true. Ruth Ann thought of the fable about the scorpion and the frog crossin' the river.

"Wonder what happened to the hand," her momma mused. "Was it cut off by farm machinery? Was he just born a freak?"

"Clarence is not a freak," Ruth Ann snapped.

"Well, well. Listen to you. You're sweet on *him*, too." Sheila cackled. "My girl is sweet on a circus freak!"

If Ruth Ann could have stood up, bed and all, she would have. She'd have whacked her momma with the headboard. Since that was impossible, she lay there and simmered.

"That ain't smart, Ruthie. Do yourself a favor and go for a man who's got both hands. That boy's never gonna make a proper livin', walkin' 'round like that. Nobody's gonna hire him, if ever he could leave here—"

"Clarence," said Ruth Ann, "can do anything—*anything*—that a man with two hands can do."

"Oooh, she's gettin' tetchy," Sheila jeered. "Aw right. Let's see 'im do push-ups."

Ruth Ann turned her head and squinted at her mother. "I'm tellin' you: he *can*."

"Let's see 'im drive."

"He *does*."

Let's see 'im..." Sheila racked her evil brain for something she knew Clarence couldn't do. "Huh."

"Conduct a symphony? He could. Shoot a gun? He could. Do carpentry work? He'd find a way, I promise you."

"My, my. You have gone an' fallen for that red-headed circus freak. You gonna marry him an' pop out some little one-handed ankle-biters?"

Ruth Ann searched her mind for a word that could describe

someone as horrible as her momma, someone who took joy in hurting others, in stepping on their soft spots and grinding in her heel. Malice came to mind. It wasn't perfect, but it was a start.

"You know what, Momma?" she said. "I think I *will* marry him. Long's he don't run screamin' for the hills at the prospect of you for a mother-in-law."

Ruth Ann lay next to Sheila for three days. It was seventy-one hours too long.

Mrs. Jekyll had been there right as she'd woken up: sayin' as how she was proud of her daughter for attacking the good doctor and amused by it. But Mrs. Hyde had returned soon enough, with gusto and gravy.

The next morning, Sheila turned her face toward Ruth Ann. Her eyes had morphed from shrewd little raisins to the dead black holes on a shark. They were empty of pride, empty of maternal feeling, empty of humanity. "You are one dumb little twat. You know that?"

Ruth Ann sighed. "Sure, Momma."

"You walked right into the jaws of the trap."

"And which trap is that?"

"Mr. Block flashed his green eyes and his pretty-boy smile at you, and you all but dropped your knickers scramblin' to do whatever he said, thinkin' he was like a hero from a fairy tale," Sheila scoffed.

The truth didn't just hurt. It sizzled along the edges of the fresh open wound. But at least now she knew better. Clarence was the hero from a fairy tale.

"Thinkin' a lawyer actually cared about you or your case. You a dumber piece of white trash than has ever walked God's green earth."

Ruth Ann was still tied to the bed. She couldn't escape the words or the bizarre, misplaced hatred that spewed out with them. She took a deep breath. "I'm your daughter, Momma. So what does that make you?"

"I'm at least *smart* white trash," Sheila hissed. "And if I could get up outta this bed, I'd slap your face so hard, it'd kiss your own backside."

"But you can't." Ruth Ann said it deliberately, tired of her verbal abuse.

"I'll be up soon enough, missy, so you'd best watch out. In the meantime, you got only your ownself to blame that the Block-head brought your Annabel here, so's they could fake some test and call her an idiot. And worse, you got your ownself to blame that he found our Bonnie and brought her here to the butcher. *It's your fault*, Ruthie, that she'll never have no babies."

The words were worse than a blow; they were a breaker crashing over her.

Ruth Ann lay there on her back, drowning in them. She couldn't seem to get oxygen under the weight of them, couldn't move her arms or legs or raise her head above them to gasp for forgiveness. All she could do was writhe in misery and guilt and truth.

"You set her up for it," Sheila spat. "You walked right into the trap Esquire set and drug her in, too, by her pretty blond braids..."

Ruth Ann thought of the day Block had brought Bonnie to the Colony—how petrified she'd been, how she'd clutched Calico Bear and wouldn't utter a word. How she, Ruth Ann, had never been so glad to see anyone in her life...besides maybe Annabel. How she'd felt so connected to Bonnie, felt such love and sympathy for her, felt safe at last to *feel* something, anything at all. Because she knew instinctively that her baby sister wouldn't attack her just for the crime of loving her.

So Ruth Ann had made Bonnie feel safe. She'd betrayed her by doing that.

She wished she could really drown in Sheila's horrible words. Just go under and breathe them into her lungs until, clawing for the surface, she lost consciousness and they no longer had the power to hurt.

It's your fault, it's your fault, it's your fault, it's your fault, it's your fault…

"I shoulda used a coat hanger to get rid of you," Sheila said.

Coat hanger, coat hanger, coat hanger, coat hanger, coat hanger…

Ruth Ann released her mind into a helium balloon that floated far above their beds in the Distressed unit. There it could bob in the breeze, be bathed in sunshine or starlight, divorce this place and everyone in it.

"Yeah, Momma," she said. "You should have."

"I knew you was gonna be trouble. I knew you was gonna bring nothin' but misery and shame. I knew you warn't gonna be worth the effort I made to push you out…"

With her mind up in the balloon, Ruth Ann could almost admire her mother's sheer viciousness. A body had to work hard to conjure up that much venom, especially for her own blood. It was quite somethin', the force and habit of her hatred.

Ruth Ann clung almost absentmindedly to the memory of them all sitting with Momma in the pale green armchair as a family: Bonnie, Annabel and finally, amazingly, Ruth Ann herself. Had that really occurred—that warmth and connection?

Thirty-One

It was a week later that Mrs. Parsons sent word to Ruby that Ruth Ann was to get cleaned up and come to Tremont House to see Mr. Block.

Ruth Ann, glad to be untied, upright, bathed and in a clean pinafore, didn't say a word of greeting to the traitorous sow in the lace collar. She did get a cheap thrill when she realized that Mrs. Parsons was afraid of her.

The story of her attack on Doc Price must have gone around the Colony like wildfire, since Mrs. Parsons instantly backed away from her once she came through the front door and looked as though she'd lunge for the telephone at the slightest wayward move on Ruth Ann's part. It was somewhat, somehow…*delicious*…to be feared.

She curled her lip at the woman. "Why, how downright lovely to see you this fine morn', Mrs. Parsons. I thank you ever so for makin' me look like a slut in the courtroom, when you know I was only expressin' my misplaced gratitude to Mr. Block that afternoon. I surely won't ever forget your kindness."

Mrs. Parsons put a hand up to her lace collar and smoothed it. Then she smoothed her hair. Then she swallowed and backed up another step.

Your head looks like it's on a doily, restin' on a servin' platter. Wonder what you'd say if I told you that, Mrs. P?

"I—I—" the woman said.

Ruth Ann raised her eyebrows and waited.

"Mr. Stringer—he asked me to testify if I had ever seen any improper behavior on your part with a gentleman."

"Oh, I see. And did you tell Mr. Stringer that 'twas Mr. Block kissed *my* hand first? When I done hired him with his own money?"

"Well, Mr. Stringer didn't ask me—"

"No, o' course you didn't see fit to mention that."

"Well, but—"

"You know what, Mrs. Parsons? I would sure like a nice cuppa tea and a biscuit or two."

The woman's mouth dropped open.

"I think it's the least you could do, don't you, Mrs. P?"

"I don't serve the likes of you, Ruth Ann Riley!"

"Well, then. Maybe you'd best serve the hates of me...otherwise they might just find you in your bed asleep at night, huggin' your guilty conscience like a pillow." Ruth Ann smiled at her, real polite.

Ruth Ann sat on the same silk-upholstered settee and sank back into the butter pillows, but took no pleasure in them this time. She felt a different person from the girl who'd so readily given her hope and trust to Wilfred Block, Esquire.

Lo and behold, she got her tea—with sugar, no less—and two fine shortbread biscuits, with strawberry jam.

In due course, Block arrived in his shiny black Model T, hat set at a more rakish angle than it had been on the way to the Amherst County Circuit Court.

He entered the parlor with gravitas, turned down the offer of tea from the now-simpering Mrs. Parsons and soberly handed his coat, hat and driving gloves to her before turning to his client. "Ruth Ann. I trust you are...well? I was told of an incident..."

"I'm fine, thank you." She took a sip of her tea. "But my sister Bonnie is not." She set the cup down in its saucer and stared him right in the eyes. "Doc Price must-a done her surgery the day after he testified in court, and afore I got back."

Block averted his gaze and became unaccountably fascinated with his own waistcoat.

"That tells even a feebleminded gal like me that Doc knew which way the judge was leanin' on the case."

Block sat down in the chair opposite her. "No, Ruth Ann. That's an assumption on your part—"

"And you did, too."

"Now, the Virginia legislature passed a law that upholds such surgeries as the one performed upon young Bonnie, so—"

"Don't you stand there and flap your gums at me, all legal-like."

"I *beg* your pardon? Dr. Price did nothing wrong—"

"Nothin' wrong? There's *nothin' wrong* in *slicing open an eleven-year-old child* for no good reason? No reason other than to stop her havin' a baby that the good Lord might put there someday? Who gave Doc Price the right to play God? You tell me that, Mr. Block!"

"My dear Ruth Ann—"

"Don't you 'my dear' me, *Wilfred*." She used his Christian name deliberately, even if it felt strange coming out of her mouth.

He gaped at her.

Shocked, was he? Why was it fine for him to call her Ruth Ann, while it was some kind of terrible manners for her to call him Wilfred? Who had set him above her, anyways? Why was he all high and mighty, while she was some kind of lowly serving wench? How had God decided that he would go to university an' law college, while she could only finish the sixth grade? How had God decided that his father would survive to pay for that college, while hers would not?

And did everything boil down to dollars?

She thought of the one he'd dropped on the rug, right there. How it had hooked her like a trout and then he'd reeled her in. Self-loathing almost suffocated her.

The silence between them stretched on. "I understand that you are…emotional…about your younger sister, Ruth Ann—"

"Do you? Congratulations, Wilfred. You'd have to be a damn turnip not to."

"But this hostility is—"

"You used me. Plain and simple. You're using all of us."

"I—I—what hysterical nonsense is this?"

"You're using Momma, you're using me, and shame on you: you're using my little Annabel. And don't think I'm so feeble-minded as not to notice that you surely didn't fight real hard for me in that courtroom, Mr. Block."

His face went pale. "What gibberish are you spewing now, Miss Riley?"

She'd somehow scored. "It ain't gibberish. I ain't hysterical. And guess what, *Esquire*? I ain't feebleminded! I done some thinkin', while I was tied to my bed in the loony bin. I done a lot of non-loony thinkin'. And it just don't make sense that I done real well in school, an' finished the sixth grade, but all's a sudden, when I'm old enough to milk a cow an' do the wash an' cook a supper by my ownself, that it don't make no sense to leave me in school, on account of I can now earn my keep. And did you know that the Dades rented me out to other families, too, for money?"

"Miss Riley, I must say, how is it possible that you blame me for a decision that was made years before we met?"

"I ain't blamin' you for that. And I ain't blamin' you for the Dades kickin' me outta their home after I got taken 'vantage of and got knocked up, neither. I ain't blamin' you for them all's a sudden declarin' me feebleminded an' stickin' me here in this Colony where I don't belong, just on account of I had to be hid from decent folk.

"But I sure as hell *do* blame you, Esquire, for pretending to work *for* me, when we both know now that you were workin' *against* me in that courtroom." Ruth Ann was surprised to find that her voice was trembling.

"Balderdash! Ridiculous nonsense. How dare you?" he blustered.

"How dare *you*, Block? Don't you lawyer fellas swear some kinda oath to do your job right?"

Block's face had gone pale; now it turned green. Another score for her. She was definitely onto something.

"I *have* done my job right, and I will continue to do it. I came here to tell you, Ruth Ann, that your case will now go to the Virginia State Court of Appeals."

"So you lost." She said it flatly.

"The judge decided in favor of the law," he corrected her.

"Right. You lost. Only question in my feeble mind, now, is whether you done lost *on purpose*."

Block turned the same beet color that Doc Price had, when she bearded him in his examination room. "You have the *effrontery* to suggest that I would—"

"Ain't got no clue what that word means, Esquire, but I'm pretty darn sure you ain't got my *backery*. Otherwise—a man like you—you'd be a lot more put out that you lost in court. Not down-right chipper to be appealin' to a new judge, a higher judge."

Mr. Block looked down his too-handsome nose at her, his green eyes unable to disguise his dislike of her. Low-class country girls weren't s'posed to speak truth to power, 'specially power disguised as kindness and charity, and Esquire—he didn't like it one bit.

"This interview is at an end," he snapped. "I will write my

briefs on your behalf and submit them to the court. I will keep you apprised of the decision."

"So I don't go to this higher court with you, Mr. Block?"

"There is no need for that. The court of appeals will rule solely based on the written transcripts, the exhibits and the legal briefs."

"But what if I want to get up in front of them judges and tell 'em like it is?"

"It's too late for that. The court of appeals is merely reviewing the lower court's decision to see if it agrees or not."

"Too late," she said flatly. "Well, ain't that convenient, Mr. Block. So now I just sit here at the Colony and wait?"

"Yes. And if the court of appeals shall uphold the circuit court's decision, then we will wait yet again while the Supreme Court decides whether to hear the case."

"How long's all this likely to take?"

"It's a matter of weeks for this appeal to be decided. With the Supreme Court, it may be a matter of months—or years."

"Well, I s'pose I'll pass 'em the usual way: doin' a few tons of laundry, choppin' and cookin'. Weedin' the gardens and harvestin' the vegetables. Canning what we don't use in the kitchens. And what will you be doin' to pass the time, sir?"

"I am very busy in my legal practice, as you know, young lady."

Ruth Ann nodded. "Oh, indeed. Writin' up your legal papers to do your best by your clients. Enjoyin' the company of your dear friends Mr. Stringer and Doc Price."

The lawyer's face went from beet-colored to eggplant-colored. "I *beg* your pardon?"

"Well, an' you should, Esquire," Ruth Ann said calmly. "You should. I surely wish I'd never met you, sir."

"Likewise. Good day, Miss Riley."

"Good day, Mr. Block." Ruth Ann didn't get up from the settee as he stalked to the door. She calmly finished her shortbread biscuits and tea.

Mrs. Parsons made sheep's eyes at him while helping him with his coat and seeing him out. As his motorcar purred to life, she whirled. "You were unconscionably rude, Ruth Ann!"

"Was I." Ruth Ann got up and walked calmly over to her.

Mrs. Parsons backed up three steps and eyed the telephone again.

"Well, I quite enjoyed it." Ruth Ann handed her empty plate, cup and saucer to her.

Mrs. Parsons goggled at this fresh outrage. "You don't deserve for that fine gentleman to work on your case, and that's a fact," she spat.

Ruth Ann's mouth twisted. "You're quite right, ma'am. I don't deserve it." And she brushed past her, opened the door and walked out without another word.

After an interview with a head doctor on staff and a solemn promise of good behavior, Ruth Ann was allowed to visit Bonnie and go back to living in the female dormitories. Evidently, the Distressed unit needed her bed for someone even crazier than she was. Sheila would get a new victim to gnaw upon.

When Ruth Ann went to the infirmary, the attending nurse eyed her as if she had escaped from the zoo. Clearly, once again, the rumor of her attack on Dr. Price preceded her.

But Bonnie lit up at the sight of her. "Ruthie! Where did you go? I missed you."

"Hi, darlin'." Ruth Ann kissed her on both cheeks and hugged her for good measure. "I, well, I had to go somewhere for a few days."

"Back to the courthouse?"

"Somethin' like that. How are you feelin', honey?"

"I'm good. It doesn't hurt as much down there. And look!" Bonnie held up Calico Bear, who was now smartly dressed in a burlap coat with neat lapels and two brown buttons. He also wore a matching burlap hat with a feather in its band. "See what Glory and Izzie made me? And Clarence found the fabric and the feather for the hat."

A lump swelled in Ruth Ann's throat, making it impossible for her to speak. Despite the tiff they'd had, Glory had come through. She hadn't taken out her anger at Ruth Ann on her helpless little sister. And she'd set a good example for Izzie, who desperately needed one.

"Doesn't he look nice?"

"Calico Bear looks like the cat's pajamas," Ruth Ann managed, when she could speak. "He sure does. Did you say thank you to Miss Glory and Izzie and Clarence?"

"Yes. And Clarence brought me chocolate cake from the kitchens today."

There were dark brown crumbs scattered across Bonnie's white blankets. "I can see that. Was it good?"

Her little sister nodded. "I had it with fresh milk that Izzie got from the cows."

Bonnie glowed. The color had come back to her cheeks, and she looked like herself again: a Swedish doll from a bandbox, not a pale, listless wax figure.

It's your fault, Ruthie, that she'll never have no babies. Sheila's words echoed through her mind again and again. *Your fault. Your fault. Your fault.*

Ruth Ann sat down on the bed next to Bonnie and took her small hands. She squeezed them. And she looked into those blue eyes, the eyes that told her she walked on water. *Float like a witch, more like.* The trust and love she saw there gutted her more than anything nasty that Sheila could say.

"What?" Bonnie said, puzzled.

"Nothing, darlin'." There was simply no way to tell an eleven-year-old that she'd never be a mother and that her sister was partly to blame for that. It wasn't a conversation that she *ever* wanted to have, but one day she'd be obliged to. "I'm just so glad you're feelin' better."

"Did Dr. Price take out the disease? Is it all gone now?"

Ruth Ann bowed her head. "It's all gone now."

Ruth Ann found Glory in the kitchens, covered in flour and kneading bread.

"Hi," she said to her, awkwardly. "Thank you for making the coat and hat for Bonnie's Calico Bear."

Glory looked up at her but didn't stop kneading. Tension rose in the air along with the loose flour. "You're welcome," she said, after a pause that made Ruth Ann think she might not speak to her at all. "Couldn't disappoint the poor mite, now, could we?"

She was so relieved that Glory wasn't just lookin' right through her an' stayin' mute that her knees almost gave way. She flattened her hand on a cabinet door to steady herself. "There's lots of adults who disappoint children, Glory. I'm just glad you're not one of 'em. It was real nice, what you did."

"Well, Clarence brought me the fabric, and Izzie was dyin' to help." Glory took her hands off the dough and dusted them on her apron, searching Ruth Ann's face. "You all right? The grapevine's been buzzin' and you been missin' from your bed. They say you got locked up with your ma."

"That's where I was. But I'm out now—thank the good Lord. Doc Price coulda left me there a lot longer."

"They're sayin' how he coulda left you there all your life, after what you did. Declared you a dangerous lunatic."

Ruth Ann nodded. "I'm not sure why he let me out, truth to tell. I just got told they need the bed for some other crazy."

"You're not crazy."

"No. But I did go right 'round the bend when I heard what Doc done to Bonnie. Never been so mad in my life."

Glory compressed her lips, took the dough in both hands and started slammin' it on the kitchen counter. *Blam! Blam! Blam!*

Made Ruth Ann want some dough to abuse, too.

Then Glory started punchin' it with her fists. *Thwack! Thwack! Thwack!*

Ruth Ann hesitated. "Lookit, Glory—when we argued—"

"I still want to see my baby." Glory caressed the dough now as if it were a newborn.

"I know, and I wasn't meanin' to say I won't help you. We just got to be smarter about it than we was before, with Annabel. I been thinkin'. If you are the poster child for good behavin' here at the Colony, and you was to ask, real polite, if you could write a letter to Lily's foster mother, I'll bet you they'll say yes. An' then maybe if she writes back, you can ask if you can see Lily sometime."

Glory's lips quivered. "An' what if the answer is no?"

"Well, then we'll come up with a different plan. I promise you that one day I'm leavin' this place for good, and I'll help you get out, too, if you want."

Glory stopped kneading the bread. "Where you gonna go?"

"I don't rightly know. But I do know that I don't belong here. I ain't feebleminded, no matter how many times they tell me I am. I can read, I can write, I can do my figures. They just brought me here because I got knocked up and couldn't be around decent folk. I'm bettin' that's what they did with you, too."

"They brought me here on account of my daddy beat me black and blue and kicked me to the curb. Didn't have noplace else to go."

Ruth Ann remembered the details in Glory's file. The notations about the bruises. "But your file says your daddy's whereabouts are unknown."

"I know exackly *whereabouts* he is," her friend said bitterly. "In his own home, whereabouts he's always been. He just don't want his whore of a daughter there with 'im."

"Oh, Glory…"

"I'll tell you whose whereabouts really are unknown," she continued. "And that's my baby's father. Mr. Marriage Proposal an' Scram. Didn't take so well to my daddy comin' for 'im with a shotgun."

"Did you go to school, Glory?"

"Sure. Through fifth grade."

"An' you can read an' do figures?"

"Yeah. I ain't the sharpest knife in the drawer, but I'm at least *in* the drawer."

Ruth Ann laughed, but the funny faded pretty darn quick. "Then you ain't feebleminded, neither. You're just like me—they had to put you somewheres."

"But…" Glory punched the dough again. *Thwack!* "But we ain't *things*. Objects to be *put* somewhere. In a drawer or in a closet or in a Colony."

"Oh, now, Glory." Ruth Ann shook a finger at her. "We are farm animals for breedin' and for labor. We are weeds, choking off the garden vegetables. Don't you go thinkin' that we're actual *people*."

Her friend gave a wan smile. "No, indeed."

Thirty-Two

The Colony had changed under the supervision of Carlotta, who was even-tempered and still led a Bible study once a week in the dorms. A good number of the girls preferred it to the Sunday sermon in the Colony's chapel.

Carlotta was no pushover, but she was fair, and she'd never struck so much as a horsefly in her life. She praised instead of criticizing. She delegated tasks to those who were most suited for them and actually exhibited gratitude on their completion. She created a lending program for the books in Tremont House's library and encouraged the girls to read. Ruth Ann no longer had to sneak books off the shelves, stuff them under her apron and read them in a corner or in the laundry at night.

Ruth Ann petitioned Carlotta for the Fawleys' address on Glory's behalf. She helped Glory write her letter to them, asking about baby Lily and whether she might perhaps be allowed to meet her one day. They posted it and waited.

Ruth Ann continued to teach Clarence to read, and he enjoyed Huck Finn every bit as much as he had Tom Sawyer. He liked Charles Dickens's *Oliver Twist* and *A Tale of Two Cities*, then branched out to *Treasure Island* and *The Count of Monte Cristo*.

Bonnie's taste ran more to *Anne of Green Gables*, *A Little Princess*, and *The Secret Garden*.

Glory and Izzie liked to sew, rather than read, though Izzie allowed that *The Wind in the Willows* was a fine book.

Louisa, Izzie's doll, and Calico Bear became quite the fashion icons, with an extensive new wardrobe. Louisa had rolled stockings with tiny garters, three different cloche hats and a flapper dress with a tiny set of opera-length pearls. Not to be outdone, Calico Bear had a shirt, trousers with suspenders, overcoat, newsboy cap and even—courtesy of Clarence—a minuscule pocket watch and cigar.

Louisa and Calico Bear liked to arrive at Colony social events arm in arm, and they were the envy of all the girls there. So eventually Glory and Izzie found themselves leading sewing workshops—which was fine with Carlotta as long as everyone also did mending work and made napkins, tablecloths and sheets.

And the day came when Clarence was pressed into service, since of course Calico Bear and Louisa needed a house to live in…and so did the other dolls and creatures who began timidly to emerge from pockets, pillowcases and crevices, since Mother Jenkins was no longer there to burn them or give them away.

Clarence could indeed do carpentry work with the help of clamps, and he enlisted other young men to assist. Izzie insisted on learning how to use a hammer, planer and saw herself—outdoing most of the boys who felt such things were their domain.

It was November of the next year before Ruth Ann saw Mr. Block again. She was summoned out of the laundry and came running up to the main building with sweat circles under her arms and burns on her calloused hands. Mrs. Parsons turned up her nose at Ruth Ann's appearance, while Mr. Block looked down his.

Ruth Ann resisted the urge to raise up an arm and fan the fumes at them both—them that worked in nice, cool surroundings without the taint of physical labor. She did park her sweaty behind right down on the settee without bein' asked and leaned against the butter-feather pillows while Esquire told her that the Virginia Supreme Court of Appeals had upheld the circuit court's opinion.

"Miss Riley, we are very disappointed," Block said in professionally somber tones. He wore a suit more beautiful than himself, and that was sayin' something. But come to think of it, he looked more like a sculpture than a man. And whereas she'd once found his face mesmerizing, the perfect symmetry of it now put her off. His cold green eyes made her feel like prey; his chiseled lips looked machine-cut.

"Quite disappointed," he repeated.

"Are you, now?"

"Of course." But Esquire could not seem to meet her eyes. "I argued that the circuit court had erred in its judgment and order, and I raised three constitutional objections upon your behalf, regarding due process under the Fourteenth Amendment, equal protection under the Fourteenth Amendment, and cruel and unusual punishment under the Eighth Amendment."

Ruth Ann tried to be more polite. "And just what does all that mean, Mr. Block?"

"What it means is that the law must treat you equally to every other citizen of these United States, and that it must not impose cruelty upon you in performing the operation."

"All right. Well, if not every woman in the country has to have it, then they're not treatin' me equal, are they?"

"That is what I hope the United States Supreme Court will decide."

"An' as for it bein' cruel, just ask my ma, my little sister an' my friend Glory how nice it is to have your belly sliced open. It hurts like the dickens for two weeks."

"Again, we can only hope that the court will understand that."

"An' how long will it take the Supremes to decide?"

Mr. Block coughed. "The, ah, Supremes, as you call them, must first decide whether to hear your case, Ruth Ann. Then, assuming that they decide in the affirmative, it may take months before they reach a decision."

"And can I go talk to them this time?"

"No, Ruth Ann, I'm afraid not. As with the prior appeal, the case is decided upon the written records, the arguments the attorneys file in briefs and the judges' interpretation of the law. But, in light of our last discussion, I did also say in my brief that you didn't have enough opportunity to object to the evidence presented at your trial or to argue against the testimony of the expert witnesses brought in by the State."

"All right."

Block raised his eyebrows and waited. Waited for what? For her to say thank you?

Grudgingly, she did. Perhaps he was trying to do right by her? Perhaps she'd listened too much to Momma and jumped to conclusions she oughtn't? Ruth Ann doubted that strongly. And she had a mountain of washing still to do.

"You're welcome, Ruth Ann." Block stood, his gaze once again leveling on the sweat stains under her arms. Not a drop of perspiration marred even his forehead, despite the heat of the afternoon and his three-piece suit.

She wanted to ask him if he'd like to step into her shoes for a few hours, swap the law for the laundry. See if he didn't perspire a bucket or two.

But she was beyond her aggression and temper of a year ago. She knew lashing out only got a body locked up and tied to a bed or sedated. Anger wasn't the way to get out of the Colony. Good behavior was.

"I shall keep you apprised," Mr. Block said.

Up-rised? She riddled on the word as he stood up. She figured she'd done uprised already. She was all through with that.

He eyed a bleach stain on her skirt as Mrs. Parsons brought him his coat and hat. "In the meantime, don't let me keep you from your…duties."

Ruth Ann was clearly dismissed.

"Thank you, Mrs. Portman," he said, as he made his way to the door.

"Parsons, sir. It's Mrs. Parsons."

Block didn't bother to respond.

At the board meeting five months later, Dr. Price claimed his seat at the head of the long walnut table, releasing an expansive breath. He would at last be on the map of medical history—there was no doubt. This court case was leading to the culmination of his professional dreams.

The rest of the gentlemen filed in, graciously providing Mrs. Parsons with their coats and hats. She had laid out refreshments, as usual, but this time on the sideboard were several chilled bottles of prohibited French champagne.

Mrs. Parsons disapproved strongly of spirits, but today she turned a blind eye to the bottles and made sure the crystal flutes on their silver serving tray sparkled under the light of the chandelier. This was a momentous occasion, after all.

Anselm Stringer came in, looking dignified and august, repressing a touch of smugness. He went immediately to talk with Dr. Price, while Mrs. Parsons greeted Wilfred Block and took extra care with his fine leather gloves, shaking off his hat and going so far as to brush the shoulders of his coat for him before she hung it up.

"Thank you, Mrs. Pressley," he said, without noticing.

"It's Mrs. *Parsons*, sir," she corrected.

"Yes, yes, of course." With an absent smile and a brush of his sleeve, he was off to the table, interrupting Stringer and clapping Dr. Price on the shoulder.

Mrs. Parsons stared after him, looking a little less enamored than usual. In fact, she looked quite cross. She smoothed her lace collar, checked her hair in the reflection of the breakfront at the far end of the room and collected from it, of all things, the crystal salt and pepper shakers. These she slipped into the pocket of her apron. How curious.

But Price was soon distracted by his guests and faintly amused when Wilfred had the gall to slip into the seat at his right hand, forcing a clearly annoyed Anselm to sit to Price's left.

Once everyone else was seated, Dr. Price nodded at Mrs. Parsons. A house boy uncorked the champagne and aided her in pouring it into the glasses. It popped, bubbled merrily and frothed away.

With a lovely, genteel smile, Mrs. Parsons personally served the three of them: Price, Block and Stringer.

"Thank you, dear lady," Dr. Price said.

Stringer murmured his thanks.

"My deepest gratitude, Mrs. Porter." Block accepted his flute with a flourish.

She nodded. "Of course."

Once every man at the table had a glass of the bubbly, Dr. Price stood. "I'd like to make the very happy announcement that thanks to Anselm Stringer and Wilfred Block, our case, *Riley v. Price*, will shortly be considered by the Supreme Court of these United States!"

"Hear, hear!" a banker shouted, as they all began to clink glasses.

"Marvelous news!" This from a real estate mogul.

"Congratulations, good fellows!" warbled a professor.

"Hip, hip hooray!"

Clink, clink, clink. And more *clink*s.

Stringer allowed himself a modest smile.

Block looked like a panther who'd just been served veal scallopini topped with foie gras. The man was truly insufferable. But a means to the end. Dr. Price kept his expression benign as they all took a long, celebratory draft of champagne.

And then, inexplicably, Wilfred Block blew most of his out of his nose, then awkwardly gargled the rest before spitting it onto the fine walnut table.

"Good God, man, what's the matter?" Price asked.

"Did you sneeze while swallowing?" Stringer queried.

The banker laughed. "Drinking problem, old sport?"

Tomato-faced, Block sputtered and fished out a handkerchief, spitting into it and then mopping his mouth. His livid gaze searched and then settled upon none other than Mrs. Parsons.

Dr. Price cast a discreet glance at the remainder of Block's champagne and beheld a peculiar white residue in the bottom of the flute. And a few faint black specks chasing one another through the bubbles. And it was then that he understood .the seasoning in her apron.

Naughty, naughty, Mrs. Parsons.

He fought to not laugh as Block excused himself for the gents'.

Then he picked up the man's glass and tilted it at her, crooking a finger.

Meekly she came over. "Yes, Dr. Price?"

"Let's get him a new glass of champagne, shall we? I discern some, ah, *dust* on the rim of this glass."

"Oh, *dear*. My sincerest apologies! Yes, of course, Dr. Price."

After Wilfred recovered and reappeared, she made herself scarce until the party was under way again.

The old pastor, seated at the opposite end of the table, hadn't touched his champagne. "I don't drink," he said. "For the record, it's against the law...not that I'll snitch to the Temperance League. But isn't it a bit early to celebrate, gentlemen? After all, we don't know what decision the court will make."

Anselm Stringer addressed him. "The court is packed with progressives such as Taft, Brandeis and Holmes. The only justice we're concerned about is perhaps Butler, since he's not...one of us. He's a *Catholic*." Stringer pronounced the last word with distaste.

"We feel very confident about the outcome of *Riley v. Price*," Block said, picking up his new glass of bubbly and peering closely at the contents before he drank. He glared at Mrs. Parsons, who eyed him back limpidly. "The science is irrefutable. The research is sound. The witnesses are plentiful. The arguments are eloquent."

"You're not afraid that it's bad luck to celebrate beforehand?"

Block shook his head and smirked. "Bad luck for Ruth Ann Riley, perhaps."

As the afternoon wore on, he consumed very little food and more than his fair share of champagne, beginning to stagger about like a bantam cock with a peg leg. Finally, Dr. Price took one arm and Anselm Stringer the other, as they helped Block to the door.

"Let me get your coat and hat for you, Mr. Bleak," cooed Mrs. Parsons.

"It's Block." He eyed her coldly, glassily. "Diju...s-season my drink, madam?"

"I beg your pardon, sir?" She looked at him quizzically, while Price stroked his beard to hide his smile.

"Diju…" He pointed at her. "Salt 'n' pepper?"

"My dear sir, I think perhaps the spirits have gone to your head," she suggested gently.

"Mrs. Parsons!" He waggled his finger. "You *know*…whah you did."

"I do?" She blinked and looked askance at Dr. Price. "The gentleman's none too steady on his feet, Doctor. Shall we have Clarence drive him home?"

Price stroked his beard again and nodded. "I think that's an excellent idea, Mrs. Parsons. Thank you."

Once the door had closed behind Block, he turned toward her and lifted an eyebrow. "Don't forget to return the salt and pepper shakers to their rightful place, madam."

A renegade dimple made an unexpected appearance next to her normally prim mouth. "I'm sure I don't know to what you're referring, Doctor."

"Tell it to the pastor, Mrs. Parsons," he said dryly.

Thirty-Three

S ix months later, Ruth Ann was chopping a great pile of onions, potatoes and carrots for stew when Clarence came running up, breathless, with the newspaper. He slapped it against the window next to where she was working and jerked his head in a gesture that she should come outside.

That, of course, set some of the gossips a-goin', but Ruth Ann just ignored them. She washed her hands at the sink and wiped them on her apron before going outside to see what Clarence was waving around.

His copper hair was a tousled mess, his eyes were the gray of the sky before a storm and his face had paled under the scattering of cinnamon freckles. "Ruthie, I don't think it's good news. Doc Price and them two lawyers who're always at them board meetings were just crowin' over it, along with about a gallon o' their 'iced tea.'"

Ruth Ann took the newspaper he handed her with shaking hands.

Three Generations of Imbeciles Is Enough!

So says Supreme Court Justice Oliver Wendell Holmes, Jr., in an historical and groundbreaking

Supreme Court decision that weighs the rights of the individual against the rights of society. This is a great victory for progressive reform in these United States, and the Post wishes to recognize it as such.

Justice Holmes has written the majority opinion for Riley v. Price, a case that upholds the Commonwealth of Virginia's right to sexually sterilize the feebleminded and degenerate of society so that they cannot reproduce more of the same.

This case is about applying the science of good breeding, or eugenics, to mentally, morally and physically unfit wards of the state. These individuals either cannot or will not support themselves. They live at great cost to the state and are a menace to society.

Proponents of eugenics theory have long argued that sterilizing these problem citizens is akin to weeding a garden or genetically engineering healthier stock or plants. Doing so is simple, quite safe and is similar to the principle of compulsory vaccination: to ensure the public health.

Ruth Ann Riley, the plaintiff in Riley v. Price, is the second in three generations of feebleminded women of loose morals. Her mother, Sheila Riley, has been estimated to have a mental age of eight years. Ruth Ann herself has been estimated to have a mental age of nine years. She has already given birth to one illegitimate child, daughter Annabel Riley, who, in the opinion of a social worker, a nurse and a doctor, is also not of normal development.

For this reason, in the Court's estimate, Ruth Ann

Riley is the probable producer of degenerate or feeble-minded offspring and should be sexually sterilized. Three generations of her family have been marked by feeblemindedness—the first two by immorality; the third, also a female, is at high risk of such.

Mr. Justice Holmes, arguably the preeminent legal mind of our times, has written the opinion for the eight-to-one majority. Justice Butler dissented.

"What's it say?" asked Clarence anxiously.

Ruth Ann swallowed hard. "So Mr. Justice Holmes is sayin' my family's got all the real, real stupid people it needs, and we don't need no more."

"Well." Clarence sounded angry. "Who asked him?"

Ruth Ann grimaced. "We did. Leastways, my fine lawyer did."

"So then he's sayin' Doc Price can do that surgery on you, Ruthie? Same's what he done to Glory and Bonnie?"

"Yeah," she whispered. "I still don't rightly know what *degenerate* means, but it ain't good. Offspring, even though it sure sounds like a handspring, is babies. Mr. Justice Holmes is basically sayin', Clarence, that it's better for the world to stop people like us from havin' babies."

Clarence stood stock still for a long moment. "That's what justice says?"

"Yeah." Ruth Ann had gone back to that numb place where she couldn't feel anything. She almost wished she had a hot iron to drop on her toe. But she was long past that.

"Well, we ain't stupid, just not schooled much. And we ain't no criminals, neither. So I don't think that's very *just* justice," Clarence said.

"Nor do I. But it ain't up to us feebleminded folks," Ruth Ann said bitterly. "People like them make up the justice, and people like us put up with it."

Clarence grabbed the newspaper and flung it to the ground. He took her hand in his own larger one and squeezed it. "Ah, Ruthie."

She closed her eyes and let him draw her forehead against his shoulder. She let him slip his arm around her waist.

"It'll be okay," Clarence promised. "You'll see."

It wouldn't be okay, but it was nice to hear the words, just as it was nice to have a shoulder to lean upon. They were in short supply, shoulders like Clarence's.

"Yeah," she said, "I s'pose it will be. If I have the surgery, Mr. and Mrs. Dade'll let me come back to their home, and then I'll be able to raise my little Annabel. Doc Price said so in court."

Clarence stiffened. "Ain't they the people what put you here in the first place?"

"Well, yeah...but that was on account of the baby. They didn't want no gossip goin' 'round about their good name."

"An' you think they've changed their minds about that? Why would they?"

"I—well, Doc Price said so. In court."

"And Mrs. Dade is the one who found you Esquire, isn't that right?"

"Well, yeah."

"Then I wouldn't trust that woman as far as you can throw her, Ruth Ann. Not to mention that fine nephew of hers who treated you so nice."

She winced. Blocked the memories yet again.

She tried not to think about being naked and helpless and once again under a man's power, even if he was a doctor. Even if the violation to her was for the good of society, and not for the pleasure or sick malice of the man.

But dark panic rose within her, spiraled up from a place deep inside, though she did her best to shove it right back down.

Clarence seemed to feel it right through her chest, through their clothing and through his own body. "Hey," he murmured. "Ruthie, what is it?"

Talking about problems only made them more real. Didn't do a body the slightest bit of good. "Nothin'," she whispered.

"Nothin's got you shook up pretty bad," he said. "Nothin's got your heart racin', fit to gallop right out of your chest."

She struggled to articulate the jumble of thoughts and emotions rushing through her mind and body. "Clarence, what happens to a woman if you take away what it means to be a woman?"

"Ah," he said. "And what makes a woman a woman?"

"Havin' babies," she said simply.

He held her away from him and looked deep into her eyes. "I think there's a lot more to a woman than that, don't you?"

She shrugged miserably.

"Take you, for instance, Ruthie. You'll always be everything it means to be a woman, whether you have more babies or not. You're strong. You're beautiful. You're smart. You're kind. You're one of the hardest workers I ever seen. You're a good friend, a good daughter, a good sister...I can go on and on."

Her eyes filled and streamed. "You're forgettin' de-botched and de-generous an' unfit an' imbecile." She smiled through her tears.

"No, on account of you are none of those things." Clarence wiped the tears away with the pad of his thumb—first the left eye, and then the right. "I don't care who says 'em: Doc Price or the Chief Justice o' the Supreme Court or even the Devil his ownself. Those things just ain't true."

"How do you know they ain't true, Clarence?"

"I know it because I *see* you, Ruthie. I see exactly who you are, right down to the core. I see your hopes and dreams and frustrations and temper. I see your tenderness and loyalty, your laughter and your love, and I also see when the hurt gets too much and hardens into hate for those who done you wrong. I see you. And you...I think you see me, the same way."

She nodded, more tears streaming down her face in rivulets, pooling in the corners of her mouth. Her breath caught in her throat as Clarence bent his coppery head forward and kissed them away.

"Now," he said when he raised his head again. His eyes twinkled with mischief. "I hear tell that you got plans to marry me, Ruth Ann Riley. It's hot gossip, all over the Colony. So when you gonna pop the question? Interested parties want to know."

She stared at him in horror. How had he heard about her shameless declaration? Who had told him such a thing? It had to have been Sheila, confound her. Her no-good, rotten, de-botched and de-generous momma.

Meanwhile, Clarence was grinnin' as wide as an alligator. Look at all them white teeth of his! Who knew the man had so many?

Ruth Ann gathered the scraps and shreds of her dignity about her. "I have *no* earthly idea what you are talkin' about, Clarence! Wherever did you hear such a...such a fantastic tale?"

"A little bird told me," he said, still showin' off every fang he could.

Little bird? More like a monstrous big buzzard.

"Well," she mustered. "Little birds has got little brains, so I wouldn't listen to 'em if I were you."

Clarence disappeared all them teeth and pulled a long face,

long as a donkey's. "You wouldn't? You would scotch the rumors and dash a fella's hopes?"

Ruth Ann drew herself up as tall as could be, squared her shoulders and raised her chin. "I do not know what kind of rattle-trap gossip you been listenin' to, Clarence, but I can tell you one thing: I am not so hard up as to have to beg *any* fella to marry me."

"Oooh, is that the way of it, then?" he asked.

Was that still a twinkle lurkin' in his eyes? Was he laughing at her? The man had a nerve.

"Yes, sir, it is." And without another word, Ruth Ann turned on her heel and marched back into the kitchens.

Thirty-Four

Doc Price didn't give her any advance notice of the surgery. One day in October, Ruth Ann was working in the kitchen when she was summoned from her baking duties. She was instructed to walk down to the Hallifax Infirmary for a test.

She exchanged a glance of alarm with Glory. They both knew what was going to happen. Glory dropped her rolling pin and left her pie crust on the butcher block to come and give Ruth Ann a hug. "Gonna be okay, Ruthie," she whispered in her ear. "I love you, honey. Now you just be brave, and you'll be up an' about in no time. Just like me. Good as new."

Glory flashed her a too-bright smile when Ruth Ann pulled out of her embrace. "It don't even hurt that much," she lied. "I was just bein' a sissy."

Ruth Ann nodded, though she well remembered Glory's face, white and waxy with pain.

She could handle pain. She always had been stoic that way. What was harder to handle was the idea of never having a family of her own. "Glory," she said urgently. "Will you tell Clarence?"

Glory nodded. "I surely will."

"Where are Bonnie and Izzie?"

"They're off picking apples."

"Well. You let them know I'm fine, all right? Bring them down to visit after a couple of days?"

"Sure thing. It's all gonna be okay." Glory gave her another quick hug, and some of the other girls nodded and shot her glances of sympathy.

Ruth Ann stepped outside and was surprised to see Ruby standing there, along with a very large gentleman with bulging muscles. She understood immediately and shot them a grim smile. "You here to make sure I don't go bananas and stab some poor soul with a butcher knife?"

Ruby blew out a breath. "Somethin' like that. I'm sorry, child."

Ruth Ann lifted a shoulder, then dropped it again. "It's fine, Ruby."

"It ain't fine," she said angrily. "It's playin' God and messin' 'round with Mother Nature. It's askin' to pay a heavy price on Judgment Day, you mark my words."

"What I mean is that I won't make no scene, Ruby. You won't have to knock me down, nor hogtie me, nor carry me down there to the Stringer-Smythe Buildin'. I'll walk."

"You's different, chile, from last year. You surely is. What's come over you?"

"I'm tired of this surgery hangin' over my head, like some sword on a rope. I cain't avoid it, been tryin' too long. Now I just want it done and over with. An' then I want outta this place. I want to go home. To my sweet Annabel."

"The Dades gonna take you back in?" Ruby said, her voice full of doubt.

"Doc Price said so in court. Said they'd like to have me back, long's I ain't no danger to society an' all."

"Hmmm" was Ruby's only response.

They all walked toward the infirmary together.

The fall leaves had broken out in brilliant color: yellows, oranges, and deep crimson vied to celebrate their last hurrahs before they'd drift silently to the ground and darken to brown.

A chilly autumn breeze blew the branches of the trees so that they waved their mantles of leaves like flags, doing their best to ward off winter. But winter would come anyway, just as it always did. Sometimes gently, with plenty of notice and last-minute appeals. And sometimes swiftly, with a vengeance, freezing everything in its tracks, leaving all living things in its wake frostbitten—white and icy and petrified.

Ruth Ann spied a solitary birch tree that was utterly bare already, save for one stubborn gold leaf clinging to a branch, refusing to turn and refusing to fall. A squirrel sat chattering on a lower branch, cheeky and gesticulating with its tail.

Another tree, this one a red maple, was bursting with rich, scarlet leaves.

Nature makes about as much sense as human beings, Ruth Ann mused. Some trees got no more than one leaf. Others got hundreds. God struck some women barren and blessed others with a dozen children. Some poor souls died in infancy or before the age of ten; others lived to be ninety or a hundred years old.

She tried to imagine a tree goin' in front of a court of other trees, though. And makin' a case for the right to have leaves and blossoms and seeds to create other trees.

She tried to imagine nine great old trees putting their branches together in a huddle and shaking them no in a great fuss…then standing tall and tellin' the other trees that no, they'd decided to deny them their leaves and blossoms and seeds.

I am plumb crazy…

No, I ain't. What has happened to me and is still happenin' to me is what's crazy. Ruby is right. It goes against the laws of nature and of God.

But I don't expect that either Mother Nature nor God is gonna jump on into Doc's operatin' room and disrupt my surgery. The likelihood of that is not great.

The same two nurses who'd defended Doc Price from her were present, their expressions just as starched and white and disapproving as their caps and uniforms.

"Does she need a sedative?" one said to Ruby.

"No, she doesn't," Ruth Ann replied tartly.

Ruby shot her a warning glance.

The other nurse produced a clipboard. "You are here, Ruth Ann, for a salpingectomy."

That word again.

"I figured as much," she said.

"Would you like to have your mother present? We can send for her."

"*No*," Ruth Ann said, belatedly adding "thank you."

The nurse shot her a funny look. But Ruth Ann didn't bother to try to explain to a stranger.

"We'll put you in a hospital gown, and then you'll lie down here on the operating table. We will give you anesthesia, which is something to make you sleep. Dr. Price will do a very short, simple operation on your fallopian tubes, and then you'll wake up good as new. All right, dear?"

Don't you call me dear. Last time I was here, you slammed my face into a wall.

"Yes, ma'am," Ruth Ann said.

"You may go," the first nurse ordered Ruby and Mr. Muscles.

Ruth Ann wished more than anything that she could have another of Ruby's big, wonderful, kindly hugs. But it just wouldn't do, here in front of the medical staff. It was already close to revolutionary to have a black woman working here at a colony for whites—even if they were feebleminded, epileptic or degenerate.

Ruby sent her love with her warm, compassionate and lovely brown eyes. Moisture had gathered in them, it was true, but there was still plenty of room for love.

Ruth Ann didn't understand how she did it, but she felt it seeping into her, caressing her skin and sending the good kind of shiver down her spine. The love felt like a soft red blanket, and Ruth Ann wrapped herself in it, snuggled down. She used it to ward off all the forbidding white and the cold steel and the horrid reality that they were going to cut her open and mess about with her organs. She used it to deny that no children would populate her future.

She used it to stay calm and warm as Doc Price came in and flapped his gums about all manner of medical mumbo jumbo, and the nurses settled a mask over her face and told her to count backward from twenty.

You don't scare me, Doc. I'm gonna wake up and leave you all behind. Nineteen, eighteen, seventeen, sixteen, fifteen, fourteen, thirteen...

Somebody had drawn a nasty smile across her belly with a white-hot poker. Ruth Ann woke soaked in sweat and in blinding pain. The kind of pain that made a person wish she'd never wake again. Oh, dear God, where was the blessed, black numb unconsciousness? *Bring it back, please...*

She gasped for relief.

"Ruthie!" Clarence's voice penetrated the pain. "Oh, thank the good Lord. You've gone an' woke up at last." His voice was unsteady. "I was afraid you'd not ever wake again. You been so still and pale as death."

She wanted to tell Clarence how glad she was to hear his voice, rough and husky and full of some unnamed emotion—as well as relief. She wanted to say, *Thank you for being here, at my side. Thank you that I didn't wake up alone.*

But the pain torched her powers of speech; all she could do was moan.

"Ruthie? You all right?"

"*Noooo.* Oh, God, Clarence, it hurts…"

"Nurse!" he called. "Nurse—she's awake, but you gotta give her somethin' more for the pain."

Ruth Ann was dimly aware through the shrieking of her nerves that someone in white bustled around next to her, shoved a thermometer into her mouth and took her blood pressure. Then a needle went into her arm, and everything blessedly faded to black again.

When she next woke, she had no idea how much time had passed.

"Ruthie?" Clarence's voice came again. "How you doin'?"

"I think Doc done confused me with a cantaloupe," she rasped in a voice that didn't sound like her own. "Am I in two halves? Or am I still a whole body?"

Clarence sucked in a breath and visibly swallowed fury.

"You m-mad at me, Clarence?" she asked. What had she done now?

"No, Ruth Ann," he said, his mouth working. "O' course not. I'm mad at what they done to you. I'm mad at Doc Price. I'm mad at these nurses what act like it's normal, all in a day's work. I'm mad at God for lettin' this happen. But I ain't mad at you. So never you mind. It don't matter."

His eyes changed slowly back from stormy dark to rainwater gray. "Aw, poor Ruthie. I'm so sorry, brave girl. But leastways it's over now."

Except for the pain. The pain most certainly was not over. It still burned in a horrible smile across her lower abdomen. She did wonder if her legs got out of bed, whether her top half would follow.

"It's over," he repeated. "Doc done his so-called simple operation on you."

"Simple operation?" She laughed weakly. "He set fire to my insides. *He* oughta feel it."

The storm came back to Clarence's eyes, and he cursed under his breath. "Yeah. He oughta. It hurts somethin' fierce, even on a man. Recovery time ain't as bad, though. I'll give you that."

He spoke as if he knew from personal experience. "Clarence?"

He changed the subject before she could ask. "Do you want some water, Ruthie?" He held a cup to her lips when she nodded. The water tasted like cool heaven, flowing past her parched lips and down her throat.

She swallowed, wincing at another chain of pain set off by the movement. Amazing how everything in the body was so intricately connected. Then she looked over at him, noticing how he stared into space, taking his mind somewhere else. Just as she did.

"Clarence...did Doc do it to you, too?"

A muscle clenched in his jaw. He refused to meet her gaze. Didn't answer.

"Did he?"

After a long moment, he swung back to face her, his expression bleak but defiant. "Yeah."

"Oh...Oh. I'm sorry—"

He punched the air with his stump. "Cain't have no circus freaks reproducin' more of their kind, eh, Ruthie?"

"Don't call yourself that. Don't you talk about my friend Clarence that way!"

He shot her a look of puzzled amusement. "Your friend Clarence?"

"Mmm-hmmm."

Without comment, he offered her more water.

"How long you been here?" she asked, wincing again as the swallowing kicked off more pain.

"Thirty-nine hours and twenty-three minutes," he said, after glancing at the clock.

"Thirty-nine...!"

"Been here since they wheeled you back from the OR." He smiled. "With one or two breaks when Glory and Bonnie and Izzie came to see you."

"I slept that long?"

"Well, you woke up shortly after the operation when the anesthesia wore off. But then they gave you morphine. So you sure have. Been talkin' in your sleep, wailin' in your sleep."

She didn't like to hear that. It made her feel even more vulnerable—mentally exposed. It was bad enough that she'd been physically exposed—stark naked and unconscious on a table, unable to move or protest or stop anything from happening to her body. She'd been no better than a carcass missin' a soul, a doctor and nurses slicin' and pokin' at her.

But now Clarence had heard her dreamin'...was nothing private anymore?

He seemed to sense that he'd made her uncomfortable, and he changed the subject. "Lookit: I brought you pink roses. You like 'em?"

Sure enough, at least a dozen of the most beautiful roses she'd ever seen hugged each other in a water pitcher on her infirmary nightstand. Their petals were like graceful folds of velvet. "Oh, Clarence," she breathed. "Those are...they are the loveliest flowers I ever seen. Wherever did you get 'em?"

Unmistakable mischief lurked in his eyes, and he tugged at his earlobe before answering her. "From somewhere's they got too many, and don't deserve to have any."

"What does that mean?"

"You really want to know where these beauties come from? You sure?"

She nodded.

"Well, I took me a moonlit stroll t'other night, when I knew Glory was sittin' with you for a spell and holdin' your hand. I walked me over to the Stringer estate—"

Ruth Ann clapped a hand over her mouth. "You did not!"

"Oh, yes, I did. An' that jackal lawyer's wife grows her a mighty fine garden. Afore I knew it, them roses were just flockin' to me, clamorin' to get rolled in some newspaper and come to visit you. Never knew roses could be quite so purposeful. But they was just bound and determined to come look in on you, Ruth Ann, and cheer you up." Clarence's eyes danced.

She did her best to look shocked and horrified, but she smiled instead. "Well. You tell 'em thank you for me. They're real pretty. I never had me any roses before."

"Never had you no roses? That is a scandal. What type o' fellas you been steppin' out with?"

She squinted at him. "No type. Don't need me any fellas. They are nothin' but trouble."

"Is that so?"

"Yep."

"All fellas?"

She slid him a look from under her lashes. "Most all of 'em."

"'Cept maybe…me?"

"Maybe," she allowed.

He smiled at her.

She smiled back.

Then he began to fidget. "You hungry, Ruthie? You want me to ask one o' the nurses to bring you somethin' to eat?"

Ruth Ann shook her head. "Thank you, though, Clarence. You sure are sweet."

"Sweet on you, Ruthie. And that's a fact." He took her hand and squeezed it.

"You shouldn't be sweet on a...a...Franken-female."

"A what?!" He hooted with laughter. "That's ridiculous."

"No, it ain't. I'm missin' parts now, an' got cuts and stitches, like Frankenstein's monster in Mary Shelley's book."

Clarence waved his stump at her. "I ain't read Miz Shelley's book. And I'm still sweet on ya—but then again, I'm just a circus freak who's no longer even a man."

Ruth Ann was outraged. "Don't you dare say that!"

"Well, then, don't you call yourself a Franken-female."

He had a point.

"We got a deal?" He squeezed her hand again and bent his head close to hers. "Deal?" he murmured.

She could fall into those rainy gray eyes. She nodded, and Clarence sealed it with a kiss, warm and firm and tender.

Ruth Ann found herself slipping into unconsciousness again and wondered if she'd dreamed his presence. Would he be here when she woke up?

Clarence was right there, sure and steady, the next time she drifted awake and gasped again at the searing pain in her lower abdomen. The first thing she saw when she opened her eyes was his dear, stubborn, freckled face, those sterling eyes fixed on her own. "I didn't dream you..."

Clarence smiled faintly and shook his head. "Hey, Ruthie," he murmured. His eyes darkened to stormy gray as he registered her agony. "How you feelin'?"

"Truth? Like I been sawed in half," she said, averting her gaze from him and looking in wonder at the bouquet of velvety pink roses.

His lips flattened and empathy and anger suffused his face. "I'm so sorry. I'd do anything to take away the pain. Anything."

She inhaled the scent of the flowers, forced her stiff, dry lips into a smile. "I know you would. Thank you."

"You hungry?" Clarence asked.

Ruth Ann shook her head.

"You gotta eat something soon. You don't eat it your ownself, they'll send a nurse to pour soup down your gullet from a beaker." He winked.

The thought of food was not appealing.

"Glory's got good news. She wanted me to tell you that she heard back from the Fawleys. They're gonna let her see little Lily."

Oh! Ruth Ann smiled. "So glad."

"She's makin' you a blackberry tart, just so's you know. Some of the other girls asked Carlotta if they could make you lemon snaps. She said yes."

Ruth Ann marveled at this. "Things sure have changed 'round here since Mother Jenkins went away."

"Thank the good Lord," Clarence said fervently. "If I'd heard once more that she'd laid a finger on you, I was gonna plot her murder."

Ruth Ann clapped a hand to her mouth, which hurt like the dickens. "Clarence, don't say such things."

He looked at her solemnly. "Well, all right. But I was."

"Shhhh!"

Footsteps echoed on the tiles behind him, and one of the more crotchety nurses said over her shoulder, "She's here in bed twenty-three. But, ma'am, I tell you this is no place for a toddler."

Ruth Ann couldn't believe it: Mrs. Dade had come to visit her. And in her arms was a wriggling, on-the-verge-of-a-tantrum Annabel. *Oh!*

Her eyes were the startling blue of a jay. And her hair…a rich chestnut. Scraped into two tight little pigtails on either side of a center part. She sported the same dent in her chin as Sheila…a portent of trouble. And there was a fresh smear of dirt on her little pinafore. She kicked her feet into Mrs. Dade's belly as the woman gasped.

Clarence stood up and doffed his cap. "Ma'am."

"Mrs. Dade!" exclaimed Ruth Ann. "*Annabel…*" Tears welled in her eyes.

"Down!" the child hollered, wriggling and kicking some more.

"Stop it at once, you little de—" Mrs. Dade broke off, crossly.

Demon? Ruth Ann was quite sure she hadn't meant to say *delight*.

Mrs. D took another kick to the kidneys, and gasped as Annabel shrieked and almost tumbled out of her arms.

Ruth Ann instinctively lunged to catch her and yelped at the vicious pain it caused.

That got Annabel's attention; the toddler hung by one arm and one leg and stared curiously at the strange lady in the white hospital bed. Ruth Ann stared back at her, mesmerized. Longing to take her into her arms and cuddle her—pain or not.

"How are you, dear?" Mrs. Dade almost growled, looking as though she'd like nothing better than to drop the child on her head.

Dear? Had Mrs. D lost her marbles?

"F-fine," Ruth Ann said, faintly.

"*Dowwwwn!*" shrieked Annabel, contorting like a wild orangutan.

Mrs. Dade looked to be on the verge of having kittens. She snapped the child upright and held her aloft by the shoulders. "Stop it, you horrid little hooligan," she spat. "Behave yourself!"

Annabel wailed and kicked Mrs. D in the stomach yet again.

Clarence stepped forward, smiling, his arms outstretched. "Mebbe I could spell you for a bit, ma'am?"

"She doesn't care for strangers," Mrs. Dade began, eyeing his stump with ill-disguised distaste. But she almost threw the child at him, her relief palpable.

"Hello there, baby doll," Clarence crooned, as Annabel quieted immediately in the crook of his arm and honked his nose. "Yes, thag you," he told her, "thad's one o' by best features."

She pulled on his left ear next, and to her delight, Clarence clucked like a chicken.

Annabel promptly pulled on his right ear, whereupon he mooed like a cow.

Entranced, Ruth Ann didn't even register that Mrs. Dade was speaking to her.

"Did you hear me? Something is very wrong with that child," Mrs. D said emphatically.

Ridiculous. Annabel was perfect, as anyone could see. She just didn't take well to disapproval and scolding. Who did?

"She's so beautiful," breathed Ruth Ann. "I can't wait to come home and take care of her…I just can't wait!"

Mrs. Dade lifted her eyebrows. "Are you daft?"

"It shouldn't be more than three weeks," Ruth Ann went on eagerly, her pain forgotten. "I'll be good as new, Doc says. Can I share my old room with her?"

"What on earth are you talking about, Ruth Ann Riley?"

"They said…" Ruth Ann faltered under Mrs. Dade's stare. "In court, they said…that if I agreed to the surgery that…"

Mrs. Dade clutched her pocketbook against her, her fingers whitening as she shook her head. Her expression was not without pity, but her next words were devastating. "I believe there has been some sort of misunderstanding. Elijah and I cannot take you back into our home, Ruth Ann. That is simply out of the question."

She may as well have been speaking a foreign language. "But—"

"I don't know who told you that it was even a possibility," Mrs. Dade went on, "but it can never happen…"

Ruth Ann watched her mouth move, one word blurring into the next: sour and incomprehensible, like curdled cream.

Clarence's big, warm hand settled on her shoulder and squeezed.

"…whatever would the neighbors think? Absolutely, categorically not. I'm sorry, Ruth Ann. Whoever told you that is rather heartless, I must say."

Ruth Ann had forgotten to breathe. When her body forced the issue, the air turned to gunpowder in her lungs, exploding as she choked on it, coughing and crying out with the pain.

Alarmed, Clarence thrust Annabel back into Mrs. Dade's arms and called for a nurse.

"Oh, dear. I just thought I'd visit, let her see Annabel while I'm here…I have an appointment with Dr. Price," her former foster mother said.

Two nurses came running. One shoved a needle into Ruth Ann's arm.

Before she lost consciousness, she heard Mrs. Dade say again, "There is something *very* wrong with this child. She's no relation to me. With that gene pool…I should have known better."

Annabel kicked and shrieked in the background.

Ruth Ann simply wanted to die. The last wraith of her hope had vanished.

Thirty-Five

D r. Price steepled his hands upon his massive desk while Mrs. Dade squirmed in the visitor's chair on the other side of it.

"I simply cannot keep her, Doctor. Annabel is...uncontrollable."

"She is a toddler," Doc pointed out. "They're not known for either grace or etiquette."

As if to emphasize these words, Annabel screeched like a dragon and went flying by the window, a laughing Glory in hot pursuit. She'd been assigned to babysit during this meeting.

"Doctor," Mrs. Dade said, "I should think that you, of all people, would understand that the child's geneplasm is...polluted. It is for that reason that the court sided with you on *Riley v. Price*."

He sighed and nodded. "Of course, Mrs. Dade. I sympathize with you. But I fail to see how I can help you."

"To be blunt—" Annabel took this moment to plaster her hands and face against the window, staring in at them with her nose and mouth squashed against the glass. "Stop that! Stop that at once, young lady!"

Glory peeled her off the glass and carried her away, shrieking and kicking, but she'd left disgusting smears upon it.

Mrs. Dade turned back to Dr. Price. "To be blunt, Doctor, my husband and I simply cannot handle this child any longer. Our nephew Patrick was found badly beaten and half dead in an alley recently…" She wiped away a tear. "I'm nursing him full time. We'd like you to take Annabel off our hands."

"Dear lady, I am sorry for your troubles, but I simply can't do that. We have no toddlers or babies in custody at the Colony. No child care."

Mrs. Dade looked down at her lap. "Doctor, I know that normally we would go back to the social worker on a matter like this. But Ruth Ann…she was apparently told by someone that following her procedure, she'd be allowed to return to our home to help care for Annabel."

Doc felt a flush rising in his face. He inserted a finger under his collar to loosen it, to no avail.

The woman before him seemed to sense his guilt and honed in on it. "She was very hopeful that she could do so. I had to dash those hopes."

"That must have been very difficult for you," Dr. Price said, grasping a sheaf of papers and straightening them.

"Well, it was. So I'd like to suggest—"

"No."

"Please hear me out. The child's mother and her grandmother are both here at the Colony—"

"The grandmother is a lunatic. The mother is a moron."

"—so she has an established family unit. There are other girls and women here who could help look after her."

"No, madam. I'm afraid this establishment simply does not function that way."

"Even temporarily? Because now that Ruth Ann has undergone the surgery, she's no longer a danger to society. She can be released, right?"

Dr. Price pursed his lips. "Theoretically."

"Why not put theory into practice?"

"She'd have to find a means of supporting herself."

"Yes. Or marry."

"I doubt she has many prospects, madam."

"I think there's a boy here at the Colony who's sweet on her. I met him at her bedside in the infirmary."

"You don't say."

"Clarence, I believe his name is?"

"The young man with only one hand? You must be joking."

Mrs. Dade shook her head.

"But how would he earn a living, with only..." Doc trailed off. "You know, against all odds, he's actually quite handy around here. It is possible that he could fend for himself—possibly even support a wife and daughter."

"And Ruth Ann—she could help out. She has domestic skills."

"Hmmmm." Dr. Price eyed Mrs. Dade and drummed his fingers upon the desk.

"So she can be given custody of her child, then, surely? Especially as she will never be able to have another?"

Doc leaned back in his chair and thought about it. "I suppose it's not altogether outside the realm of possibility."

Mrs. Dade looked quietly triumphant. "It would make me feel much better about all of this...to reunite them. I love the babies. And I'm happy to take in a child who's a little older and can be reasoned with, trained to help out. But for toddlers—and that one in particular—I have no patience."

Dr. Price gazed out the window, at the sight of Glory swinging Annabel in a circle, the two of them giggling madly.

"We haven't formally adopted her. So there wouldn't be any need to petition the court, because Ruth Ann is her biological mother, correct?"

He silently nodded his assent.

"So surely it's not complicated."

Dear Lord, was the woman trying to leave Annabel here *today*?

He frowned at her. "I'll need some time to think about this, madam."

She sighed, but nodded. "I understand. But surely you can see that this is the best possible solution?"

Dr. Price stroked his beard, then looked down at his papers again. "You may very well be right, Mrs. Dade. I'll be in touch with you shortly."

When Ruth Ann awoke, Clarence was somehow *still* there.

"Mornin', sleepyhead," he said.

"It's mornin'?" She took in the dim, gray light and the rustle of patients in the beds down the hall from them. She didn't much care. She would be stuck here for the rest of her days, separated from the only child she'd ever be able to have.

"Yep," said Clarence. "Brand-new day."

She shrugged. His gray eyes held a twinkle that she found downright annoying, given the circumstances.

"Them nurses keep tryin' to hustle me out of here," he said, "but I begged 'em to let me stay. I couldn't leave, what with you rehearsin' in your sleep an' all."

"Rehearsin'?" She was puzzled.

"Oh, sure. You are plumb dedicated to gettin' things just right." Clarence nodded. "An' I respect that about you."

"Gettin' what things right?"

"Your marriage proposal to me, o' course," Clarence said. "What else would you need to get right?"

"My...my..." Words failed her.

He raised his eyebrows and grinned at her.

"No!" Ruth Ann, scandalized, tried to sit up. Big mistake. Pain scorched through her in waves.

Clarence paled and swore under his breath. "Don't you move again, Ruth Ann," he said. "Aw right? Promise me."

"Yes," she said weakly.

"You want some water?"

She shook her head.

"Okay. Now, where was I? Oh, yeah. So you, Ruth Ann, were most certainly rehearsing your marriage proposal to me in your sleep."

"What?! No, no, no, I was not!"

"Were, too. You said to me, 'Clarence,' you said, 'you are the handsomest fella in all of these United States.'"

Ruth Ann managed a snort.

"'And the smartest fella, too—'"

"Even in your wildest dreams, Clarence—"

"'And the most likely to succeed in anything you choose to set your mind to, in particular circus-juggling…'"

"Stop it," she cried. "Laughing hurts."

"'And the heir to a great fortune and a castle in Europe—'"

"Oh, right."

"'And because, Clarence, you're a secret prince who done switched places with some low-born, one-handed fool—'"

"My, I do have quite the imagination," Ruth Ann said.

"That you do. So anyways, where was I? I mean, where was you? Oh, yes. You says to me, 'Clarence, because of all them things, I just cannot live without you. Will you do me the great honor of marrying me?'"

"I never said any of this. I never asked you," Ruth Ann said emphatically.

"I am quite sure that you did."

"Nope."

"Let's look at the evidence," Clarence suggested. "Who was under anesthesia? Me or you?"

"Me," she said reluctantly.

"Ah. And who was on morphine, me or you?"

"Most likely me."

"And who was asleep for thirty-nine hours and twenty-three minutes, me or you?"

"Me."

"Correct. Now, here's the kicker: do you have any witnesses at all who will testify that you did *not*, in fact, ask me to marry you?"

"No."

"Well, then. I rest my case. You did."

"Did not. I'm the girl. You're the boy. The boy does the asking."

"Well, all right. Seems silly to me," Clarence said. "But if you feel strongly about it, then I'll go ahead and ask you, instead."

"I didn't say…! Oh, Lord. I'm very confused," wailed Ruth Ann.

"Ruth Ann Riley," said Clarence, dropping to one knee. "Will you marry me?"

She gaped at him. "Clarence, what are you doin'? You get up off that floor this instant."

"No. Not until you say you'll have me." And Clarence pulled a ring, of all things, out of his pocket. It was a simple gold band with a tiny heart-shaped red stone set in it. It was the most beautiful thing Ruth Ann had ever seen, besides maybe Clarence's rainwater gray eyes.

"Where'd you get that?"

"Stole it."

"What?!"

"Kiddin'. I done saved me up a bushel o' tips over the years, from the motorcar polishin' an' such. I come by it honestly, I swear." His eyes held no humor now.

She swallowed the lump that had grown in her throat. "You really want to marry me?"

He expelled an exasperated breath. "No, Ruth Ann. I just go around collectin' pretty rings for my ownself. I figured I'd wear this one on my fourth toe."

"Clarence, be serious!"

"I am serious as all get out. Will you be my wife, Ruth Ann Riley?"

"But I cain't...you know I cain't...give you children."

"And I cain't give you none, neither."

"I thought I was goin' to go back an' live with—" Her voice broke. "The Dades."

"Those folks don't deserve you, and that's the truth." Clarence looked away into the distance, his jaw hardening. "I'd like to tell 'em just how much they don't."

Then his expression altered, softened, and he turned back toward her. "How 'bout you live with me instead? And we petition to get Annabel back?"

"*Oh!*" Ruth Ann couldn't speak more than that one syllable.

"You like that idea?"

Her eyes filled, then overflowed. She nodded.

"It may be one helluva fight. You know that, right?"

She nodded again.

"You up for it? Once you get up outta this bed?"

"Clarence," said Ruth Ann. "Really? When have you *ever* known me to stop fightin'?"

"Well, I'd really like for you to stop it right now, at least long enough to let me put this ring on your finger and tell you that I love you."

Ruth Ann gazed at him fondly through her tears. Clarence got back up off the floor. He took her left hand in his and then gently slid the ring onto her fourth finger, where it winked and glimmered under the hospital lighting.

"I've loved you since I first saw you," Clarence said, a bit too casually. "Loved you when I drained your toe. Loved you when I wheelbarrowed you to the dairy. I just didn't know you loved me back, not until—"

"Not until when? How did you know?"

"When you defended me to that old vulture what's goin' to be my mother-in-law," Clarence said with a grin.

"You *heard* that?"

"I did."

"You were eavesdroppin' on a private conversation!"

"How could I not, when the woman accused you of bein' sweet on me afore I got a yard out the door? I had to know the answer, Ruth Ann. You'd a done the same thing."

She glared at him, but didn't deny it...and then Clarence kissed her glare away. He kissed her pain away. He kissed her until an outraged nurse discovered them, squawked and threatened to report their immoral behavior.

Thirty-Six

D r. Price wore a three-piece suit with lots of authority and a kind smile.

He no longer looked like God to Ruth Ann. She was sure the Almighty didn't hang out here at the Virginia Colony for the Epileptic and Feebleminded.

A month had passed since her surgery. Outside, the wind had picked up, sending mini-tornados of leaves spiraling. Clarence hadn't raked them, because he wasn't here. He'd petitioned to leave the Colony two weeks ago and received permission.

Ruth Ann no longer cared what a storm might do to the mountains of laundry outside on the lines. She was here to discuss her own departure.

Doc checked his gold pocket watch and wrote down the time, while she turned the gold ring on her fourth finger, then turned it again so that the tiny ruby heart glimmered up at her.

She was glad to be here, the focus of his attention, on account of that meant he was takin' her wish to leave seriously.

Doc asked her questions and she answered them directly. She kept her mind here in the present, in the room.

"What's your name?"

"Doc, you surely know my name by now."

"Yes, but for the exit interview, I must ascertain that you know it, too. What is your name, patient #1743?"

She restrained herself from rolling her eyes. "Ruth Ann Riley."

"How old are you?"

"Nineteen."

"Do you plan to marry when you leave the Colony?"

"Yes, sir."

"To whom will you be married?"

"To Clarence, my fiancé."

"Where is he now?"

"At work in Lynchburg."

"And what is his employment?"

"He has a taxi and delivery service," Ruth Ann said proudly. "His own motorcar." With funds he'd saved from years of tips from visitors whose cars he'd polished, he had bought it used from a widow who didn't drive.

"And does he bring in sufficient income to support you both?"

"Yes, sir. He also does odd jobs."

"Where will the two of you live?"

"In the boardin' house where Clarence already rents a room."

"And he is willing to adopt little Annabel?"

"Yes, sir. He already thinks of her as his own."

"You are aware that you have been sterilized, Ruth Ann? And Clarence as well?"

She managed her answer without bitterness. "Yes, sir."

"And you are aware that this means you will never have more children."

Ruth Ann took a deep breath. *A lot you know, Doc. There's plenty of children out there just like me and Bonnie who need a home and people to love 'em, not use 'em for domestic help. We will petition the court for custody of Bonnie, too, if need be.*

What she and Clarence did with their lives after they left the Colony was none of the good doctor's business. But she nodded. "Yes, sir."

"Ruth Ann, do you feel capable of managing a household—such as it is, a room in a boardinghouse—on your own, given your mental state?"

She felt the old fury and helplessness rising but tamped it down. It would do her no good in this exit interview with Doc Price. She drowned her anger as she might have a pair of dirty trousers or a soiled pinafore in the laundry water. "Oh yes, sir. I got good trainin' an' all with the Dades and here at the Colony. Washin' and gardenin' and choppin' and cookin' and cannin'... I can do it all myself."

"Yes, indeed." He gave her that kindly old uncle smile. "You should be very proud of yourself, Ruth Ann."

She looked at all them diplomas on his wall: the one from some Latin preparatory school, the one from the two Johns Hopkins and the one from Harvard. *And you should be right ashamed o' yourself, Doc. All that knowledge, used to hurt people in the name o' the greater good.*

He snapped his fingers, recalling her attention. "Ruth Ann? I just paid you a compliment."

"Oh. Yes, sir. Thank you, sir." She forced herself to smile gratefully at him. The scar on her belly twinged and smiled at him, too.

He rounded his massive desk and stood next to her, gazing down fondly. "The Colony has done right by you, my dear. You have flourished here. And though you may be feebleminded, I have every confidence that you will succeed in building a life on the outside, you and Clarence."

Yeah, Doc? I got every confidence that we will, too. No thanks to you.

Doc Price dropped a hand on her shoulder and patted it.

She flinched, then froze and looked up at him. To her astonishment, he was misty-eyed.

He stroked his beard. "I know we've had our... misunderstandings...Ruth Ann. But you are one of God's children, one of *my* children, here at the Colony. And it is my life's work to take good care of my flock."

His self-delusion was downright appallin'.

I may be a child of God, but I surely ain't your child, nor am I a sheep. And in my "feebleminded" opinion, Doc, God is gonna have something to say to them lawyers an' you on Judgment Day for carvin' on His children. But that's neither here nor there...So please, will you stop gum-flappin' so I can get outta *here and go there?*

"I am sorry to see you leave," Doc said. He actually seemed to mean it.

Please, Lord, help me to not laugh...

"But it is the right thing for you to do."

Now that I'm no longer a danger to society, an' all?

"So I will approve your petition to be discharged from the Colony, Ruth Ann."

"Thank you, sir."

Doc nodded and patted her shoulder again. "You'll come back to visit your mother?"

"Yes, sir. And—once Clarence an' I got enough saved for a place of our own, can Bonnie come to live with us, too?"

"I think that's a splendid idea, Ruth Ann." Doc drew out his pocket watch and checked it. "Our time is up, my dear. I have to see another patient now."

An' good luck with that, Doc. You still, to this very day, do not truly see me.

She got up obediently. "Goodbye, Dr. Price," she said.

"Goodbye, my dear."

And in less than five seconds, Ruth Ann and her disrespect were outside his door, dismissed for the last time. She stood there for a moment, releasing the breath she hadn't been aware she was holding. Then she went to find Bonnie, say goodbye to Glory, Carlotta and the other girls and gather her things.

The bright blue Virginia sky was cloudless, the sun shining down upon her face in a warm welcome to the future. In the distance, the laundry swayed upon the lines, trousers kicking in the breeze and skirts dancing. A line of crisp white shirts flung up their sleeves at her, as if to salute.

Ruth Ann raised her hand and waved goodbye.

Epilogue

June 1949

Ruth Ann's hair lifted in the warm breeze as she planted Virginia bluebells and peonies in the flower beds that bordered the little white cottage she and Clarence now called their own. True to her dreams, her husband had added on a front porch with some help from a neighbor, built two rocking chairs for it and painted the front door, shutters and window boxes bright blue.

A home of her very own...It still occasionally brought tears to her eyes. She'd never seen anything more beautiful in her life—other than her daughter, Annabel, of course. Her daughter was now a young woman with a teaching certificate, married to the headmaster of a nearby school.

Annabel's darling baby, Grace, was as lovely as her mother, with the same dent in her chin they'd both inherited from Sheila. A dent that spoke of strength and grit and determination—the resilience they'd need to take on life.

Grace cooed and gurgled from her comfortable spot on her mother's lap. Annabel sat in one of the rockers, smiling at Ruth Ann. "I love the way you look in that hat, Ma."

Ruth Ann sat back on her heels and touched the straw brim of it. "So fancy. Too fancy for gardening." It was decorated with a grosgrain ribbon and a cluster of cherries with silk leaves. Imagine. A girl from the Colony owning a hat such as this.

Clarence whistled as he eased out the screen door with the blueberry pie she'd left cooling in the kitchen. His once-copper hair was streaked with silver and his freckles had faded somewhat, but he was still handsome. "Ain't nothin' too fancy for my Ruthie." He winked. "You look almost as fine as this here pie."

"That's for supper, and you know it," Ruth Ann said. "Bonnie's coming by with her husband after their visit with Momma. Ruby, too."

"Mmm-hmmm." Clarence still cradled the pie.

"You put that back straightaway. You hear?"

He gazed at it sadly. "Well, but my tummy's rumbling somethin' fierce, and them little ol' blueberries? They started singin' to me."

"Is that right?" Ruth Ann said, in a tone that told him she wasn't buying it. "What were they singing?"

Clarence didn't miss a beat. "The Sugar Blues."

"The Sugar Blarney, is more like it." She stuck her spade in the dirt and brushed off her hands.

The right corner of Clarence's mouth quirked up. Of course, there was no *wrong* corner to her husband's smile. It still got to her—still made her heart roll over, even after all these years. Ruth Ann tried, unsuccessfully, to bite back her echoing smile.

But he spied it and knew in that moment that he'd won. "No, I promise you…these berries got musical talent. They got soul. And they are positively clamorin' to meet up with the trombone and the trumpet in my belly."

Annabel laughed, and baby Grace did, too, as her mother tickled her stomach. "Ma, let him have some pie. He pinned up all the sheets for you on the line in back."

Ruth Ann's breath caught. Clarence knew how much she hated doing laundry since she'd done so much of it in her youth. That softened her up more than his blatant wheedling. She got to her feet and shook out her skirt, then wiped her hands on her apron. "Give that here, Clarence. I'll cut you a piece. You want coffee with it?"

"Well, now. I reckon I wouldn't turn it down." His gray eyes danced, caught the sunlight and turned to silver.

"Annabel, honey? You want pie? I made a second one. I knew he would do this."

"That's all right, Ma. I'm just going to sit here a spell with the baby. But thank you."

Clarence slid an arm around Ruth Ann's waist once they got inside. "You do look fetching in that hat, my girl."

Though she was decades past blushing age, she felt her face heating. "Only thing I'm fetching is pie, and I'm an old crone, you goof."

"But you're *my* crone, Ruthie," he teased.

She swatted him lightly and took the pie from him in order to slice it.

"And I thank the good Lord every day—twice—for that." His voice thickened.

Ruth Ann turned to look at him, and he took her in his arms, tipping the hat to the back of her head. There was a lot more to her these days, but he didn't appear to mind.

The laughter had disappeared from his eyes, but the sterling remained there, as it would until the day he died. Clarence kissed her, and she felt cherished. She laid her cheek on his chest, listening to the beat of his heart, feeling more content than she'd ever dreamed she would have a right to feel.

Outside the window, silhouetted through the screen and the

lace curtains, she drank in the sight of her daughter once more. So bright and fresh and pretty, with her whole life ahead of her, little Grace in her arms. Annabel turned the baby around to face her, and bent toward her, whispering earnestly.

Ruth Ann couldn't make out the words between them. But she smiled, aching, as the last two drifted to her ears: "I promise."

There were all kinds of promises in the world. Some were false. Some were made in earnest, but easily betrayed. Some were awkwardly, imperfectly fulfilled. But the promise made by a mother to love her child…the promise that began in utero, via the umbilical cord that linked them…that promise could never be broken.

a mother's promise

READING GROUP GUIDE

BUCK V. BELL:
THE HISTORY BEHIND
RUTH ANN'S STORY

by K.D. Alden

This novel is based upon the tragic life of Carrie Buck and her true legal case, *Buck v. Bell*.

From the moment I encountered her—heard her actual voice in an NPR podcast—I felt compelled to bring Carrie alive on the page, writing in her own, simple point of view about a complicated topic. I also yearned to give her a happier ending than she had in real life.

Why was this story such a must for me to write? I, too, struggled with fertility issues—though not at governmental whim. My husband and I then experienced a sequence of disastrous attempts at adoption and finally gave up. I was left so numb that I was unable to write for several years. Then, by pure chance, a friend urged me to listen to an episode of Shankar Vedantam's *Hidden Brain*, "Emma, Carrie, Vivian: How a Family Became a Test Case for Forced Sterilizations," which aired on National Public Radio on April 23, 2018.

I ran to my laptop, flipped it open and began writing chapter one of this book as though the story were being channeled through me. I have never in my career had a stranger, virtually mystical, experience! It was only after completing chapter three that I began to research in earnest and plan out the rest of the novel.

As I read further about Carrie Buck and her Supreme Court case, I reeled at the ramifications—for the individual, for American society, for World War II Europe, and even in terms of U.S. immigration today.

Much of the science and philosophy behind the "progressive" eugenics movement is far too unwieldy to weave into the narrative of this particular book, though there are some excellent nonfiction sources to explore that I read voraciously and with a growing outrage at the injustice done to Carrie.

Actual Colony board meeting minutes do show that the two lawyers and the doctor were in cahoots, and that Carrie Buck's lawyer utterly betrayed his client's trust and interests.

Carrie's mother and sister were indeed both residents of the Colony, her mother having been admitted in a disheveled, malnourished state, with track marks on her arms and a suspected history of prostitution.

But as a work of fiction, *A Mother's Promise* does differ in certain ways from Carrie Buck's actual life, though it is inspired by it.

Here are some of the "dramatic licenses" I took as an author.

1. Most institutions never explained what they were doing to the patient when they underwent sterilization. I chose to have Dr. Price tell Ruth Ann.

2. Unlike Ruth Ann, Carrie Buck never attempted to escape the Virginia Colony for the Epileptic and Feebleminded. She trusted "her people" there to make good decisions on her behalf.

3. I made Mrs. Dade's character more sympathetic than she was in real life, so that the twist at the end of the novel is even more shocking.

4. I chose to depict Ruth Ann's mother as a violent lunatic. She was not so in real life, and they did not have a bad relationship, nor was it Carrie's fault that her mother was transferred to the Colony. But I wanted to emphasize that not all genetic traits are passed along to offspring, as eugenics philosophy held at the time. I also wanted to highlight just how alone and defenseless Ruth Ann was during her ordeal at the Colony.

5. Ruth Ann's younger sister, Bonnie (based on Carrie's sister Doris Buck), was in reality sterilized shortly *after* Carrie. I reversed the order for dramatic purposes in the story. (Doris was told that she'd had an appendectomy for medical reasons. She only found out the truth thirty years later. She and her husband burst into tears upon being told, because they'd unwittingly been trying to conceive children all of their married life.)

6. Tragically, the real Annabel (Carrie Buck's only child, Vivian) died at the age of eight. I just couldn't do that to Ruth Ann in the novel. I desperately wanted her to have a happier ending, being allowed to adopt her one child and her baby sister.

7. Clarence is ficticious, in yet another of my attempts to rewrite Carrie's story with a more positive ending. But

Carrie did marry twice after she left the Colony, the second time after she was widowed.

8. There was no actual Mother Jenkins character at the Colony, to my knowledge. It's not my intention to depict the place as all bad. Socials and dances and outings to see picture shows were offered to the patients/inmates, though they did indeed work for their room and board.

9. I've altered some facts and timelines for dramatic and plot purposes. I've adapted the Colony setting to the needs of the novel and created buildings that did not actually exist. I had the surgeries occur on premises, and not at nearby hospitals.

10. I also have not mentioned the notorious "blind room," which existed to punish wayward inhabitants. But there is a haunting, brilliant and evocative book of poetry by Molly McCully Brown titled *Virginia State Colony for Epileptics and Feebleminded*, which does.

MORE INFORMATION ABOUT THE EUGENICS MOVEMENT AND *BUCK V. BELL*:

Buck v. Bell has largely been buried, since this case in particular, and eugenics in general, are now seen as shameful examples of how American society has, on occasion, gone wrong. And nobody has wanted to sully the reputations of such luminaries as Oliver

Wendell Holmes, Jr., Louis Brandeis, and other supporters of the movement such as Theodore Roosevelt, Alexander Graham Bell, and the Carnegie Institution, to name only a few. It's not my intention to blacken their legacies. These were great men, but they were products of their heritage, privilege and times.

The worst repercussions of the eugenics movement and *Buck v. Bell* are even more shocking than the sterilization of approximately 70,000 innocent American citizens. Eugenics led to the Immigration Act of 1924, which was meant to stop Eastern Europeans and Jews from entering the country, as they were considered of "inferior" stock and might "pollute" the gene pool of the United States. This act, endorsed by Hitler in *Mein Kampf*, made it extraordinarily difficult for Jews to flee to America during World War II.

Adam Cohen points out in his extraordinary book *Imbeciles: The Supreme Court, Eugenics, and the Sterilization of Carrie Buck* that Anne Frank and her family might have survived had they been allowed to come to this country.

Fortunately for my own family, my grandfather was born an American citizen to German Catholics, but my Jewish maternal grandmother would have been exterminated had she remained in Europe. My mother and her siblings would have been sterilized had they stayed there, because they were of "mixed" blood. And I myself would not exist.

All of this is disturbing enough. But Harry S. Laughlin, director of the Eugenics Record Office at Cold Spring Harbor, New York, was so proud of his research—and his recommendation that approximately *15 million* American citizens should be sterilized in order to "protect" the gene pool—that he shared it with Nazi scientists. He was quite proud of the fact that they used his model eugenics law as the basis for their own, which led to the forced sterilizations of over 375,000 more people under the Third Reich. Worse, the Nazis prosecuted at the Nuremburg Trials cited American law (and *Buck v. Bell* in particular) as part of their defense strategy.

Curiously enough, Laughlin either hid or was not aware of the fact that he himself had epilepsy, which wasn't revealed until he had a public seizure while driving in Cold Spring Harbor, New York.

Eugenics began to fall out of favor in the United States in the late 1930s along with the rise of the Nazis, whose actions became indefensible in the eyes of most. The Carnegie Institution withdrew its funding for Laughlin and his research. But the eugenics laws remained on the books in most states until the 1970s, despite a solid challenge to *Buck v. Bell* in 1942 in Oklahoma.

Buck v. Bell is still, shockingly, the law of the land. It was cited in 2001 in a Missouri case by the Eighth Circuit Court of Appeals, which ruled that "involuntary sterilization is not always unconstitutional." And from 2006 to 2010, *150* (!) inmates of California prisons were sterilized.

Three generations of this imbecilic law are enough. When will *Buck v. Bell* **be overturned?**

DISCUSSION QUESTIONS

1. At the beginning of the novel, did you believe that Ruth Ann Riley was, as she's been told, feebleminded? If so, when did you realize that perhaps she wasn't?

2. Do you think that having a baby out of wedlock is as shocking today as it was in the early twentieth century? Why did people feel the need to segregate "fallen" young ladies from the rest of society?

3. Ruth Ann was the victim of rape, yet nobody seemed to either believe her or care. The authorities still considered her "fallen." Why? How do you think that affected her? Were you surprised that she still loved her baby so much?

4. How did you feel when Ruth Ann tried to recover Annabel from the Dades? Was she really capable of caring for a baby on her own? Was it right of social services to place Ruth Ann's baby with the Dades, in a "swap" of one child for another? Was it right for the Dades to profit off of Ruth Ann's labor, since they provided room and board for her?

5. How did you view the relationship between Ruth Ann and her mother? Is Sheila mentally ill? Or just impossibly angry at what life has done to her? Do you feel that she's right to be so nasty to Ruth Ann? Do you think that she still loves Ruth Ann in any way?

6. The term *eugenics* refers to the "science of good breeding." Do you think it's possible to breed out less desirable traits in human beings—or breed *in* more desirable ones? Aside from religion, what are the ethical and moral issues at stake?

7. What do you think about the underlying financial concerns that drove some of these "progressive" ideas? Do you think these money issues still affect policy-making and politics today?

8. What do you think of the Supreme Court's decision to uphold the state's right to sterilize individuals against their will?

9. Do you think that these gentlemen were well-intended? Patriotic? That the end justified the means?

10. Despite losing her long court battle, Ruth Ann finds happiness with Clarence, eventually leaves the Colony and is able to adopt Annabel and Bonnie. Did you find the ending of the book satisfying? Why or why not?

In the actual writ of opinion for *Buck v. Bell*, Justice Oliver Wendell Holmes, Jr., describes the reasoning behind the Supreme Court's decision to uphold the findings of the lower court. The bold-face sections are of particular interest (they are not bold in the original).

It is beyond unfortunate that the trumped-up "evidence" that Carrie and her infant daughter Vivian were feebleminded was never questioned by her own attorney. If the "evidence" had been invalidated, then Carrie could not have been judged to be the "probable potential parent of socially inadequate offspring." She could not have been found to be "manifestly unfit" to reproduce.

If anyone had cared to listen to her true story of rape, Carrie also would not herself have been found to be an example of "degenerate" offspring, since her pregnancy was in no way her fault. She never committed a crime, nor was she an imbecile, unable to feed herself. Both she and her daughter, Vivian, received good marks in school. People who knew Carrie in later life noted that she didn't seem mentally disabled in any way and in fact looked forward to reading the newspaper every day and doing the crossword puzzle.

Opinion

HOLMES, J., Opinion of the Court

This is a writ of error to review a judgment of the Supreme Court of Appeals of the State of Virginia affirming a judgment of the Circuit Court of Amherst County by which the defendant in error, the superintendent of the State Colony for Epileptics and Feeble Minded, was ordered to perform the operation of salpingectomy upon Carrie Buck, the plaintiff in error, for the purpose of making her sterile. 143 Va. 310. The case comes here upon the contention that the statute authorizing the judgment is void under the Fourteenth Amendment as denying to the plaintiff in error due process of law and the equal protection of the laws.

Carrie Buck is a feeble minded white woman who was committed to the State Colony above mentioned in due form. She is the daughter of a feeble minded mother in the same institution, and the mother of an illegitimate feeble minded child. She was eighteen years old at the time of the trial of her case in the Circuit Court, in the latter part of 1924. An Act of Virginia, approved March 20, 1924, recites that the health of the patient and the welfare of society may be promoted in certain cases by the sterilization of mental defectives, under careful safeguard, &c.; that the sterilization may be effected in males by vasectomy and in females by salpingectomy, without serious pain or substantial danger to life; that the Commonwealth is supporting in various institutions many defective persons who, if now discharged, would become a menace, but, if incapable of procreating, might be discharged with safety and become self-supporting with benefit to themselves and to society, and that experience has shown that heredity plays an important part in the transmission of insanity, imbecility, &c. The statute then enacts that, whenever the superintendent of certain institutions, including the above-named State Colony, shall be of opinion that it is for the best interests of the patients and of society that an inmate under his care should be sexually sterilized, he may have the operation performed upon any patient afflicted with hereditary forms of insanity, imbecility, &c., on complying with the very careful provisions by which the act protects the patients from possible abuse.

The superintendent first presents a petition to the special board of directors of his hospital or colony, stating the facts and the grounds for his opinion, verified by affidavit. Notice of the petition and of the time and place of the hearing in the institution is to be served upon the inmate, and also upon his guardian, and if there is no guardian, the superintendent is to apply to the Circuit Court of the County to appoint one. If the inmate is a minor, notice also is to be given to his parents, if any, with a copy of the petition. The board is to see to it that the inmate may attend the hearings if desired by him or his guardian. The evidence is all to be reduced to writing, and, after the board has made its order for or against the operation, the superintendent, or the inmate, or his guardian, may appeal to the Circuit Court of the County. The Circuit Court may consider the record of the board and the evidence before it and such other admissible evidence as may be offered, and may affirm, revise, or reverse the order of the board and enter such order as it deems just. Finally any party may apply to the Supreme Court of Appeals, which, if it grants the appeal, is to hear the case upon the record of the trial in the Circuit Court, and may enter such order as it thinks the Circuit Court should have entered. There can be no doubt that, so far as procedure is concerned, the rights of the patient are most carefully considered, and, as every step in this case was taken in scrupulous compliance with the statute and after months of observation, there is no doubt that, in that respect, the plaintiff in error has had due process of law.

The attack is not upon the procedure, but upon the substantive law. It seems to be contended that in no circumstances could such an order be justified. It certainly is contended that the order cannot be justified upon the existing grounds. **The judgment finds the facts that have been recited, and that Carrie Buck is the probable potential parent of socially inadequate offspring, likewise afflicted, that she may be sexually sterilized without detriment to her general health, and that her welfare and that of society will be promoted by her sterilization**, and thereupon makes the order.

In view of the general declarations of the legislature and the specific findings of the Court, obviously we cannot say as matter of law that the grounds do not exist, and, if they exist, they justify the result. We have seen more than once that the public welfare may call upon the best citizens for their lives. It would be strange if it could not call upon those who already sap the strength of the State for these lesser sacrifices, often not felt to be such by those concerned, in order to prevent our being swamped with incompetence. **It is better for all the world if, instead of waiting to execute degenerate offspring for crime or to let them starve for their imbecility, society can prevent those who are manifestly unfit from continuing their kind.** The principle that sustains compulsory vaccination is broad enough to cover cutting the Fallopian tubes. *Jacobson v. Massachusetts*, 197 U.S. 11. **Three generations of imbeciles are enough.**

But, it is said, however it might be if this reasoning were applied generally, it fails when it is confined to the small number who are in the institutions named and is not applied to the multitudes outside. It is the usual last resort of constitutional arguments to point out shortcomings of this sort. But the answer is that the law does all that is needed when it does all that it can, indicates a policy, applies it to all within the lines, and seeks to bring within the lines all similarly situated so far and so fast as its means allow. Of course, so far as the operations enable those who otherwise must be kept confined to be returned to the world, and thus open the asylum to others, the equality aimed at will be more nearly reached.

Judgment affirmed.

MR. JUSTICE BUTLER dissents.

FURTHER READING

Shankar Vedantam, *Hidden Brain*. "Emma, Carrie, Vivian: How a Family Became a Test Case for Forced Sterilizations," National Public Radio, April 23, 2018

Three Generations, No Imbeciles: Eugenics, the Supreme Court, and Buck v. Bell, by Paul A. Lombardo

Imbeciles: The Supreme Court, American Eugenics, and the Sterilization of Carrie Buck, by Adam Cohen

A Whisper Past: Childless After Eugenic Sterilization in Alberta, by Leilani Muir

Eugenic Nation: Faults and Frontiers of Better Breeding in Modern America, 2nd edition, by Alexandra Minna Stern

American Eugenics, by Nancy Ordover

The Virginia State Colony for Epileptics and Feebleminded, by Molly McCully Brown

ACKNOWLEDGMENTS

I'm deeply grateful to:

V. S. Alexander, for tossing me the ball.

Evan Marshall and Martha Jewett.

Paul Lombardo and Adam Cohen, for their remarkable books, invaluable to my research.

Wanda Ottewell, for pushing me further in the draft stage of the manuscript.

Leah Hultenschmidt, for taking a chance on me and for deft editing and guidance.

Sabrina Flemming, for fielding all sorts of odd things and laughing at my terrible jokes.

Daniela Medina, for creating more than one incredible cover.

Rita Madrigal, for stellar copyediting. Any mistakes are my own.

Jodi Rosoff, for spreading the word.

The entire team at Grand Central Publishing and Forever.

Readers everywhere who, in the midst of this chaotic world, still find time for books.

This novel wouldn't exist without any of you! *Thanks* is an entirely inadequate word.

ABOUT THE AUTHOR

K.D. Alden is the pseudonym for an award-winning, bestselling author of more than twenty-five novels for New York publishers. While she's created hundreds of characters under multiple names, she herself has only one personality. This is her first historical novel.

For all the latest news from K.D. Alden, visit:

KDAlden.com
Instagram @KDAldenauthor
Facebook.com/KDAldenauthor
Twitter @KDAldenauthor

YOUR
BOOK
CLUB
RESOURCE

VISIT
GCPClubCar.com

to sign up for the **GCP Club Car** newsletter, featuring exclusive promotions, info on other **Club Car** titles, and more.

 @grandcentralpub

 @grandcentralpub

 @grandcentralpub